Any Minor World

Craig Schaefer

Demimonde Books

Copyright © 2022 by Craig Schaefer

All rights reserved.

No portion of this book may be reproduced in any form without written permission from the publisher or author, except as permitted by U.S. copyright law.

CONTENTS

1. Chapter 1 — 1
2. Chapter 2 — 7
3. Chapter 3 — 13
4. Chapter 4 — 19
5. Chapter 5 — 25
6. Chapter 6 — 31
7. Chapter 7 — 37
8. Chapter 8 — 43
9. Chapter 9 — 49
10. Chapter 10 — 55
11. Chapter 11 — 61
12. Chapter 12 — 69
13. Chapter 13 — 73
14. Chapter 14 — 79
15. Chapter 15 — 85
16. Chapter 16 — 91
17. Chapter 17 — 97
18. Chapter 18 — 101
19. Chapter 19 — 107
20. Chapter 20 — 113

21.	Chapter 21	119
22.	Chapter 22	125
23.	Chapter 23	131
24.	Chapter 24	137
25.	Chapter 25	143
26.	Chapter 26	149
27.	Chapter 27	155
28.	Chapter 28	161
29.	Chapter 29	167
30.	Chapter 30	173
31.	Chapter 31	179
32.	Chapter 32	185
33.	Chapter 33	191
34.	Chapter 34	197
35.	Chapter 35	201
36.	Chapter 36	205
37.	Chapter 37	211
38.	Chapter 38	217
39.	Chapter 39	223
40.	Chapter 40	227
41.	Chapter 41	233
42.	Chapter 42	239
43.	Chapter 43	245
44.	Chapter 44	251
45.	Chapter 45	257
46.	Chapter 46	263
47.	Chapter 47	267
Afterword		273

Also By Craig Schaefer

Chapter One

Out on the desert's edge, where a hangover sunrise made the air ripple and tumbleweeds rolled across the empty interstate, the price of a human life had been written in stone: one brick of cocaine, wrapped in thick plastic, in trade for one body, still breathing. Roy Mackey brought the coke. He was here for the body.

He stood out in the motel parking lot, waiting, head throbbing. He tasted grit on his teeth, and last night's tequila. A prickly heat had him sweating, plastering his ocean-blue cotton shirt to his back, and when he rubbed the dark stubble on his cheeks his fingers came away clammy.

This handoff should have gone down an hour ago. Could be lots of things. Maybe they overslept. Maybe they had car trouble. Maybe they scoped him out from a distance, decided he was a cop, panicked, killed the kid, and ran for the border.

Roy tried not to think about maybes. Worry was a waste of time if he wasn't doing anything useful with it.

A distant mirage of blurry steel caught his eye. A dirty white pickup was coming his way. It got off the highway on the access road and turned its bug-encrusted grill toward the motel. Roy held his ground and waited. Soon he made out three figures in the front seat: man behind the wheel, woman riding shotgun, the kid squeezed between them on the bench seat.

They parked, sloppy, the nose of the pickup straddling the faded white line. Roy didn't approach the truck. He just kept his face polite, neutral, empty, his open hands in plain sight. Junkies were unpredictable at the best of times, and these two had every reason in the world to be jumpy. They left the kid in the pickup. That was fine: Roy wanted him at a safe distance if anything went sideways.

And it went sideways quick. The man had shaved his face for the first time in years—he had a beard on all the wanted posters—and he'd paid for it in lost skin and shredded acne. He flashed a .32, keeping it low and pointing it at Roy's belly. His traveling companion had a piece of her own, a bulky revolver that looked too heavy for her needle-scarred bird-arms to lift. They had a dozen good teeth between them.

"You got the stuff?" the man asked.

Roy nodded, amiable, and shot a glance at the door of Room Three. "In there. Door's unlocked. You go in, I take the kid and leave—"

"You don't *dictate*," the man said, raising the gun a little higher. "You don't dictate *terms* to us, mister. You think we won't plug you right here and now? Inside. You lead the way."

Roy knew he meant it. These two had developed a taste for blood on their little cross-state rampage, starting with a county sheriff they left dead in a ditch, and one more body wouldn't mean anything to them one way or another. They also didn't care much about witnesses. He wasn't concerned they'd kill him to keep him quiet; he was concerned they'd kill him just for kicks.

He brought them inside. The air conditioning was dead and the morning sun had turned the east-facing room into a sauna. More sweat pooled at the base of Roy's spine, refusing to turn cold. As promised, the brick of coke sat out on the window-side table. The woman shut the door behind them, sullen, glaring death in Roy's general direction.

"Go ahead," he said. "Check it out. Do a taste test, if you want. It's real."

"Better be," said the man.

He set his gun on the table. Roy almost went for it then and there, but the woman by the door still had hers and she would put a bullet in his spine before he could reach it. A switchblade flicked open in the man's hand, the tarnished, dull blade scissoring a jagged cut through the plastic around the brick. He scooped up a fingernail-thin line of coke with the knife, held it under his chapped, bloodshot nose, and snorted it right off the steel. He shut his eyes, nodding hard and fast, his body vibrating like he'd stuck his finger in an electric socket.

"Yeah. Yeah. It's good."

"It's good?" asked his traveling companion, her head tilted and eyes dull.

"I said it's good. Clean the rocks out of your ears."

"What about him?" she said.

Solid question, Roy thought. Once the switchblade went away, he figured the man would reach for one of two things. If he was ready to leave, he'd reach for the coke first. If he had some evil on his mind, he'd reach for the gun. It wasn't an exact science, but Roy had handled enough negotiations to learn how people telegraph their intentions. Then the man opened his mouth and removed any doubt.

"We're takin' this. The kid, too."

He reached for the gun.

The chair next to the table was lightweight aluminum, a cheap cigarette-burned cushion on battered spindly legs. Roy swept it up and swiveled on one foot, whipped out his arm, and let the chair fly. It hit the woman in the belly. She doubled over with a grunt and yanked the trigger, her revolver roaring loud enough to make Roy's ears sting. The bullet scorched a trench into the dirty carpet.

A thin strip of duct tape held Roy's insurance policy against the underbelly of the table. He'd spent an hour that morning practicing, reaching for it blind until he could count on muscle memory to get the job done. The tape tore away and a slender black handle dropped into his hand. His fingers curled around the textured grip. With one hard flick, three feet of flexible steel—an ASP tactical baton—telescoped out and locked into place.

The baton hissed down, cracking the man's knuckles, splitting skin and spraying blood. He dropped the gun and went for the switchblade with his other hand. Roy had two seconds of breathing room and he used them to cut his threats in half: the woman was winded, wheezing, trying to square him in her sights with her finger on the trigger. Roy lashed the baton across the crown of her head and she dropped like a sack of rocks, gashed scalp bleeding onto the carpet. She clutched herself, went fetal, and made hiccupping moans.

Her lover came at Roy with the knife in his good hand, spearing wildly at the air between them. Roy jogged a half-step back, stealing distance, and swung the ASP underhand. The flexible steel cracked up between his attacker's legs like a bullwhip. He hit the floor with both knees, eyes bulging and face beet-red as his cheeks puffed up.

"Stay down," Roy told him. "I wouldn't mind beating on you all day long, but I've got places to be."

Roy collected both pistols and confiscated their keys. He left the switchblade and the brick of cocaine. That gunshot would attract attention—his damn ears were still ringing—and Roy figured the state police would be down here in ten minutes or less. Let these two tell any story they wanted; his fingerprints weren't on anything and he'd paid for the room with cash. He left the coke to add one more charge to their rap sheet. He left the knife to give them another way out, if they felt so inclined. Roy was a generous man.

The kid was still in the cab of the pickup, roasting in the desert heat. He jumped, panicky, and turtled his head down into the neck of his faded superhero t-shirt when Roy climbed into the driver's seat.

"Relax," Roy told him. "I'm taking you to your mother. Your mom's been worried sick about you. I'm a friend of hers; she asked me to come and pick you up."

The engine came to life with a hoarse, sickly cough and the AC vents sprayed hot air across Roy's sweaty face. He checked the rearview, listening for sirens in the distance. He heard them; they were coming from the south. He'd go north, then. One quick detour and he'd get the boy home in time for supper.

"What about my dad?" the kid asked.

As Roy pulled out of the parking spot, he shot one last look at the motel room door.

"You shouldn't have to hear this from me," Roy told him, "and I'm sorry for that, but your dad's a real piece of shit."

The kid stared at him, wide-eyed.

"It's fine," Roy said. "My dad was a real piece of shit, too, and I turned out all right."

Some tears of gratitude and one envelope stuffed with cash later, and Roy was feeling all right. Mostly for the cash, but he wasn't made of stone. He figured he'd feel even better with a drink—and now he could afford one—so he found a roadside bar just off the highway with a parking lot full of long-haul semis. It was after sundown, the desert turning bone-cold. He was halfway to the front door, country music drifting out on the white glow of electric light, when his phone started to ring. He didn't recognize the number, but he picked up out of curiosity.

"Yeah?"

The voice on the other end was precise, cultured, carefully bland and stripped of any trace of a regional accent, as if the man wanted to be perfectly understood and then utterly forgotten.

"May I speak to Roy Mackey, please?"

"I might be able to find him. Who's asking?"

"Ah, yes. Of course. I represent a legal firm in need of some assistance. *Special* assistance."

"I flunked out of law school," Roy said.

"We're well aware of your talent for off-the-books negotiations, Mr. Mackey."

"And you think you know about me because..."

He trailed off, an invitation for his caller to provide a reference. One he could believe in.

"Adam Darger, with Hillside's Global Fine Arts section. Hillside Insurance was extremely pleased with your work."

Good, but not good enough, not enough to earn his trust. Roy was technically a criminal. One who wore an off-white hat, but getting results meant going off the books; that was why his clients hired him in the first place. And he was picky about his clients.

"Tell me more," he said.

"A Renoir, stolen from a private collection," his caller said. "Not only did you recover it in perfect condition, saving Hillside from having to pay out on a multi-million-dollar theft policy, your discretion kept the situation far from the ears of the press and the authorities alike."

All true. Whoever this guy was, he knew his business. And Roy's business, too.

"Where do we meet?" Roy said.

"This particular task is time-sensitive. We have a vested interest in—"

"*Not* on the phone," Roy said.

The stranger cleared his throat. "I understand. Can you come to my office in Miami? We'll pay your way, of course; I can wire funds for a plane ticket to the bank of your choice within the hour. All I need is a name, account, and routing number."

"Account is under the name 'Carter McCoy,'" Roy said, rummaging in his pocket for a folded scrap of paper. He read off two strings of numbers, and the voice on the line repeated them back in a monotone.

"Excellent. I'll give you the address. And of course, we'll send over extra money to cover your cab fare."

"And who am I talking to?" Roy asked.

"Do clients trust you with their real names?"

"Some do, some don't. None of my business either way, but I have to call you something. Go by any name you want."

"Excellent," said the voice. He sounded vaguely pleased. "Then you may call me Mr. Smith. It's a pleasure to make your acquaintance, Roy. My firm and I are looking forward to working with you."

Chapter Two

A redeye flight transformed the desert nightscape into an East Coast sunrise, fire boiling across the brass-colored face of the ocean as Roy's plane touched down at Miami International. He knew he must have slept, at least a little bit, but the flight was nothing but a memory of droning fuzzy floating nothingness. Chasing dreams while they raced just ahead of him, luring him deeper into the darkness behind his bloodshot eyes.

Roy traveled light. He slung a dusty black gym bag over his shoulder by its frayed canvas strap as he shuffle-stepped his way off the plane. Miami International was waking up, shops along the concourse rolling up their grates and flicking on the lights. He found a spot where he could get a tall cup of black coffee and a chocolate glazed donut—*breakfast of champions*, he thought—then splashed lukewarm water on his face in a bathroom that stank of industrial-strength disinfectant. Same routine he'd performed on a hundred mornings in a hundred airports. He couldn't quite remember if he'd done Miami before; he thought the closest he'd gotten was Fort Lauderdale, but the layout here felt familiar and he'd been swaddled in a layer of *deja vu* from the moment he landed.

Airports and hotels were liminal spaces. Transitory, temporary. Sometimes, when it was early enough and he hadn't had his coffee yet, Roy wondered if they were all connected down at the roots. Like if he walked the right combination of halls and airport lounges in Atlanta, he might end up in Houston, or Vancouver, or a maze of empty white concourses and blank, flickering signs, all flights canceled. He wondered if anyone had ever done that by accident, *gone wandering* and been swept away, too far from home to ever make it back again.

The idea had a certain appeal to it.

Cabs lined up in a haze of morning smog and the odor of engine exhaust clung to the back of Roy's throat. He hopped into a tornado of ice-cold air conditioning and tried to get comfortable on the lump of a loose seat-spring as he gave the cabbie the address for the meet.

He'd expected downtown, a glass and granite tower, something on a penthouse floor with expensive furniture. Instead, he got squawking seagulls and the tang of salt, white sand and crystal-clear water. "Mr. Smith's" office was on Miami Beach at the Fontainebleu Marina. Fontainebleu was like a car show, swapping the wheels for sleek yachts and double-decker party boats. Roy didn't know boats, but he had to figure the cheapest one in sight cost seven or eight figures, easy. Smith's people, whoever they were, weren't afraid of flashing money around. Normally he'd take that as a good sign.

Normally, he didn't have a pinched-skin crawling sensation at the back of his neck just before a face-to-face with a new client. The cab dropped him off, leaving him at the edge of the marina under a high morning sun. The wintery cold stayed with him, stubbornly clinging to his bones despite the rising heat.

He'd almost walked into a setup, once, early in his career. He crossed some dangerous people with one of his recovery jobs, and he had been sloppier back then, easier to find; they tracked him down and made him a bogus offer. Roy got the jitters that night something fierce and vanished before anyone knew he was there. He only found out later that the "meeting place" was a soundproofed room with tacked-up plastic sheeting and a meat hook.

This was different. The prickling along the nape of his neck wasn't fear for himself. His instincts weren't warning him about an ambush, or a police sting, but something was *wrong* here. Something crawled, unseen, behind the million-dollar floating toys, slinking under the champagne sparkle of the water. Some kind of apex predator.

Roy had dumped the confiscated pistols from his last job before getting on the plane to Miami—he didn't need to be caught carrying a couple of spree-killers' guns—but his tactical baton rode snug and compact against his hip. The cool, textured grip rubbed against his fingertips, reminding him that he had options. Roy was a predator, too.

The tail of the *Oceans Beyond* rose from the water on a pair of upside-down shark fins, the boat shaped like a curved lozenge in ivory white and stainless steel. Dwarfed by most of its neighbors, but still worth more than Roy could earn in a lifetime. He stood at the base of the gangplank and cupped his hands to his mouth, calling out for permission to come aboard.

"Granted and gladly," said a man on the rear deck. Same bland, anonymous voice as the phone call, and he had a face to match. Mr. Smith could have been anyone in the marina, dressed in a crisp white linen shirt and khakis. He could pass for a millionaire or a busboy or anything in between. Roy had trained himself to look for signifiers. You could tell a lot about a person from the tiniest details, from the cut of their hair to the price of their shoes. Smith didn't have any. At all. The man was a walking blank, and Roy wasn't sure he'd remember the man's face come tomorrow.

They shook hands on the deck, standing on polished pale wood that reminded Roy of a bowling-alley floor. An elegant white couch curved against the chrome railing, along with a small triple-shelf bar service laden with high-end liquor and cut crystal glasses.

"Drink?" Smith asked, gesturing with a slender hand. "You strike me as a whiskey man. Two fingers, neat?"

Direct hit, but Roy shook his head. "Not on the job. Thank you."

"Good. Keeping a clear head. We like that."

"We," Roy echoed.

"The legal firm I represent—whose name doesn't need to come into this, as I'll be your primary and only point of contact—has its fingers in quite a few global pies. Heavy industry, pharmaceuticals and biotech, government contracts; this could become a fruitful long-term relationship for both of us, if you prove yourself capable."

Roy nodded at the twin tiers of cabins, stacked like the levels of a ziggurat with a staircase rising between walls of dark onyx glass. "Looks like you're doing all right for yourselves."

"Assets, we own in abundance. Money is easy. Influence is hard. And at the moment, we find ourselves lacking a competent, discreet investigator. Certainly lacking one with your background and skill set. We've been alerted to an opportunity, and it's time-sensitive."

"I'm listening."

Smith drifted over to the bar service, so slowly Roy barely noticed him moving at all, as he spoke.

"One of our smaller clients is Red Harvest, a publishing firm that specializes in genre fiction. Some award winners, some airport trash. I'll let you guess what sells better. There's an issue with one of their authors."

"Missed their deadline?"

"Terminally late. Have you ever heard of a writer named Carolyn Saunders?"

Roy combed his memory and shook his head. "Can't say."

"She's not exactly a household name. Red Harvest was hoping to hook jumper cables to her flagging career, and they succeeded beyond expectations: her last book, *The City at Midnight*, is a certified hit."

"And that's a problem?"

"She took a hit, too. From a semi, which collided head-on with her car at roughly sixty miles an hour." Smith drew a pale finger across his throat. "Saunders died on a vacation up in New York the same week that the book came out. Of course, dead artists always bring in more cash than live ones. What's missing is what every best-seller needs: a sequel."

"You need a spirit medium, not a PI."

"Not at all. Publishing is a slow business; Saunders turned in her manuscript well over a year ago, at which point it entered the endless cycle of editing, layout, cover design, all the bits and pieces. She was contracted for *two* books, and began work on the second right away. By all accounts it was coming along smoothly, and *The City on Fire* should have landed on her editor's desk."

"Before she died."

Smith shrugged with a *what-can-you-do* look. "Inconvenient, but we're certain about two things. *The City on Fire* exists, a finished manuscript or close to it, and our client wants it."

"What if it's not done?"

"That's what ghost writers are for," Smith said. He turned over a single crystal glass and reached for a slender frosted-glass bottle. "They can hire someone to mimic her style and wrap up the last few chapters if need be. The important thing is getting a sequel into production while the first novel is still hot. The recovery requires a person of your talents, capable of things a normal insurance investigator can't or won't do."

Breaking and entering, for starters, Roy thought. The manuscript was probably sitting snug on Carolyn's hard drive. Red Harvest might have the legal rights to the book, but that didn't give them the right to break into a dead woman's house and loot the place. That was where he came in. Compared to his last job, this would be a cakewalk.

"Let's talk about my fee," Roy said.

Smith tilted the frosted-glass bottle. Liquor, clear and sparkling as the water lapping against the hull of the yacht, tumbled into his glass. Roy caught a stringent smell, harsh, laced with old, dried herbs. Smith corked the bottle and reached into his breast pocket, taking out a folded slip of paper. He passed it over to Roy.

Roy unfolded it, read the number, and almost walked out then and there.

The offer wasn't too small. It was too big. Big enough to trip his alarms and set his skin prickling all over again. Mr. Smith was pitching an easy search and recovery job—one day of work, tops—and offering him contract-killer money for it. Either his firm was so flush with cash that they could burn it by the bushel, or Smith was making an amateur mistake. Or something else was going on, something behind the curtain, and he should walk away right here and now.

"Do we have a deal?" Smith asked.

Indiana. The dead writer had lived out her last years in Indiana, on the edge of a cornfield. Smith had a dossier all ready, snug between manila-folder covers, and Roy flipped through the pages of dense type on the flight. A stewardess came by with the drink cart and cracked open a tiny airplane bottle of whiskey, pouring it out into a plastic cup for him.

Had he said yes? He couldn't quite remember. He must have, though, because here he was. On another plane, rising above another fluffy layer of clouds, listening to the drone of the jet engines and the faint, trembling quiver of the wings. Maybe it was a foregone conclusion. This was what he did: one job after another, one foot in front of the other, always moving and somehow standing perfectly still.

He drank his whiskey, leaned back, and sank into a restless dream. He fell through the bottom of the plane, down through a kaleidoscope of freezing rain, of broken and falling glass, of hot wet blood and the smell of gunsmoke.

"You were the last one, you know that? The last one I ever thought would betray me."

Roy felt the weight of the gun in his hand. One bullet left. He was deciding where it should go. The ferret-faced man grinned up at him with bloody, puffed-up lips and a cracked front tooth.

"We were brothers. Guess this is what I deserve. Trust is a bitch."

"What you deserve—" Roy said. Then he ran out of words and pressed the muzzle of his gun against the man's sweat-slick forehead.

The broken smile didn't falter, not for a second. "That's on you. You get that, right? My hands are clean. But what you did to her...that's forever, pal. Try to blame me all you want, but what you did to her is a forever thing, and there's no taking it back now."

Roy leaned in, pushing the muzzle hard. The ferret's face tilted back, wet eyes and bloody face raised to heaven as the storm thundered down.

"Go on," he whispered. "Go on, Roy. Pull the trigger. You know you want to. Let's go all the way tonight. Pull the trigger."

An electronic chime snapped Roy's eyes open. He breathed pressurized air and stared dead ahead until his heart stopped pounding. The plane was over Indiana, fields and ribbons of lonely road as far as the eye could see, and the pilot gently banked into his landing approach.

At least this'll be a quick job, he thought. *In and out. Easy.*

Chapter Three

Carolyn Saunders had secrets.

Roy didn't know that right away. Didn't even guess it. He did some due diligence on his phone while he waited for Budget to find him a cheap rental. She lived, she wrote fantasy novels for a small but enthusiastic audience, and she died. Everything about this job, save for the crawling at the back of his neck and how he was getting paid way too much to get it done, looked crystal as the water off Miami Beach.

Miami was half a nation away now, and he'd left the coast for the flat, endless heartland of America. He drove down a stretch of Indiana highway, cornfields and farmhouses to the left and right, more pavement dead ahead, nothing to indicate his passage but billboards and mile markers. An hour slid by in the stillness between off-ramps. When another rose up, promising food and rest, he almost took it. But his GPS put him twenty minutes from Carolyn's last known address, so he stayed the course. Better to get the job done. Break in, grab the book, get out, go enjoy a fast-food dinner and a palatial sixty-dollar motel room.

Carolyn's place was a lonely farmhouse, tethered to an access road by a ragged strip of rough dirt. No neighbors for miles in either direction, no cars in the driveway. Good. It didn't seem like she had any living relatives. All the same, he parked a little down the road, at the edge of a cornfield, and turned on his emergency flashers. He propped up his hood up before hoofing it back to the house. If anyone did come along with questions, he had a ready excuse at hand.

The lock on the front door had been picked. More than once, and inexpertly, judging from the scrabbling, fumbling scratches on the steel. Roy crouched, studying the lock, his brow furrowed, hopes of a quick payday slipping away fast. This wouldn't be the first time an opportunist saw an obituary and made a move on the dearly departed's hearth and home while everyone was distracted by grief. Robbing the dead was a game for junkies and two-bit thieves who couldn't hack a serious burglary. Either way, they'd grab anything that was easy to move and might sell for a few bucks. Kitchen appliances, tools, watches and jewelry. Computers. Roy hoped for the best, but he resigned himself to canvassing every pawn shop from here to Chicago.

Whoever broke in was considerate, if amateur; they locked up after themselves. Thirty seconds with a pick and a tension rake undid their good deed. The tumblers clicked, rolling over, and he was inside.

One glance at the wreckage beyond the front door, the shattered furniture and broken glass strewn across the cheap, rumpled rug in Carolyn's living room, confirmed Roy's suspicions. Then twisted them. Thieves looking for an easy score would swoop in quick, maybe rip the drawers apart rummaging for the good stuff, but they'd be in and out like a swarm of magpies. This was different. Thorough. Deliberate. The invaders had cut open the pillows of Carolyn's sofa, gutting the stuffing, searching for hidden treasure inside. A glance into her bedroom confirmed the same: they'd even shoved her mattress against the wall, carving it like a Thanksgiving turkey and ripping the innards out by the fistful, tossing it to the floor in rough chunks.

Magpies never dug this deep. This wasn't an attack of opportunity. It was a professional search by determined hands for something in particular. Something small, something precious. Roy moved on. The dead writer had left a sink piled with dirty dishes in the kitchen next to a trash can that stank like a compost pile in the dog days of summer, bad enough to make him bury his nose in the crook of his sleeve, but the things that remained told a story. A waffle maker, a vintage toaster oven, a spilled drawer of antique silverware; all of it was cheap, easy to move, easy to pawn for a few quick bucks with no questions asked. Carolyn had a taste for the good stuff, too: the cupboard under the sink held a battlefield of bottles, most of it blended scotch and expensive imports, another treasure that few opportunists would leave behind.

Her office had been stripped bare. Just a desk, yanked-out drawers, nothing but a few lonely fountain pens remaining. Her desk sported a clean square in the middle of a dusty plain, perfectly shaped for a computer, gone now. They'd stolen her PC, her papers, her notebooks...they'd stolen *her*. All the things that weave the story of a life.

A crazed fan, maybe? Carolyn wasn't popular enough for her memorabilia to make bank on the black market, but Roy could imagine a determined collector swooping in to grab her true valuables for their private collection. *Like her last, unpublished novel*, he thought. His jaw clenched tight enough to ache, and he had to rub it with one absent hand, massaging the rough stubble until his muscles started to relax. The fan theory was the only thing that fit the evidence, which meant he wasn't going to solve this puzzle with a quick drive to the local pawn shops.

He almost walked out. But something was nagging at him, the empty office whispering that there was still something left to find. Instinct. He always tried to listen to his instincts. He stood in the center of the floor and made a long, slow sweep, turning in a circle, gazing at the walls and bare carpet as if he had just entered the room for the first time. In Zen, they called it the beginner's mind: the art of abandoning preconceptions and seeing things with fresh eyes. Roy tried studying Zen, once. He made for a lousy student in the end, but he still found a treasure or two to take with him when he left.

And there it was. The back wall, lined with seventies-era wooden paneling, sported a hair-thin crack running from the floor to a few inches from the ceiling. Now that he saw it, he could follow the concealed line and the cunning bevel-cut that kept it hidden. The outline of a door. He curled his short-cropped fingernails into the crack and gave it an experimental tug.

The wood pulled away from the wall with a suction-pop of air. The hidden room beyond was about the size of a walk-in closet. Roy tugged a string and a bare, dangling bulb sputtered to life.

This room had been ransacked, too. More carefully, more thoroughly, than the rest of the house. The carpet held indentations where boxes once sat, heavy ones, long enough to leave their ghosts behind. A corkboard dominating most of the side wall had been stripped bare of all but a handful of colored thumbtacks and a dangling piece of scarlet string.

The idea of a writer using a board to pin up notes and ideas made sense. Hiding it in a secret room, not so much. Unless she had some other business going on. The sun outside the window simmered low, drawing long amber shadows across the cornfield. There wasn't anything left to find here. Just a Carolyn-sized hole in the world, carved away with a purpose in mind. Roy wiped the doorknobs down and locked up on his way out.

He found a motel twenty miles down the road, so old that it still advertised *Color TV in Every Room!* on its marquee as if it was a recent invention. His room's rickety lawn-sale furniture was about that ancient, too, but the sheets were clean and the air conditioning worked, and he didn't need anything else for a decent night's sleep.

Not just yet. He peeled off his shirt on the way to the bathroom, pulled the shower handle and listened to the rattling pipes while he stripped. Water rained down, icy cold then hot enough to fog the mirror. He stepped under the spray and let it hammer his aching muscles, sluicing away sweat and road-grit, and walked backward through the day in his mind's eye.

The devoted fan theory was still the only idea that fit. The only intruder who would raid a dead writer's house and make off with her papers and her PC while leaving the rest of the goods behind. A hell of a lot harder to track down than an opportunistic junkie or a petty crook—this was a small town, and he could get a list of the local wash-ups just by asking around—but he still had one advantage. Collectors *talked*. They tended to be proud of their collections, the rarer the better. And what was more unique than a book that had never seen the light of day?

He toweled off, piled up the pillows, propped himself up in bed, and clicked on the TV. A talk show played out on the wavy screen, celebrity interviews filling the silence with meaningless background noise. Roy rested his phone on one bent knee and tapped out Carolyn's name.

A deeper dive, now, focusing on her fans. That and her most recent work. Considering Mr. Smith talked it up as a big hit, he expected to find more than he did. More than a general sense of disappointment. *She left the last Donatello book on a cliffhanger, and then gives us this?* One disappointed forum-dweller wrote. *It doesn't read like one of her novels. The characters are different, the setting, everything.*

Even the good reviews were tepid, most of them expressing similar thoughts: they wanted her old characters back and her old style too. From a look at the sales numbers, at least the ones he could find on public display, *The City at Midnight* was far from a best-seller. The small press behind it, Mr. Smith's patron, was a garage operation that put out a handful of boutique titles a year. Nobody was hotly anticipating *The City on Fire*'s release, and the unpublished sequel didn't even merit a casual mention on Red Harvest's website.

"The hell is your game?" he murmured. Smith offered him a fortune to track down a sequel nobody wanted to a book nobody read. Anything but a blockbuster in the making, like he'd claimed, and Red Harvest didn't have the money to hire a law firm that operated off a yacht in Miami Beach.

This would be a good time to walk away, he thought. Murky client, murkier job, some kind of scam in motion. He felt like a pawn in the plan, and pawns were born to be sacrificed. But he kept digging. He didn't have anything else to do tonight but dive down the rabbit hole, and he could afford to sleep on his decision.

RIP-OFF, blared one review, the capital letters and the one-star rating catching his eye. *This entire book is blatantly plagiarized. Saunders didn't even bother changing the names of the characters. Check out The Midnight Jury by Chandler Hawks and you'll see what I mean. How did she think she was going to get away with this? Total hack, would give negative stars if I could, and I hope they sue her into the ground.*

Too late. A truck already did that job, leaving her six feet under with a flop as her epitaph. All the same, her fans were *fans*. Dedicated to her books, immersed in picking apart her tangled skein of lore. If Saunders was a plagiarist, after this many books and this many years, someone would have caught her before now. Curious, Roy went on the hunt.

The Midnight Jury wasn't a novel. It was a comic book, published a decade ago by an outfit called Bang Pop Comics. It was the only thing Chandler Hawks ever wrote, at least under that name, and the series abruptly ended with the third issue even though Roy found old, floating previews, soliciting a never-released fourth. The covers were lurid, painted to resemble vintage forties-era pulp magazines. They featured an avenging angel in a dark blue trench coat and fedora, features concealed beneath a flowing silk scarf. The Midnight Jury dispensed justice with a pair of .45 automatics, swooping from the crumbling urban skyline and facing off against a rogue's gallery of miscreants and monsters. The taglines were breathless: *The Midnight Jury versus Trigger Mortis! Only One Can Keep Their Head!* And *When Noir York Sleeps, Nightshade Stalks—and SLAYS!* Half-smiling, Roy clicked over to the back-cover blurb for Carolyn's *The City at Midnight*.

Once the champion of Noir York, an avenger who stood against the teeming metropolis's hidden horrors, the Midnight Jury has vanished. Crime rules the streets and the nights are filled with terror and bloodshed. As the dark lords of the city carve out their territories, guns blaze from the shadows. Is this a new challenger, or in the city's greatest hour of need, has the Midnight Jury returned to pass judgment upon the guilty?

He downloaded the book to his phone and went looking for a site where he could find some scanned copies of the comics. This rabbit hole kept getting deeper, and he had already taken the dive. Too late to back out now.

Chapter Four

The voice from the tenement stairwell was like frost over fire, an icy sheen holding back a torrent of white-hot rage: "You should have stayed dead, Jury. Let me fix that for you."

A dark blue trench coat fluttered in the corner of the assassin's eye, leaving only a shadow behind. Trigger Mortis's rifle kicked, clattering, a three-round blast blowing the antique banister to splinters and chewing up the faded linoleum floor. The assassin crammed his shoulders into the corner of the room, face slick with sweat under his skull-faced mask, heart beating hard and fast.

"You should have stayed dead!" he roared, his nerve starting to crack. The only response was a peal of hollow, mocking laughter—from above him, not below. Trigger looked up as a dark figure plunged toward him, like a raven with oily blue-black feathers, blotting out the light.

Roy's fingers tapped against the screen of his phone. Drumming while he thought. Perplexed. He'd found scans of Chandler Hawks's comic books on a vaguely illicit website and was alternating between strolling through the lurid four-color pages and browsing Carolyn's last published book. Over in Issue Two of the comic, the Midnight Jury was investigating a string of random murders in a Noir York high-rise, intent on proving that the building's owner—losing money due to rent control—was killing his most inconvenient tenants.

The landlord sent in the Roach, a gas-masked contract killer equally comfortable with poison and flame, dispensing both from the custom-built "extermination rig" on his back. As they played cat and mouse in the halls of the run-down residential tower, the Midnight Jury's thoughts splashed the page in dripping bubbles of black ink.

Calm. Deep breaths. You've trained for this. Roach, and the monster who hired him, are used to preying on the vulnerable and the weak. They think they're immune. Safe from the cops, from the courts. Tonight they find out how wrong they are. It's time for this city to learn...that the Midnight Jury is now in session.

Roy shifted on the mattress, his head propped up on the pillows. The television had faded to a soft, anonymous drone on the edge of his hearing, human voices reduced to comforting and meaningless sounds. One small piece clicked at the corner of the puzzle.

"It's a *sequel*," he said out loud.

Carolyn Saunders had lifted...well, *everything* from the comics. Same characters, same setting, in an act of plagiarism unprecedented, as far as Roy could tell, in her entire career. Everything but the plots. In the comics, the Jury was an up-and-coming crusader in a city without heroes, building a name and a rogue's gallery of foes. In *The City at Midnight*, the Jury had passed into legend, and then memory, vanishing for years—just like the comics, and their abrupt ending—before returning with a literal bang. Something Mr. Smith said about the missing manuscript, back on the yacht, came back to him.

"What if it's not done?"

"That's what ghost writers are for."

What if Carolyn wasn't a plagiarist after all? What if she'd hired Chandler Hawks for the job, to write a follow-up to the comics that ended too soon? Roy's research couldn't find a reason for the series to get the ax after its third issue. It looked like a fourth was supposed to have been released, and possibly more, but none ever made it to the shelves.

And if Hawks wrote the first book, putting it out under Carolyn's more-established, better-known name, he was almost certainly the man behind the sequel. *Find Chandler Hawks, find the book*, Roy thought. *Or at least some solid answers*.

He set his phone down at his side, clicked off the end-table lamp, but left the television on. The faint glow of the screen and the chatter of a talk show chased him down into restless dreams.

Worthy didn't want this job. He didn't ask for this job. He didn't *need*— —well, that part wasn't true. But he would rather have been just about anywhere but down in the bowels of a Longacre Square porno theater, the floors sticky under his square-toed shoes, the air thick with stale sweat and a few odors he didn't want to identify. The house lights were up but the pimple-faced projectionist had vanished ten minutes ago and the movie was still playing, showing close-up penetration in gynecological detail. The soundtrack of breathy, faked moans was a poor accompaniment to the pair of dead bodies, slumped side-by-side in the middle row.

Worthy hooked a finger around the starched collar of his uniform shirt. It was hot as the devil's asshole in here and he was supposed to have been off the clock an hour ago. Now he had to wait for the medical examiners, for a detective or at least a sergeant, someone who could give him the thumbs-up to leave. Then it was back to the station house for paperwork and paperwork about the paperwork and maybe he'd get to sleep sometime before dawn.

"Sweltering in here," Kinbrook said, the rookie peering over the seats at the two stiffs like he'd never seen a body before.

"Yeah," Worthy said.

"Makes the murder rates go up," he said.

Worthy tilted his head, keeping one eye on the theater door. "What does?"

The rookie straightened up. He jerked a thumb at the two corpses.

"Heat. The hotter it is, the higher the rates of violent crime. Come summer, when the city's really on fire—"

"Rook?" Worthy said, cutting him off. "Do me a favor. Read less. Think less. You'll go further in this job if you do, trust me on this."

"Sir?"

"Look at the Lieutenant. Not two brain cells in that man's head and he keeps getting promoted. That's a role model to live by."

The static-laden moaning on the speakers rose to a crescendo, then stopped. It was a short-lived mercy. Now the actors were talking. *I've never seen one that big,* the actress purred. Worthy studied the dead man on the right, the one with a butcher knife buried in his sternum. His buddy had a clump of blood-matted hair and crushed bone where the back of his head should have been, and a dimple of an exit wound in the middle of his forehead.

Two attacks, two weapons, from two different directions. And he should have been off the clock an hour ago.

The door at the top of the ramp swung open. Worthy didn't think his hopes could sink any lower, but this night was happy to dash his dreams. It wasn't a medical examiner. It was *the* medical examiner, the city coroner herself, sauntering down the aisle in a long and tight white jacket and scarlet-bottomed Louboutin heels. Her hair was a pinup bob of raven black, and her eyes were all kinds of wrong.

Of course they're contact lenses, he remembered arguing in the precinct locker room one night. *Nobody has violet eyes. That's not a real thing.* But Owens insisted he had a buddy in the 38th who knew better, and swore she was born that way, some kind of mutation. The desk sarge had come in and given them all a dressing-down for talking about things above their pay grade.

"All you gotta know when it comes to the Doc is this: you stay polite, you speak when you're spoken to, and you never, ever, walk into a room alone with her. She doesn't come down to scenes herself, not unless she's got a special reason, so if you're lucky you'll never even meet her."

The sarge wouldn't elaborate on any of that, and Worthy didn't ask him to. Ten years behind a badge had left him with enough nightmares to last the rest of his life; he wasn't in the market for any new ones. But here was the coroner, toting an alligator-skin doctor's bag, casting those weird violet eyes his way with a flutter of lashes.

"Officer...Worthy, is that right? I try to know who's who around here."

"Yes, Doctor Contraire." He cupped his hands behind his back, standing at parade rest, and mentally begged the rookie to pick his jaw up off the floor. Not that he could make things any more awkward, with the voices begging some mustachioed stud to *do it harder, daddy* crackling over the theater speaker system. Worthy was going to find the projectionist and wring his scrawny neck. If nothing else, it'd give him an excuse to get out of here.

The coroner set her bag down on the edge of a folding seat and put her hands on her hips. Her violet nails, impeccable, matched her eyes.

"Well, boys? Tell me what we've got."

The rookie snapped to attention. "Two dead bodies, ma'am!"

Worthy stifled a groan. They were clearly recruiting the best and brightest these days.

"I was hoping for a little more detail," she said. She looked to Worthy. "You're a man of worldly experience, Officer Worthy. Tell me what you see. I'm curious. Come on, Officer...fill me in?"

He turned to the two stiffs. It wasn't his place to offer opinions, and he'd be lucky if he didn't get a talking-to when the detective in charge finally showed up, but an honest answer felt like his safest option right now.

"Manager called in a gunshot a little past twenty-two hundred hours. By the time we arrived on scene, everyone but theater personnel were long gone." Worthy pointed to the dead man on the left. "He's wearing disposable gloves, easy to pull on in the dark. From the angle of the knife wound, I think he waited for the house lights to go down, then stabbed the first victim."

The coroner stared at Worthy like he was a prime cut of steak, grilled to perfection.

"And met his own demise...how?"

He slipped into the row behind the corpses. "We found the slug. It exited down here—see the torn fabric, in the seat in front of him? For that angle to work, he had to have been leaning forward when someone shot him in the back of the head. My best guess is, he showed up for some kind of handoff, stabbed his contact instead of paying him, then leaned over to pick the goods up off the floor."

Worthy cocked his fingers into a gun, taking careful aim with one eye squinted shut.

"Another perp, keeping a low profile right about here, opened fire and made off with the loot. This wasn't a crime of opportunity. The shooter had to have known the meet was going down, might have even known that victim two was planning to bushwhack victim one. He waited until there was only one target left and took his shot."

"I do love a good surprise," Dr. Contraire said, leaning in. She inhaled, deep, sniffing the air as if the corpses gave off the bouquet of a fine wine. Then she reached into her pristine white coat and tugged out a small lollipop. She unwrapped it, crumpling the paper, and contemplated the cherry sphere before popping it between her lips. The stick dangled from one corner of her mouth like a cigarette.

"It's just a theory," Worthy said.

"I like it. I'm keeping an eye on you, Officer."

That was the last thing he wanted.

Second to last thing. The last thing he wanted stood in the open doorway at the top of the theater ramp, a tall, lean silhouette. A nightmare walking.

Chapter Five

Dr. Contraire opened her alligator-skin bag. She produced a pair of rubber gloves and pulled them on, letting each one snap against her wrist while she casually sucked on her lollipop. She barely glanced up at the new arrival. Worthy's mouth went bone-dry. He wasn't sure where he should look: not at her, not at him, and he didn't want to look at the corpses. The rookie was smart enough to stare down at his shoes. Smarter than Worthy gave him credit for. Maybe he'd make a decent cop after all, if he survived this.

The man in the doorway strode down, sanguine, his footsteps punctuated by the slow and steady tap of the ivory cane in his hand. The curled handle, filigreed in gold, bore the face of a roaring lion. He wore a tailored suit in pure vanilla-ice-cream-white, with a thin black tie and the dark puff of a silk handkerchief poking from his pocket.

"Gentlemen," he said. "Do you know who I am?"

They'd have to be deaf, dumb and blind not to. Then again, Worthy knew more than few people who went through life that way on purpose. It was safer than the alternative.

The rookie answered for him, his voice soft: "You're Duke Ellery."

The Illustrated Duke had a face to match his street name. Every inch of skin, from his pale blond hairline to his chin, down his neck to where his flesh vanished under the neck of his imported linen shirt, was tattooed. Letters in careful rows curling around his face, unreadable words in dead languages. He was tattooed in Sanskrit and Aramaic and Egyptian hieroglyphics. Latin circled one of his ears, spiraling inward like a chant made flesh, while Sumerian adorned the other. His hands curled around the handle of his cane, one over the other, sporting more ink. Each finger bore a forgotten name, each name ending in a small sigil, spiky and oddly angled and swirling, resting neatly upon his fingertips.

The coroner plucked the lollipop from her mouth. Then she took a scalpel from her bag with her free hand, raising it, studying the blade in the projector's flickering light. Duke Ellery curled one arm around her waist and pulled her close, almost hauling her off her feet. She grinned, feral, and touched the sharpened steel to his cheek.

He mirrored her smile and then, rattlesnake-fast, grabbed her knife hand by the wrist and yanked it back. He pressed his lips against hers, a long and furious kiss, as one of her legs slowly curled and lifted off the floor.

We are so dead, Worthy thought. He'd heard the rumors that the medical examiner's office was in bed with Duke's gang. He never gave it another thought because he didn't *want* to give it any thought. Now the knowledge was thrust upon him, along with the consequences.

Duke broke the kiss, purring in her ear before looking over her shoulder at the two cops. "My sweet Mary. Lips like butterscotch and wasp venom. Are these officers being helpful?"

"Very," she said.

"Very?" he echoed. Something different in his tone, now, and Worthy's churning gut told him what the question meant.

She took her time, deliberating, making them wait. Worthy felt like a gladiator, waiting for the turn of a thumb to decide his fate.

"Very," she said.

"I'm glad to hear that," Duke replied. "I am a taxpayer, after all. Gentlemen? Your work is finished here. You can leave, with my thanks."

"We're supposed to guard the scene until—" the rookie stammered. Worthy slapped him across the shoulders, shutting him up. Duke just chuckled, a low and rumbling sound, something like thunder at the edge of the savannah.

"There's no need to file any kind of a report on this," Duke said, "and I believe you'll find that your commanding officer has already written up your shifts for you. It was a very uneventful night. Nothing you need to remember, nothing you need to talk about. To anyone."

"We understand," Worthy said. The rookie, to his credit, was smart enough to clam up and nod along.

"Excellent. You'll find a little something extra in your pay envelope on Friday. A tip of the hat, from the Duke." He lifted his hand, tattooed fingers tugging down the brim of an imaginary hat. "You can go now. Be seeing you, Officer Worthy."

Worthy's face was slug-belly white, washed in sweat. He didn't say a word until he and the rookie were outside, out on the street, and back in their squad car. Normally he felt safe behind the wheel, with the shotgun clamped to the dash in easy reach. He wouldn't feel safe again anytime soon.

"Was that—"

"No," he said, sticking a finger in the rookie's face. "You shut up. You shut up and you *keep* shutting up. Nothing happened tonight, just like the man we didn't meet said, in the place we were never at. Get it?"

He stared at Worthy, silently asking for permission to speak.

"That, you can answer."
"Yeah. I get it, okay?"
"Good. Go back to shutting up now."

Duke studied the two corpses. He poked at the protruding handle of the butcher knife, curious. Then he said the name that was on both of their minds.

"Verna Bell."

The coroner's eyes narrowed to furious violet slits.

"You should have given her to me. I was right about her all along."

"Mary, baby, you have a track record of crying wolf. Don't pretend you weren't just hungry to get her on your table in the morgue. Every time you want a new plaything, you smell treachery in the air. Wild coincidence, truly."

"I was right," she said. "This time I was right."

"Greedy little thing," Duke murmured, and it wasn't clear which woman he was talking about. He turned. "Shame. Lance was a good bagman. Always brought back the goods, by hook or by crook."

"Until Verna popped a slug in the back of his head. What's with the kitchenware, anyway?"

Duke shrugged. "The other corpse is an antiquarian of local repute. He wasn't actually meeting the person he thought he was; Lance took him out and stepped in to take his place. I'm assuming negotiations went badly. Lance had a fondness for cutlery, something of a calling card. When Verna ransacked my study, she helped herself to my appointment planner. She must have cracked my code."

"What'd she get her hands on?"

"Nothing," Duke said. "In fact, come along. Entertain my hunch."

The theater had a fire exit down to the left of the screen, sign burned out, alarm long dead. It screeched on its hinges as Duke pushed it open with the tip of his cane. They stepped out into the back alley together. Fresh rain clung to the black asphalt, pooling in puddles that caught the neon of Longacre Square and glowed like a rainbow of dirty gemstones.

"Check that dumpster," he said, cane-tip pointed at an overflowing, rusted-out bin.

Mary gave him a sour look. "Why me?"

"Because, baby. You're the one wearing gloves."

She glanced down at her hands, decided she couldn't argue with his logic, and hauled the lid back. The search didn't take long. Her smudged gloves pulled out a dirty cardboard box, one flap covered in cinnamon-colored stamps from the far corners of parts beyond. Inside, on a bed of foam peanuts, nestled a small leather-bound book with a scuffed and unlabeled cover.

"She only cracked half my code," Duke said. "Enough to know that Lance was picking up a book for me. A rare import."

Mary tilted her head, puzzled. The lollipop stick dangled from the corner of her mouth, turning with a stroke of her tongue. "And then after putting a slug in your boy, she dumped the goods and ran? How's that make any sense?"

"Wrong goods, wrong night. That little number is the private journal of an archaeologist who, allegedly, solved the Araby Configuration and lived to talk about it. Priceless, to the right people—myself included. But Verna was hunting bigger game."

Now Mary followed him. "She thought this guy was bringing in the Argisene Grimoire."

"Poor, disappointed Verna," Duke said. "Imagine her dismay. Kills a man in cold blood and doesn't even get what she wanted."

"Yeah. Poor, poor, Verna. My heart bleeds. Speaking of…"

He waved a hand in the air and turned, his cane tapping along the wet pavement.

"She can run. What she can't do is hide. Believe me, I know the full scope of Ms. Bell's talents. She's capable of opening a door, but she can't close it behind her."

"And you know where she's running to?"

"Only one answer tells me true. Without the Argisene in her hands, there's only one play she can make: she's after the same prize we are. Which will tie this whole mess up in a delightful shiny bow, when we find them both in the same place. It's a two-for-one special."

He paused, turning to the coroner.

"Round up the crew."

"All the regulars?" she asked.

"My best people."

"They don't all work together so nicely, you know. Like cats and dogs, that lot."

"Nothing soothes bad blood like the promise of good money. Make it clear that this is a special job. Top priority, top pay to go along with it. I expect them to play nice and share their toys."

"A couple of our boys are cooling their heels up at the nuthatch," she said, twirling a finger around her ear. "Want 'em to sit this one out?"

His hand rested on her shoulder, massaging it, thumb rubbing in a slow and soothing circle. She closed her eyes.

"And miss all the fun?" he asked. "Perish the notion. Be a dear and break them out for me, would you?"

She leaned into his hand. "Anything for you, Duke."

"Those are the magic words I love to hear. Trust me: Verna was an unforeseen hitch, but nothing more than that. A bump in the road. Soon enough we'll have everything."

"The world, and everything in it," Mary sighed.

"The world and everything in it. After all..." he asked with a gleam in his eye. "...who's going to stop us?"

Chapter Six

Roy didn't call himself a private investigator. Lack of a license aside, he didn't do divorce work or background checks for suspicious bosses. He was strictly rescue and recovery. Same bag of tricks, though, and the same imperative when it came down to details: when he didn't have enough information to assemble a complete dossier on his target, he went looking for an expert opinion.

In this case, the expert worked behind the counter at Speedway Comics in downtown Indy, about an hour's drive from Carolyn's last known address. When Roy was a kid, his local comics shop was a dimly lit dungeon with dingy carpets and a funky, musty smell that clung to his allowance-bought treasures. The world had shifted when he wasn't looking. Speedway was more of a boutique, with track lighting and clean-swept beechwood laminate, and it smelled faintly like potpourri.

A few things stayed the same. Roy had to smile at the cardboard stand-up of Superman launching into the air, throwing a heroic punch. He recognized maybe half of the costumed heroes on the New Release racks. The art had improved over the decades, but the stories felt like home, the kind of stuff he used to read under the covers with a flashlight long after he should have been asleep. There'd be a diabolical villain, a sinister plan, a crusading hero who kept getting up no matter how many times he got knocked down. After a last-second escape or a titanic fight, the world would be saved once more.

Until another villain came along in next month's issue, anyway. For all the chaos in Superhero Land, nothing ever really changed. Roy found some small comfort in the consistency. Real life was a messier place, and it could turn on you in a hot second. And when the real world changed, it broke; nothing ever went back together again, not perfectly, not without some cracks to remind you of the damage.

The clerk behind the counter looked like he should be selling stocks instead of comic books. Crisp as the pages around him in a pressed button-down shirt and a bow tie. He pushed his glasses up on his nose and Roy saw him mentally composing his sales pitch. No doubt he'd made Roy for an outsider, anything but a regular in these parts.

"Not sure if you can help me," Roy said, cutting to the chase, "but I'm looking for information on an obscure title."

"Are we talking Bronze Age obscure, or Golden Age obscure? You might be surprised, we've got some crazy stuff in the short boxes in back."

"Series called *The Midnight Jury*. Only three issues ever came out, about a decade ago. Not sure who the artist was, but they were written—"

The clerk snapped his fingers and grinned like a winner on trivia night. "By Chandler Hawks. A definite rarity. Please, tell me you found a complete set, and tell me they're in mint condition. I'll make you an offer on the spot."

"Hard to track down?"

"Small press, small print run, and it never got the attention it deserved before its untimely demise."

"Why'd it get canceled?"

"Not canceled," the clerk said. "A casualty of war. The entire industry hit a recession. Some publishers found a way to survive—mostly by grabbing a chunk of that Hollywood money—and a lot of them didn't. From what I heard, the fourth issue of *Midnight Jury* was well on its way to print, and a fifth already written and inked, when Bang Pop ran out of cash and crashed overnight."

"I'd like to read those missing issues," Roy said.

"You and me both, but it's never going to happen. Bang Pop is long gone, their entire inventory got pulped in the liquidation, and Chandler Hawks could have been literally any writer in the industry."

"You think it was a pen name?"

"Had to be. The whole series was drenched in noir tropes, and the first issue of *The Midnight Jury* heavily referenced *The Big Sleep*." The grin was back, thrilled at the chance to share some obscure bit of lore. He held up two fingers, curling them as he broke down the name. "1946, Warner Brothers. Based on the novel by Raymond Chandler, directed by Howard Hawks."

That wasn't what Roy wanted to hear, but only a fool ignored the facts when they were laid out right in front of him. If "Chandler Hawks" was Carolyn's silent collaborator, finding him—or her—was his best shot at finding the missing manuscript. Except Hawks could have been anyone, a forgotten nobody or a superstar, safe in anonymity. Which put Roy back at square one all over again.

Hell, he thought, *maybe Hawks WAS Carolyn. That'd be a kick in the pants.*

He wasn't ready to call this a dead end, not yet. He had one last angle of attack. First, though, he had a hunch to settle. Out in the parking lot, face tilted up to catch the warmth of the noonday sun, Roy basked for a minute like a lizard on a rock. Then he did some quick research on his phone. Red Harvest Publishing's contact information was publicly listed; so was the office number for their general counsel.

"This is Frank Bigelow, with Bigelow and Halliday," he said, putting on the hint of a southern accent. "We're the executors of Carolyn Saunders's estate, and I was hoping you could clear up a bit of confusion."

"Of course," the company lawyer said. Her tone of brisk sympathy was about as calculated as Roy's mild country twang. "We were all so sorry to hear about her accident. How can I help?"

"Well, we were contacted by a gentleman who says he's working for y'all, a Mr...Smith, I think his name was? He's helping to track down the manuscript for *The City on Fire*, but we couldn't find anything about it when we took an inventory."

The pause in her voice told Roy everything he needed to know.

"There must be a mistake," she said.

"You didn't hire him?"

"There's nothing to hire anyone for. There's no book."

Roy squinted up at the sun.

"No book," he echoed.

"*The City at Midnight* underperformed. By, well...a lot. It wasn't exactly her most popular novel. We *had* contracted her for two books, but once the sales numbers came in, we cut our losses. *The City on Fire* was canceled, and we let her keep the first book's advance money. Call it a peaceful divorce."

They hadn't bought it. That didn't mean she hadn't written it. Mr. Smith had commented on the glacial pace of the publishing industry when they met, and right now that felt like the only part of his spiel that Roy could actually believe.

"Any idea if she'd been working on the sequel, at least up to when her contract got the ax? A first draft, maybe?"

"It's possible. Likely, even, but she never turned anything in."

Meaning the only copy would probably be sitting on Carolyn's personal computer. Her stolen computer. Ray cursed under his breath, thanked her, and ended the call.

Mr. Smith knew the book existed, or he wouldn't have tapped Roy for the hunt. But Red Harvest hadn't hired him, and they didn't *want* Carolyn's unpublished opus: they wouldn't even pay him for the paper it was printed on.

Roy thought he knew every scam on the street, but scams all had one thing in common: a profit motive. No matter how he came at it, he couldn't see any way for Smith to earn a dime even if Roy did manage to find the missing and unlamented manuscript. Only one theory even came close to making sense: Smith was a hardcore super-fan with more money than sense, looking to score a truly one-of-a-kind piece of Carolyn Saunders memorabilia. But if that was the deal, why bother misrepresenting himself or lie about the nature of the job? Roy had dug up stranger things for people with dodgier motives, and anyone with the juice to find him would know that.

Curiosity had Roy on a leash. He felt it tethered to his throat as he plunged down the rabbit hole, rope spiraling down after him into the dark. Maybe it would last forever. Or maybe it would run out and yank, sharp and hard and fast, snapping his neck before he reached the bottom. Leaving him dangling there, dead and blind, a warning to anyone else who dove in looking for answers.

Wouldn't help. Once you jumped into the rabbit hole, there was only one way you could travel: straight down, all the way to the end of the line. A hot breeze ruffled Roy's hair, tinged with the smell of gasoline. He chased the only solid lead he had left. Bang Pop Comics might have collapsed in the recession, but there had to be an old-timer or two still kicking around, somebody with a memory for details. Hopefully somebody who could pin "Chandler Hawks" to a real name for him.

He found an answer quick. And an opportunity. Roy wanted a better read on Mr. Smith, some insight into the nature of his game. Now he had a perfect excuse to give the man a call.

"Mr. Mackey," he said, picking up on the second ring, "I do hope you're calling with good news."

"Solid progress. I've found someone with a connection to the manuscript. If we're lucky, they have a copy, and I can wrap this up by tonight."

"I don't trust in *luck*," Smith said. He pronounced the word like it personally offended him, the closest he had come to any display of a personality. "I trust in the talents of professionals. Professionals like yourself."

"Well, there's just one hitch. Ideally this meet would go down in person, but they're out in Los Angeles—"

"So fly there."

Simple as that.

"If you'll recall, I'm in Indiana at the moment. On short notice, the cheapest flight is going to run me four hundred bucks, easy."

"I didn't mean to imply that I expect you to pay your own way," Smith told him. "Obviously, the firm will compensate you. Email me a receipt for your tickets and I'll wire you the payment. Same bank as before?"

"Same one," Roy said. He could chalk this up as one suspicion confirmed: Smith was willing to throw cash at him without a second thought. He wondered how far he could push it. "And lodgings?"

"We don't want you to sleep on the streets, or go hungry. Whatever you need, pay for it. I don't expect you to call me for every little thing. Consider yourself pre-authorized to spend any funds you deem necessary, and send me the receipts. As long as you get results."

"Is the publisher on board with that kind of expense?" Roy asked, playing dumb. "Travel costs can add up fast."

"The publisher is ready to make a small fortune when you deliver their next best-seller. The fans are waiting, Roy. The fans are *hungry*. We can't deny them their pleasures, now can we?"

"Wouldn't dream of it," he said.

Chapter Seven

Bang Pop Comics was the brainchild of two entrepreneur brothers, the Zielinska twins. The elder Zielinska (by twenty minutes or so) was dead. He'd survived the collapse of Bang Pop and three other business startups, but he hadn't been able to beat cirrhosis of the liver. The younger brother scraped whatever pocket change he could from the wreckage of their publishing house and set sail for the lights of Hollywood.

Or as close as he could get, anyway. Neil Zielinska's new business was registered to a residential loft just a brick-toss from Skid Row. The cab driver at the airport asked Roy to repeat the address, twice.

"You know it's gonna be after dark by the time I get you there, right?"

"That's fine," Roy said.

"What I'm saying is, it might be hard finding a ride back out again."

"I don't mind walking."

The cabbie shot him a look in the rearview mirror.

The street outside Zielinska's was an open-air misery market. Ragged puptents dotted the dirty sidewalk, hard-up survivors shuffling past or curled up in dirty sleeping bags, shivering in the sunset heat. Roy didn't look and he didn't linger. He made a beeline for the address, which was marked in tarnished brass numbers over a battered awning.

As he was walking in, a woman was storming out, stomping down the stairs in chunky sky-high wedges. They clacked on the dusty steps like gunshots and a leopard-print purse, matching her barely-there skirt, swung with dangerous weight.

"You're a real prince, Neil," she shouted over her shoulder. "A real goddamn peach of a prince."

The surviving Zielinska brother chased after her, keeping a safe distance from her purse. He wore an off-the-rack suit that didn't fit him, the sleeves too long and the trousers too short, all in avocado green.

"Baby, come on, it was a minor financial hiccup, I'll call the bank and get it sorted out. I'll make this right, I swear."

"What are you going to do, write me another check? Hey, maybe you can send me a fax while you're at it. Or record it on an 8-track. Old bastard hipster wannabe."

He waved a finger at her back. "I'm not old, and those cassettes belonged to my father. The 8-track is a severely underappreciated medium with excellent sound quality."

Roy held up a hand in greeting, then ducked to one side, pressing his back to a row of dented mailboxes to evade the stampede.

"Mr. Zielinska?" he said. "We spoke on the phone, about an hour ago."

"Right, right. One second. Hey, baby? Come back upstairs, let's talk this out. I hate it when we fight."

The woman barely paused on her way out, firing a glare at Roy.

"*Don't* let him write you a check."

Then she swept outside, leaving Neil halfway down the steps, broken-hearted in her dust. He spread his empty hands and mouthed a silent plea at the door.

"This a bad time?" Roy asked.

Neil shook off his despair and forced a smile. "Nah, never a bad time. You are..."

"Frank Bigelow, with Bigelow and Halliday," Roy said.

"Okay, good, just making sure. I been getting phone calls all morning and...you know what? Don't worry about that. Come on up. If somebody knocks on the door, we'll just be real quiet until they go away."

There were two flavors of money trouble, in Roy's experience. The kind where a debt collector calls you on the phone, and the kind where they show up on your doorstep after sundown. One could break your credit score, while the other favored kneecaps. It wasn't hard to guess what kind of trouble Neil was in. Roy followed him up the stairs.

"So this is about some kinda...probate?" Neil asked, looking back over his shoulder.

"We're representing the estate of Carolyn Saunders."

"So you told me, but I gotta say, the name doesn't ring any bells. Did she leave me anything?"

Roy kept him in suspense.

The streetlights outside couldn't penetrate the windows that lined one wall of Neil's loft, glass caked with streaks and swirls of dried soap. The best they could manage was a cold and muted glow. Roy took the place in, one quick sweep: a California King bed with rumpled gray satin sheets, dirty dishes in the sink, cereal boxes and a pizza carton on the kitchenette counter. Three handles of cheap booze scattered here and there, two of them running on empty. Neil had settled into a life of perpetual bachelorhood, and Roy didn't see his status changing anytime soon.

ANY MINOR WORLD

The back wall of the loft, old bare red brick, thrummed with muffled bass. The music throbbed along the floorboards, tingling the soles of Roy's feet. Neil grimaced. "My neighbor. He's either deaf or hosting a rave in there. Seven nights a week, this goes on."

"Call the cops?"

"Not in this neighborhood. So, ah...about this chick's will?"

"I had some questions," Roy said, "about Bang Pop."

Neil shuffled over to the kitchenette, grabbed a nearly tapped-out bottle of scotch and rummaged in the cupboard for a glass.

"That was my brother's idea. Bless his soul, he had great ideas but his timing was garbage." He wiggled the bottle. "You want?"

"No thanks."

"We get into comics, the industry hits a recession. We get into skin flicks, and everybody starts watching porn online without paying for it." Neil looked Roy up and down, lingering on his biceps. "You're a pretty big guy. You ever, y'know, do any acting?"

"I don't take checks."

Neil splashed his scotch into a water-spotted glass, shaking the bottle to get the last few drops out.

"You published a series called *The Midnight Jury*," Roy said. "By a writer calling himself Chandler Hawks."

"Sure. Good stuff. Wasn't a best-seller, but then again, none of our titles were. We were carving out a healthy little niche for ourselves until the bottom dropped out."

"Did you ever meet him in person?"

Neil sipped his scotch. He contemplated the glass, thinking back.

"Her. The pen name was my idea; I figured readers would be more responsive to that two-fisted pulp action stuff if they thought a guy was writing it. We never met face-to-face, but we talked on the phone. Young chick, sweet voice. Name was..." He scrunched up his brow. "...Lucy, Lucy something. I don't remember, it's been a lot of years and a lot of drinks since then."

"Would it be in your company paperwork?"

Neil chuckled. "Like I saved that stuff. Nah, the corpse of Bang Pop Comics is rotting in a landfill somewhere in Cincinnati. My accountant might have something, old payroll records, but..."

He gave Roy an expectant look.

"But?"

"But," Neil said, "you're asking a lot of questions and haven't gotten around to the 'how this does me any good' part yet. Don't get me wrong, I don't mind a friendly chat. But digging up the past sounds like actual work. I try to stay away from work in general, and when I do it, I like to get paid."

Roy had ginned up a story on the cab ride over. On past jobs, "Bigelow and Halliday" had become everything from a courier company to a talent agency. His imaginary employers were very flexible. Right now, the probate angle was working fine.

"Our client left a large sum of money to Chandler Hawks. We're not sure why Ms. Saunders recorded the pseudonym instead of a real name, but this puts us in a bind. I have to find the woman behind the disguise so I can give her the happy news."

"A...large sum, you said?"

"A large sum," Roy repeated. "And if you help us out, I imagine 'Lucy something' will be happy to share a finder's fee. For your time and trouble."

Neil almost reached for his phone. Then he paused, calculating.

"I mean, this is a whole lot of speculation and 'maybe.' You could sweeten the pot a little."

Roy took out his wallet. All he had on him was a single folded twenty; he took it out, wrapped it around one finger and held it up, asking a question with his eyes.

"That'll do," Neil said.

Lucy Something was Lucy Langenkamp, and Neil's records coughed up an address in Phoenix. Roy slept on the plane. He dreamed of engine fires, and woke to turbulence over the endless jagged teeth of the Rocky Mountains. He slept again and dreamed about a woman he used to love.

My hands are clean. But what you did to her...that's forever.

His nightmares collided at thirty thousand feet. Roy stood in the husk of a jetliner, choking on smoke while shattered consoles spat sparks and flames roiled in the cockpit. Below was the city to end all cities, studded with mammoth art deco skyscrapers and elevated trains running on curling spaghetti tracks suspended far above the filthy streets. Clock towers and corporate embassies like cathedrals, with tarnished chrome gargoyles and vaulted stained-glass penthouse windows.

Perez was down on his knees, looking just like he had the last time Roy saw him. Bleach blond, ferret-faced and feral. He grinned, showing bloody teeth.

"You were the last one, you know that? The last one I ever thought would betray me."

"Shut your goddamn mouth," Roy said, playing his part from memory. The revolver in his hand weighed twenty pounds. He let off the pressure by pressing the muzzle tight against Perez's forehead.

"My hands are clean, but what you did to her..."

The plane's dying engines shuddered and spat fire. The floor lurched under Roy's feet as the nose started to pitch, leaning into a dive.

"Noir York," Perez said, breaking from the script. "Ain't it beautiful? They say this city can make a new man out of you. That you can be anyone you want to be."

The plane veered downward, going vertical, screaming as superheated wind whipped through the smoke and flame. Dream logic kept Roy on his feet.

"But it's no place for you and me, is it, pal? You couldn't change if you wanted to. And me, well, I'm dead."

Windows flashed by, gleaming like diamonds in the dark. A neon sign roared past, longer than the jet, pinned to the side of a granite tower. The city opened its jaws wide.

"Remember, Roy. Dead is forever."

He didn't sleep any more after that. Roy spent the rest of the flight staring at the window, watching his own faceless reflection in the glass.

Chapter Eight

Lucy Langenkamp had lived in Phoenix a decade ago. Some people stayed in one place their entire lives. She hadn't. Roy found a cheap apartment building at the address Neil gave him, a dirty white stucco brick surrounded by a lawn of yellow, dying grass, but the tenant in 1208 was a half-blind elderly German man who had never heard her name. Roy's next stop was the management office.

The leasing agent didn't want to cough up a resident's personal information, even a former one, without anything short of a court order. Roy was glad he'd stopped at the airport ATM. He didn't have a subpoena up his sleeve, but he did have a bribe. While the leasing agent rummaged through her files, Roy sent a quick text to Mr. Smith: *In AZ, looking for someone who might have worked on the book with Saunders. Send money.*

Smith's response was fast, faster than most people could type. *Done*, he wrote. *Name of this person?*

Roy hesitated.

His fingertip hovered over the screen. Normally he'd tell a client anything they wanted to know; after all, they were paying him to get results. But Mr. Smith wasn't a normal client. He'd sent Roy hunting for a manuscript that might not exist, on behalf of a publisher who didn't hire him and didn't want to buy it.

Fair's fair, Roy thought. *You're gonna lie to me, I'll lie right back. At least until I figure out what your real angle is.*

Uncertain, he wrote. *He might be using an alias. Will follow up as soon as I know more.*

The leasing agent came back with the goods. Lucy moved out three years ago, but she'd left a forwarding address. Lucy left Arizona behind to seek her fortune three hundred miles north, in Las Vegas. Roy booked a shuttle flight and sent the receipt to Mr. Smith.

Every airport was a little different. Each had some kind of tell, some way to let Roy know he hadn't come full circle and landed in the place he started from. Sometimes there'd be far-off forests outside the big plate glass windows, sometimes fresh, fluffy snow, sometimes dirty concrete and cold rain. This was the airport with the jangling, flashing slot machines in the concourse and the rust-red mountains in the distance.

He thought he passed himself in the crowd. His twin lumbered past him, unkempt dark hair, bristle on his cheeks. Roy registered the oddity and his brain froze for a second. He shook it off, stopped dead and turned back to look.

Nobody. No one even remotely his height in the passing throng, no one with his broad shoulders, his rolling gait. *I need sleep*, he thought. Not airplane sleep. Real sleep in a real bed.

It would have to wait. First he needed to find Lucy. Then the real problem: figuring out what to do about her. And about Mr. Smith.

Lucy Langenkamp didn't have a view of the mountains. The blinds in her lab were pulled low, dirty plastic blocking out the sun. Even if she opened them, all she'd get was a view of the side alley and a whitewashed brick wall with a No Parking sign. Her light came from muffled overheads and the pinpoint beam on her head-mounted magnifying lens. Her eyes were big almond orbs behind the visor, wide and alert, and her brush whisked gently across a rugged old canvas while she perched on a swiveling stool.

Her free hand reached out, picked up a jar, held it to her lips. The stench of turpentine and dirty paint-water hit her nose just before she took a swig. Wincing, she set it down and fumbled for the mug of coffee right beside it.

This portrait had been a beauty once. Early twentieth century, maybe late nineteenth, judging from the oils and the canvas. That and the rich emerald ball gown on the seated woman in the picture, her warm smile smeared by smoke from a house fire. Lucy traced the cut of her gown to a particular Parisian fashion house, helping her nail down the provenance of the portrait and get another clue to the identity of the artist whose initials, once elegantly scribed in silver in the bottom-left corner, had been charred nearly black.

"Don't worry," Lucy said to the woman in the portrait. "I'll save you."

The restoration was slow, methodical. From the sweep of an infrared scope to a spectroscopic analysis, Lucy saw beyond the damaged artwork to the untarnished jewel beneath and inked a road map to renewal. Then came the gentle stripping of the old varnish, replacement with fresh layers, and the alchemical sorcery of mixing period-correct pigments to find a perfect match for colors you couldn't buy in any modern store. Her instruments and tools paved the way for her palette and brushes, working together in elegant symmetry. A yellow sticky note, dangling from the bottom corner of her wooden easel, summed up her thoughts on the subject.

Art + Science = Magic

"You've got a great smile," she murmured, whisking a fresh brush across her messy palette. "Let's fix that up for you. Nothing a little time and attention can't—"

The door to her lab swung open. Mr. Gillibrand didn't knock. He never knocked, operating on the assumption that whatever he needed was the most important thing in the office at any given moment. After all, he was fond of pointing out, the name out front was Gillibrand's Art Restoration. If that didn't mean he called the shots around here, what did? Lucy couldn't argue with his logic.

"Going to need you to stay late tonight," he said. "Pasquale's running behind on his restoration job for the Carmine account, and it's all hands on deck."

"How late?"

His expectant stare pinned her like a bug. She squirmed on her stool, fighting to hold eye contact. *Don't look down*, she told herself, *don't look down.*

"Until it's done," he said. "I don't know, talk to Pasquale. They're coming to pick it up at ten sharp tomorrow morning, and it has to be finished. Pull an all-nighter if you need to."

"It's just that, um—" *don't look down, don't look away, be confident—* "I sort of had plans for tonight."

Gillibrand snorted out a laugh. "What, you got a hot date or something? Come on, Lucy. You don't have anything going on tonight."

Her gaze dive-bombed to the floor at her feet.

"It's my sister's birthday," she stammered out. "I was going to take her out for—"

"I really need you here. Come on, you're my best team player. I need you on this. Yes? Yes. Good. I'll tell the Carmines they can come by tomorrow to get their...family painting or whatever it is. Ten o'clock sharp!"

Then he was gone, the deadline echoing along with the final-word click of her lab door falling shut.

"The power of negotiation begins with the power of one word," said the soothing voice in Lucy's earbuds. "The power of *no*. Mastering this simple, two-letter word will pave your way to personal and professional success. Go ahead and give it a try, right this minute: say 'No.'"

Lucy shrank a little, winding her way down a sunbaked sidewalk east of the Vegas Strip in the city's University District. She could see the sleeping monoliths of the casinos, silent in the breath-stealing noonday heat, looming in the distance over the city's sports arenas and the university campus. Her little chunk of the district offered cafes and boutiques, small art galleries by day and live music by night, close enough to the Strip to draw a tourist crowd but far enough to be priced for local wallets.

No, she mouthed, her pale lips pursed in a tight *O*. No sound behind it, not even a breath, but a passerby still gave her an odd look. She pursed her lips tight, clicked off the recording, and ran nervous fingers through her mousy brown hair.

Jenna was waiting for her at Firehouse Subs, part of their usual lunch spot rotation. Tuesdays were always at Firehouse Subs, when she had time to take a lunch break at all. Lucy gave her a wave and put in her order. The counter-man was already assembling her usual—Virginia honey ham on a toasted roll with lettuce, tomatoes, and onions—before she had a chance to order.

She had been thinking about trying something different for a change, but it was nice to be remembered, and she'd have to interrupt his work, so she didn't say anything. It was fine. She liked her usual order.

"He's keeping you late again," Jenna said as soon as Lucy sat down. Jenna was bright and brassy as her copper-blonde dye job, and her fingernails glittered in a rainbow riot of color as she poked a straw into her bucket of soda.

"How can you tell?"

"You get this look on your face. It's always the same look."

"It doesn't happen that often," Lucy said.

"Three times in the last two weeks," Jenna fired back. "Girl, you are *salaried*. He doesn't pay you overtime and he doesn't pay bonuses."

"We get a Christmas bonus."

Jenna stared at her. "Two hundred bucks and a toaster is not a Christmas bonus. You've got to quit that job."

"I like my job."

"No, you like your career. Enjoying what you do is not the same thing as enjoying the place where you do it, or the stingy asshole who pays you to do it for him. You can do better."

Lucy unwrapped her sub, picked up half, and tried to disappear into silence for the space of a long bite. Her friend waited for an answer, expectant, not letting her off the hook.

"I don't know if I can. Gillibrand's hired me fresh out of college and I don't have much of a track record. Or credentials! Credentials are important too. What if I quit and nobody else will hire me? I'm safe where I am."

Jenna's plastic fork plowed into her salad, spearfishing for a chunk of grilled chicken.

"People in prison are safe, too," she said.

"Well, actually," Lucy said, "prisons are pretty dangerous—"

"You know what I mean. You're in a rut. It just *feels* safe because you're deep down in it, so deep you can't even see the sun." Jenna reached across the table and put her hand over Lucy's. "Hey. I get it. Change is scary. But you deserve better than this."

Lucy made some reassuring noises and pretended to agree.

She wrapped up the other half of her sub and took it with her. It was Tuesday, which meant Steamboat would be sitting in his usual spot on the skillet-hot sidewalk, cross-legged on a ratty blanket in his old green fatigues, with a sign that said Homeless, Veteran, Please Help God Bless. Lucy wasn't convinced he'd ever seen a steamboat, let alone captained one up and down the Mississippi before falling headfirst into a bottle, but he always had a good story to tell.

"Miss Lucy," he said, tipping his watch-cap.

"Hey Steamboat, you hungry?"

She knew the answer, and he gladly accepted the other half of her sub. No time for chat today; the sooner she got back to the lab, the sooner she could get a head start on her plateful of extra work. Jenna, headed the same way, waited until he was out of earshot before speaking up again.

"Really? On what Gillibrand pays you, you can just throw away half of your lunch?"

"I didn't *throw it away*. Besides, I wasn't hungry."

"Uh-huh," Jenna said.

Lucy gave her a sidelong glance. "What's that supposed to mean?"

"I worry about you. You're too goddamn nice."

"That's a bad thing?"

"In this town?" Jenna laughed. "Nice people get rolled in Vegas. You need to toughen up."

"I'm tough. I mean, when I need to be. I can be tough."

"Uh-huh."

Neither woman noticed the plumbing van with dirt-caked California plates and amber-tinted windows revving to life in their wake. Or how it prowled behind them, crawling well below the speed limit, keeping pace from a distance.

Chapter Nine

Roy found Lucy's name on the mailbox in the cramped vestibule of her new apartment building. She was still in town and moving up in the world, if only by a ladder-rung or two. Decent neighborhood, not far from the university, a stone's throw or a quick cab ride from the glitz of the Strip. Roy idly wondered if the locals even cared about the Strip, or if it was like a tourist beach in Florida: a place you'd visit once or twice and then forget about entirely. Maybe he'd ask Lucy when they finally met, before he got down to the important questions.

The landlord was out, so Roy knocked on a few doors. One neighbor had never seen her, another described Lucy as "a nice, quiet kid" and said she was some kind of restoration expert, but he didn't know where she worked exactly. That was a little more to go on, at least. Roy asked for a physical description.

"You're supposed to give her a chunk of money, and you don't even know what she looks like?" the neighbor asked, dubious now.

"It's a written will. All I've got is a name and address. I tried to call her, but she must have changed numbers at some point; the one I have doesn't work anymore."

The neighbor didn't know her number—that was too much to hope for—but he gave Roy enough of a description that he might be able to pick Lucy out of a very small crowd.

Roy was making extra work for himself. He knew that. The best, smartest thing to do was to camp outside Lucy's apartment door, cool his heels, and wait. She was probably at work, she'd be home in a few hours, and he could invite himself inside and find out what she knew about Carolyn's lost manuscript—or at least why Carolyn had apparently stolen the characters from her comic books. Easy.

Instinct drove spurs into his hips. Everything about this job felt hinky, weird from the start and getting weirder every step of the way. It took a minute for him to register what was really nagging at him, tugging at the back of his brain like a loose thread on a sweater.

Mr. Smith had been a constant presence on his phone, asking for updates, pushing for results. Right up until Roy sent him the receipt for his shuttle flight to Vegas. Since then he hadn't called, hadn't texted, and Roy doubted the man was sleeping. He wasn't sure why Smith had gone silent, but he didn't like it.

Finding Lucy's place of business was Private Investigator 101. He grabbed a list of local art-restoration houses—more than he expected, but not too many to canvass by phone—and called each one, posing as a client. On the third try, Gillibrand's Art Restoration, a bored receptionist passed him through to Lucy's voicemail.

He didn't leave a message. He didn't know if she would call him back and besides, this felt like a face-to-face situation. He hailed a taxi on the corner.

Lucy said her goodbyes at a traffic light—she was headed east, Jenna's office was a few blocks west—and resigned herself to a long afternoon and a longer night of working on another restorer's late project. Again. At least she knew the painting would be in good hands, and that had to count for something, right?

She tried to imagine, as she walked, what would happen if she just said no. She was the best restorer on Gillibrand's staff. She turned in her projects ahead of schedule, above expectations and under budget, and repeat clients asked for her by name. Gillibrand never acknowledged that, but they both knew it was true. So what was he going to do if she put her foot down and said she couldn't work late tonight, that she'd promised her sister a birthday dinner and that was that? Fire her? No. He was stingy, not stupid.

But he'd bluster, and yell at her, and...and it was just easier to stay late. Just easier, that was all.

"The art of negotiation begins with setting firm limits," said the voice in her earbuds. She'd daydreamed her way through half a chapter of her audiobook, lost in thought. She glanced down at the screen of her phone, tapping it twice, bumping the recording back a bit.

She was distracted enough not to notice the plumbing van with the tinted windows rolling up on her. Not until the side door rumbled and whipped wide and a flash of dark motion flickered in the corner of her eye. A beefy hand clamped down on her wrist, squeezing hard enough to make her eyes water, and the phone dropped from her fingers to shatter, bouncing and broken, on the sidewalk at her feet.

Roy wasn't distracted. Not one little bit.

He was closing in on Gillibrand's Art Restoration when he spotted a woman who could be Lucy—at least going by her neighbor's sketchy description—coming toward him from the opposite direction. Then he noticed the van.

California plates in Nevada weren't unusual; people drove across state lines for business and pleasure all the time. Neither were the tinted windows. When you were working in desert conditions, fighting the heat was a matter of daily survival. It was the pace—careful, deliberate, so slow that delivery trucks and cabs were winding around it—that put his nerves on edge. He knew an impending snatch-and-grab when he saw one. He knew because he'd organized a few of his own.

The driver was either timid, an amateur, or both. What should have been a smooth, brisk roll-up on the target was a slug-slow crawl that made the van stand out like a sore thumb. More importantly, there was only one target in sight on the nearly empty sidewalk. Lucy.

The van jolted to a stop and the panel door rattled open. A man in a black ski mask fired out like a cannonball, one hand on Lucy's wrist, yanking it behind her, the other clamping down over her mouth before she could scream. Roy broke into a run, silent, feral, a predator on the move. Three steps and the handle of the ASP baton was in his hand. Five and it snapped to its full length, black and gleaming under the high noon sun.

The thug in the mask hauled Lucy backwards, dragging her by her heels and wrestling her into the van. He had a buddy, jumping out while he struggled to get in. His buddy had a mask and a gun. Roy shifted targets on the stride. The gunman's finger was mid-squeeze on the trigger, his pistol's barrel aimed straight for Roy's belly, when the ASP whipped down with a subsonic crack and shattered his wrist into torn flesh and chunks of bone. He didn't stop, turning his hip and throwing an elbow that spattered the shooter's nose and drenched Roy's sleeve in hot blood.

The piece hit the sidewalk, barrel twirling like a lethal game of spin-the-bottle, as the wounded man fell back into the van and landed on his ass. The driver, too confident or too dumb to wear a mask of his own, looked back and screamed for them to get moving. Roy looked him in the eye, marked his face, burned it into memory, then got back to work.

The first thug let go of Lucy's wrist. He went for the sidearm on his hip, snug in an open-carry holster. One of the fingers cupped around her face slid too close to her mouth. She opened wide and chomped down. He yowled and shoved her away, giving up his best advantage. She hit the sidewalk, sprawling, landing hard enough to skin her forearm bloody.

"He boke my fuggin *node*," whined the injured shooter, his face a scarlet mask as he rocked back and forth, clutching his wrist. The driver dove for something in the glove compartment. Roy assumed a gun. That made three, with one coming up fast right in front of him and one still spinning on the white-hot pavement.

Roy was big. That meant people thought he was slow, in the head and on the move. He liked proving them wrong. In a heartbeat he calculated how much time he had, what he could reach, what he could do, how to survive the next ten seconds.

Surgery, he thought, dropping the baton to free up his fists.

His shoe lashed out, smacking the thug's gun hand and driving it toward the sky before he could pull the trigger. He fired, the shot echoing with a clap of thunder. Roy heard a window shatter somewhere above his head and behind his back, and pedestrians broke into a panicked stampede. He closed in, unrelenting. Next his heel came down on the thug's kneecap. It shattered with satisfying precision. So did a pair of ribs, snapping under concrete-knuckled punches. The driver had his gun out now, Roy could see in his peripheral vision, a nasty squat machine pistol. He tried to take aim, looking for an angle that wouldn't hit his own guy.

Roy wouldn't give him one. He turned, pivoting a step to the left, using the first thug as a human shield as he brutalized him with a knuckle-punch to the throat. Tenderized by pain, he gave up the pistol in his hand with a simple tug, just like Roy knew he would. He spun it around, took another sidestep, and opened fire.

Roy's bullet blasted into the driver's shoulder, punched through, and turned the side window into an amber spiderweb of cracked glass and blood-spray.

"*Go*," screamed the shooter with the broken nose. "Forget it, just fugging *go*!"

The wounded driver slumped against the wheel and slammed on the gas. Horns blared as the plumbing van fired into traffic like a torpedo, leaving Lucy behind. And the man who'd tried to kidnap her, who stared up at Roy with wide, terrified eyes behind his ski mask. No honor among thieves, at least not *these* thieves.

He lunged for the pistol on the pavement. Roy's heel came down hard on the gun, stopping it mid-spin. His free hand clamped down on the scruff of the man's neck.

"Figure somebody must have called 911 by now," Roy said, yanking him along like a dog. "Gives us a few minutes before the cops get here. C'mon. Let's have a quick chat. Just you and me."

Lucy pushed herself up off the sidewalk, gritting her teeth, dazed. She barely noticed the stinging pain along her arm or the warm trickle of blood leaking down into the curl of her palm. All she could do was watch as the stranger who had swooped in to save her disappeared into the mouth of an alley, dragging the beaten kidnapper like a trophy of war. The van was already long gone, swallowed whole by traffic.

There were plenty of smart things she could do. She could call the cops, run into her office and barricade the door, maybe hail a cab and get as far away from here as possible. Those were smart choices. Those were safe. Following her rescuer and his prey into that alley was the farthest thing from safe she could possibly imagine.

And yet.

Sometimes, every now and then, she heard a voice at the far edge of her mind. Felt it, more than heard it, and it always offered a warning: *If you take this path, your life will change forever. Nothing will ever be the same.*

She always assumed that instinctive voice was a warning, steering her away from danger. All of a sudden she wasn't so sure. Maybe it was an invitation.

Lucy held her breath. Soft on her feet, craning her neck to peer around the corner first, she followed them.

Chapter Ten

Roy collapsed and concealed his ASP. The two guns he'd taken, a nine-millimeter and a revolver, were both in crap condition and worth maybe twenty bucks apiece to some aspiring hood. He slapped them down side by side on the lid of a garbage can, then wiped his prints off with the tail of his shirt. The injured thug bled on the alley pavement at his feet, his back propped against the bare brick wall. He whimpered a little but he didn't say a word. Roy wasn't sure if the guy was scared or defiant, clinging to the last scraps of his pride. One easy way to find out, though.

"I'm short on time," Roy said, plucking his cuff buttons one by one and rolling back his sleeves. "You may or may not be short on time. We'll see how it goes. Can you walk?"

"My knee," he groaned. "I think it's busted—"

"So you can limp. Good. I'm going to ask you some questions. You're going to give me some answers. If you tell me what I need to know, I'll be on my merry way and you'll be free to do whatever you want to do. Which right now, let me assure you, is to hobble out of here as fast as you can manage before the cops show up. The faster you talk, the faster you walk, and the better your chances of spending the night in a hotel room instead of a jail cell."

"I ain't telling you any—"

He didn't finish the cliché. Roy had been expecting it, that last obligatory wall of defiance, and he'd been studying the downed man's chest. Two snapped ribs. Couldn't risk hitting those, might drive a broken bone into his lungs and then he wouldn't be talking at all. Roy picked his target and dropped hard, putting his plunging weight behind a full-force punch to the gut.

The thug doubled over and puked, retching onto the dirty ground. Roy waited patiently—as patient as he could manage—for him to stop spitting and sputtering.

"We understand each other?" Roy said. "Sure. We understand each other now."

He spotted Lucy standing off to one side in the corner of his eye, watching with a look of bloodless horror on her face. She didn't make a sound, didn't budge an inch. Roy nodded in her general direction.

"What were your intentions for the young lady here?"

The thug's resolve crumbled like an eggshell.

"We were supposed to grab her," he wheezed. "Not hurt her. Just snatch her off the street and take her to the place where we stole the van. Five g's if we grabbed her, two if we got you."

Roy wasn't expecting that. "Got me?"

He nodded weakly at his left front pocket, and then looked up with a question in his eyes.

"Go ahead," Roy told him, "but if you come out holding a weapon, I'm taking those fingers with me when I leave."

"Boss didn't tell us you were crazy," the man grumbled, digging in his pocket. "He said you used to be a cop."

Roy's expression darkened. "Long time ago. Show me what you want to show me. Stalling hurts you, not me, understand?"

He unfolded a photograph. Long-range, taken with a telephoto lens. Roy recognized himself in the picture. Him and Mr. Smith, talking business on the back deck of his company yacht. Someone had been spying on their meeting, and probably listening in the whole time.

"There's been somebody tailing you since Miami," he said. "Switching off, so you wouldn't notice. Every step of the way."

"And her?" Roy asked, nodding again to Lucy. "You got a picture of her in your pocket?"

"No." He coughed into his hand, leaving crimson flecks in his palm. "That was a special order. Boss called in half an hour ago, gave us her name, where she works, what she looks like, all we needed to scoop her up."

About the same time Roy figured Lucy's identity out for himself. He led them straight to her. Damn it.

"So you were supposed to snatch both of us and..."

The thug shook his head. "No, not like that. We were supposed to grab her. We were supposed to *get* you."

He explained the difference by cocking his trembling fingers like a gun, and putting them to his head. Roy's blood was already cold. Now it became a river of ice, flowing hard over furious, jagged rocks.

The next question was obvious: "Why?"

"Didn't ask, didn't want to know. Come on, man, my crew does stickups and shakedowns. A seven thousand dollar payday doesn't happen for dudes like us. We weren't gonna risk that kind of money by sticking our noses where they didn't belong. All I know is that he wanted her alive, and you gone, and those were, what do you call it...non-negotiable terms. He said if she got one scratch on her, we'd be walking dead men."

Roy had been imagining sirens, anticipating their arrival in the distance. Not his imagination, now: he could hear them closing in, pushing through the sluggish afternoon traffic on their way to the scene of the crime. Not much time left.

"Funny how things turn out, huh? Okay, last question, and this one's real important. Who hired you?"

He hesitated, like he might find some way out of this—some way to escape Roy's wrath *and* his employer's—and then his shoulders sagged. His gun finger raised, slow, and pointed at the photograph in Roy's hand. It took Roy a second to put two and two together. Then the jagged rocks under his icy river rapids rose another inch, close to breaking the surface.

"Mr. Smith," Roy said. "He hired you to kill me."

"Only after we made the snatch. I guess he was waiting for you to put the finger on her first, so he knew he'd have the right chick." He shot a nervous look at the alley mouth. "C'mon, man, it wasn't personal, business is business and I told you everything you wanted to know. You gotta let me go before the cops get here. You promised."

"Sure," Roy said through gritted teeth. "A deal's a deal."

Roy's heel slammed down on the thug's good kneecap. He let out one sharp, shrill scream then passed out from the pain, slumped motionless against the garbage can.

"Go ahead and walk that off," Roy told him.

He turned to Lucy. She still hadn't budged, hadn't said a word. She looked like a rabbit getting ready to run.

He held out his hand to her.

"Come on," he said. "I won't hurt you. Name's Roy Mackey. I was hired to find...well, I was hired to find a missing book, but it's a long story and I don't have time to walk you through it right now."

She glanced at the photograph in his fist. He'd crumpled the picture, balling it into a piece of trash, without realizing it.

"You said his name. It was him, wasn't it? The man who sent those kidnappers was the same one who hired you."

Which makes you my responsibility, Roy thought. *Hell, this whole mess is my responsibility now. And I'm not even getting paid.*

Unless he wrung the cash out of Smith's broken body, every penny he was promised plus damages. A mental image that had a definite appeal to it.

"He screwed me and he wants you," Roy said. "This guy met me on a forty-foot yacht, just to show off. He's got serious cash and resources behind him. Trust me, Smith's not going to stop with a few low-rent shooters. He'll try again, and next time he'll try harder."

"The police can protect me," Lucy said.

Roy tilted his head at her. "You really believe that?"

Her silence was all the answer he needed.

"Come with me," he said.

She took a halting step toward him. "Where?"

"Away from here. First thing I have to do is get you off the grid, someplace safe, where Smith can't find you."

"And second?" she asked.

"Second," Roy said, "I need to arrange a meeting with my former client, so I can get some real answers out of him. A very private, very personal kind of meeting."

"Mistakes were made," Mr. Smith said.

And not by me. But he left that part unspoken, buried as deeply as his seething, roiling anger, firmly concealed behind his genial gray mask. When addressing the Board, hiding your emotions was a key survival tactic.

Facing their hologram projections, today. He stood on a low dais in a room of featureless white plastic, the lenses of cameras and projectors and light-cans aimed with precision from overhead railings. A neon-blue wireframe of a room half a world away stretched out before him, faceless grid people sitting along a graph-paper conference table. Windows, before they faded halfway into stardust at the edge of the projection, showed the blurry glow of a foreign skyline.

Distance offered no sense of safety. Half the people at that table could destroy him with the press of a button. The other half had more potent—and more painful—methods of getting the job done.

"As I was saying," he continued, "we *have* positively identified our operational target."

"And positively lost track of her," said a woman at the table, her voice rippling with digital interference.

"Our outside assets lost track of her," Smith replied.

"Explain that," said a man at the table's far edge, half of his body cascading into neon static. "Once you found the target, why use outsiders instead of retrieving her yourself? This mission was placed in your hands, Smith. Along with our trust."

"She lives in Las Vegas," he said, as if that answered everything.

From their confused, irritable silence, it clearly didn't. Mr. Smith took a deep breath.

"Vegas is New Commission territory. A criminal syndicate that has remained stubbornly, proudly free of our influence. Their people know my face and they know my closest associates. Going there in person was too much of a risk, so I hired some regional talent with no connection to our organization. I was assured that they could handle the job."

"Sounds like you could have killed a pair of birds with one stone," one of the directors said.

"Under normal circumstances, perhaps. However, the Vegas mob is sizable, plugged into every local information channel, and several ranking members are *enhanced*. If they got wind of what we were after, not to mention what the target is capable of, they'd intervene for their own profit. I was hoping to stay under the radar and avoid unnecessary complications."

"I agree with your priorities," the first woman said. "Vengeance can wait. Tell us where we stand right now."

"My hired help was picked up by local authorities shortly after the mishap, one at the scene, two in heavy traffic a few blocks away. I've ensured that they know nothing and cannot hurt us—"

"Eliminate them," snapped a digitally-masked voice.

As I was about to say, Smith thought, biting off the words before they could reach his lips. "I've reached out to a skilled freelancer who's done good work for us in the past. All three will be dead by morning. Accidents."

"And the target?"

"Through our banking intermediaries, I have frozen Ms. Langenkamp's bank account and both of her credit cards. She won't get far."

"*Alone*," the woman stressed, "she won't get far. But she's not alone, is she?"

Mr. Smith clenched his hands behind his back, squeezing until his fingers ached.

"Roy Mackey is more difficult to pin down. That said, I chose him for more than his detective skills. I studied the man for a month before reaching out to him. I know how he thinks, how he reacts...I know what his next move will be, and who he'll likely reach out to for help. All contingencies have been planned for well in advance."

"You didn't plan for Las Vegas."

Now he squeezed his hands and bit the inside of his cheek.

"I thank you for your continued trust," Mr. Smith said, "and I look forward to repaying you with results. Soon."

"So do we," one of the directors replied. "And I don't have to tell you what will happen if you fail us, Smith. The future of this entire organization is in your hands. Don't forget it."

The projection flickered and died, neon wireframes collapsing to the floor in a shower of sparks before fading and vanishing. Smith stood alone in the white plastic room, eyes forward, quietly furious.

"Believe me," he said to the empty air, "I won't. *Sir.*"

Chapter Eleven

"So this woman—" Lucy said.

"Carolyn Saunders."

Lucy usually took the bus home. Roy had vetoed that and hailed a taxi. She sat beside him in the backseat, tapping at her phone, her brow furrowing as she read the blurb for *The City at Midnight*.

"These are *my characters*," she said.

"And you didn't work with her?"

"I've never even heard of her." Lucy's head dipped closer to the screen, peering into it like it was a crystal ball, searching for answers. "So this Mr. Smith said he was hired by the publisher—but he wasn't—and he wanted you to find this unpublished sequel..."

"*The City on Fire*. Which may or may not actually exist. I'm leaning toward 'not' right about now. I've got a working theory."

Lucy glanced up at him. "Which is?"

"It was never about the manuscript. He wanted you, right from the start. Smith knew there was a connection between Saunders's last book and the comics you wrote as 'Chandler Hawks,' and he probably thought the same thing I did at first: that either you two were friends and she had done it with your permission, or you had ghost-written the book for her. Digging into Saunders was just a way of tracking you down. Unmasking the person behind the pen name."

"Why not ask her?"

"Saunders died in a car accident not long ago, up in New York State. Allegedly. I'm questioning everything right about now."

"I know the feeling. So who is this Smith guy? The real him."

"If I knew that, I'd know why he wants to grab you," Roy said. "Don't suppose you've got any insights there?"

She buried herself back in the screen of her phone, head down, shoulders tucked in. Trying to vanish in plain sight.

"Me? I'm...I'm nobody. There's no reason anyone would want to hurt me."

"He wanted me hurt. You, he wanted alive and intact. That speaks to a special motive." Roy squinted, studying her. "You got any relatives with money? Someone who might pay to get you back?"

"My dad's a postal worker, my mom's a housewife, and my only sister is a nurse. We do okay, but we're a long way from rich. I had to get a scholarship just to attend college, and I paid for anything it didn't cover out of my own pocket. Heck, that's why I wrote those comics in the first place. Not that I made all that much money before the publisher went belly-up."

"Think back," Roy said. "There's something special about you."

Her eyes flicked toward the side window, away from him.

"There really isn't. I promise. Maybe it's something to do with my job, one of the pieces I've restored?"

Roy shook his head. "If Smith knew that much about you, he wouldn't have needed me to track you down. Whatever he knows begins and ends with Chandler Hawks and those stories you wrote."

"It was just a lucky break. Bang Pop Comics was holding an open submissions contest, I entered, I won. They put out three issues and I only got paid for two of them."

They fell into a thoughtful silence, two trains running on parallel but separate tracks, marking time by the thrum of the taxicab's wheels.

"So what now?" Lucy asked.

Good question. Roy would have felt better if he knew what he was trying to protect, and why. Mr. Smith's scam had been inscrutable back when Roy thought he was after a worthless sequel to a book nobody bought. Now that he knew the man's real target was a mousy little art restorer whose only claims to fame were a few comic books she wrote in college, it was even harder to find a profit motive. He knew what Smith was doing. He knew how he was doing it. The *why* danced around him, as vital to discover as it was impossible to grasp.

Information was leverage. And considering the man wanted him dead, Roy needed every advantage he could get.

"When we get to your apartment, I have to make a couple of phone calls. While I'm taking care of that, I want you to pack a bag. Fast."

"Pack?" she said.

"Like you're going away for a weekend trip. Take everything you need, anything you can't leave behind, but keep it light."

"Where am I—"

Roy inclined his head, just slightly, toward the silent cab driver sitting up front. Lucy got the message.

The cab dropped them off outside her apartment building. Roy got out first, sweeping the parking lot and windows with a practiced eye, hunting for an ambush. By now, Smith would know Lucy's address; their best hope was getting in and out before he managed to scramble another hit squad. Roy had half a mind to skip the visit entirely, but he knew Lucy wouldn't be back home for a while—if ever—and she already looked like she was about to crack under the stress. Having some of her own things around, her own clothes, might make exile a little easier to take.

Once she was out of sight and out of reach, one less thing to worry about, Roy could go on a hunting trip. Miami was nice this time of year.

They took the stairs up. Nobody in the second floor hallway, just a stretch of old, worn blue carpet under faded dome lights. A few of Lucy's neighbors had put out their kitchen-sized trash bins for collection, overflowing with bulging plastic bags, and the air carried the tang of sour milk. The keys jangled in the lock, longer than they needed to. Her fingers were shaking.

Roy put his hand on her shoulder. Steadying her.

"Easy. Nobody is going to hurt you. Not while I'm around."

He hoped he wasn't making empty promises. She took a deep breath and looked back at him.

"Who *are* you?"

I'm the guy who just accidentally screwed up your entire life, he thought. *Yours and mine both. I'd like to say I don't make a habit of this kind of thing, but...*

"Just a friend," he told her.

The keys turned and the door swung open. She led him inside.

Her apartment was small, shabby-chic, still furnished with the remnants of a college life left behind: milk-crate cubbies, a beanbag chair, a maroon and gold Arizona State pennant on one wall next to a pair of framed diplomas. The rest was a mix of IKEA build-it-yourself furniture and thrift store discoveries bought on the cheap, all lovingly restored and white-glove clean.

"I should—" she said, freezing up in the middle of the room.

"Pack," he said. "One bag, clothes, toiletries, anything you can't leave behind."

"You say that like I'm not coming back."

"Just for a few days," he assured her. She disappeared into the bedroom, leaving him alone with his lies. He took out his phone and dialed an overseas number from memory; this wasn't the kind of contact you saved on a list.

"Shanghai Noodles," said the tinny voice on the line. Dishes clacked and steam hissed in the background.

"I need to place an order for pickup. The number two dinner special. Name's Mackey. M-a-c-k-e-y."

"Yes, sir, I have you in our system. Always happy to serve a returning customer. How many entrées would you like?"

"One," he said. Lucy would go into exile alone, safe underground while he took care of things. For both of them.

He gave them an address, made up off the top of his head. All that mattered was the city and state.

"Las Vegas," repeated the voice. "Very good, sir. We have a franchise in your area, and you can come in for your order this evening. One number two special will total ten dollars, plus sales tax. Is that agreeable?"

Ten dollars meant ten thousand. Roy's stomach went sour. He had a nest egg, an emergencies-only account, and paying for Lucy's safe extraction would drain it dry. No more reserves, no safety net, no fuel in the tank for a quick getaway. He'd be back to zero and scrambling for every spare dime.

For a second, he thought about walking. This wasn't his business, wasn't his fight— *But you made it her fight*, he told himself, casting a dark glance at the bedroom doorway. Lucy was puttering, in and out of sight, tossing clothes into an open suitcase on her neatly made bed. She wouldn't survive for ten seconds on her own, and that was on him. His responsibility, and his responsibility to fix.

But you don't have a great track record when it comes to playing the white knight, do you, Roy? The inner voice crept up on him, dragging a cold and bony finger down his spine. *She'd be safer without you, and you know it.*

He shook it off. "Ten is fine," he said.

The voice on the line gave him a pick-up spot and told him his order would be ready at seven, which meant he needed to have Lucy there at six o'clock on the dot. The extraction team would be gone by five minutes after six, with or without their precious cargo.

"How's it coming?" he called out.

She poked her head out. "Almost done. Do we need to pack food?"

"They'll take care of that."

"Who's 'they'?"

"Friends of mine," Roy said. "I'll explain on the way. Finish up, we've got to get moving."

She ducked back into the bedroom, and he made a second call. Now the background noise was muted industrial rock, an electric guitar thrashing over meat-grinder synths. The voice on the other end sounded like a kid who had just grown his first mustache.

"Hey."

"Hey," Roy said. "Need you to run a background check for me. Guy named Smith. Says he's a lawyer, but I don't know if that's legit or what firm he's repping."

"Oh, no problem, I mean 'Smith' is such a rare and unique name. Come on, toss me a bone here."

"I met him at the Fontainebleu Marina in Miami, on a yacht named *Oceans Beyond*. I figure it either belongs to him or his people."

"Now *that* I can work with. Slip-rental registries are easy to crack."

"I need it fast," Roy said. "Anything you can dig up. I've got a phone number for him, but I assume it's a burner."

He read off the digits anyway. "You pay extra for speed," his contact said.

"I also need you to put this on my tab. I'm good for it."

"Your what?" the teenager sputtered. "This is a cash business, my dude. There are no tabs."

"I'm good for it, I said. And you owe me."

"Nuh-uh. You can only play that card so many times—"

"This is me being nice," Roy said. "I'm using the carrot. You want me to get out the stick, I'll get out the stick. Either way, you're going to give me what I want."

Roy listened to the sullen silence, counting silently. *One, two, three...*

"I'll put it on your tab," the voice said. "And you'd better pay me by the end of the month. Plus ten percent."

"Pleasure doing business," Roy said.

He made one last call. On impulse, though he told himself he had a good reason.

"Mr. Mackey," Mr. Smith said, not even sounding mildly surprised.

By now, Smith had to know that his hitters had failed, and that one of them had squealed before the cops scooped him up. Roy reasoned there was no harm in laying a few cards on the table, and there was always the chance that he might rattle the man into revealing something he could use.

"You tried to kill me, Smith."

"You served your purpose."

"Most people pay me once the job's done. It makes for a friendlier relationship."

"And I would have been happy to. Believe me, I don't like ending contracts in bloodshed, it tends to make things messier than they need to be. But you, my friend...well, I hope you'll forgive the terrible cliché, but you know too much. You're far too dangerous to be allowed to live."

"I know Red Harvest Publishing never hired you, and that they canceled Carolyn's contract," Roy said. "The sequel doesn't exist. You never wanted it in the first place. You wanted Lucy."

"Quite."

And I led you right to her, like a chump, Roy thought. His grip tightened on the phone.

"Don't see why that's worth killing me over," he said.

Smith's chuckle was soft, genial. "Is this where I'm supposed to tell you the rest of my assuredly-diabolical plan? No, Mr. Mackey. I'm not a comic book villain, and we both know you certainly aren't any kind of a hero. What you are is a cog in a vast machine, part of a design you are incapable of understanding. Sometimes cogs break and need to be discarded. Don't take it personally."

"You tried to kill me. Don't take it personally when I return the favor."

"You wouldn't be the first to try."

"I won't be sending second-rate hired help," Roy said. "I'll do the job myself. And I won't miss."

He hung up the phone.

Lucy came out of the bedroom dragging a rolling carry-on suitcase, the gray fabric sides bulging and ready to burst.

"Anything you *didn't* pack?" he asked.

She stopped in the middle of the living room and let the suitcase thump onto its belly. Then she crossed her arms, tight, and fired a glare at him.

"Hey," she said. "I almost got kidnapped less than an hour ago, by men with guns, apparently because some dead writer I've never heard of ripped off some comic books I wrote in college. I'm a *little* stressed out right now. And maybe this 'man of mystery' crap works for you, but it's *not* working for me, okay? So cut the attitude."

Roy had to smile. She had some fire in her, after all.

"Sorry," he said. "Really. I'm used to this kind of thing. Sometimes I forget that other people aren't."

She looked dubious. "You're used to armed men jumping out of vans and trying to kill you."

"You'd be surprised."

The fire alarm went off.

Roy shot a look at the kitchen doorway, but the wailing from the hall outside—a strident ear-piercing whine that set his teeth on edge—told him it was the building-wide system. He wanted to think it was a coincidence. He knew better than that. He held up one hand to Lucy, gesturing for her to stay put, and moved to the door in three brisk steps.

No sign of fire in the hallway, but a filmy gray haze of smoke kissed the air, carrying the faint scent of hickory. Neighbors poked their heads out, looking back and forth, concerned and curious. Then the stairwell door at the far end of the hall blasted open under the kick of a steel-toed boot.

The man on the other side—if it was a man—filled the doorway. He was shrouded in glossy black leather, a butcher's apron over shapeless, baggy coveralls, with knee-high boots and elbow-length gloves. Under a drooping hood, the muzzle of a vintage gas mask poked out beneath the long, insect-like ovals of lenses darkened to an onyx sheen. He wore a bulky twin-tank rig on his back, corroded steel and buckled leather straps, connected by a hose to a long exterminator's spray-wand in his beefy grip.

He was surreal, a figure from a comic book standing in broad daylight. And Roy knew exactly which one. He'd seen the man before, in the second issue of *The Midnight Jury*, battling Lucy's own man of mystery across the four-color pages.

"*Roach?*" Lucy whispered, standing at Roy's shoulder. "Why...why is he dressed up like Roach?"

The masked man raised his spray-wand high and squeezed the trigger. A gout of blue-hot flame fired from the nozzle, washing across the roof of the hallway. Soot and curls of black smoke rained down around him.

"Okay," Roy said. "Grab your bag. We're leaving."

Chapter Twelve

One of Lucy's neighbors down the hall, the one who had pointed Roy her way earlier in the day stepped out of his apartment. He turned to the leather-shrouded exterminator, whose bulk still filled the stairwell door.

"Hey," he shouted over the shrieking whine of the alarm. "You with the fire department? We gotta evacuate or what?"

Without a word, Roach—*the psycho dressed up as Roach*, Roy reminded himself, grounding himself in the real world—pointed his wand in the man's face and squeezed the trigger. Instead of fire, a stream of pea-soup fluid sprayed out in a foamy torrent.

The neighbor shrieked, shriller and louder than the klaxon, and clutched his face. Gobs of melted flesh and bubbling fat drooled between his fingers, his hair smoking and sagging on his skull. He staggered back, hit the wall and collapsed, thrashing on the blood-flecked carpet.

Roach gave the fallen man another quick blast. Acid washed across his arm, burning through cloth and skin, melting down to bare his scarlet, glistening bones. Exposed muscles twisted and snapped, boiling and charred black. The exterminator stepped over him. A burbling, wet chortle echoed from beneath the vintage gas mask.

"There you go," he said, his voice a low, gristly wheeze. "Stop, drop, and roll."

Roy slammed the apartment door and flipped the deadbolt.

"Not getting out that way," he said. "Got a fire escape on this floor?"

"Those stairs he's blocking *are* the fire escape," Lucy said, wide-eyed. "Don't you like, have a gun or something?"

Roy shook his head, darting to the living room window.

"Don't like guns," he said. "Guns only say one thing, and it's usually the final word in a conversation. A tactical baton is more eloquent. Sends exactly the message you want, no more and no less."

But his ASP was worthless unless he could get into close range, and the hulking brute in the hallway—with his homemade fire-and-acid murder rig, just like Lucy dreamed up in her comic books—wasn't going to give him that chance. The window didn't offer much of an alternative. It wasn't built to open, and even if it did, all it offered was a straight drop from the second floor down to the hard, hot pavement below.

More screaming erupted in the hall outside, punctuated by gouts of flame. Wispy fingers of smoke pushed their way under the apartment door, rippling against the eggshell-white wood like a mirage. Roy sprinted into Lucy's bedroom, skirting her bed and checking her other window. This one was a worse prospect than the first, looking down over asphalt littered with glittering broken glass.

No way out through the windows, no way out through the hallway. *No way out unless we make our own*, Roy thought.

"He's going to kill us," Lucy mumbled, petrified and staring at the door. "I don't want to die like this. Not like this."

Insight sparked with a white-hot flash. Roy didn't know where Mr. Smith had dug this maniac up, or how he had gotten him over to Lucy's address this soon after his first crew failed, but the wounded thug's alleyway confession was fresh in his memory.

"All I know is that he wanted her alive, and you gone," he told Roy. *"He said if she got one scratch on her, we'd be walking dead men."*

Roy turned to Lucy. "He's not here to kill you. This is a kidnapping. The costume, the whole getup, he's just trying to scare you."

"Well, it's *working*," she said.

"People who are afraid are easy to control. Smith wants you alive. Come here." He put his hands on her shoulders and squeezed, looking her in the eye. "I can get us out of this, but I need your help. Can you be brave for me?"

She bit her bottom lip. Then she nodded, firm. He believed her. Something about the look in her eye, the faintest hint of long-buried steel, told him that he could count on her.

Now he just needed to prove that she could count on him.

The apartment door rocked under a brutal kick. Then a second. The third blew it open, reeling on twisted hinges, letting in a storm of roiling smoke and furnace heat. The hallway behind Roach was blazing, flames rippling along the ceiling and dripping down the walls. He had left contorted, charbroiled corpses in his wake. People Lucy knew, neighbors, friends.

Her throat was dry. It hurt when she swallowed. She stood on the far side of the living room, in her bedroom doorway. Far enough, she hoped, to escape the killing spray of his exterminator's wand. The ragged leather hood lifted, and she saw herself reflected in the bottomless black ovals of Roach's gas mask.

She knew this nightmare. Every beat of it, burned into her childhood memories. Normally by now she'd wake up in a cold sweat. But she wasn't waking up, and pinching herself didn't do a thing. She focused on what Roy told her. *Stay calm, stay confident, keep his attention focused on you.*

"Lucy," he wheezed. "You look just like I imagined. You have an appointment with the Duke, little Lucy. He doesn't like to be kept waiting. Will you come willingly...or shall I melt your pretty legs away, and drag you by the hair? He didn't say I had to bring *all* of you along."

"You're too late," she stammered, trying to keep her chin high. She decided to play along. If he was going to pretend to be a monster from her stories, she knew exactly how to act out her part. "I sent up the signal. The Midnight Jury is coming to stop you."

That mocking, wet chortle slithered from under his mask.

"The Jury is long gone, Lucy. Long gone, and the city is our playground now. I'll show you. So sorry, so sad, your hero is dead."

Roy lunged in from the left with his ASP already extended and raised high. The baton slashed the air and whipped across Roach's mask, the black steel tip cracking into the middle of an oval lens. The onyx glass shattered, loose shards spraying into the assassin's eye. He stumbled back, flailing, reflexively squeezing the trigger. A gout of acid splashed across the wall, drawing a ragged gash of curling, bubbling paint.

"*Burn* you," Roach hissed. He tried to turn but Roy was already ahead of him. He guessed the exterminator getup would act like armored padding: the ASP would only be good for a precision strike or two and would feel like a light slap everywhere else. He gripped his backup weapon, grabbed from a block on Lucy's kitchen counter, in his other fist. The steak knife blazed down, aiming for one of the hoses dangling from Roach's back. It hit the corner of a tank, steel clanging against steel, sending a jolt up Roy's wrist.

Roach pivoted, his gloved hand clamping down on Roy's throat with crushing force. The two men faced one another through the broken window of the gas mask. Roy saw fresh blood on the other side, drooling down gutters of old, twisted burn tissue like raw hamburger meat, and a bottomless pit of madness in a single, lidless eye.

"Hold still," Roach said. "Burn you good."

Roy flipped the knife in his hand. He drove it upward, spearing through the black apron and into Roach's hip. Only half an inch penetrated the leather but it was enough to make him let go of Roy's throat, his fingers spasming. Roy ripped the knife free, giving it a twist for good measure, sidestepped, and hacked at the swinging hose again. The line ruptured, spraying fuel in all directions, a deadly, wild rain begging to become an inferno.

"My *rig*," Roach howled, spinning like a dog trying to catch its own tail. All he managed to do was cover half the living room in gasoline, the chemical stench burning Roy's nose hairs. Roy tightened his grip on the knife and tackled him blade-point first, using his own weight to drive it all the way into Roach's gut. The men fell together, landing on the carpet. The nozzle sprayed acid like a fountain, painting the ceiling, drawing jagged and hissing lines across Lucy's bookshelf and pitting the face of her television set. The screen caved in on itself in a torrent of black smoke.

Roy tore the knife loose, rose to his knees, and brought it down one last time, holding the blade in a two-handed grip that made the muscles along his arms stand out like steel cords. The knife punched through the assassin's chest, buried to the bloody wooden hilt.

He didn't check to see if the man was dead or dying. No time for that. Roy jumped up and reached for Lucy's hand. She was a step ahead of him, her paralysis shattered, charging for her kitchen.

"What are you—" he started to ask, hearing water flood into the kitchen sink. Lucy emerged with a pair of dishcloths, soaking wet, and offered him one. She nodded to the open doorway. The corridor beyond was a wasteland of fire and corpses and killing smoke, almost too thick to see the stairwell, and salvation, on the other side.

"For the smoke," she said. "Press this over your mouth and nose, and stay low."

He didn't need to be told, but he was impressed that she didn't need to be told either. Roy had figured Lucy for a country mouse: no fight, all flight, if she wasn't too petrified to escape danger on her own. But while he was tussling with the costumed freak, she was putting together an escape plan. They stood at the edge of the blaze, side by side.

"You all right?"

She answered him through the wet towel, clamping it over her mouth. "Scared shitless," Lucy said. "So let's do this before I lose my nerve."

Chapter Thirteen

Lucy and Roy plunged into the maelstrom. The heat hammered them in waves, driving the air from their lungs and replacing it with killing smoke, the black tendrils seeping through their makeshift masks and plunging itching, burning fingers down their throats. Roy hacked into his wet cloth, doubled over, charging a few feet ahead of Lucy with his eyes on fire. He forced them to stay open, watching the spreading flames all around and hunting for a way out.

For one stomach-lurching moment, he thought he lost Lucy. He didn't see her behind him in the tempest, didn't see a way forward—and then her hand squeezed his forearm, turning him, pointing him in the right direction.

The floor dropped out from under him. Then he caught himself on the railing, his foot coming down on the first step of the stairwell. Five more little leaps of faith and he ducked under the worst of the smoke, his blurry, itching eyes starting to clear, the way to freedom just below.

Lucy's shoulders shook, a string of lung-rattling coughs exploding into her hand. Roy turned back and she mutely waved him ahead, giving him a weak thumbs-up.

Tougher than I thought, too, he reflected. *Still have to stash her someplace safe while I take care of business. She's not ready for more of…whatever the hell that was, back there.*

Not sure I am, either. But 'Mr. Smith' is going to have some answers for me, even if I have to beat the truth out of him.

Might do that anyway.

They emerged into fading sunlight, the strobe of emergency lights, and the dry desert air. It was dirty, but Roy gulped it down, breathing it in until his lungs were ready to burst. People milled, confused, at the edge of the sidewalk, and firefighters waved stragglers to a safe distance while they rolled hoses up the building's front walkway. A high window exploded, spitting flame and glass.

"This way, this way," barked a firefighter, ushering Roy and Lucy along. "Over here, we got two ambulances stationed and more on the way.

They'll check you out and take you in for emergency treatment if you need it."

Balls to that, Roy thought, and the look on Lucy's face told him she was thinking the same thing. They needed to get as far away from here as possible, as fast as they could manage it. All the same, he asked her, "You okay? Can you walk?"

The wet cloth dropped in her limp hand and she tilted her head back, drinking the air like it was champagne.

"With all this adrenaline?" she said. "Pretty sure I could run a marathon right now, but don't test me on that."

She stopped dead at the end of the block. Roy followed her gaze across the street, to the truck parked against the opposite curb. It was a beater, a rust-spotted ancient Ford with a sixties-era body bolted to a mismatched forties-era grill. Faded pastel paint on the side read *Burdock's Extermination Services*, above the smaller cursive motto, *The FRIENDLY Exterminator!*

Roy knew where he'd seen the truck before, a perfect twin down to the exact colors, the last spot of rust, the tarnished streaks on the old hubcaps. He'd seen it in *The Midnight Jury*.

"Keep moving," Roy told her. Cops were working the crowd, asking who saw what and when, and the last thing they needed right now was police attention. The best the cops could do is waste their time; at worst, they'd toss him and Lucy into separate interrogation rooms and turn them into sitting ducks.

Lucy put one foot in front of the other, but she couldn't keep her eyes off the truck. "This makes no sense."

"Like I said. He was trying to confuse you, to scare you, so you wouldn't fight back. I knew this bounty hunter once, made his money tracking down real bad guys, the kind who'd put a bullet in you just for making eye contact. When he was out on a capture job, he dressed up like that guy from the slasher movies, the one with the hockey mask."

"Jason Voorhees," Lucy said.

"Him. He'd wait until his mark was half-asleep, then jump out of a closet, waving a machete and screaming like a lunatic. Said it worked every time."

"Problem with your theory."

"Yeah?"

"You think Mr. Smith had a hitman dress up as Roach to intimidate me, right? So he could grab me and I wouldn't fight back."

"Makes sense to me."

"Except he just found out my name—my real name, and where I live—earlier today. Think about how long it would take to put together a perfect costume, and an extermination rig that really works, just like in the comics, not to mention an exact copy of Roach's truck. I know people who are into cosplay, and they spend *months* on their outfits. And if he had this whole production ready and waiting for me, why would he send the guys with ski-masks after me first?"

She fell silent. Roy didn't have an answer for her, and he didn't try to fill the silence.

"Jesus," she said. "I knew most of those people. He killed my neighbors. He didn't...he didn't have to do that."

"He paid for it," Roy said. He wasn't sure if the man was dead when he left, flat on the floor with a steak knife jutting out of his chest, but the smoke and the fire would have put a definitive point on things. Lucy looked back, the distant flames and the emergency lights flashing scarlet in her haunted eyes.

"He'll be back," she said, her voice almost too soft to hear. "The bad guys always come back."

"Not in the real world," Roy told her.

Dead is forever, he thought, and set his sights on the glow of the Vegas Strip.

"Cosplay," Roy said, breaking a long silence.

They took the monorail. It wasn't a city-wide system, just a four-mile serpent of concrete and steel that snaked its way behind—and through—the monoliths along the Strip, offering door-to-door transport between most of the major resorts and casinos. It was an easy way to beat the desert heat, and as far as Roy was concerned, a handy escape from the crowds on the street. He didn't know how many more lunatics were on Mr. Smith's payroll, or how many were on their way, making a beeline for Sin City.

He leaned into the standing bar, adjusting his balance as the monorail made a tight turn. White neon flashed in the tall windows around them, the city coming to life while the sunlight started to fade. Lucy looked up from her seat, curious.

"What about?"

"Something you said, about knowing people who are into cosplay. That's...people dressing up like superheroes, right?"

"Characters from comics, games, movies, you name it."

"And that's a big thing now?"

Lucy shrugged. "Sure. Some people build entire careers around it. It's an art form. Why?"

"I think that's what we ran into, back there."

"How do you mean?"

Roy had been trying to wrestle the sequence of events, since the moment he and Lucy met, into something that made sense and didn't look too much like a pretzel. He thought he'd figured it out.

"Bear with me. What if that getup wasn't for you at all? What if a killer latched onto your comics, and decided he was going to model himself after Roach?"

Her brow furrowed. "A real-life supervillain?"

"Why not? It's doable, right? Roach isn't superhuman. He's just an ordinary hitman with a costume and a nasty way of murdering people; he's a serial killer who gets paid to do his thing. He can't climb walls, like Doctor Contraire, or conjure up demons—"

Lucy broke into a bashful smile. "You read my comics? You actually read them."

"All three issues. I was looking for clues at the time."

"Sorry about that." She ducked her head.

"Why? I thought they were pretty good. Anyway, my point is, if you were a killer who wanted to dress up like a comic book character, you'd probably pick one who you could actually copy. I don't know how he built that flamethrower-acid thing, but I figure any talented mechanical engineer could whip up something that looked and acted like the one on the page."

"That doesn't solve the timing problem," Lucy pointed out.

"Maybe it does. Picture this: Smith sends his gunmen. Big fail. He knows he needs to step up his game, fast, before I take you out of his reach. He talks to whoever lines up his underworld talent and they say, 'Hey, we've got this weirdo who's *obsessed* with Chandler Hawks. He'll snatch her for free.'"

Lucy tapped her fingertip against her chin, thinking.

"*I'd* hire him to kidnap me," she said.

"Right? He probably blazed out here as fast as that junker of a truck could carry him, not hard if he was already working on the west coast. I bet if we look up cases of arsons and acid attacks over the past few years—"

The buzz of his phone broke his train of thought. His intel buddy, hopefully calling back with the dirty details on Mr. Smith.

"Hey, glad you called," Roy said. "While I've got you, I need you to look up some crime stats. No rush."

"Man, *fuck* you," the teenager spat.

"Excuse me?"

"Do you have any idea what you just did to me?"

"What," Roy said, "about this Smith thing?"

"And his yacht, and the five-star alert I triggered just breathing on it. Online. From a thousand miles away. Which is closer than I want to get to any of this."

"Any of what? Calm down. Calm down, take a deep breath, and start from the beginning."

"Like I have time for that? No, I'm clearing out. Burning this place behind me, salting the Earth, don't look for me, I'll find you. Maybe."

Roy stared at the flickering lights outside the monorail window, catching the faint reflection of his ghost in the glass. This wasn't right.

"Kid, you've dug up dirt on Mafia families for me. When I said that working with me could be dangerous, you laughed in my face and said nobody could trace you, not even the NSA and the CIA combined. Now you're spooked and I didn't think you could *get* spooked. What the hell did you find?"

He didn't answer right away. The line went silent, save for the grinding, electronic pulse of the kid's music and a metallic pounding noise, like he was taking a hammer to a hard drive.

"The Network," he said.

"Bullshit," Roy fired back.

"Mr. Smith is a Network operative. Hell, apparently he's *the* Network operative. Their number-one fixer."

"There's no such thing as the Network," Roy told him. "You know that. Everybody knows that."

"Well, I just spent the last hour following a trail of corpses, all tied back to that thing that 'everybody knows' isn't real. I'm telling you, Mr. Smith is Network property. Know what happens to people who find out about the Network? They recruit you or they kill you. And if you get in their way, you die slow."

"Yeah, I know all the tall tales," Roy said. "I was hearing them over rounds of cheap booze before you were old enough to grow pubes. Trust me: the Network isn't real."

"Well, I'm clearing out before the not-real Network sends not-real killers to nail my ass to the wall. Literally. Stay safe, Roy. I'd say I liked working with you but that's a straight-up lie. And if you've got any sense that hasn't been punched out of you by now? Run. Drop whatever you're doing, drop whoever you're with, and run."

He hung up the phone. Ray stared, expression blank, at the dead screen.

Lucy had been listening. "What's the Network?"

He sighed and dropped into the seat beside her, leaning as the monorail took another shuddering turn.

"Underworld fairy tale. It's like the Mafia of Mafias. A global conspiracy with its tentacles in organized crime, world governments, the media, you name it. They're invisible, all-powerful, and run the world with an iron fist."

"Sounds like the Illuminati," Lucy said.

Roy nodded. "Same kind of bogeyman, but this one sprang up in local hood circles. It was a grift, originally. People would claim to be repping the Network, and demand 'tribute' from small-time skells."

"And that worked?"

"Rarely. But you know the Nigerian Prince email scam? Same principle: most people laugh it off or see right through it, but you only need a few suckers to turn a decent profit. Along the way, someone noticed that a lot of the con artists working the Network grift wound up dead. The messy kind of dead."

"Ah," Lucy said, eyes lighting up as she put her mental pulp-writer hat on. "And of course, those gruesome murders were a message from the *real* Network, warning the scammers—and the entire criminal underworld—to never take their name in vain."

Roy snapped his fingers. "You got it. And so, an urban legend is born. But there's nothing to it."

"You sure?"

"I've been a lot of places, met a lot of people, seen a lot of things," Roy said, stretching. "The Network isn't real. Smith is just a crook with a lot of money and a motive I haven't figured out yet. But I will. Count on that."

The automated speakers chimed. The monorail slowed down, rumbling softly as it pulled into a beige-tiled tunnel. A pre-recorded voice announced their arrival at the Monaco.

"This is us," Roy said.

Chapter Fourteen

"I don't really gamble," Lucy said, slipping off the monorail at Roy's side. A broad hallway led them past theatres and shops, a miniature boutique mall bolted onto the hip of the casino's main gallery. Soon it opened up into a wonderland of flashing lights and trilling bells, the deep maroon carpet swirling with crowds. Stray gusts of nervous energy washed across the room, a psychic whirlwind roiling with the invitation to come and play.

"Neither do I. We're here to meet somebody."

"Friend of yours?" she asked.

He waggled a hand from side to side.

"A friend for pay," Roy said. "Wouldn't give me the time of day otherwise, but I wired her ten grand to arrange safe harbor, so safe harbor is what you'll get. She keeps her word like it's a holy vow."

The blood drained from Lucy's cheeks. She walked closer to Roy, dropping her voice.

"Ten grand? As in ten thousand dollars? I can't afford that!"

"You don't have to," he said. "Like I told you, I already paid."

"But I can't pay you back—"

"And you don't have to. Hey."

He tugged her to one side, out of the flow of human traffic, their faces bathed in the light from a vacant slot machine.

"Listen. I got you into this," Roy said. "What happened to you today, that's my fault. That's all on me."

"You couldn't have known."

"Doesn't matter. I got you into this, and that means it's my responsibility to get you out. Step one is tucking you away someplace safe. Step two is tracking Smith down."

"And step three?" she asked. A little hesitation made her voice hitch, like she was afraid of the answer.

"Step three," he said. He reached out and squeezed her shoulder. "I make sure that Mr. Smith, and anyone with him, can never come after you again."

She nodded, mute.

Roy's hired friend was waiting at a small bar tucked into the tail end of the casino floor. Her sinuous shape and the flare of her emerald jacket's collar gave her the look of a hooded cobra, and she cast lazy, hungry eyes at them over her cocktail as they approached. Her hair was so blonde it was almost ice-white.

"Been a while," she said, nodding to the empty stools on her left. Roy sat down. Lucy hesitated, until he urged her on with a subtle wave.

"Too long," Roy said.

"Introduce me to your friend."

"Lucy?" Roy nodded. "Hawke. Hawke, Lucy."

"Is that a first name, or..." Lucy asked. Hawke cocked a lopsided smile.

"Oh, she's *new*. It's not a name at all, honey. We never met and we never will. All the same, I'm about to become your new best friend."

"Hawke's a lady of many talents," Roy explained, "one of them being the safe passage of people and things under the radar."

"You're a smuggler," Lucy said.

"I'm a concierge with an exclusive clientele." Hawke set her cocktail glass on the bar. "Here's how this works: I'll bring you to a safe house where you'll stay, toasty and warm, until Roy handles whatever cowboy business he needs to handle. You'll be blindfolded on arrival and departure. You won't ask questions. If any part of this arrangement is not to your satisfaction, the door is over there, feel free to walk out now."

"She's fine with that," Roy said.

"I need to hear it from her."

Lucy swallowed hard. Her head bobbed. "Agreed."

"Spiffy. Then I suggest we get this traveling carnival on the road. Roy, where are you off to?"

"Miami."

"Let me give you a ride to the airport."

"You charge extra for that?" he asked.

She winked. "You can owe me."

"Never heard you say that before."

"And you never will again."

She slid off her stool, her every movement serpentine, and beckoned with a curl of her fingers. Lucy followed, entranced, with Roy at her side. Hawke led them down a side concourse to the casino's parking garage. The jangling electronic trills faded away, swallowed by the echoing rumble of engines. Her car was a white Lincoln, windows tinted, the paint caked with rust-brown desert dust. A man sat motionless in the driver's seat. Dark glasses shrouded his eyes, the same shade as his suit, and he didn't say a word when Hawke got in beside him. Lucy and Roy climbed in back. As she sank into the leather bucket seat, she cast a questioning look at him. Roy patted her hand, reassuring.

"Go," Hawke said.

The driver fired up the ignition and rolled out. The Lincoln merged into the endless traffic on Las Vegas Boulevard, anonymous in the infinite curling stream of hot steel and scarlet brake lights. Roy leaned closer to Lucy, pitching his voice low.

"This should only take a couple of days. You'll be all right."

Lucy's lips parted, slightly, then closed again. He gave her time, knowing the question she wanted to ask. She finally found the voice for it.

"Are you going to kill him?"

Roy had been thinking about that.

Killing changed a man. Killing turned a soft mattress into a battlefield, every dream a rocky hell-ride to the places you never wanted to go back to. Roy had enough of that weight to carry and he didn't want one more pound of it. That said, he knew some men weren't satisfied with anything short of a bullet; they'd kill you or you'd kill them and that was all there was to say about it. He wasn't sure what kind of man Smith was, when push came to shove.

"First thing I need to do is find out why he wants you," Roy said. "Once I know that, maybe I can negotiate a peace. Find some other way to give him what he's after, in trade for your safety."

"And if you can't?" she asked.

Roy leaned back in his seat and watched the traffic crawl by.

"If I can't, then I'll have to consider my other options."

He left it at that, and she didn't press.

A jetliner came in low, shimmering the darkening sky. Roy saw the airport up ahead, and he resigned himself to another night of restless sleep in the sky. Then the driver flicked his turn signal, taking a left at the next light, breaking from the flow of heavy traffic and pulling off onto a long and lonely stretch of local access road.

"Hawke?" Roy said.

"Have to make a pit stop on the way," she said. "Just be a second."

"Since when do you take on more than one client at a time?"

"Needs must," Hawke said.

There was nothing down this way but shopping cart nomads and motels where you could rent a room and a warm body, both by the hour. They were plunging fast into the ugly side of Vegas, where all the gold and glitter shone in the distance, close enough to see but too far to touch.

"Hawke," Roy said.

"Needs must, Roy. You know that phrase? 'Needs must'?"

"That's half the phrase," Lucy said, breaking her silence.

Hawke eyed her in the rearview mirror. Roy turned, curious.

"Shakespeare," Lucy said. "From *All's Well that Ends Well*: 'I am driven on by the flesh, and he must needs go that the devil drives.'"

"Look who has an education," Hawke said.

"Hawke," Roy said.

"When the devil commands it," Lucy explained, "you have to obey."

"Metaphorically," Hawke said.

"Or not."

The Lincoln pulled into a motel parking lot. Skirting the far edge, rolling up to park behind a stretch limousine. The plates weren't livery; this was a privately owned ride, flanked by a pair of Hummers in matching funeral black. Roy knew the difference between military and civilian models, and these didn't come from any local car lot. Four men, their suits bulging with barely concealed steel, stood out in the lot and waited under the setting sun.

Roy fixed the back of her head with a thousand-yard stare. "God*damn* it, Hawke."

"I'd love to say 'all's well that ends well,'" she told him. "But."

With the Lincoln in park, the driver was free to turn in his seat. Roy caught the dark sheen of a revolver, nestled low in the man's palm, the muzzle pointed square at Roy's heart.

"I need you both to get out of the car," Hawke said.

Lucy shot a look at Roy. "'Keeps her word like it's a holy vow,' huh?"

"People change. Some more than others." Roy turned to Hawke. "How could you do this to me? We've worked together. We've got history."

"And I'd move mountains to play this out any different way, if I could. I tried. I said I'd just give them the girl, but you were a package deal."

The back door of the limousine swung wide. Mr. Smith stepped out. He fixed Hawke with an expectant, silent stare.

"Who *is* he?" Roy said.

Hawke half-smiled, looking tired.

"You know who he is."

All his angry denials didn't amount to anything in the face of the truth, and the belief he clung to was hollow, meaningless. He knew this woman. He knew she had contacts from DC to Beijing, a hundred operators at her beck and call, a thousand private numbers on her speed dial. There was only one thing, one force, that could scare Hawke into an act of naked treason.

"He arranged a demonstration," she said. "Had my entire European bureau picked up by the cops. One hour later they were all released within sixty seconds of one another, and all traces of every single arrest scrubbed clean, straight down the memory hole. You know who has that kind of juice."

The Network, Roy thought. His stomach sank.

"I won't even try to tell you this is a matter of business," Hawke told him. "This is simple survival. I feel like shit about it, if that's any compensation."

"Really isn't," Lucy said.

"I need you both to get out of the car now."

There wasn't any point fighting it. He could take a bullet from her driver, at point-blank range, or roll the dice and take his chances with Smith and his men. Roy got out of the car. Lucy followed, circling to stand behind him, shielded in his shadow.

"Ms. Langenkamp," Smith said, offering her a polite bow of his head. "It's a pleasure to finally meet. I admire your work. Please, get in the car. You'll find refreshments in the side console. Help yourself to anything you'd like."

The Lincoln was rolling away, leaving them in enemy hands. Hawke didn't look back.

"Mr. Mackey, I regret to say that this *does* conclude our business."

"Not in front of her," Roy said.

Smith paused. "Hm?"

"Do what you've got to do, but not in front of her," Roy said, nodding at Lucy. "She doesn't need to see that."

"Agreed." Smith snapped his fingers, and a pair of his suits stepped up. "If you'd be so kind as to accompany these men around the back of the motel here—"

"No," Lucy said.

Both men looked at her. She took a deep breath and lifted her chin.

"Whatever it is you want from me, if you kill him, you won't get it."

"I rather think we will," Smith said.

She glanced down, just a flick of her gaze, breaking eye contact as she instinctively shrank into herself. Then she found her steel and stared him down.

"I promise you won't."

He thought it over.

"If you're that positive," she added, "go ahead. But you can't *un*-kill somebody."

"You'd be surprised at what I can do. But...if I guarantee Mr. Mackey's safety, do you agree to cooperate? Fair is fair: if I give you something, you have to give me something in return. No escape attempts, no tricks or tomfoolery. Your word on it."

"Fair's fair," Lucy agreed.

Mr. Smith beamed and smacked his palms together.

"Deal. Would the lady *and* gentleman please get into the limousine, then? There are enough refreshments for everyone."

Chapter Fifteen

They patted Roy down before he got in, plucking away his ASP. Mr. Smith offered a flute of champagne in trade. Bubbly all around in the back of the stretch limo, Roy and Lucy facing forward, Smith facing back, raising his flute in an amiable toast.

"To profit," he said.

Lucy squirmed in her seat, staring at her own flute like she wasn't sure what to do with it. Eventually she raised it, clinking it against the two men's glasses, then took a ginger sip. Roy was less cautious; Smith had served them all from the same bottle, kept on ice in a chromed bucket in the limo's side console. Besides, he doubted the man would go to all this trouble just to poison them. He didn't know vintages, but he knew quality. The bubbly was dry and strong and tasted like money.

"Where are you taking us?" Lucy asked.

"To your new home. Well, your temporary home until we arrange for long-term accommodation, but I think you'll find it quite pleasant. Gourmet meals cooked by our in-house chef, a full media library with a private screening room and first-run movies, and spa treatments on demand."

"You running a criminal syndicate or a resort hotel?" Roy said.

"Why not do both? We have a vested interest in keeping Ms. Langenkamp comfortable and happy."

"You've got the wrong Langenkamp," Lucy said. "Whoever you're looking for, whatever it is you're trying to accomplish, I can't possibly be the person you want."

"Such modesty. By the way, I have to ask: that cliffhanger in the third issue. How was the Midnight Jury going to get out of that industrial freezer?"

"My hunch was right, you *are* some kind of psycho fan," Roy said. "Was that hitman dressed as Roach your idea, too?"

Smith blinked. "The what, now?"

"The reason my apartment, and everything I own, is a smoking cinder," Lucy said. "Thanks, by the way. Thanks for that."

Smith usually had two expressions: mild pleasure and mild apathy. For the first time, Roy caught the trace of something else in the depths of his wool-gray eyes. *He's nervous*, Roy thought. *What can make a fixer from the big, bad Network uneasy?*

And more importantly, he just gave the game away. He didn't send the cosplaying killer. Lucy's the hottest ticket in Vegas. More than one bad guy wants to get his hands on her.

Just have to figure out why.

"You...saw this man," Smith said. More of a statement than a question.

"He was hard to miss," Roy replied.

Smith shifted gears, peppering Lucy with questions before she or Roy could return fire.

"What did Carolyn Saunders tell you before she died? Clearly she didn't tell you the *real* reason she wanted to write a sequel to your comics, or you wouldn't be so filled with curiosity right now."

"I never even met her," Lucy said. "I didn't know *The City at Midnight* existed until Roy showed it to me."

"She stole your work outright? Ah, that makes sense."

"Does it?" Lucy looked doubtful.

"She was trying to protect you. From us. She wanted to reap the benefit of your skills while keeping you safe in the dark."

"What skills?" Lucy squeezed her champagne flute until it trembled in her hand. "I haven't written anything since I was in college, and the only thing I did write crashed and burned after three issues. I'm an art restorer now. I restore art. If you've got a neglected portrait that needs cleaning up, I'm your girl. Otherwise I don't know what you want from me."

Mr. Smith sipped his bubbly as he contemplated his answer.

"What I want," he said, "well...I think you'll need to be shown, rather than told. It's a lot to take on faith and I won't expect you to believe me until you see for yourself. What I can tell you is that you have a very powerful gift. I want you to use that gift for me, and for my special friends. Great rewards await you."

Lucy lifted an eyebrow. "Special friends, huh?"

"Kings," Mr. Smith replied.

The darkened partition over his shoulder hissed downward. Smith shot an annoyed look at the driver. Through the windshield, Roy saw nothing but desert road, rust-red walls of rugged stone, and the armored back end of the Hummer at the head of their small convoy. The other Hummer rode on their tail, a hundred yards behind.

"Problem?" Smith asked the driver.

"Sorry, sir. Lead car just radioed back. Spotted a wreck a couple miles up ahead. Big one, looks like a semi had a header with a tour bus. Whole road's blocked off."

"So? Go around it."

"The Hummers can handle off-roading, no problem. But the limo's going to have to take it slow in the rough. Want us to turn around, find another route?"

"No time," Smith said. He leaned back in the dark leather seat and crossed one leg over the other.

Roy saw smoke now, black and thick, curling up in the distance above the lead car. Fresh, flowing from a still-burning engine fire. He felt a spark of hope. Accidents meant firefighters, EMTs, a hope of rescue. All he'd have to do is wait for the limo to slow down and shove Lucy out. Then he could take Smith apart without worrying about her getting hit by a stray bullet.

His hope sputtered and died as quickly as it had flared up. The wreck was too recent, a fresh graveyard in the middle of a desert wasteland. It would take an hour for emergency crews to show up, if anyone had even called for them yet.

The dashboard radio squawked, the sound drifting back through the open partition, jarring Roy from his half-baked plans of escape. "Lead car here, really think we should turn around. Scene looks wrong."

Smith turned his head, lifting his chin so he could answer for the driver. "Wrong?"

"There's a survivor, a little girl—"

"Not our problem."

"Come on," Roy said. "It's a hundred degrees, and God knows what happened to her parents. You can't leave the kid out here."

"She's on top of the capsized bus," the voice on the radio said, puzzled. "She's...*dancing*."

Roy hadn't noticed, until now, how Lucy stiffened at his side. She leaned forward, eyes going wide.

"Ask if she's wearing a white dress with yellow ribbons down the front," Lucy said. "Ask if she's holding a teddy bear."

"Did you get that?" Smith asked.

"Yes, sir. Yes, she is. Orders?"

"Turn around," Lucy whispered. The blood drained from her face.

"Speed up," Smith said. "Go around the wreckage. We're already running behind schedule."

"Turn *back*."

Roy found Lucy's hand and gave it a protective squeeze. He asked a question with his eyes. She breathed a single word in response, a word he'd never heard before.

"*Rumblebones.*"

The road ahead exploded, the detonation throwing up a solid wall of dirt and sand and shattered asphalt that crested like a tidal wave. It caught the front bumper of the lead Hummer and lifted it, twisting it in the air, tossing it like a child's toy. The truck slammed back down, rolling, spewing smoke and scrawling gashes in the scrub as it tumbled out of control. The limo driver hauled on the wheel, pulling a hard right and sending the stretch ride into a lurching skid. Just before the windows whipped around Roy caught a glimpse of something behind the eruption of earth, something ancient and yellowed and vast, before it dove back beneath the desert's skin.

The spin of the limo sent Smith skidding sideways, off-balance. Roy launched from his seat and threw his momentum behind a steel-piston punch, his knuckles cracking into Smith's jaw hard enough to send a shock of pain up his arm. Smith dropped, out cold, and Roy hauled him onto the floor of the limousine. In the corner of his eye, he caught the driver's head turning.

"Eyes on the road," Roy snapped. "Get us out of here. You try anything, your boss pays for it."

The lead Hummer was out of the action, its final lumbering roll leaving it flipped over onto its roof, a wreck of broken glass and crumpled black steel. The chase car was still right on their tail. Roy rummaged through Smith's tailored jacket and dug a pearl-handled .22 out of his breast pocket. Peashooter of a gun, but it was better than nothing.

The driver was still trying to get the limo under control, the ungainly beast fishtailing as they barreled through the rough alongside the highway. The bus-and-truck crash was just ahead, smoke roiling and flames licking at the cloudless desert sky. The girl on top of the carnage was eight or nine, in pigtails, her dirty faded dress like something out of a Charles Dickens novel.

"Oh my god oh my god," Lucy breathed. "It's her. This can't be happening."

"Who?" Roy said. He was more focused on the chase car and figuring out how he was going to take out four heavily armed men with a pocket-sized gun. "You know her?"

"I *made* her."

The earth rumbled. Roy wanted to chalk it up to the bucking limo, battered tires bouncing hard against the rough scrub. Then he spotted the bulge in the sand. It was a rippling wake, an underground torpedo firing alongside them. Veering in, tight, on a collision course.

"*Brace!*" Roy shouted.

An ear-splitting roar, like rocks screaming in a meat-grinder, erupted along with the soil. A battering ram fired into the belly of the limousine, knocking it up onto two wheels. Then it began to teeter, and roll. As he tumbled, lost in a moment of dizzy, weightless free-fall, Roy gazed up at a nightmare.

The thing under the desert sands was a snake. A dirt-encrusted serpent at least twenty feet long, made of vast bleached bones and knots of leathery sunbaked sinew. The skeletal monstrosity reared up over the rolling limousine like a cobra, its jaws opening wide in hungry triumph.

Chapter Sixteen

The limousine thumped onto one side and Roy landed hard, his shoulders and neck cracking against steel, the pain stunning him to the edge of a blackout. The world went gray and red, smearing, time going sideways. Mr. Smith, still out cold, lay on top of him in a tangled heap. Lucy dangled sideways, held above them both by her seatbelt.

"Lucy—" Roy stammered, finding his voice.

"I'm here, I'm okay." Her seatbelt clicked, the fabric whistling away, and she carefully slid down from her perch. They both grabbed Smith's shoulders, shoving him off, and she helped pull Roy up to an awkward crouch.

The driver was already on the move. They heard his door thump open and saw his shoes kick at the open air as he pulled himself up and out, escaping the crash. Through the cracked, dusty glass of the limo's back window, Roy watched him run. He was a flailing puppet, his arms pinwheeling, feet off-balance and scrambling in the rough. A dark shadow soared in from above, swallowing him.

The skeletal serpent slammed down, a pillar of fangs and bone, grabbing the driver in its hungry maw. It kept going, diving beneath the sand and scrub with its prize, its tail rattling before it vanished underground. All that remained was a crater of blood and one mangled leg, ripped off at the root.

Lucy clutched herself, arms squeezing tight across her chest. Her jaw clenched so hard Roy could see it trembling. He needed a clear head. Perspective. A plan. And fast.

"What did you mean?" he said. "When you told me that you 'made' her?"

Lucy leaned, craning her neck to look up at the smoking ruins of the highway crash. The little girl was up there, one hand clutching her raggedy old teddy bear, the other gleefully pointing, drawing an invisible line across the desert. The serpent responded, shaking the earth under the limousine's side.

"She works for Duke Ellery," she said. "After the Midnight Jury busted his designer drug lab, he hired her to track the Jury down."

Roy shook his head, not following. "When? I read all three issues of the comic, and that never happened."

She turned, her face bloodless-pale, and fixed him with a look of absolute horror.

"Issue five," she said. "It never came out. It never even got drawn. It was just half a script, my notes..."

Lucy put a finger to the side of her temple.

"In my *head*. The artist never drew her. But that girl? That's exactly what Rumblebones looked like, in my imagination. That's the only place she ever existed. In my head."

Until now. Roy didn't have time to figure it out, and while he was staring into the face of the impossible, only a fool argued the facts right in front of him. This was happening, this was real. A monster made of a giant serpent's bones was churning through the desert earth and tearing men to pieces at the command of a giggling little girl, and if he didn't find a way out, they'd be next on the menu.

Mr. Smith was still out cold. Gripping the stolen .22, pearl handle hot against his clammy palm, Roy squirmed onto his back and slammed his heel against the limo's smoke-tinted sunroof. It rattled, started to buckle, and finally gave after three rough kicks, the safety glass shattering into glittering pebbles. He poked his head out, risking a quick look.

The lead Hummer was out of the action, flipped onto its back like a turtle and spitting black smoke from an engine fire. One of the Network shooters was halfway out a side window and limp, dead or dying from the crash. Another had clambered out and onto the belly of the truck, revolver out and braced in both hands, trying to track the rumbling from below with the muzzle of his gun.

Might as well bring a peashooter, Roy thought. Whatever made that monster work, he didn't see any organs, any vitals, anything to target. Just leathery sinew and brutal bone. All the same, he wasn't the expert here. He looked to Lucy.

"How do I take it down?"

"Her familiar? It's...it's ancient Egyptian necromancy. The Jury used the Staff of Ankhen-Thoth—"

"Do you *have* the Staff of Ankhen-Thoth?"

"No," she said. "I made it up. It's not real. None of this is real."

A bellowing screech, like jagged stones in a blender, made a solid argument to the contrary. Behind the crashed limo, the second Hummer had pulled off to the side; Roy guessed that Smith's men were intent on getting their boss back in one piece. The driver was huddled behind the wheel and a pair of shooters were out on foot, sticking close to their ride, hunting for a target.

Roy had an option. He didn't like the idea of gunning down a little kid, didn't like it one damn bit, but under the circumstances—

Lucy read his mind and shook her head. "Bullets won't stop her. She's a lich."

He didn't know what that was and didn't have time to ask. "Did you give her *any* weaknesses? Besides the staff of Ankh-Whoever that we don't have?"

She thought fast and snapped her fingers. "The teddy bear. Her canopic jar is stitched inside of it."

"Canopic…?"

"Her organs. Her organs aren't in her body, they're in the jar. They're weak against magic."

Roy didn't know magic. He didn't have a wand to wave, just a dinky holdout gun, and that snake was coming back around for another attack. *Out*, he thought. They needed a fast ride away from here, and there was only one in sight: the one with all the panic-mad gunmen clinging to it like a lifeboat.

"Lady," he said, "You have one messed-up imagination. Stay put, keep your head down. I'm going to get us a new set of wheels."

He grabbed Smith's shoulders and hauled him out through the shattered sunroof, one muscle-straining inch at a time, until they both rolled free onto the burning hot scrub. Roy needed to cross thirty feet of open desert to reach the Hummer, and he had one way to get close without being peppered with bullets. At least, if his hunch was right. If it wasn't, he'd be the first to know. He jammed the .22 into his belt and hoisted Mr. Smith's limp body, tossing him over his shoulder in a fireman's carry.

Then he ran. He focused on the goal, a marathon sprinter going for the gold, trying to ignore the churning of the sands all around him. He spotted the serpent's wake; it moved through the desert like the parched earth was water, drawing rupture lines as it curved around and targeted its next meal.

Him.

He's not going to make it, Lucy thought.

She saw what he was doing, bringing Mr. Smith over to his men. They wouldn't open fire on Roy, not if it meant hitting their boss. More important, Smith was their priority. She watched through the limo's back window as one of the shooters holstered his weapon, scurrying around and opening the back of the Hummer. Another reached for what looked like a first aid kit.

Then she spotted the serpent's wake. It was circling, a shark on the move, zeroing in on Roy. The body on his shoulders slowed him down, made him easy prey.

He's going to die, she thought.

Unless I do something.

"Doing something" felt like the worst idea in the world. Her muscles locked up, keeping her frozen, safe in the belly of the armored limousine. All she had to do was stay right there, make herself small, and she'd be all right. She was good at making herself small.

Heroes weren't real. They were as imaginary as...*as ancient Egyptian necromancers and giant skeleton-snakes*, she thought.

But there was Roy, trying his damnedest to do something heroic, here and now. And if she didn't do something, he was going to die in the desert.

Her paralysis broke. She squirmed out through the sunroof, grabbing the hot steel and hauling herself through. Then she got onto her feet and ran, heading straight for the wreckage on the highway. And the impossible little girl, dancing with delight on the ruin of an overturned tour bus.

Lucy's world collapsed in on itself. The vivid desert sky and the smoking wreckage became black lines, a sketch, on white paper. The lines folded, bent, blossoming into fractals, and the fractals resolved into crisp twelve-point Courier type.

Panel 1: Nighttime, establishing POV, looking upwards. RUMBLEBONES perches upon the crashed wreckage of a MetroSys monorail train in the heart of the urban sprawl. There are flames inside the windows, and the dark suggestions of dead bodies.

Lucy knew the next line. She knew it because she remembered writing it, burning the midnight oil in her college dorm room. The girl wasn't looking her way, hadn't even noticed her, too focused on steering her pet monster toward Roy. She needed to say the words. She took a deep breath, belting them out like the Midnight Jury.

"*Rumblebones*," Lucy roared in a voice she didn't know she had. "Stop this! It's me you want."

The real world and the script and the type collided, overlapping, winding around one another in a dance of realities. She saw the world in living color, the neat type tapping out in fast letters in the corner of her vision.

Lettering Note: While she's drawn like a little girl, emphasize that Rumblebones is an impossibly ancient and evil being, fueled by black magic. Consider a dripping, 'sinister' dialog style, maybe purple in a jagged cloud of black.

Panel 2: Rumblebones looks down at the new arrival and smiles. Her eyes are bottomless, hollow pits.

"It's not me who craves you, morsel. It's the Duke."

The girl spread her hands and gave Lucy a mocking shrug.

"But you, he wants alive. Only you. The rest will make worthy sacrifices."

The underground wake streaked like a bullet, churning the barren earth, on a collision course with Roy. It wasn't going to stop.

Chapter Seventeen

Roy was never great at math, but he could add two and two. Lucy had left the safety of the limo, trying to snag the kid's attention and turn her pet snake before it reached him. Nobility and guts, plenty impressive...but it didn't work.

The Network goons by the Hummer were ready to collect their boss; if they'd decided what to do about Roy, it was going to have to wait until Smith was safely delivered into their hands. Draped limp over Roy's shoulders, the man made for a decent human shield. That was the least of his problems right now, with the bone serpent burrowing its way to him like a torpedo primed to blow. He wasn't going to make it.

Not running at half speed, anyway. And not without giving the beast something to chew on.

Roy shrugged Mr. Smith's body off his shoulders. Smith hit the scrub and rolled, stirring, pushing himself up on one hand while he shook his dazed head. Roy didn't miss a step, still charging toward the Hummer. The .22 cleared his belt, yanking free, as Smith's men registered what had just happened. Too slow. Roy lined up a shot and squeezed the trigger twice. Both slugs punched into a Network man's chest, shoving him backwards, ripping up his dress shirt and baring the twisted fibers of a bulletproof vest underneath.

He'd live, with bruises, but the impact and the pain was enough to throw off his balance, almost knocking him off his feet. His buddy was faster, circling the other side of the Hummer and crouching low, using the armored truck for cover. The driver sat frozen behind the wheel.

Roy heard the avalanche roar of broken earth just behind him, echoing the bone-serpent's triumphant howl. He braced himself and got ready to die.

All of Lucy's questions came out at once in a single word, shattering the script: "How?"

"Architect," Rumblebones replied. "We are here because of you. You built the bridge. You built it all."

"I didn't do anything," she shouted up at the girl-thing. "I just wrote a stupid story, that's all it was!"

"Do you remember when you were small? You dreamed of me, then. You imagined I was the monster under your bed."

She remembered.

She sat between her parents, safe in their arms, warm in the glow of the television screen. They were watching *The Mummy*—the original one, with Boris Karloff. Her mother thought it was too old to be scary, but Lucy had been plenty scared. She carried her newborn fears down the dimly lit hall to her bedroom where she carefully balled up her feet, keeping them away from the edge of the bed, half convinced that a wizened corpse was waiting to reach up and grab her by the toes.

Years later she put pen to paper, refining her old terrors. Giving them new names and shapes and purposes, and a hero to fight them in all the ways Lucy never could.

"But you were only a nightmare," she whispered.

The little girl smiled, baring sharp and yellowed teeth.

The bone-serpent fired straight up into the air. It took Mr. Smith with it. Just behind Roy's back, close enough to pelt his shoulders with a shower of stray rubble, the beast clamped its jaws around Smith's torso and went airborne. It reached the arc of its jump, gracefully coiled in mid-air, and bit down.

Smith's legs, his arms, and his severed head spattered against the desert floor in a syrupy rain of blood and ripped flesh. The serpent kept what was left of its prize, angling downward, hitting the scrub with piledriver force and burrowing back underground. The sound of its clicking, rattling tail chased Roy as he ran. The offering had bought him a few seconds, at least. Now he had to make each one count.

The Network man behind the Hummer poked his head out of cover. Roy was already aiming down the sights of his stolen .22. The first shot went wide but the other drilled a hole through the shooter's cheek, shattering bone and teeth and sending him slumping to the ground, choking on his own blood. That left the first gunman, who was getting back up with one hand clutched to the holes in his bulletproof vest, and the driver, who was still frozen behind the wheel.

The soil rumbled, spitting up a trail of churned earth as the serpent came around for another pass.

The driver fired up his engine. No reason to stay, with their boss in ragged chunks on the scarlet sand. The shooter in the vest was more focused on Roy, lining up a shot as Roy charged straight for him. Roy was faster on the trigger. Roy drilled him in the throat, dropping him, then he opened fire on the Hummer and drew a line of chipped-glass craters across the driver's field of view. He knew he wouldn't penetrate the armored windshield, but the bullets still did their job: the driver, panicking, threw himself down in his seat.

Roy ripped the side door open before he could lock it. He clamped down on the driver's shoulder with one hand and put the muzzle of his gun to the man's forehead with the other. He was out of bullets, but the driver wasn't counting.

"Out," Roy snapped, helping him along with a hard yank. The driver fell out of the truck, hitting the ground at Roy's feet in a tangled sprawl. Roy didn't much care what happened to him, as long as he was out of the way. He climbed into the empty seat and slung the shift into first gear, stomping the gas hard enough to make the Hummer's wheels spin and spit loose dirt.

The wheels caught traction and the truck launched, firing across the badland, bouncing and jolting in the rough scrub. Lucy was just up ahead. So was the kid. Roy saw the skeletal serpent in the rearview mirror, firing up into the air with another fresh kill between its scarlet-stained jawbones. Then it arced, hit the desert flats, and burrowed deep, making a beeline straight for him.

He stomped the brakes just long enough for Lucy to pile in. She rocked back in the seat, her door still dangling open, as the Hummer took off again. Roy hauled on the wheel, rocketing past the wreckage and back up onto the highway. The truck fishtailed, threatening to roll for one stomach-lurching second, before he got it back under control. He didn't dare take his eyes off the road, not until they were clear.

"Is it still chasing us?" he asked.

Lucy turned in her seat, squinting into the dark. She shook her head. "I don't see it."

They both knew that wasn't the same thing. Roy kept his foot on the gas and the needle in the red. He didn't slow down until the last of the wreckage had disappeared into the distance, not even a lonely trickle of smoke against the clear blue sky.

Lucy vanished into her thoughts and Roy vanished into his. The desert sky at night shone with a faint and distant glow, colors streaked like jewel-toned oils across a vast, empty canvas. They barely saw anyone, or anything, just the distant red rocks and the encroaching night. Roy glanced at the fuel gauge. They'd need to find a place to refuel soon. And a safe place to sleep.

You almost got eaten by the skeleton of a giant snake, he reflected, *controlled by an ancient Egyptian necromancer in the body of a little girl. There is no such thing as 'safe,' not until I come to grips with this.*

"She said I built the bridge," Lucy told him.

He glanced sidelong at her. "Hm?"

"Rumblebones. She said they were here because of me."

He didn't have anything useful to say, so he kept his mouth shut. She shifted in her seat, looking at him.

"That wasn't a cosplayer, back at my apartment," she said. "That was Roach. It looked just like his truck at the curb, straight out of the comic, because it *was* his truck. All of my characters...they're coming to life."

All but the most important one. The bad guys were all here, spilling from the four-colored pages out into the real world, and there wasn't a fedora-wearing pulp hero in sight.

A sign up ahead pointed the way to an exit. Roy flicked the turn signal.

"Where are we going?" Lucy asked.

"Wherever this off-ramp takes us."

"And then?"

"We need gas, we need food. I assume you're going to need a few hours of shuteye and I know for a fact that I do. I'm moving on pure momentum. So we'll get out of sight. Find a place to hole up and get our strength back."

"And then?" she asked.

And then was a damn good question.

Chapter Eighteen

Once you drove far enough into the desert, far enough that you could see the stars at night, slipped free of the veil of light pollution and shining in all their scattered-diamond glory, you could still see signs of life here and there. Postage-stamp towns, some big enough for a community, some just big enough to hide a speed trap, dotted the web of old roads and old ruins. After midnight it was hard to tell the difference between a ghost town and a living one, at least until you came upon the bar or the brothel that kept the whole place in business.

Roy didn't know the name of this burg but the name of the local cathouse, the allegedly world-famous Silk Ranch, blared from a prominent sign on the outskirts of town. He decided he'd take their word for it. He wasn't interested in the brothel but the diner down the road, with bright lights and a promise of twenty-four-hour service, offered more immediate satisfaction.

"I don't know if I can eat," Lucy said.

"You can eat," he told her. "Trust me. You've still got that fight-or-flight juice in your veins. Once the last of it drains away, you need something to take its place. Just take it slow."

"I didn't do such a great job with the 'fighting' part," she said.

He pulled the Hummer into a spot toward the back of the lot, as far away from the lamplight as he could get. He doubted anyone was looking for it just yet, but eventually the Network would figure out that their prize fixer and his goons were never coming back.

"You did fine," Roy said. He would have lied to reassure her, but he didn't have to. "You stood your ground, kept the kid distracted and bought me the time I needed. Couldn't have done better myself."

It didn't look like she believed him, but she smiled anyway.

She had more questions, in the warm harbor of the diner. She held onto them until they were seated at a booth, the big plate glass window capturing the light inside so it looked like a black mirror. Her reflection reached for a laminated menu.

"So, Mr. Smith," she said. Her voice trailed off.

"Gone," he said.

"And the people he works for?"

The waitress came around, dead on her feet but powering through the tail end of her shift. Roy ordered coffee, black, and the steak-and-eggs special. Lucy stuck with ice water and asked for the buttermilk pancakes with a side of Canadian bacon.

"Good choice," Roy said, waiting for the waitress to walk out of earshot.

"Breakfast food at midnight is always a good choice," she said. Her tentative smile faded. "But...the Network?"

"Bear in mind that before today, I thought they were a myth."

"I don't expect an expert opinion," Lucy said. "But you know more than I do."

"I know how outfits like the Network operate."

He'd been thinking about that. Planning for contingencies, maybes and might-happens.

"Okay," she said, listening.

"Sooner or later, they'll realize that wherever he was supposed to take you, Smith and his gang aren't showing up. Hopefully later than sooner, but we don't know where the end of the line was meant to be, so there's no way to tell."

"And then?"

"And then they'll come looking. Have to assume Smith reported in, back when Hawke double-crossed us and handed us over. So they know where he would have left from, and where he was headed, which makes it easy to draw a road map. Then they'll find the highway crash. Tell me something: would Rumblebones clean up after herself?"

She paused in the middle of unwrapping a straw, giving a tiny shake of her head.

"I...I have no idea, I mean—"

"The character," he said. "The way you wrote her. The way you pictured her in your head. Would she have cleaned up after herself?"

Lucy sank back into her seat, thinking back. She crumpled the paper wrapper.

"No," she said. "She's sloppy, and insane. Duke Ellery only calls on her when he needs his biggest guns."

"So the Network is going to find a flipped Hummer, a crashed limo, and whatever's left of the corpses. We've got a big advantage here."

"I'm having a hard time seeing it right now," Lucy said.

"Did you catch Smith's reaction, when we mentioned Roach? He didn't send him, didn't even know about him. Rumblebones attacking the convoy is all the proof I need: they're not working together."

"So there are *two* groups of lunatics gunning for my head." Lucy stirred her straw in the glass of ice water. "Tell me why this is an advantage?"

"Number one, the Network is going to have no idea what happened. I'm pretty sure 'a comic-book character came to life and brought her pet giant snake along for the ride' will be rock-bottom on their list of best guesses. Sorting out the mess is going to take time, and that's time we can use to get off the radar."

"And number two?"

"A little professional wisdom," Roy said. "When two groups of people want the same thing, and they're both willing to go to extremes to get it, they're vulnerable. A push and a prod in the right direction can work wonders."

Lucy got it. "You want to make them fight each other."

"If we're lucky, we won't have to try. If the Network figures out even half of the craziness that went down today, and if they live up to the urban legends, they'll be out for blood. Nobody crosses the Network and lives. Not even...ancient necromancers, or whoever else is rattling around that head of yours. Hey, do me one favor?"

"Name it."

"Imagine an airplane to get us out of here. Better yet, a helicopter. Maybe it'll be waiting for us in the parking lot."

"A military helicopter," she said. "One with lots of guns and missiles."

"Perfect," he said. Then he paused. "Wait. Do any of your villains actually have a military helicopter?"

She glanced at the dark mirror of the window.

"One has a jetpack."

"On second thought," Roy told her, "don't imagine anything."

"We're a few years too late for that," she said.

Roy was right about one thing: Lucy took a few timid bites of her dinner, still insisting she wasn't hungry, then tore into the stack of pancakes like she hadn't eaten in a week. They both cleaned their plates down to the last bite. The coffee would keep him on his feet a little longer, long enough to find a bed for the night, gas up the stolen Hummer for tomorrow's escape, and park it out of sight.

He still wasn't sure where they were escaping *to*, but any random road would take them somewhere.

A roadside motel, stucco walls painted in Technicolor shades of aquamarine and pastel pink, offered the thin hope of sanctuary. At least until sunrise, anyway. Roy gave Lucy a credit card and told her to rent a room while he hid the truck.

"I can afford it," she said.

"Are you carrying cash? We have to assume your credit cards, debit cards, anything with your name on it is radioactive until proven otherwise. Last thing we want is to fire up a flare telling 'em exactly where we are right before we get some sleep. This card isn't in my name. Or in any real person's. It's got a little emergency money on it, enough to get us by for a couple of days at least."

Her hand tightened around his card.

"They can do that? Track us that way?"

"Don't know, not inclined to risk it. Same reason I'm moving the truck: if there's any kind of transponder hidden on it, pinging out a location, I don't want it stashed anywhere near the place where we're resting our heads. I'll be back in about twenty minutes."

She got a ground floor room with two queen beds, lined up side by side on the paper-thin carpet, with a view of nothing in particular. The curtains were already drawn tight by the time Roy returned, and she was sitting on the edge of a mattress with a remote in hand, glued to a repeat of the nightly news.

"They were reporting on the highway crash," she said.

Roy flipped the deadbolt behind him and checked the fish-eye peephole for good measure, scanning the desolate parking lot.

"Yeah?" he said.

"They didn't show any footage. Just said it was a tour bus in a head-on with a delivery truck, and..."

She stopped talking. She didn't have to say anything. He knew, with one look, what was tearing her up inside. Roy crossed the room and gently took the remote from her hands. He turned off the TV, plunging the room into silence.

"That's not on you," he said.

"I don't know...I don't know how many people died in the accident, and how many Rumblebones killed while she was waiting for us to show up. I guess she didn't want any witnesses. Either way, nobody—"

"Either way," he said, sitting down next to her, "that's not on you."

The thin, worn-out mattress sagged under his weight. She leaned in, her shoulder against his.

"The trap was for me."

"And what happened to those people was sad. You can feel sad about it. Just don't feel guilty, because that's not your cross to carry."

She stared down at her empty hand. Flexing her fingers, unflexing them, closing them around an imaginary pen. She scribbled on the air, then let her wrist sag back against her lap.

"I don't *know* that," she said. "I don't know why this is happening in the first place. What if it really is my fault?"

He thought about that while he kicked his shoes off. They thumped onto the carpet one at a time.

"What happened today," he said, "was...I want to say 'impossible,' but I can't, because it happened and we lived through it. I don't want to say 'magic' because I don't want to believe in magic, but I sure as hell can't figure out any rational explanation. Believe me. I tried."

"Same," Lucy said. "I could almost buy the idea that Roach was a killer playing dress-up, but that, out there on the highway—that was something completely different. I thought about holograms, about robots. Then I thought maybe they dosed us with some kind of weapons-grade hallucinogen."

"But we had the exact same hallucination, which is just as impossible. I know, I had the same ideas. Probably threw them all out for the same reasons, too."

"And what's left, the only answer that fits," she said, "is magic."

He got up, moved to the other bed, and tugged back the covers. The sheets had a musty smell, like old paper.

"We won't solve any mysteries tonight," he said. "I know it's going to be hard, but do your best to get some sleep. The more rested we are come sunrise, the better equipped we'll be."

"Equipped for what?" she said.

"For whatever's down the road. We'll find out when we get there."

He clicked off the lamp between their beds and unbuttoned his shirt in the dark.

She was quiet for a while, long enough to make Roy think she'd drifted off to dreamland. Then she spoke, her voice a faint tremor.

"Are you awake?"

"I'm right here," he said.

"When we first met, when you stopped those guys in the van from kidnapping me, the one you dragged into the alley said you used to be a cop."

The musty sheets took on an earthy smell. Like a burial shroud.

"Sort of," he said.

"Do you still know anybody from back then? Someone who might help us? Or give us someplace to hide?"

No. Nobody from those days would even admit to knowing Roy's name. Nobody but Hawke, and she'd traded his life for less than a nickel. He wouldn't expect a warmer reception from anyone else.

Thinking about the past set him on a spiral, a long slide down to places he'd rather not go. But it was all waiting there for him, vivid as yesterday, right behind his eyelids.

"Go to sleep," he said. "Tomorrow's going to be a long day."

Chapter Nineteen

"Roy? Are you awake?"

He hadn't been, but that was all right. "Sure."

"Are you real?"

The numbers on the digital clock floated in the darkness between them. 2:17 in the morning was a strange time for philosophy. Then again, maybe it was the perfect time.

"Did you ever write me?" he asked.

"I don't think so."

"There you go, then."

She was quiet for a minute. Then:

"Tell me a story," she said.

He shifted on the stiff mattress, hunting for the cooler side of the pillow.

"You're the writer," he said.

"Something I don't know about you. Something I couldn't have made up."

Roy thought about it. He only had the one story, he supposed. He wasn't sure if it was a good one, but it was his, and he was the only person who could tell it.

"Once upon a time," he said, "there was a poor kid from a shitty town who loved watching cop shows. Couldn't get enough of that stuff. See, his old man spoke with a belt wrapped around his fist and his mom popped pills behind the bathroom door, and he didn't really have anywhere to run to but the television set. So he sat there, late at night, gobbling it all up. Dreaming of this world where there were good guys and bad guys, and the good guys always solved the crime and the bad guys always went down."

"A promise of order," Lucy said.

"Are you telling this story, or me?"

"Sorry," she said. "For all of it."

"Nothing to be sorry about. It happened. But this kid, he made a mistake somewhere along the way. He thought all those cop shows were real. Don't get me wrong, it's not like he thought they were documentaries or something. More like he thought they were telling the truth about the world and how it all worked. And that was a very dangerous lie."

———⋈———

Roy's captain once told him he was perfect for undercover work. He looked exactly like the kind of cheap dumb thug that rich dumb thugs wanted to hire. Roy was never sure if he meant that as a compliment. He supposed it didn't matter either way, which was what a cheap dumb thug would think.

His first operation targeted a ring of cowboys hijacking trucks near the airport, flipping whatever they could steal for pennies on the dollar and flipping those pennies for crack cocaine. Strictly personal use. They were dangerous and sloppy and they'd already put a driver on life support with a broken skull, so time was a factor. Roy got in, he did his job and he did it well: he put faces to names, building a web from the crew to the shady pawn shops and street dealers they did business with, and lined up a string of thirty-something good arrests on the day his higher-ups brought the whole thing crashing down. He was proud of himself. A real TV cop.

The leader of the crew, who bragged to Roy's face about personally delivering the beating that stole a driver's life—he did it because he felt like "letting off some steam," and because he could—was the first to talk in the interview room. First to talk gets the first pick of plea bargains, and when the dust settled, he got off with a six-month sentence as a reward for pinning all the rough stuff on his fellow hoods.

"What were you expecting," one of Roy's drinking buddies asked, "honor among thieves?"

"I was expecting something like justice for the guy who got his brains bashed in."

His buddy stared at him, bleary-eyed, over a glass of straight bourbon.

"Guy's in a coma, he'll never know the difference. Anyway, you got in, you got out, and you got a commendation on your jacket. That's a win. Justice isn't our job, Roy. We're trash collectors. Just keep your head down, do your twenty, and collect your pension like everybody else."

Roy was good at undercover work. He studied the streets like a broker picking stocks, staying ahead of the curve, always anticipating the next job before his bosses handed it down. There was always a new crisis, always a new problem-of-the-week that someone at City Hall needed fixed before the next election, an endless game of criminal whack-a-mole. When cheap blow flooded the streets, the unintended consequence of a cartel collapsing half a world away, Roy knew he'd be called up to Narcotics.

They trusted him with a big fish: Vic Perez, the Peruvian connection himself. He was gearing up for a war with some up-and-coming rivals, so he was in the market for a few cheap dumb thugs. In a week, Roy was a new recruit. In a month, he was on the man's personal bodyguard detail. All he had to do was keep his eyes open and his mouth shut and document Perez's operation from the inside. Nothing he hadn't done before.

Then it all went to hell.

"The thing is," he told Lucy, both of them drifting in the dark, "when you go undercover, you don't just learn to think like a criminal. You become one. We'd all like to pretend otherwise, but it's hard to hang out with gangsters without doing some gangster shit. There are compromises for the sake of the job."

"Where's the line?" she asked.

"Liability. Don't do anything that'd give a citizen with a beef any cause to sue, and don't do anything so extreme that the department can't sweep it under the rug. Anything less than that is just the cost of doing business. I've smashed windows, boosted stereos, put the fear of God into a few people who didn't deserve it...but working Narcotics was a different beast."

"How so?"

"First and foremost," Roy said, "'never get high on your own supply' is a catchy slogan, but reality doesn't work that way. My whole time on that beat, I never met a single dealer who didn't partake. A lot. It was part of the culture. Also the cause of a whole bunch of bad decisions, but that's neither here nor there."

"So you had to..." her voice trailed off in a question.

"When it's offered, you don't say no. These guys watched the same shows I did growing up, and they were dumb enough to think cops couldn't break the law. So somebody tapping out a line of coke in front of you, for example, is both a gift and a test. First I was doing it to fit in. Then I was doing it because I liked it. Then I was doing it just to do it."

"Didn't anyone notice?" Lucy asked. "I mean, the people you worked with. Your department."

"They noticed I got results, and that was the bottom line. Besides, undercover work is an acting gig. Being a functional junkie is also an acting gig. Same set of skills. But my sweet tooth wasn't the real problem."

"What was?"

"Carmen."

As his bodyguard, Roy's job was to go where Perez went. Mostly that meant his sunbaked mansion, silently prowling from the wet bar to the pool and back to the bar again. Perez was high by noon and more or less stayed that way until the small hours of the morning, swinging between booze and pills and blow, between blessedly sedate and violently paranoid.

Carmen was Perez's girl, an aspiring model turned into a piece of resident eye candy. Roy was only human. He could only see her out by the pool so many times, perfecting her tan in a string bikini or less, before he had to meet her. Turned out she had been watching him, too.

They had some things in common. She liked him, he liked her. Neither of them liked Perez, but they both liked his cocaine. That was how they ended up playing house on the down-low, meeting up in the fleabag apartment Roy rented on his department stipend. He knew he was playing with fire: Perez would kill them both if he found out, and he'd kill them slow. But Roy was dumb and in love.

Not dumb enough to tell her the truth. "Never trust a junkie" is rock-solid Biblical writ, the wisdom of the ages, and those words had never steered him wrong. Roy was never quite sure if Carmen was more interested in him or in his access to Perez's stash. He didn't know whether she'd sell him out if she knew he was working undercover. So he settled that problem by making sure she never had the chance. He loved her and lied to her and he knew nothing about his lifestyle was sustainable, but he wasn't thinking about the long term anymore. One day at a time was fine, measuring out the hours between feeding his two habits.

Then his handler called for a meeting. They stood in an all-night laundromat, pretending to fold shirts while he passed down the news: it was over. Roy's work had borne all the fruit it was going to, and the brass had decreed it was time for the bust and the mop-up operation. He was done, great job.

"When's it happening?" Roy asked.

"Day after tomorrow. Same drill as always: you'll get arrested along with everybody else, to keep your cover intact. After you get processed I'll have you pulled out of holding. Keep things cool and you'll be on your way to a well-earned vacation."

Now he had a Carmen problem.

He thought he solved it the next night, awake beside her, sharing a cigarette in tangled, sweat-soaked sheets.

"Run away with me," he told her.

"You loved her that much?" Lucy asked.

"I loved her enough to get her away from me. No. I was going to disappear from her life the next day, one way or another. I just wanted her away from Perez's mansion when the bust went down. I didn't know what they'd charge her with, and there was a good chance she'd be standing right at Perez's side when SWAT stormed in. Accidents happen. I just wanted to keep her safe. I figured if she was stranded at a bus depot on the other side of town, waiting for a lover who was never going to show up, that was kinder than the alternative."

"Did it work?"

Roy stared at the shadows on the ceiling. They seemed to move of their own volition, drifting like storm clouds.

"No," he said.

The silence between their beds demanded feeding. He wouldn't tell her everything. This was his story, his alone, and he'd take it to his grave. But he could give her one last piece of it.

"I was done, after that. Said hell with my twenty years and my pension. I was just done. Managed to get clean, somehow, eventually, and I went into business for myself." He turned his head on the pillow. She was a shadow too, lying across from him, motionless in the dark. "So what do you think? Am I a figment of your imagination?"

She gave it some thought.

"No," she said. "I like stories with happy endings."

He wanted to take the cynic's way out. Answer her with some defensive tough guy panache, like *there's no such thing, princess*. But he didn't really believe that, so he told her the truth.

"This one's not over yet," he said. "We'll see how it goes."

Chapter Twenty

"I was thinking," Lucy said, raking a puddle of syrup across her plate with the tines of her fork.

They'd gone back to the diner at first light, pausing just long enough to refuel their bodies and their stolen truck. The road ahead was a big fat question mark. Or a field of land mines.

Roy sipped his black coffee. "I'm all ears."

"What if we go back to where everything started?"

"The comic books? I already talked to Neil Zielinska. He pointed me your way, but beyond that he didn't know anything."

"Before that," she said. "These characters...I told you I made most of them up when I was little, right?"

"Sure. Like turning the Mummy into a kid with a teddy bear. I've been very circumspect with my opinions on your creativity in general."

"Appreciated. Anyway, I used to fill entire notebooks with this stuff. Thoughts, ideas, snippets of stories I wanted to write but never got around to finishing. Maybe there's something in all that junk, something I forgot."

"Something that might explain what's going on here?" Roy said.

"Bingo."

"If they were back at your apartment, that's going to be a problem."

She shook her head. "The problem is, they might not even exist anymore. Can you get us to Wickenburg? It's just outside of Phoenix."

"We've been driving north, now we're driving south again. Sure. What's in Wickenburg?"

"My parents."

She called on the way. Her mother had a feather-soft voice that quavered around the edges.

"I...suppose so, dear. When you went away to college we moved all your old things up to the attic. You're welcome to take a look, if you like."

"We can be there at—" Lucy glanced to Roy, sitting behind the steering wheel. He checked the clock on the Hummer's dash and mouthed *four*. "—four this afternoon?"

"We?" her mother asked.

"A...friend of mine from work. You haven't met him."

"Well. I'll make tea."

Seven hours on the open road, sun blazing in the cloudless, arid desert sky, brought Lucy home. Wickenburg was a blip of a town that wore its Western heritage on its sleeve. Affably rustic, a modern-day frontier outpost that smelled like hickory and mesquite, where the locals had traded their mustangs for dusty pickup trucks.

The house was down a nowhere road, the nearest neighbors a mile in either direction, a saguaro cactus in the yard towering over a battered old mailbox. The paint on the slats of the Southern-style cottage had faded over the years, from pristine white to yellowed bone, and a wasp nest dangled beneath the eaves of the gabled roof. Stray gravel rumbled under the wheels as Roy pulled into the driveway. He leaned forward in his seat, checking the windows.

"You sure this is a good idea?" he asked.

Lucy pursed her lips and thought it over.

"These people who are after me—the Network, and whoever's behind my characters coming to life—they all know who I am now, right?"

"Looks like it." *Thanks to me*, Roy thought, still stinging over it. Of course, with Smith dead on a stretch of desert highway along with his entourage, ripped apart by a skeletal snake, hopefully they'd have some lead time before more of the Network's finest came hunting.

"So it wouldn't be hard for them to find out who my family is and where they live. It's not a secret. If they're going to come here, there's not much I can do about it. Except one thing." Lucy pushed her door open and slid down from the passenger seat. "If there's anything useful in my old notebooks, anything at all, we grab it and take it with us. Keep the target on me, and away from my family."

He couldn't argue with her logic. *As long as we're quick*, he thought, leaving the safety of the armored truck and stepping down onto rough gravel. *If I was hunting us, this place would be my next stop.*

Lucy's mother answered the door. Roy didn't need an introduction: the woman was Lucy's older reflection, the same eyes set into a more wizened face, her shoulders stooped under the weight of her years. Roy held back, lingering on the porch, while Lucy and her mother shared a gentle hug.

"Mom," Lucy said, "this is Roy."

She looked up at him, a glint of suspicion in her eyes. "And you are...?"

"I work with Lucy." Cover stories came easy to Roy, as easy as lying. "In the gallery, doing art restoration. I specialize in repairing fire and smoke damage."

"He's really good," Lucy put her hand on Roy's back. "I've been learning a few things."

"I'm also good at lifting weights. Lucy said she was going to dig through her old stuff and wasn't sure if it would be easy to get at, so I volunteered to help out."

"She might need you," her mother said, waving them both inside. She shut the door behind them, sealing them into the air-conditioned stillness. "That junk has been up in the attic for...I don't even know, years now."

Roy scoped out the place. The living room was cozy, the furniture all in shades of beige, a fat television sitting on a cubbyhole credenza. The cubbies were filled with trinkets, odds and ends, vacation photos and stray memories. A small, dirty teddy bear, a scalloped seashell, a postcard from Miami Beach. One picture caught his eye. Lucy couldn't have been more than six, with pigtails and a gap-toothed smile. She sat on her mother's knee.

A man grudgingly shared the frame with them, a few feet apart and looking away, like he had someplace else to be. He wore an Arizona Cardinals T-shirt, cut at the shoulders to show off his full tattoo sleeves. Cheap ink, mostly. Prison ink.

"Is Dad home?" Lucy asked. He caught the change in her tone, hesitant now.

"No, dear. He doesn't get off work for another hour or two, and, you know. He spends most nights with his friends at the Palomino."

"Still, huh?" Lucy said.

Her mother offered a weak smile. "I don't mind the quiet."

A cord, dangling from the ceiling of the second-floor hallway, pulled down to open a trapdoor. Roy and Lucy unfolded the attic stairs, and he tapped his phone to shine a light up into the darkness. Her mother left them to it, vanishing into the kitchen downstairs. Roy didn't comment on the family dynamic. He felt like he had some things in common with Lucy, but it wasn't his place to say. He just led the way upstairs, up into the gloom.

A bare hanging bulb cast light on the situation. The attic was a maze of moving boxes and loose ends. A long-neglected dressmaker's form leaned against the angled rafters, not far from the drooping neck of a plastic Christmas tree. Lucy shooed a spiderweb from her path with the back of her hand.

"I think...this might be it," she said. Roy followed her lead, pulling away a heavy cardboard box and setting it aside while she dug into the one just beneath. It was a time capsule. Old report cards, a sticker album, stray Polaroids. And notebooks. So many notebooks, from school steno books to spiral-bound ones with glossy Lisa Frank unicorn covers.

"That the stuff?" he asked.

"Jackpot," she whispered. She gingerly picked up the top notebook and flipped through pages lined with prim cursive.

Roy couldn't help with this part, but he had questions that needed answering elsewhere. While Lucy went on the hunt, he drifted back downstairs. He found her mother in the kitchen, almost done pouring a couple of glasses of iced tea. She looked to the open doorway, eyebrows lifting in surprise.

"Oh," she said. "I was just about to come upstairs."

"Thought I'd save you the trip."

"Thank you for that," she said, holding out the tall glasses. "I hate that attic. Too many spiders, and those stairs aren't kind to my knees."

"I'm not fond of spiders myself."

She gave him an appraising look as he took the glasses from her. "Have you known Lucy for very long?"

"About a year now." There were times to play a long game, and times to take a chance. To dive right in. "Can I ask you something?"

Her mother shrugged. "Sure."

"When Lucy was young, did anything...strange happen?"

"Strange?"

"Unexplainable," he said.

He wasn't expecting her face to drop like that, or the anxious look she shot over his shoulder. Her already soft voice became a gust of breath.

"How did you know about that?"

"Lucy—" he started to say.

"She doesn't remember. At least she didn't, when I asked her a while back. She doesn't remember any of it."

"Tell me."

She took a step closer, still looking past him.

"You'll think I'm crazy."

"Tell me anyway."

"When she was twelve," her mother said. "Things started...moving. Little things. The kitchen chairs would get turned upside-down. Lights would go on in rooms nobody was in. We'd all be downstairs and hear a door slam on the second floor."

"How did her father react?"

She shook her head—almost a nervous twitch—and stepped past the question.

"I talked to a specialist in these sorts of things, or at least he claimed he was. He said that sometimes, when a girl goes through puberty, she can...attract things, or make things happen."

Roy had heard something like that, somewhere. Maybe just an old movie. "You talking about poltergeists?"

"That was the word he used. One day, when she was fourteen or so, it all just...stopped. Like I said, she doesn't remember any of it. But it happened, I swear it did. Now you tell me something."

"Shoot."

"How did you know?" she asked.

"Your daughter," Roy said, casting a glance to the ceiling, "is a very special girl."

Roy found Lucy sitting cross-legged in a patch of dust, notebooks spread around her on the attic floor like tarot cards. She was lost in thought and Roy picked up one of the notebooks, curious.

"May I?"

"Sure," Lucy said. "So far I'm finding a bunch of memories, not much else."

"Good ones?"

"Just memories," she said.

He leafed through the pages of a steno book, gazing over the penciled-in block letters and a tapestry of old dirty eraser smudges. Instead of offering up a story, this looked more like some weird form of code.

Duke Ellery, it read, *(AKA the Illustrated Duke). Medium Human, Lawful Evil, Level 16 Sorcerer. STR 12, DEX 16, CON 14—*

"What's this?" Roy asked, crouching down to show Lucy the notes. This memory, at least, she could smile at.

"Oh, when I was in high school—sixteen, maybe seventeen?—I ran a homebrew RPG based on my story ideas. I wasn't having any luck getting anything written, except for one short story that got rejected by every magazine I sent it to, and I had a lot of creativity to get out."

"Gotcha," Roy said. "What's an RPG?"

"A roleplaying game. You know, like Dungeons and Dragons?"

Roy waggled a hand from side to side. "Vaguely. So you...acted these characters out?"

"Most of them. I was the DM for that campaign and..." she paused.

"You remember something?" Roy asked.

She took the notebook from him, tearing through the pages.

"Okay, so if Roach and Rumblebones are real," she said, "it's not crazy to assume that *all* of my characters are real, right?"

"I'd love to argue, but sure. Everybody except the Midnight Jury, if we can believe what Roach said back at your apartment. The Jury's missing and the cavalry's not coming."

"Maybe it is. Or at least, maybe we've got a friend out there."

Her fingertip came down on the page, drawing an underline beneath an unfamiliar name.

Verna Bell. Medium Human, Chaotic Neutral, Level 5 Wizard.

"If we can't find a hero," Lucy said, "this is our second-best hope. We need Verna Bell."

"And she's...who, exactly?"

She started gathering up the notebooks, slapping covers shut, bundling them in her arms.

"I'll tell you on the road. We've been here too long as it is, and now we've got everything we need."

Chapter Twenty-one

"Verna Bell," Lucy said once they were back on the road.

She'd hugged her mother, said a quick goodbye, and borrowed a couple of plastic bags from her recycling bin to stuff full with her plundered treasures. The bags, overflowing with notebooks, rested at her feet in the passenger seat of the Hummer.

"Who may or may not be real right now," Roy said.

He stepped on the gas. He didn't have a destination in mind, just far away from here, far enough to lead their pursuers away from Lucy's family doorstep.

"Okay, so Duke Ellery was—is, I guess I should say—the biggest crime boss in Noir York City. Half the villains in town are on his payroll. Verna Bell is one of his apprentices. Not that he teaches her all that much; she does his accounting and cooks his books to make everything look nice and legal."

Roy thought back to the impenetrable block of statistics, like one of his old baseball cards. "Didn't it say she was, what was it, 'chaotic neutral?'"

"Chaotic neutral people are...ugh, how do I word this? I wish I had my Dungeon Master's Guide. They're basically individualists who value personal freedom above everything else. They don't care about good or evil, they just want to be free."

"Doesn't sound like someone who would be happy under a crime boss's thumb," Roy said.

"And she isn't. She hoped he'd lead her to the mysteries of the universe and arcane power. Instead, she launders his money for him and runs errands. Anyway, the Midnight Jury caught her and she offered up a deal: in exchange for letting her walk, she forks over little scraps of intel now and then. When the Duke is making a big play, when a major crime is going down, that kind of thing."

"She's a rat?" Roy said. "That can't be safe."

"She's good at covering her tracks. She's a survivor."

Roy drove, drumming his fingers on the steering wheel. He shot her a sidelong glance.

"You admire her."

"I mean," Lucy said, "I didn't think she was real."

"Jury's out on that one. Speaking of—"

"Obviously, they had to be careful about meeting. Duke Ellery has eyes everywhere and he doesn't trust anyone, especially not his own people. He assumes they're all out to kill him and take his throne, and mostly he's right, they just don't dare to try."

"He's that tough, this Duke guy?"

"He can *do* things."

She didn't elaborate.

"So what's the plan?" Roy asked. "We can't just hang around and hope she finds us before anything else pops out of your head."

"I've been thinking about that. Verna and the Jury had a way to signal each other, when they needed a meeting."

"Don't tell me," Roy said. "Big spotlight on a rooftop somewhere? It's been done before."

"More like a…mystical conduit."

He shot another look at her.

"A spell," he said. "You're talking about a magic spell."

She squirmed in her seat.

"We almost got eaten by a giant skeleton-snake yesterday. Is the idea of a magic spell really all that weird?"

"You got me there," he said.

"The problem is, I never actually wrote down the details."

"Dead end?"

"Maybe not." She frowned, thinking. Then she scooped up one of the plastic bags at her feet, rummaging through her notebooks, hunting a memory.

"What are you looking for?" he asked.

"An old snippet of a story I never finished. We might just have everything we need right here."

She found the passage. She only half remembered writing it, a strange graveyard rendezvous plotted out in the nervous, over-neat cursive of a fourteen-year-old girl, but the voices on the page sang out to her.

Teach me, she thought.

"Magic," said Verna Bell, "is the science and art of causing change to occur in conformity with the will."

Rumblebones snorted. The girl-thing perched on the damp curve of a tombstone, watching her.

"You're going to quote Aleister Crowley at me? I was mastering the Fourteen Emerald Tablets and raising the dead when your ancestors were rubbing sticks together to make fire."

Verna had a stick of her own: a muddy twig, scavenged from a scattering of fallen leaves beneath the boughs of a dying tree. She traced a slow circle in the cemetery dirt.

"You're too hung up on high ritual. Effective? Yes. Powerful? Undeniably. But a witch can do one thing that a ceremonial magician can't."

"Die?"

"Work quick and dirty," Verna said, rolling her eyes. She plucked a clump of muddy grass, held it up, and let it fall, pausing a moment to study the scatter of the dew-damp blades. "Your wands and your chants, your grimoires and grim words are nothing but nattering. Lenses of focus for a forlorn and lonely light."

"Wordplay," scoffed Rumblebones.

Verna glanced up from where she was crouched in the weeds, her eyes big and curious, lashes fluttering.

"Won't you come down and play with me?" she said.

"What's the game?"

"Improvisational jazz."

"I thought you were going to cast a spell."

Verna arched an eyebrow. "Isn't that what I just said? Witchcraft is jazz."

"I prefer baroque."

"Like I always say, if something isn't baroque, break it. But if you want a Handel on magic, you have to get Bach to basics."

Rumblebones hopped down off the tombstone. "I don't care for this game."

"Bailing? But we've barely begun. This linguistic labyrinth may be leavened with levity, but leads and lures along liminal lines."

She slapped her palms together, sudden and fierce, the sound of a gunshot crackling across the empty graveyard.

"Your feet," she said, staring into the girl-thing's eyes, "are frozen."

Rumblebones jerked one knee, then another. Her white leather saddle shoes stayed pinned to the wet grass. She grimaced.

"Hypnosis. Real cute, you bitch. Let me go or I'm telling the Duke."

"As soon as my demonstration's done. The latent magic in the air here should kindle my spell's flames nicely, no elaborate ceremony required. For reagents, we'll keep it dirt-simple: something to honor the past, something to live in the present, and something to shape the future I desire. That's all it takes."

Roy drove while Lucy tapped away at her phone, exploring the long road ahead. She had an idea.

All of these things, these people from my notebooks, they're all real, she reasoned. *So did I create them somehow, or did they always exist and I just picked up on them, like an antenna tuned to a strange frequency?*

Neither possibility pointed to a reason for them to be hunting her down, turning her into a character in her own twisted tale, but that question could keep for later. She kept going, chasing her own hazy, looping train of thought.

Both possibilities take me to the same place. It doesn't matter that I didn't write down the details of Verna's spell.

"Because I'm doing it right now," she murmured. Roy gave her a look. "Hm?"

"Either I'm responsible for all of this, creating people with my imagination, or I'm just some kind of weird psychic who saw these people, *thought* it was my imagination, and wrote everything down. Right?"

"Checks out," he said.

"In the first case, I must know how Verna's spell works, because I created it."

"And in the second," Roy said, "you know how it works, because you watched it from a distance."

"Exactly."

"So," he said, "how does it work?"

Lucy sank lower in her seat.

"I'm still figuring that part out," she said. "Sorry."

She knew—she thought she knew—that she needed a few things. Beyond that she was playing by ear. Shopping ate up the rest of the afternoon and they had to drive three towns over to find what she was looking for, splitting time between a used bookstore that smelled like mothballs and a seedy comics shop where water-stained boxes gathered dust on folding card tables.

Back in the car, she showed Roy her prizes: the rare second issue of *The Midnight Jury*, sheathed in collector's plastic, and a dogeared paperback copy of Carolyn Saunders's *The City at Midnight*.

"Something to honor the past," she said, "and something to live in the present."

"I get the symbolism, but I'm not seeing how a comic book and a paperback turn into a magic spell."

She almost apologized, again. She felt sheepish, stupid—*though not as stupid as I'm going to look if this doesn't work*—and it was hard to translate the swelling pressure in her chest into words. She tried all the same.

"It's..." she touched her fingers to her heart. "It's in here. Wanting to come out. It's not something I know so much as something I feel. I have to go with my instincts, and if I second-guess myself, if I convince myself I can't then I won't be able to—"

"Hey," Roy said. She fell silent.

He checked the rearview mirror and shifted the truck into drive.

"I believe in you," he said. "You've got this. Let's go."

"I need a cemetery," she said.

"One cemetery, coming right up."

Chapter Twenty-two

Lucy needed a few more things, ideas she conjured on the way. A disposable plastic lighter, a pair of scissors, a tube of white glue. Stopping off at a drugstore rendered up all three, along with some sodas and snacks for the road. Roy felt himself flagging, the madness of the past few days draining his batteries dry, but the caffeine and sugar kick from a lukewarm can of Coke kept him on the move.

Monroe Cemetery was an oblong suburban graveyard, awkwardly squeezed between a tract-housing development and a sleepy shopping district. The sun dipped below the shaggy trees, then vanished, taking the people with it. This was the kind of town that rolled up the sidewalks after dark. That was fine with Roy. Monroe might have a caretaker—one, at most, paid to sleep on the job—but no serious security. Sure enough, right next to the *Closed at Sunset* sign on the stone fence was a wide-open gate inviting them in.

All the same, he parked the Hummer at the curb outside and they moved in on foot. He led the way, keeping to the cold, damp grass, avoiding the gravel-paved paths that unspooled between the graves like fingerprint whorls.

"Stay behind me and keep low," he whispered. His eyes, adjusting to the spreading dark, hunted for a caretaker's shack. He found it by the west-side wall, just inside the stone fencing. They went east. Lucy looked like she was hunting too, cradling her newfound treasures in a plastic bag tight against her chest.

"Here," she said. Roy looked back over his shoulder. She'd planted herself in the middle of a shady triangle between three intersecting paths. The stones there were old, tiny and worn, so eaten by weather and time that nothing of their engravings remained. Whoever slept under their feet was long-forgotten now, left to rot beneath a tangle of overgrown grass.

"Okay," Roy said. "You need me for this, or...?"

She shook her head. Quiet for a moment, as if making up her mind.

"No. I have to do this myself."

He wouldn't pretend not to be relieved. Running into magical creeps from the pages of a pulp comic was bad enough; actually *doing* magic felt like one more irreversible step into another world. He liked his own world just fine.

"I'll stand guard," he said, backing off to one corner of the triangle. "Do your thing."

He could see the distant slanted roof of the caretaker's shack from here, and a light burning behind a dirty window. The only sounds were the faint cries of night-birds and the plastic rustle of Lucy's bag as she set it down. She knelt on the wet grass, brow furrowed, deep in thought.

Roy didn't much like graveyards, and he didn't like having time to do nothing but think. The combination of the two led him down a path he didn't want to take, straight to the question nagging at his mind since this whole mess started.

Mousy little Lucy Langenkamp imagined a world, and that world came true. Or it was always out there, alongside theirs, and she discovered it like some kind of psychic astronaut. Either way, they weren't alone in the universe. There were other worlds and undiscovered countries out there.

So was there a world where Carmen went to the bus station instead of the morgue?

And if there's a world where she lived, he thought, *is there another me there? And was he smart enough to meet her at the bus, to run away with her and leave everything behind?*

And are we happy right now?

Pointless. He was torturing himself and he knew it. Carmen was dead and he was a living shadow, like the pools of inky darkness gathering around his scuffed leather shoes. That was life.

The flame of a butane lighter flickered just over his shoulder, turning his head. Lucy was doing her thing.

For reagents, we'll keep it dirt-simple: something to honor the past, something to live in the present, and something to shape the future I desire.

Verna's words, summoned from the pages of Lucy's old notebook—or Lucy's words, put in Verna's mouth, and she couldn't be sure which was which and who was who—echoed in Lucy's ears. She had the past, in the form of one of her old comic books, and she set it before her. Down on the grass, to the left of her bent knees. The present came courtesy of the stranger who had stolen her work and her words. She placed *The City at Midnight* on her right, her fingertips gliding over the paperback's glossy cover.

That left the future. She hadn't figured that out yet. She was playing improv jazz, going by instinct and feel.

She knew that threes were important. She knelt at the intersection of three paths, encircled by three old gravestones. Past, present, and future made three. And for conjuring Verna Bell...

She took her scissors and flipped through the pages of Carolyn's novel. Verna appeared as a minor character, a *femme fatale* and Cassandra-style prophet. Lucy found her name and carefully cut it out. Then she ripped a blank page from the back of her spiral notebook and glued the scrap of paper to the sheet. She repeated the process two more times. Past and present mingled, new paper on old, drawing an uneven column of names in crisp block type down the faded page. Lucy breathed the words out loud as she read them.

Verna Bell
Verna Bell
Verna Bell

A car backfired on the street outside the graveyard, a shotgun crack that jolted her to the core. Her muscles locked up in rebellion, keeping her still, down on her knees, the conjuring unbroken.

The night wind ruffled the pages of her comic book. The cover flapped aside, opening to the dramatic splash page of the Midnight Jury battling a skull-masked assassin. The Jury was in mid-leap, nightingale trench coat fluttering in the vigilante's wake, twin .45s blazing.

The future, she thought.

Roach claimed the Jury was long gone or dead. But that couldn't be true. Lucy wasn't naive; in the real world, the bad guys won all the time. The meek didn't inherit, the meek got crushed while their heroes fell, and all you could do was hope for the best. But Noir York wasn't the real world. It was *her* world.

And I like stories with happy endings.

She took her scissors to the comic page, cutting around the Jury's shadow, snipping the edges of his fluttering coat. She added the cutout to the ragged notebook paper with three dabs of glue. The Jury was real, the Jury was alive, and Verna Bell would lead the way. Lucy flicked her lighter and the tiny flame cast her face in shifting shadows.

"I summon thee," Lucy whispered.

She touched the flame to the notebook page. It caught, curling and smoking.

"I summon thee."

The fire spread, consuming the image of the hero and Verna Bell's triple name. Ashes fell and embers danced, captured by the graveyard wind.

"I summon thee."

She let go of the page just before the fire could reach her fingertips. The final scrap fluttered away and burned. A fresh gust of wind stirred the embers and lifted them, swirling, like a swarm of fireflies.

For a heartbeat, the embers took on the suggestion of a familiar shape. A brim pulled down low, a rugged face cloaked in shadow, a pair of guns clenched in leather-gloved hands. Then the sparks fell and faded, cold and dead before they touched the wet grass.

Lucy knelt there, waiting, listening. She didn't feel quite the same. Something was off-kilter inside of her. Or something off-kilter had finally been set to rights.

"We can go now," she said.

Roy turned, looking down at her from his sentry post at the corner of the triangle.

"Did it work?" he asked.

She wanted to hedge her bets, to demur and wave away what she'd just done. The idea of taking pride in an accomplishment, or even acknowledging that she might have done something right in her life, felt like rampant, inexcusable ego. All the same, a tiny voice inside of her said that *something* had changed. She'd reached out to the other world, and something, someone, had heard her call.

"I think it did," she said. "We just have to wait and see if she comes to meet us."

They didn't have to wait long.

Roy found a motel half a mile from the cemetery. No frills, but the room was clean, and he found a parking lot down the street to stash the truck overnight. If the Network was still on their heels, they hadn't caught up yet, but Roy didn't want to make it too easy for them. Lucy was already asleep when Roy got back to the room, and he quietly undressed in the dark.

He woke to freezing cold.

The clock said it was half past one. He sat up, shivering so hard his teeth chattered, and scrambled for his clothes. He heard Lucy stirring while he yanked his undershirt on.

"It shouldn't be—" she murmured, half awake.

"Get up, get dressed. Something's wrong."

This was midwinter cold, and the air conditioning wasn't even turned on. Roy tugged on his pants, stepped into his shoes, and buckled his belt as he crossed the motel room carpet. He left the light off and tugged the drapes aside. Frost kissed the window glass.

Lucy came over to stand at his shoulder. There was someone out in the parking lot, a lone figure in a puddle of lamplight. Roy cursed under his breath and used the elbow of his shirt to rub away a clear circle in the middle of the frost.

"They found us," Lucy whispered.

"Well," Roy said. "That sure as hell isn't anybody named Verna."

The young man in the spotlight had stepped right out of the 50's, with his greasy coal-black hair in a pompadour wave. He wore a leather jacket and jeans and cradled a Louisville Slugger in his hands. He could have been trying out for the cast in a revival of *Grease*, if it wasn't for his wounds. A long, jagged gash carved its way along his forehead just under his hairline, matted with dried gore. Another sliced a trench across his pale, bloodless throat. He grinned at the window, flashing a single gold tooth, and called out to them.

"C'mon out, Lucy. Ditch that zero and get with a hero. It's prom night, and I'm saving the first dance for you."

Roy let the curtain fall shut.

"Who's your friend?"

"Griffin Malone," Lucy said, staring at the curtain. "The Living Dead Boy."

Roy gritted his teeth. He took a deep breath.

"And he does what, exactly?"

"He's a debt collector. He's...well, he's strong, and he's really tough."

"That's it?" Roy said. "No giant monsters, he doesn't shoot laser beams out of his eyes or turn people inside out or anything like that?"

Lucy's head gave a tiny shake.

"Great," he said, crossing the motel room in two brisk strides. "The C-Team is here. Okay, here's the plan. Catch."

He tossed her the keys to the Hummer. They landed, jangling, in her cupped hands. Roy grabbed one of the wooden chairs next to the motel room table and flipped it upside down.

"Watch for an opening," he said. "The second you get one, run and get the truck. Don't stop for anything."

"What are you going to do?" she asked.

Roy's heel came down hard on a chair leg. It splintered, tearing against the bolt that held it to the lacquered seat. One more stomp broke it free. Roy scooped up the chair leg by the narrow end and tested its weight.

He gave it one slow and easy swing, like a bat, and thumped the broken head against the palm of his hand.

"Recent events have left me with some frustration to work out of my system," Roy told her. "So I'm going to go out there, I'm going to politely introduce myself to Mr. Malone, and then I'm going to beat the undead shit out of him. It'll be good for my overall sense of well-being."

Chapter Twenty-three

Roy didn't consider himself any kind of strategic genius. He could put together a plan of attack when he needed one—metaphorically or literally—but he liked to keep things simple when he could. A desolate parking lot in the back half of nowhere, the weight of a broken chair leg in his clenched fist, and somebody to use it on. Simple.

All the same, as the pale, scarred dead man turned to greet him with a smug look on his face, Roy didn't charge into the fight. He kept his distance, sidestepping, slowly circling him. Turning him away from the motel room doorway and opening up a chance for Lucy to run. *Need to keep his attention on me*, Roy thought.

"You know you're not even real, right?"

Griffin squinted at him. The lazy, dumb smirk never left his bloodless lips.

"Real as you, pops," he countered. "Flesh and bone. Try me and find out."

Roy had just wanted to rattle him a little. Didn't work, but now he saw an opportunity. Knowledge was more than power: it was a matter of survival, and he and Lucy needed every scrap they could get.

"You're literally a comic book character," Roy said.

"*You* are," he fired back.

Okay, not a deep thinker. Roy kept circling, a shark with a makeshift bat, his weapon a poor twin to the Louisville Slugger in the Living Dead Boy's grip.

"I'm serious," Roy said. "Nobody told you? Where do you think you came from?"

"Richmond, Noir York born and bred. Heart of the Apple, baby."

"And where are you, right now?"

Griffin didn't follow, or he didn't want to. He looked around the parking lot and waggled the tip of his bat.

"Nowheresville. What's with the Twenty Questions?"

"Call it a philosophical quandary," Roy said. "How about the girl? You want her. Do you even know why?"

This one, Griffin could answer. "Cash money. All the reason anybody needs to do anything."

"Can't argue that, but I'm talking about the bigger picture. Why Lucy?"

"The Duke wants her. And what the Duke wants, the Duke gets."

"You're not even a little bit curious?" Roy asked.

"What's to know? Big man said to scoop the chick up, gentle as I can—no damaging the merchandise—and bring her to him. He's got his reasons."

Roy tilted his head. "Bring her to him where, exactly?"

Griffin's smug smile came back in full force.

"Oh, I get it. You want to muscle in on my action. Nice try, pal."

"Maybe we could split the bounty," Roy said. "Why don't you take me to this Duke guy and introduce me. We can work something out here."

"I got a better idea."

The business end of the Slugger pointed straight at him.

"How about I bash your brains in, break both your kneecaps, and take whatever I want?"

"That's an option," Roy said. "Might not go the way you're hoping, though. You sure you want it like this?"

"Pretty sure I—"

Roy didn't let him finish the sentence. He charged in, swinging the chair leg, backing up the swing with a bestial grunt. It slammed upside Griffin's head with the hollow crack of wood against bone, sending him staggering, blind for half a second. Long enough for Roy to spin the chair leg around and use it like a battering ram, sending it straight into Griffin's gut and driving the air from his belly.

The kid was faster than he looked. Roy ducked under the Slugger, driven back a few steps by a sudden, furious onslaught. Griffin was swinging wild, no art or style behind the attack, just fury and murder-lust. Roy held up the chair leg like a shield, parrying another brutal swing, and a hairline crack blew down the wood like a fault line opening wide.

It wouldn't last much longer. Neither would he.

———⋈———

Lucy had been watching from the motel room doorway. She caught what Roy was doing—circling, holding Griffin's attention and turning him in the other direction. She froze on the threshold, biding her time. Then she waited. Then she waited some more.

She knew what kept her pinned. All her childhood nightmares were coming to life. All of them. And if Griffin Malone could track them down, anyone else could be out there in the dark, lurking and watching and hungry for her. She was going to have to run two blocks down a dead-quiet street with a single lamppost to mark the gulf of shadows, all the way to where they stashed the Hummer, and make it back again. Alone.

Roy and Griffin had gone from conversation to all-out battle. She didn't like her guardian's chances. Roy was tough, she knew that from experience, but now he was up against a juggernaut who could barely feel pain.

Which means he needs me, she told herself. *NOW.*

Her paralysis broke, and she ran.

Lucy barreled down the sidewalk, scouting ahead in the gloom, hunting for the vacant lot where Roy had parked their stolen prize. There it was, sitting alone at the lot's edge, wheels halfway deep in scraggly yellow weeds. Not a soul in sight. She almost let herself breathe. Almost. She fumbled with the key remote, unlocking the doors as she ran up on the truck, barely breaking her stride. Then she jumped inside, yanked the door shut behind her and slammed the locks down.

Safe.

She didn't have time to catch her breath. She fired up the engine, putting together a piecemeal plan in her head. Then she heard someone whisper her name.

The voice was coming from the back seat.

Lucy's gaze flicked to the rearview mirror. She caught a glimpse of bottle-glass-green eyes, glittering and segmented like a fly's. There was a faint rustling sound. Then the back seat exploded with vines. They unfurled and whipped the air, flooding the truck cabin, an eruption of plant life that stank like grave dirt and manure. The vines, thick as Lucy's fingers, snared around her. They pinned her upper arms to her chest and squeezed until she saw spots. Vine-tips snapped at her face, poking toward her eyes, a threat of pain to come.

Fetid breath washed hot across her shoulder, riding on a silken whisper.

"Say my name, Lucy. You know who I am."

She did.

"Charikleia," Lucy breathed. The vines that trapped her gave an encouraging squeeze. "The Dark Dryad."

"Very good. You and I are going to go on a little trip together. You're not going to give me any trouble at all, are you?"

The foul air had become sweet. Fragrant, the alluring scent of roses in full blossom, a field of grass on a warm summer day, a mug of mulled cider by a Winter fire. An offer of comfort, of solace—

A lie, Lucy knew. The odor hadn't changed, her perception of it—decreed by the swirls of wild magic that trailed the Dryad's rippling tendrils—had. The flowers in Lucy's mind bloomed with the power of suggestion.

"No trouble," Lucy stammered.

The words came out unbidden. The problem with knowing you're under hypnotic attack, she realized, was that it didn't actually help. She knew what Charikleia was capable of. That didn't mean she could fight her off.

But it does. She created the monster in the back seat. Her powers, her weaknesses, her hungers, her fears. She just needed to find a way to turn that knowledge into a winning edge. And fast, with Roy's time running out and her willpower slipping away with every breath she took.

Have to focus, she thought. *Think, think hard, keep your mind busy. Don't let her in.*

She looked to the passenger-side floor, where her notebooks lay, half-sliding from their plastic bag. Then her gaze shifted to the console between the front seats. The odds and ends for her improvised ritual were still there: the tube of glue, the scissors.

The lighter.

She blurted out the first thing that came to her mind, desperate to keep Charikleia talking. "The Jury. What happened to the Midnight Jury?"

"Gone, my poppet. Gone without a trace and it irks me: the Jury was one of my favorite playmates. It's funny, you know. We rogues spent so many years bragging and boasting of all the things we would do, if it wasn't for the city's protector getting in our way. Know what we do now that the Jury is missing? More or less the exact same thing as always. It's just *easy* now. Boring. But you're going to change the game."

Lucy's fingers inched toward the lighter.

"How?" Lucy said. "I don't understand what Duke Ellery wants from me."

The Dryad's soft laughter felt like warm ocean wind washing over Lucy's entire body, while gentle fingers trilled down her spine.

"Forget the Duke," Charikleia said. "He's short-sighted. Talking about saving one world when there are so many more for the taking. No, when I say that you and I are going on a trip, I mean you...and I. I found you, and I'm keeping you."

Four inches. The lighter was four inches away from her outstretched fingertips. It felt like a mile.

"He won't like that," Lucy said. "And what do you mean, save a world?"

"Lucy, when you were young, did you ever own a pet?"

"Sure. One dog. A couple of cats."

"And, at any time, did any of your pets ever ask you questions?"

"I...don't think so," Lucy said. "They couldn't talk."

The thorny tip of a vine drew feather-light strokes down the nape of Lucy's neck.

"Exactly," Charikleia said. "Please take that as the perfect model for our new relationship. You don't need to ask questions. You don't need to *think*. Just...lean into me, and let go. Wouldn't it feel nice to let go?"

It would. Damn it, it would. The Dryad's psychic tendrils turned Lucy's thoughts fuzzy around the edges, and she couldn't be sure what she wanted or what Charikleia wanted, or where to find a dividing line between them.

"Now say, 'Yes, Mistress Char.'"

Two inches. The lighter was almost close enough to grab, but Lucy's fingers didn't want to do it. They fought her, trembling and frozen.

"You imagined me," Charikleia added. "Don't pretend you don't want to play with me."

"You don't know me," Lucy stammered back.

"Don't I? Maybe I imagined you, too. Or maybe I'm just inferring. You can learn a lot about an artist from the art they create."

"That wasn't art," Lucy protested. "That was a pulp comic that I wrote because I needed tuition money."

"If a commercial motive means something can't be art, that eliminates most writers, painters, and musicians in all of recorded history. In *both* our worlds."

"That's not what I meant."

"Then choose your words more carefully. I hope you're not suggesting that I'm anything but a masterpiece."

Lucy saw one of Charikleia's eyes in the rearview. Glittering, alien and unblinking, staring straight into the core of her soul. *Just don't look down*, she prayed. She was only going to get one chance to escape; the Dark Dryad wouldn't give her another.

"Poor, confused Lucy," Charikleia cooed in her ear. The words slid into her brain, silky soft, a ribbon around her thoughts. "It's all right. I'm going to make all your troubles go away. No more stress, no more struggle. Just lean back and surrender. All you have to do, from this day forward...is obey me."

Lucy's fingers strained. She willed them to move toward the lighter, bit by tiny bit.

Just a little closer, she thought. *One more inch.*

Chapter Twenty-four

The baseball bat crashed against Roy's shoulders and drove him down, one knee cracking hard on the black asphalt. He wheezed, fighting to keep conscious through the waves of electric pain, and gripped his chair leg in both hands. Then he came up charging like a bull, head down, and rammed shoulder-first into Griffin's belly.

Griffin staggered back. He bent his arm and brought his elbow down like a hammer. Fresh explosions went off in the back of Roy's skull and between his shoulders. He tried to get his arms around Griffin's waist but the dead man's knee fired up, jarring him loose.

"How long, old man?" Griffin grunted. They clinched, each one trying to grapple the other, both of them hurt and bleeding and winded. "How long can you keep this up?"

That was a damn good question. *Lucy,* he thought. *Where are you?*

Charikleia's mass of vine-tendrils taunted and threatened Lucy, going from violently stabbing at her face—always stopping a fraction of a hair away from her wide and terrified eyes—to gently stroking along her shoulders, her arms, a single stray vine sliding down the back of her blouse and nuzzling, like a damp and clammy finger, against her spine. One faceted insect eye, a glittering sapphire in the dark, burned in the rearview mirror.

"Why do you resist?" the Dryad asked, her voice riding on a hypnotic current. "You're trying to run from me, but would anything be worse than going back to your old life?"

She was trying to reach the lighter in the center console, actually. But she was pinned to the driver's seat, hugged by vines and held by her creation's magical voice, and her odds didn't seem much better than if she had tried to run. Either way, her body was all but frozen, flesh and bone rebelling against her while her pulse pounded a staccato beat in her ears.

"Like I said," she stammered, "You don't know anything about me."

"I know everything about you. Lucy Langenkamp, a true city mouse. Diagnosed with social anxiety and depression, single, stuck in a dead-end job—"

"I like my job."

"You like *art*. You hate your job and you hate your boss. Yet no matter how much abuse he piles on your shoulders, you smile and take it. You're afraid of confrontation, you're afraid of *everything*, you always were and you always will be. You've squandered your talents and you don't even know the depths of your own power. The best thing you could do with your life is surrender it to me. At least I'll make good use of it."

The tendril invading her blouse slid lower along her spine, sinuous, a snake against her skin. Charikleia's harsh tone melted to a soft seduction.

"I can show you such sights, Lucy. I can treat you to so many pleasures. All you have to do is lean back, close your eyes, open your mind and let me inside."

Lucy closed her eyes.

In the darkness, the world became sound and scent and sensation. The passing clouds of rose perfume, the fingertip-tendrils against her skin, the rustling of leaves and bark. She felt her muscles loosen, responding to the Dryad's call, like slipping into a warm bath.

"I have to confess," Lucy said.

"Tell me everything. Hold nothing back."

"You have a good point."

"Yes," Charikleia hissed. "You'll make a wonderful pet."

"I didn't mean that part," Lucy said.

Her fingers closed around the lighter.

"I meant, I should really start sticking up for myself."

One flick and the lighter sparked to life, a tiny flame against the darkness. Lucy grabbed hold of the closest tendril with her other hand, squeezed it tight, and put the fire to its tip. It caught like dry tinder. The Dryad screeched, letting her go, and Lucy dove down across the front seats as the truck became a frantic, furious storm of hissing and snapping vines.

Her bag of notebooks was down on the floor, on the passenger side of the truck. She reached for it, hand outstretched and fingers straining. One of Charikleia's vines cracked like a bullwhip across her shoulders, drawing a burning line along her skin. Another came down on her lower back hard enough to tear her blouse and fleck the seat with blood. Eyes stinging with tears, Lucy grabbed the closest notebook she could reach.

It was part of her history, her life, maybe a key to the mystery she'd been dragged into—and it was her only weapon. She touched the lighter to it.

The old, dry paper between the cardboard covers went up in a tiny inferno. Lucy dropped the lighter and brought up her forearm as another vine came lashing down toward her face. It sliced across her wrist, drawing a ragged red welt. She turned and tossed the lit notebook into the back seat.

The scent of roses became blazing wood and rot. Charikleia caught fire, howling as the truck filled with billowing clouds of gray smoke. All Lucy could see was the Dryad's blazing silhouette behind the smoke, a slender woman engulfed in a serpentine nest of burning vines. Charikleia shoved her way out the back door, tumbling to the vacant lot and rolling, slapping at herself, trying to put out the fire.

Lucy gritted her teeth, stared dead ahead, and stomped on the gas.

The Hummer lurched out of the lot, jumped the curb, and swung hard, swerving onto the empty street. She heard the Dryad shouting out behind her, the last of the flames sputtering out as she rose to her full, towering height.

"When the Duke gets his hands on you, you'll *wish* you'd given yourself to me," Charikleia screeched.

"Maybe," Lucy said.

Maybe.

Roy was out of gas.

He was on his back in the motel parking lot, gasping for breath, his muscles raw and aching. Scarlet trickled down his cheek from a split bottom lip, and his right eye throbbed with a shiner in the making. The splintered remnants of his chair leg, broken down the middle and useless, lay beside him.

Griffin had a face like a tenderized steak. Roy had gotten some good punches in. But the Living Dead Boy was the one still standing, looming over him with the Louisville Slugger braced in his murderous grip.

"Not gonna lie," Griffin said, "you gave me a pretty good fight. Still gonna bash your brains in, though."

He hoisted the bat, gripping it in both hands. Roy had to smile. Griffin hesitated, uncertain.

"What's so funny?"

"Just something I realized. I've been going through the motions for the longest time now. Just...waiting to die, I guess."

"This is your lucky night."

"But maybe..." Roy said. "Maybe I just needed a reason to stick around."

His heel fired out like a piston, driving into Griffin's knee. He yelped, almost dropping the bat, hopping backwards as his pale face twisted in pain. Then in rage. He raised his weapon high over his head.

"I was going to make it quick," he said. "Now I'm going to take my time, you son of a—"

The blare of a horn cut him off. The sudden flare of high beams washed over him, pinning him in the spotlight and heralding the roar of a turbocharged V8 engine powering two and a half tons of military-grade steel. The Hummer blazed across the parking lot, Lucy at the wheel with her foot on the gas. Griffin had a heartbeat to react.

"Oh," he said.

Lucy slammed the brakes a second before she plowed straight into him. The Hummer squealed, spinning and drawing dark furrows in the parking lot tarmac, while Griffin went flying with a brutal *thump* and the crunch of a crumpling bumper. He launched, landed hard, and rolled off into the shadows. His baseball bat stayed behind, pinned under the front wheel, wet with his own wine-dark blood.

Roy got up. He hobbled to the passenger-side door, wincing with every step, and dragged himself into the truck.

"What kept you?" he said, slumping back in his seat.

"Ran into somebody."

As she pulled out of the parking lot, getting back on the road to nowhere, Roy gave her a sidelong look.

They drove for a while with no destination in mind, chasing the moon down backwater roads. They both had some thinking to do.

A lone pair of headlights shone in the back distance. Lucy didn't pay any attention at first, not until she noticed how fast the other car was gaining on them. Roy sat up a little, noticing how she tensed, and he checked the side mirror.

"Could be a cop," he said. "Were you speeding?"

"Not in a stolen truck. I mean, I've never stolen anything before, but even I know that."

"Keep the needle steady. Let's see if he lights us up."

Lucy gave him a nervous look. "And if he does?"

"We'll play it by ear. Relax. Pretty sure the worst is over, at least for tonight."

The headlights loomed closer, sheathed in fog and radiator steam. They grew into an outline, too big to be a patrol cruiser. Some kind of old van. It looked familiar, but he couldn't place the silhouette. Then he remembered where he'd seen it before. The van, parked outside Lucy's blazing apartment. The old Frankenstein-rigged junkyard Ford with a mismatched front and back, the worn paint on one side reading "-*Burdock's Extermination Services*." And then the smaller cursive motto, "*The FRIENDLY Exterminator!*"

"Roach," Lucy breathed.

"Drive," Roy told her.

Chapter Twenty-Five

They barreled through the dark, Roach's monster machine hot on their heels and gaining ground. Lucy stepped on the gas, pouring on speed, answered by a throaty, rattling roar from the killer's engine. The exterminator van's body was a battered, stitched-together antique, but whatever Roach had under the hood was more than equal to the chase. His headlights loomed larger in their mirrors, closing the distance between them.

Roy didn't like their odds. His last weapon had been a busted chair leg, and he'd left it back in the motel parking lot, nothing but a useless handful of splinters. Now he had nothing but his fists. Most of the time he wouldn't mind, he was good with his fists—but normally he wasn't facing a psychopath who dealt in acid and flame.

They had to stay ahead of him, stay mobile, and find a way off this endless, empty highway. Find an urban tangle somewhere, a place to corner hard and fast and lose him in the alleys. The starless night, still and wide and deep, offered nothing but table-flat countryside and farmland with fallow fields of sleeping dirt.

"Give me a heads-up here," Roy told Lucy. "Does he have any tricks that he didn't show off in that comic I read?"

Roach answered for her.

A long slot behind his van's iron grille dropped open with a rickety clunk. A second later, a buzzsaw blade fired like a bullet, deadly teeth spinning as it chewed through the air. It hit the back of the Hummer, throwing sparks and gouging a long furrow of black paint before it spun away into the ditch at the side of the road. Lucy jerked the wheel in a startled swerve, fighting to get the truck back under control.

"Hold it steady." Roy looked back, squinting, and put a firm hand on her shoulder. "Don't let him close the gap. You can do this."

A second blade came screaming through the shadows. It ricocheted off the back bumper, just above the tire, with a sound like a dentist's drill.

"He won't give up." Lucy squeezed the wheel until her knuckles turned white.

"He can't stop us, either. This isn't the rich boy's toy version of a Hummer. It's the real deal: up-armored, bulletproof, and ready for battle. If that's the best he's got, he can't put a dent in this thing."

The van shuddered, a long wedge of rooftop ratcheting back, rolling like a shutter. In its place rose a long rust-flecked tube of dark steel, mounted on a gimbal. The ball of the gimbal let the tube move, smoothly swaying from side to side, forward and back as if limbering up. Then it took aim.

"Forget what I just said." Roy cursed under his breath. "Swerve. Swerve a lot. And please tell me that isn't a goddamn rocket launcher."

Lucy leaned into the wheel, dragging the Hummer from one side of the empty highway to the other and back again, fighting to stay ahead of the turret.

"He doesn't use guns. Or explosives. They don't hurt people the way he likes."

"Then what the hell is—"

The tube erupted with a plume of oily smoke. The rear window of the Hummer imploded, showering the back of Roy's head with pelts of rounded safety glass. The missile—a harpoon, three feet of jagged metal festooned with spikes and curling, tearing razors—plowed into the console between Roy and Lucy's seats. The radio sputtered and died in a cascade of static.

The harpoon was tethered to a thumb-thick rope of old, gnarled leather. The rope tugged hard, wrenching the head of the harpoon free. It slithered away, out the destroyed back window and back to its nest. Getting ready for a second shot.

Roy scouted the road ahead. He pointed left. "Up here. Get us off the highway."

"There's no way out," Lucy protested. "There's no exit for another twenty miles—"

"We can go off-road. Not sure he can. See that farm up ahead? Cornfield. Hit it."

"I'm pretty sure that's illegal."

He stared at her.

The tube spat smoke and the harpoon came screaming at them. It drove into the Hummer's roof, piercing armored steel. It cratered just above Roy's head, the harpoon's tip stopping an inch from his scalp. He sank lower in his seat as the tether ripped the missile free, calling it back once more.

Lucy veered left. There was a stomach-lurching drop as the Hummer shot off the highway, landing in rough dirt, the engine shifting into overdrive while the tires fought for traction. The cornfield was just ahead. Behind them, Roach's death van overshot them and then veered off the road, fishtailing, falling back but still in pursuit. They hit the edge of the corn and plowed straight through, the tall stalks blotting out the world and slapping the windows as they left a trail of flattened, broken crops. Lucy didn't need to see to know they were in trouble; the throaty diesel growl behind them, gaining fast, told her that much.

Roach put on a burst of speed. He swerved again, rolling up alongside their truck. The turret turned on its mount, tilting to aim downward. Soon they were neck and neck in the corn, twin streaks of destruction, both pouring on the gas. The turret zeroed in on its next target: the driver-side window. And Lucy's face.

Lucy hit the brakes.

The van shot past them as the turret fired. The harpoon missed the window and speared the hood, driving deep. It ripped free with a plume of oil from a ruptured tank. Half of the emergency lights on the dashboard flickered to life at the same time, the Check Engine signal strobing a high alert.

"*No kidding!*" Lucy shouted at it, clutching the wheel in a death grip. Roy clung to his seat, bracing his feet against the floor mat as the truck started to judder and the engine whined like a wolf in a trap.

"He's up ahead," Roy said. "Try taking a right, maybe we can lose him."

The wheel didn't budge in Lucy's hands, locked up tight. "Steering's dead!"

She hit the brakes. The dying truck did the rest of the work, sputtering to a stop at the heart of the cornfield.

The world went very quiet.

Either Roach's van had completely overshot them, off in the far distance now, or he'd stopped, too. And he was out there, somewhere in the swaying corn. Coming for them.

Roy opened his door. Softly. Lucy did the same, casting a nervous look his way. Roy put his finger to his lips. She nodded.

They both dropped down to the soft loam, leaving the doors open as they circled around. Roy pointed back the way they'd driven in: the trail of crushed cornstalks didn't offer much protection, but he figured it'd be faster and quieter than shoving their way through the field, and they might hear Roach coming. Lucy fell in at his side. They moved as quick as they dared. Stalks crunched under their feet, rising above the trill of insects and night-birds.

A louder, heavier crunching echoed at their backs. Ten feet behind them, the rippling of the tall stalks was their only warning of Roach's arrival. That, and the hiss of gas from the deadly nozzle of his murder-rig. He lumbered out into the open, turning to face them, draped in his leather aprons and his gas mask. He gave his trigger a squeeze, firing a lance of flame into the air over their heads.

"How are you not dead?" Roy asked. There wasn't any sign of the wounds Roy had given him, the knife in his chest as they left him to die in the fire. The shattered onyx lens over one eye had already been replaced, good as new.

"Ask you the same question," Roach grunted.

He took a step toward them. Roy moved up, planting himself in front of Lucy, using his body as a human shield. Not that it would help much. He glanced back for just a second, pitching his voice low.

"If anything happens to me, you run."

"But—" she started to say.

"You *run*. Run like hell and never look back."

She didn't need to see him burn.

"Little risky back there," Roy said, trying to keep Roach talking while he figured out a plan. "You could have hurt Lucy. I thought you needed her alive."

"Live bounty," said the muffled voice behind the mask. "Good, high bounty. But thought...maybe I don't need the money. You *hurt* me."

"Welcome to the real world," Roy said.

Roach squeezed the trigger again. The nozzle spat a torrent of sickly green fluid. It splashed across a row of cornstalks and they withered in clouds of foul, rotten-fish-smelling smoke, collapsing to the steaming dirt.

"Let you decide," Roach grunted. "Fire, or acid. How do you want to die?"

"How do I want to die?" Roy thought it over. "In bed, of natural causes. Preferably after enjoying a prime porterhouse steak and a bottle of good whiskey."

"Funny. Let's see how funny you are when you're melting."

Roy only saw one way out. Not a good one. He was going to have to rush him. If he could close the distance before Roach opened fire, he might be able to tackle him and beat him down. If he couldn't—if he was too slow, if he swerved the wrong way, if he was one second off his game—he was going to die in this cornfield. And he was going to die badly.

And then he'll chase Lucy down, he thought. *No. Not letting that happen. I lost Carmen because I fucked up when she needed me most. My fault. Never again. No one else dies on my watch.*

He braced himself, watching for the sway of the nozzle, getting ready to charge. His mouth went dry, his vision narrowing to a tight and focused funnel. Dead ahead, fast as he could, live or die.

The wind picked up. The twinkling sound of crystal chimes rang out across the cornfield. Roach's mask twitched, his head lifting, sniffing the air like an animal. The odor from his killing rig, a mixture of diesel fumes and rot, faded as a new aroma wafted over the corn. A rich musk perfume.

"N-no," Roach stammered. "No claim jumping! I was here first."

A snatch of wordless song, lilting and winding on the wind, chased the perfume's scent. Roach took a step backward.

"He'll know," Roach said. "I'll tell. Tell the Duke I had them first. You can't buy back his good graces anyway. You're on the outs."

"And I'll tell him that you were going to burn our darling Lucy instead of bringing her home," came a reply from beyond the corn. A woman's voice, leisurely and relaxed, a little on the husky side. "What do you think he'll do to you then?"

Roy was frozen where he stood. He knew that voice.

Roach hop-stepped backward, shaking his mask, the nozzle of his weapon swaying wildly from side to side. He didn't pull the trigger. "Bah. Not worth it. Get you later. Find you and hurt you."

"You can try," said the unseen woman's voice. "Run away, Roach. Run away before I teach you what it truly means to burn."

The killer turned and lumbered off. Half jogging, the bulky tanks on his back swaying with his heavy, rolling gait, he let out a stream of muffled, mumbling hisses from behind his mask. Roy and Lucy stood and watched him disappear into the corn.

The stalks rustled, closer, and their rescuer stepped out into the moonlight. Roy's heart shattered like glass. He knew that voice. He knew the careless spill of her raven hair, her deep baby blues, the pout of her pomegranate lips. He knew her vintage black dress and her kitten heels and all the territory underneath.

"Carmen," he breathed. "How...how are you here?"

"Sorry," she said, more interested in looking Lucy up and down. "Wrong person."

His stomach dropped. His dead lover had just walked out of the corn, and she was treating him like a complete stranger.

"Carmen, it's me. It's Roy."

"Sorry, pal. I don't know you. Must have me confused with somebody else." She fluffed her hair with the tips of her scarlet fingernails. "My name is Verna. Verna Bell."

She circled around him, stepping up to Lucy. Verna was a head taller, and the two women stared into each other's eyes for a moment, silent. Then Verna reached out, cupping Lucy's chin in her fingers.

"And you," Verna said. "You must be God. Pleased to meet you."

Chapter Twenty-six

The Gran Isle train station, out on the city's ragged eastern coast, had been built in the heyday of champagne and easy money. Crystal chandeliers dangled from the great vaulted ceilings, and the curved arches of the gallery were lined with mosaic tiles in an endless checkerboard of ivory and amber. Art deco sconces in the crowned form of Lady Prosperity, Noir York's patron goddess, were set between the maps and directional signs and vintage cigarette ads. Her figure, immortalized in shining chrome, offered to guide weary travelers home with frosted, glowing globes of light. Far above, a cold and greasy rain pelted down on the skylights, turning the city's skyline into a dark blur of endless monoliths.

Twelve times a day, the number nine train from Brookside to Berwyn rattled past, shaking dust from the walls as it throttled up, never stopping. The passengers didn't see a thing, thanks to the plywood barricade that isolated the farthest track from the rest of the station, sealing it in darkness. Gran Isle Station had shut down a decade ago, a casualty of budget cuts, and came under private ownership shortly thereafter.

On the trackside tiles where commuters once milled in their overcoats and fedoras, sixteen television sets stood. Arranged four by four, lopsided and mismatched, leaning against one another in a teetering pile. All sixteen were on, each turned to a different channel. And ten feet away, in an armchair upholstered in shabby, water-stained burgundy velvet, the Illustrated Duke watched the world as it fell apart.

He slouched, narrow-eyed and frowning, one hand dangling over the armrest with a cut-crystal glass of bourbon. The ancient glyphs inked along his slender fingers danced and writhed, marching like ants across his skin. The tattoos on his face itched as they trembled, reacting to the storm outside and the storm in their master's head. Under his sharp-collared suit jacket and unbuttoned, dangling white silk shirt, the tail of a tattooed salamander curled around his left nipple. A Latin incantation rode the lizard's back, letters rearranging themselves, transforming into a warning in forgotten Sanskrit.

The clashing noise of the televisions washed over him in a comforting cacophony. A wall of sound, voices weaving and overlapping and crashing over him. He thought about his childhood trips to the beach. He would lie on the dirty white sand, letting the waves rush over his body, feeling the pull of the ocean as they rolled back again, gently tugging at him. He had no idea then what he would someday become. Not until the voices, deep beneath the sea, began to whisper through the water.

The second television from the left, bottom row, caught his eye. A reporter shivered in a fur parka, hood pulled down against a rabid winter wind, cars in the background swallowed by snow drifts. The far south side was in trouble.

Not as much trouble as the west end. Another television, far right, top row, was a shaking, blurry mess as a cameraman ran for his life. For one fleeting moment he turned the lens behind him, capturing the screaming mob that filled the cobblestoned street. Their bloody mouths, the black pits of their eyes, their hospital gowns and autopsy scars.

Behind the Duke's velvet throne, a steel-jacketed door rumbled open and shut again, accompanied by the hollow echoes of stiletto heels against the tiled stairs. He didn't need to look.

"Honey, I'm home," Mary called out. The white-jacketed mortician sucked on a fresh lollipop, stick dangling at one corner of her mouth, as she drifted across the antique train station. Her hands curled around Duke's shoulders, practiced fingers rubbing the knots from his muscles.

"You're late," he said, "and you smell like blood."

"Sorry, sweetie. Work was murder."

He glanced over his shoulder at her.

"*Metaphorical*," she said. "We can't keep up with the parade of stiffs this week. I'm running out of slabs. Might have to start taking the extras home and popping 'em in the freezer."

"You already do that."

"That's dinner. I mean the bodies folks'll actually miss. You hear about the mess over in Richmond?"

Duke's free hand dangled over his armrest. He snapped his fingers.

A small, misshapen creature, a naked and grotesque parody of a human with skin like mottled clay, scurried from the shadows of the train station. It carried a remote control, almost as big as itself, over its head like a trophy. Duke plucked the remote from the imp's hands and sent it away with a wordless nod. The bottom left television was showing NY News on the Nines, and a click of a button silenced all the other screens at once.

"—pandemonium in Richmond tonight, as an attempted bank robbery led to a shootout in the streets. The aftermath left twelve dead, including the alleged thieves, and fifteen in critical condition."

"Bad days," Duke murmured, sipping his bourbon. "Bad days and strange days, all around."

The reporter on the scene stood in front of a police-tape barricade, rain pelting down on the transparent canopy of her umbrella. She stared, solemn, into the camera's eye.

"And once again, as the crime wave gripping our city spirals completely out of control, the people cry out: where is the Midnight Jury?"

"There was a time," Duke said to the television, "when I would have enjoyed this."

"In other news, a shocking breakout at Corum Asylum—"

He muted the TV, leaning back into Mary's hands. "You did as I asked."

"Don't I always?"

"Sugar doll, you twist wishes like a genie with a mean streak."

"But you keep me around," she said.

"You're good with your hands."

"I gave 'em their marching orders and sent them through the gate. All but Trigger Mortis. I've got him on our side, watching for any unplanned arrivals."

"You put *Trigger* on guard duty." He shifted in his chair, looking back at her again. "He does grasp that I need Lucy Langenkamp *alive*, yes? If she dies, we're all in for a world of hurt."

"Cool your jets. I told him to keep his guns in his pants. Observe, follow, and report."

"He's never been good at following orders. Especially ones that don't involve eighty-sixing somebody."

Mary's hands slid across his lapels and then downward, tracing the lines of his unbuttoned shirt, the pale silk and the flesh underneath. Her cheek, baby-soft and flecked with freckles of dried blood, nuzzled his.

"Honey," she said, "far be it from me to criticize how you run your business—"

"Mm-hmm."

"—but have you considered that the sheer number of sociopathic murderers on your payroll might be the root cause of a few of your problems?"

"Like you?" he said, tattooed lips curling in an affectionate smile.

"I'm not a sociopath." She twirled the lollipop with her tongue, shifting the stick from one side of her mouth to the other. The tip brushed against his ear. "I'm a psychopath. Not the same thing at all."

"Noted. I don't suppose we've heard any good news from our friends on the other side?"

"Bupkis." She stood up and circled the chair, taking his glass. A bar service stood off to his right between a pair of chrome wall sconces. "Well, only that Lucy's in the wind. And she got herself a friend. Rumblebones says she almost snatched her, but some guy, a heavyweight bruiser, made off with the prize."

"And does this...'heavyweight bruiser' have a name?"

"Rumble's working on that. She's good and pissed off. In other words, highly motivated to get results. Meanwhile, no word at all from Griffin Malone or the Dryad. Wherever they are, whatever they're up to, they're not reporting in."

Duke frowned at the wall of television screens. "Griffin is loyal but stupid. The Dark Dryad is smart but duplicitous. Could I get just one associate with all the good qualities, none of the bad? I know I'm a demanding boss, but am I asking for too much here?"

Mary's lab coat flared as she turned on a heel, with a glass in one hand and a bottle in the other. A waterfall of amber splashed down into the cup, rolling across the wet crystal like an ocean wave.

"Baby," she said, "I am the complete package."

"Don't I know it."

"So why keep me on the bench while you let the second-stringers play? I don't mind being your cheerleader—and I got the outfit to prove it, back in the bedroom—but I do my best work in the field. Hands-on, preferably red and wet."

"I need you on this side of the gate, ready to act on my behalf. Right now I have every road agent, gutter magician, antiquarian, and rogue librarian scouring the city. The Argisene Grimoire is here. Somewhere. The second it's found—"

"I swoop in for the kill?"

She sauntered back to the armchair, hips swaying, sharp scarlet nails curled around his glass of bourbon. He took it with a nod of thanks and raised it in a toast.

"We get Lucy, we get the book, and I get everything I ever wanted."

Mary straddled his legs, easing herself down onto his lap. One hand cradled his shoulder, squeezing tight, and she brushed her forehead against his.

"We get," she whispered, "everything *we* ever wanted."

"That's what I said."

"But there's a fly in the ointment. A bee in the butter."

"Verna Bell." Duke turned his head and put the glass to his lips. "I don't think Rumblebones would mistake her for a large and muscular man."

"He might be working for her. We don't know how many pies she jammed her thumbs into before she turned traitor."

"And if she wants the big prize, she's going to have to lure Lucy over to our side of the gate. Might as well leave her on our doorstep with gift wrapping and a big shiny bow."

She tilted her head. "Then why so glum, chum?"

"Because another possibility suggests itself. Verna has one other option, and she knows it. She can save herself. Just herself, at the price of a few billion lives."

"You think she's that ruthless?" Mary said.

"I never thought she was. But then, I never thought she'd bite my hand after I spent so many years feeding her. When she finds Lucy, she'll have a choice to make. She can go for the prize, same as us. And that means keeping her alive at all costs until she gets her hands on the Grimoire."

"Or?"

"Or," Duke said, "she can put a bullet in Lucy's head and decide things once and for all. She'll be penniless, alien, and adrift in a strange land, but she'll live. And our world dies."

Chapter Twenty-seven

She wasn't Carmen.

Roy knew this. People didn't come back from the dead, and when Verna Bell looked his way she had the eyes of a complete stranger. It didn't matter that he knew her voice, the way she walked, the tiny mole on the slope of her left shoulder. He knew her perfume and her lips and all her dark territories. But she wasn't Carmen.

She led them through the cornfield. Her car was waiting. It was a Ford Century, a vintage dreamboat with fins and chrome piping over pastel blue paint. A pair of bulbous headlights rose up over a broad, shark-mouthed grill. Roy wasn't much of a gearhead, but he knew enough about cars to know that this one hadn't rolled off any mundane assembly line. Not in *this* world, at least.

She wasn't Carmen. She was Verna Bell. Chaotic Neutral Verna Bell, the Midnight Jury's inside woman, the *femme fatale* traitor on Duke Ellery's payroll. Lucy asked the most obvious question before he could.

"Is the Jury with you?"

"Sorry, kid. I'm the only cavalry coming. Nice work with that summoning spell, by the way. You lit up like a beacon from a hundred miles away. Downside is we have to get you out of here, and fast. Soon as Duke realizes you slipped the net, he'll send his serious heavy hitters."

"How is this happening? How is any of this happening?" Lucy's hands clenched and unclenched with nervous energy. "You aren't *real*."

Verna circled the sedan. She popped the locks, then paused, looking at Lucy over the hood.

"I can sing, and I can dance. And if I can sing and I can dance, stands to reason I can do anything I want to do, doesn't it?"

Lucy nodded, uncertain.

"Your mother and father made you," Verna said. "Are you real?"

"Yes, but—"

"Well, you're *my* mother. Save the philosophy for the open road. We need to burn rubber before Roach finds his spine and comes back for another go. Don't spread it around, but I'm a lot better at bluffing than I am at fighting."

Roy got in back, sliding onto a long slick vinyl bench the color of vanilla ice cream. He leaned to one side, checking out the dashboard. It sported big dials and polished chrome needles, and the speedometer marked intervals from zero to three hundred. Lucy reached behind herself and paused.

"Where are the seat belts?"

Verna snickered and turned the key. The sedan fired up in a grinding roar, like a jet engine packed with broken glass.

"This is a Century," she shouted over the din. "You get into an accident in one of these babies, they just hose out the interior and sell it to the next customer."

The noise faded to a glass-rattle growl as she pulled away from the roadside, off the dirt shoulder and onto the empty highway.

"I have a million questions," Lucy said.

"I might have one or two answers." Verna caught Roy staring in the rearview mirror. "Paint a picture, it'll last longer."

"You look like someone I used to know," he said.

"You ever notice how, when you're dreaming, everybody has a familiar face? Your mind is a pirate. It can tell a crazy story, but not from whole cloth. It takes bits and pieces from the waking world and puts 'em in a blender. Far as I can tell, this business works more or less the same way."

"This business?" he echoed.

"Building a world." Verna gave Lucy a sidelong glance. "You've got a talent for big dreams. Here, this is the best way I can explain it. And bear in mind that I had to work it all out on my own, and there's plenty I haven't figured out yet. You ever play with a prism, like a piece of cut crystal?"

"Sure," Lucy said.

"What happens when you shine light through a prism?"

"It changes," she said. "White light enters one side and spills out in a rainbow on the other."

Verna nodded. "Refraction. So, wrap your noodle around this: *you* are a prism. The source of the light, that's something I haven't sussed out yet. Call it magic, call it willpower, call it the stuff of creation. Point being, it's just floating around out there, waiting to be tapped."

"Potential energy," Roy said.

"That's right. But Lucy, here...she's a prism. So when it passes through her noggin—getting a high-octane boost thanks to a precocious, turbo-charged imagination—what comes out on the other side is a rainbow. *My* world."

"But...how?" Lucy said. "And why me? There's nothing special about me."

"Agree to disagree on that one. But I don't think it's *only* you. There's something special about stories, special enough that we've been dreaming them up and telling them since the first humans sat down around the first campfire together. A good story has a way of shining a light in the dark, teaching us things about ourselves, maybe even showing us what it means to be human in the first place. And a good story is always true, even when it's all made up. Did Carolyn Saunders manage to track you down before she kicked the bucket?"

"I had never even heard of her, not until I found out she was writing sequels to my comic books."

"Carolyn was an odd duck with an odd skill. Her head was a radio for stories, and it had one hell of an antenna. I was experimenting with some of the weirder books in Duke's occult library, hoping to reach you. I got her instead. She was trying to help. Anyway, she had a theory, and it checks out. Carolyn believed that *every* storyteller is a prism. That the very act of weaving a tale is what creates a refraction-world."

"That's hard to swallow," Roy said.

Verna's lips twisted into a sarcastic smile. "Why? Because everything you've seen up until now is so rational and easy to believe?"

"You're telling us that every story ever told is a world of its own," Roy said. "All of them? Like...there's a world where Luke Skywalker is zooming around in his X-Wing, and another where Captain Ahab is hunting for Moby Dick."

"That's the gist of it. But there's an intangible factor in play, too. Most refraction-worlds are just like the light from a match passing through a prism. Never built to last, and when the match flickers out, so does the rainbow. Poof. Gone, like it never existed at all. But every once in a while, maybe once in a generation, maybe less, you get the perfect storm. A powerhouse of natural talent, a childhood spent dreaming and longing, and a wicked imagination all come together to build a stable, permanent refraction."

"No one's ever described me as a 'powerhouse' before," Lucy said.

"I'm living proof. I'm betting a lot of weird stuff happened around you, when you were a little kid. Things moving around, doors slamming on their own. Did you live in a haunted house?"

Lucy shifted in her seat, silent now. Roy answered for her.

"Her mom called it a poltergeist."

"More like our young Lucy was a font of wild psychic energy and it was looking to bust out any way it possibly could," Verna said.

"You mentioned Carolyn was trying to help you find her," Roy said. "Was that why she wrote that novel? Trying to draw Lucy out from behind her pen name by inviting a lawsuit?"

"The thought did occur to us, but that wasn't the main reason. More like slapping a band-aid over a gaping chest wound. I didn't hop between dimensions just to say hello and introduce myself. I need your help. We need your help, and by 'we' I mean everyone. Remember what I said about how only a tiny few refractions manage to survive?"

Lucy nodded.

"Ours *isn't*, not anymore," Verna said. "Our world is dying. And we need you to fix it."

Roy leaned forward in his seat. "When you say 'dying'—"

"Literally. One slow piece at a time at first, but the disasters are picking up speed like a rock rolling down a mountainside. At first it was little things: an earthquake here, a bad flu season there. Then it was epidemics and typhoons, and that was just the warm-up act. Now we've got ghost-storms. Dead bodies crawling out of their graves. There's a new plague making the rounds that boils the blood in your veins. I figure we've got a few months, tops, before an extinction-level event wipes us all off the cosmic table for good."

"But I didn't do that," Lucy protested. "I never imagined anything like that. I never would, even before I knew you were real. That's not the kind of story I like."

"I'm betting it's the opposite problem. When was the last time you wrote about us?"

"The comics, I guess," Lucy said. "That was years ago, though. My big chance at success that never went anywhere."

"Uh-huh. You were disillusioned. You put away your pencils and your notebooks. But crafted things need love and care. If not, entropy always finds a way in. Carolyn hoped that if she put her typewriter in gear and wrote a story of her own, she could revitalize our world. She slowed the tide a little bit, but she couldn't stop it. For that, we need you. We need our creator."

Lucy's brow furrowed. "You want me to...write a new comic book?"

"This is the tricky part. Tricky mainly because I'm playing it by ear. I've got a few ideas that might work, though, and you'll like my solutions a lot better than you'll like the Duke's."

Roy almost didn't want to know. "What's his solution?"

"He has this theory that if someone from a refraction-world steals the powers of its author, they'll assume complete control of the refraction itself. He won't just stabilize our world, he'll rule it with an iron fist." Verna flicked a glance at Lucy. "He wants you inside of him. By which I mean...he wants to eat you."

Lucy bit her bottom lip.

"I want you to come back with me," Verna said. "Across the veil, back to my home."

"Back to where the leader of the psycho brigade is aiming to bake her into a home-cooked meal," Roy said, his voice flat.

"Do you think you're any safer here? Do you *feel* particularly safe?"

She had a point, Roy grudgingly conceded. "And then?"

"I'm hunting for a book. A very special, very rare book. It's called the Argisene Grimoire, and legend has it, it's a conduit to the entire multiverse. With access to that book and Lucy's brain, I think I could do something truly remarkable."

"But my brain stays in my head, right?" Lucy said.

"Cross my heart," Verna replied.

Chapter Twenty-eight

"This book," Roy said. "The, ah—"

"Argisene Grimoire."

"You need it, but you don't have it."

Verna shifted in her seat. Her fingers flexed on the steering wheel and the alien Ford let out a thunder-crack bellow as it lurched into the next gear.

"I've got a line on it. Just, it might take some doing."

"Define 'some doing.'"

"A little heavy lifting." She looked away from the road, a long desert chasm cast in the pillars of the high beams, just long enough to bat her eyelashes at him in the rearview mirror. "Nothing we can't handle. You've got muscles for days. I don't imagine you're any stranger to strong-arm work."

She's not Carmen, he told himself, repeating it like a mantra. *She's not Carmen.*

This has to stop, Roy told himself.

Admitting it felt like some kind of progress. Wasn't that what they preached to the drunks in AA? That you have to admit you've got a problem before you can fix it? Back when he was undercover, face to face with the slowly unspooling disaster he called a life, Roy told himself *This has to stop* at least three times a day. The problem was he never got any further than that. Step two, he figured, was defining exactly what *this* meant, and there were too many candidates to count back then.

It could have been the undercover work. The constant stress, the daily fear of being discovered, the room covered in plastic sheeting that was waiting for him if Perez ever found out his loyal bodyguard was a rat.

He pored over every stray word, every glance in his direction, hunting for invisible threats and making up monsters in the shadows.

It could have been the blow. Everyone in the narcotics game was hooked on something—money, power, chemicals. Roy used to be hooked on his childhood fantasies of truth and justice, law and order, and when they came into hard contact with reality they shattered like glass. Vic Perez was happy to provide a replacement to fill the emptiness. Theoretically, Roy knew he had a problem. He'd gone from doing it to fit in with Perez's crew, to doing it because he felt like it, to snorting maintenance lines three times a day. The powder kept him moving, active, on task and feeling good. He liked feeling good. He knew it couldn't last, no high ever did, but for now he was fine, skating just ahead of the crash.

It could have been Carmen. Roy didn't mind flirting with death. Working his way into Perez's confidence, his home, and his criminal empire was like swimming in shark-infested waters. It would only take one wrong move to drag him under. The only way he could possibly make his life more dangerous would be to steal Perez's girl.

So he stole her.

Or she stole him. Either way, every time Perez turned his back Carmen was over at Roy's place, sharing his blow and wrecking his bed. Every once in a while he'd sober up long enough for reality to come barging in: one day his assignment would end, his mask would come off, and things with Carmen would finish one bad way or another. But then she'd flutter her eyelashes, nuzzle his neck and whisper *I love you*, and the inevitable day of reckoning looked a thousand miles away.

They built a tiny world together. Just the two of them. And when his world was all wrong, she just needed to smile his way and everything turned right again. He remembered one afternoon, a Tuesday, lying tangled in rumpled sheets, dirty sunlight pushing through the window blinds. The cheap cotton smelled like sex and sweat and cheap perfume. Carmen stretched out next to him and lit a cigarette.

"Is this perfect?" he asked the ceiling.

"Don't know," Carmen said. She took a drag and blew a thin plume of smoke up to heaven. "Never been to perfect."

"I just don't want this to end."

"Who says it ever has to?"

Run away with me, he thought.

"Close enough to perfect," she decided out loud.

Their hands found each other under the twisted sheet. "Close enough."

"I need to get back," she said. "Before he misses me."

"Five more minutes?" he said.

"Five more minutes."

"I mean, if you don't *want* to help," Verna said. She trailed off, expectant.

"I didn't say that. I just want to know more about how we're going to get our hands on this rare, magic book, since it's the key to your whole plan. You're asking me to take Lucy into a world that's literally falling apart at the seams—"

"I have to go," Lucy said. "This is my fault."

"We don't know that," Roy said.

No one replied. He looked to Verna for some backup. She focused her attention on the highway.

"I thought I had a line on the book," Verna said. "I spent months reading Duke's mail, intercepting his messages, figuring out his whole scheme. He put feelers out all over the underworld. He had a courier coming in hot, delivering the book to a middleman, so I paid them a visit right before hopping over to this side of the gate. Figured I'd grab the grimoire, pick up Lucy, and make some magic."

"What went wrong?" Roy asked.

"Wrong *book*. Either I botched cracking Duke's code, or the courier was pulling a fast one. I tossed that thing in the trash. By that point, though, Duke knew I'd betrayed him. I had to move."

"You went on the run."

"Racing, romping, running ragged," she said, her voice sliding sideways into a staccato chant, "ruminating on the road. But with your kindly consultation I can the prize be showed. Your argent attention and admiration—"

"*Verna*," Lucy said. Her voice rang out, sharp, breaking Verna's vocal stride.

Verna gave her a sidelong glance, suddenly uncertain. "What's up, cupcake?"

Lucy had a problem.

She could take a few things on faith, as crazy as they were. Her imaginary world was real. Her imaginary world was dying. She had to help. But she had never invented anything called the Argisene Grimoire. Didn't mean it didn't exist, and it didn't mean Verna wasn't telling the truth. But.

Lucy knew some things.

"Roll for initiative," Lucy said, the teenage girl breaking into a rare mischievous grin.

Polyhedral dice clattered across a dining room table, the surface strewn with cans of Mountain Dew, character sheets, and maps sketched out on scraps of graph paper. The four hapless adventurers of the Vernon High School Drama Club groaned in unison.

"I'm covering the north exit with both pistols," Ty said. "That barricade won't hold for long. If any of Duke's men come through the door, I'm opening fire."

"We are so screwed," Gabe mourned. "I'm checking the windows. Is there any way down from the outside?"

Lucy slid a twenty-sided die, transparent and filled with pink sparkles, in his direction. "*Maybe*. Give me a perception check."

Jenna folded her arms and slouched back in her chair. "I'm not taking my eyes off of Verna."

"You notice she's edging toward the fire exit," Lucy said.

"'Hold it right there,' I shout. 'We came in together, and we're leaving together. It's the only way we're getting out of here in one piece.'" Jenna paused. "Wait. Who's holding the bag of diamonds right now?"

Lucy rolled a die behind the cardboard wall of her gamemaster's screen.

"Before you can react," she said, "Verna whispers a string of sibilant words. They dance around you, drifting like smoke, slipping into your minds. As you listen, your limbs feel sluggish, like they're filled with lead weights."

"Her hypnosis attack," Ty groaned.

Lucy's grin turned wolfish. "Everybody make a saving throw versus magic."

"Should have known it was a double-cross," Jenna grumbled, reaching for the dice. "If I've said it once, I've said it a dozen times: *never* trust Verna Bell."

"Nothing," Lucy said, meeting Verna's eyes.

There was plenty she wanted to say. Starting with *I wrote you. I know when you're using hypnosis on people. And you just tried it on Roy.* Speaking up had broken the spell before it could take root, but it didn't change the fact that Verna had done it.

But if she said so, Roy might leave in anger. Or kick Verna out and insist that he and Lucy go it alone. And Lucy didn't like either of those options. There was a long and dangerous road ahead, and she needed every asset and every ally she could get.

So do I warn Roy in private, where we can plan a strategy? Or do I confront Verna and remind her that I know her tricks? Lucy's stomach twisted in knots. She hated confrontations. She wasn't good at speaking up, or dealing with people, or...any of this, really.

But I'm going to have to learn, she thought. *And quick. Too many people are counting on me.*

The sedan roared across the Nevada state line, fast enough to rattle the sign at the side of the road and kick up a swirl of desert dust.

"The gateway is north," Verna said. "We're a couple of hours out. I think we should find a place to stay, get some sleep, and cross the portal in the morning."

"Agreed," Lucy blurted. Rest was the last thing on her mind, and she didn't think the adrenaline in her veins would let her sleep a wink, but this was a chance to set things right. She could give Roy a diplomatic warning about Verna behind closed doors. And she could give Verna a less-than-diplomatic one.

Lucy hated confrontations. But she had to do this.

"Still waiting to hear the rest of your plan," Roy said.

Verna drummed her fingers on the steering wheel.

"By now, Duke either has the book, or he knows where it is and his people are closing in." She nodded, resolute. "We're going to steal it from him."

Roy leaned forward in his seat, looking to Lucy. She understood. He was asking for an expert opinion.

"He's the biggest crime boss in Noir York," Lucy said. "He has a small army of henchmen, he owns the police and the mayor's office, and he's a sorcerer who can conjure demons. And you want us to rob him."

"We have two advantages," Verna said.

"Which are?"

"Number one," she said, "almost all of Duke's elite agents are over on this side of the portal, chasing *you*. Once we cross over, if we cover our tracks, it could be anywhere from hours to days before he finds out and calls them all back. He's understaffed and most of his heavy hitters are occupied."

Lucy pursed her lips. She had a point. Roach, the Dark Dryad, all the rest of her walking nightmares—they'd be off on a wild goose chase, hunting for Lucy on the wrong world. That still left all of Duke Ellery's *ordinary* thugs and gunmen, but it was still an advantage.

"What else?" Lucy said.

"Number two, contrary to what you might have been told, I know a little secret. The Midnight Jury is not dead. Far from it."

"Then why—"

"It's complicated." Verna's eyes sparkled in the dark. "But if anyone can convince the Jury to put on the coat and fedora, pick up the old guns, and get back into action, I'm thinking it's you."

Chapter Twenty-nine

The bright lights of the Vegas Strip burned on the horizon, but they stayed out of reach. Tonight's road ended at the outskirts of the city, at a seedy motel by the airport. Roy booked two beds for himself and Lucy and put Verna in the room next door. The beds smelled musty and mildew spotted the tiles under a dubious, rust-flecked shower head, but all they needed was a few hours' shelter and rest before stepping into another world.

"I don't mind the digs," Verna said. "Trust me, compared to some of the dumps I've slept in back home, this is the Ritz. But we need to play this smart."

Roy was a step ahead of her. "We set a guard. One of us stays awake and watches for trouble, and we switch off in four hours so both of us get a little shut-eye."

"What about me?" Lucy asked.

"You need as much rest as you can get," Roy said. "Anything could happen tomorrow, and I mean anything. We need you bright-eyed and ready for it."

"But I can help. You need rest, too."

"I can manage," he said.

Lucy folded her arms tight across her chest.

"I'm not made of glass," she said. "I can help."

"Like the man said, you can do the most by saving your strength." Verna jerked her thumb over her shoulder toward the motel room door. "I'm going to take first watch. I'll come and wake you up in four, big guy. Get some beauty sleep."

Lucy waited until the door shut behind her. She slid the deadbolt and turned to Roy.

"We need to talk," she said.

Roy listened, his hands becoming fists as Lucy spoke and then slowly, reluctantly unclenching. He looked away from her, his gaze fixed on something a few miles or a few years away.

"She tried to cast a spell on me," he echoed, repeating the words like he couldn't quite parse them.

"I think she was worried you might ditch us. You didn't sound like you were down with the plan."

"I'm not," he said, "because so far I haven't seen much evidence that there *is* a plan, beyond 'let's go to Lucy's imaginary world, try to find a magic book and hope we figure something out.'"

He looked at her and reached out. He took her small hand in his, beefy fingers curling, gentle.

"But I would never leave you behind," he said.

"I know," she said.

"You're my responsibility. I dragged you into this mess."

She shook her head. "You didn't, though. Yeah, you kinda accidentally helped the bad guys track me down, but they weren't even half the problem. If you hadn't stepped in when you did, Duke's people would have found me. And I'd be...gone by now."

Her other hand closed over his. She gave it a tiny squeeze.

"You don't owe me anything, Roy. All debts have already been paid. And whatever's waiting for us on the other side, there's a good chance none of us are coming back. If you don't want to come with us, I would never hold that against you." Lucy gave him a nervous smile. One corner of her mouth twitched. "I can't lie, I'm scared to death. But I have to do this. That world, all those people—that's *my* responsibility, not yours. If you need to go, go."

He fell silent for a moment.

"She looks just like Carmen," Roy said.

"Verna."

"I know she's not. Like she said, these story worlds, refractions, whatever you want to call them, they're built out of dream-stuff. They take faces from our world, but that's where it stops. She's not Carmen. In my head, I know that."

He fell silent, sorting things out in the quiet. Lucy gave him time.

"I told you about my last job," Roy said, "working undercover."

"You lost her," Lucy said. "That guy, Perez, he—"

"No," Roy said.

He'd begged Carmen to stay away, but he couldn't tell her why. She didn't listen. She had shown up like usual, lounging at Perez's poolside in her little red bikini, offering Roy what looked like a silent apology with her eyes while her lips cooed sweet nothings into Perez's ear. Then she and the kingpin adjourned to the upstairs bedroom.

It was all right. Roy had a plan. Once they came back downstairs, he'd corner Perez in the kitchen, away from his other bodyguards, and drop him quietly. He'd be breaking cover, endangering the investigation, but at least he could grab Carmen and drag her to his car if he had to. They'd be long gone before the fireworks started.

Then SWAT hit the steps of Vic Perez's mansion with a hardened steel battering ram, while a truck with a chain winch ripped the garage doors off like a can opener. The raid was going down early. Three hours early. None of these guys knew Roy was an undercover cop. He had his orders to stay safe in the chaos: drop his weapon, kick it away, kneel and lace his hands behind his head. They'd arrest and process him, and his handler would come pull him out of the holding cell once the dust settled. He'd done it a dozen times at a dozen other busts.

But Carmen was upstairs in a bedroom with a coked-up lunatic and too many guns in easy reach, and all of a sudden his orders didn't mean anything at all. He drew his pistol, a nine-millimeter Beretta, and charged inside. A storm of sound—SWAT barging in, Perez's men trying to get out, fleeing like rats from a ship they knew was sinking fast—swirled around Roy and fogged his head and pumped his veins full of white-hot adrenaline. He knew this house like the back of his hand. He knew the rooms the raid would hit first, where not to go, the safest way to the top. The action was still downstairs by the time he rounded the third-floor staircase.

He heard gunshots from below, the tin clatter of cheap automatics, the heady bass boom of SWAT shotguns tearing through walls, doors, bodies. He pushed it all behind him and kept his eyes on the door dead ahead. One kick and it blasted wide, swaying on a bent hinge, Roy firing through like a cannonball.

He jolted to a stop on the snow-white bedroom carpet. Perez, draped in a leopard-print robe that dangled half open, had his arm around Carmen's neck and the muzzle of his revolver pressed to the side of her head. Her eyes were wet, a dark line of mascara dripping down one cheek.

"Let her go," Roy said. He dropped his act, took off his mask, and aimed his pistol for a kill shot. Tried to, anyway. Carmen was too close, the situation too dangerous to open fire.

"I had a hunch," Perez said, grinning wildly. He was twitchy, tweaking, a cornered animal looking for one last bite. "Didn't want to believe it. We were close, me and you. Real close."

"I won't tell you again." Roy closed one eye and focused his world into a target, sharp and tight. It was still a bad shot, with Perez weaving and dragging Carmen around like a rag doll. Roy just had to hold him, pin him here until the SWAT team made it upstairs, keep him talking and keep Carmen alive for a few more minutes.

"You spied on me, robbed me, stole my *fucking* girl—" he gave Carmen a rough shake, his arm squeezing harder around her throat. "You know what, Roy? Hell with it. Let's go down together, huh? Just the three of us, together. Carmen goes first."

He saw Perez's finger on the trigger. Saw it start to curl, an execution in slow motion. Roy did the only thing he could do. He aimed for Perez's face, the only part of his body that wasn't hidden behind his human shield, and he shot first.

Carmen's head snapped backward, riding on a gout of ruby blood. The blood hit the snowy carpet, spattering like a spilled glass of wine, just before her body did. Her eyes were wide open. Fixed on Roy.

He didn't remember much of what came next. He charged, beat the revolver out of Perez's hand and kept beating him. Perez never stopped smiling, even when he was down on his knees, his teeth broken and running with scarlet spit. Roy loomed over him and pushed his gun into the ferret's battered face.

"That's on you," Perez said, eyes flicking to the corpse beside them. "You get that, right? My hands are clean. But what you did to her…that's forever, pal. Try to blame me all you want, but what you did to her is a forever thing, and there's no taking it back now."

Roy leaned in, pushing the muzzle down hard. Perez's neck bent back, his wet eyes and bloody face raised to heaven.

"Go on," he whispered. "Go on, Roy. Pull the trigger. You know you want to. Let's go all the way tonight. Pull the trigger."

Lucy stared at Roy, wide-eyed.

"Did you—"

"Don't ask me that," he said, his voice soft.

"It was an accident. You didn't mean to hurt her."

"I shouldn't have been there. I should have let SWAT handle it. They might have sent in a negotiator or something, solved it some other way—"

Lucy squeezed his hand between hers, holding it on her lap.

"You can't know that," she said. "Going down that road of 'maybes,' you could just as well say he would have killed Carmen before anyone got up to the bedroom. You were the only one close enough to help her. You tried your best. That's all anybody can do."

Roy lifted his other hand, waved it at nothing.

"I said I'd never let that happen again. Working for myself, freelance, made it easier to keep my promise. Every job, every late night phone call and redeye flight, every envelope stuffed with rumpled cash, put me a few more miles ahead of the past. All I had to do, to stop seeing her every time I closed my eyes, was keep moving."

"And now someone who looks just like Carmen is here, and she needs help, and it's life or death," Lucy said. "I can't imagine how that feels."

Roy looked to the motel room door. He shook his head.

"Same body, same strut, same careless flip of her hair. Different heart. Different soul. As much as I want to forget, she's not Carmen. And I can't tell you how much I'd love to forget, and pretend, and get lost in her. For the first time, all over again. But I know better."

He turned his head, gazing down into Lucy's eyes.

"I'm here for you, not her."

"I already told you," she protested. "You don't owe me anything."

"I know," Roy said. "But you need a helping hand, and I've got two to offer. That's the only reason I need. Besides, don't I have to play my part?"

She furrowed her brow. "Meaning?"

"Seems to me, the parade of sideshow freaks and monsters aside, what we've got here is a classic film noir. Duke Ellery's the mob boss, Verna Bell is the *femme fatale*—"

"Don't call me the damsel in distress," Lucy said.

"Wouldn't dream of it. What you are is the client with a problem. A problem too big to tackle all on her own. That's a long way from being a damsel in distress."

Lucy took that in. "That sounds a little better. Which makes you...?"

"Isn't it obvious?" Roy broke into a sad-eyed smile. "I'm the down-on-his-luck PI who takes the case. If I walked away now, the whole story would go wrong. And we can't have that, can we?"

She shared his smile, leaning closer. "I guess not."

"We'll see it through to the end. You and me." He looked to the door. "But first things first. I need to have a little chat with Verna about appropriate behavior."

"Let me," Lucy said. She just blurted the words, too fast to reel them back in.

"You don't exactly enjoy confrontations."

"I don't," she said. Understatement of the century. "I kind of do everything humanly possible to avoid them."

"So why not let me handle it?"

Lucy let go of his hand. She stood, facing the door, the parking lot—and Verna—just a few steps away. Her mouth went dry, her pulse going jittery.

"Because sometimes you have to do things you hate if you want to get better at them. If you want to grow. I don't know what's waiting for us on the other side, but I do know it's going to be anything but easy. I have to be at my best. That'll take more than a few hours of sleep. I have to look at the things I'm afraid of and take them head-on."

She walked toward the door. She turned back to look at Roy, her smile wan.

"Besides," she said, "I'm technically her mother. She has to listen to me."

She hoped.

Chapter Thirty

Verna was a shadow in the sleepy gloom, holding her post at the far edge of the motel parking lot, well away from the flickering lamp that hung over the driveway. When she stood perfectly still, it was hard to see her at all.

Lucy circled the lot, footsteps light, ears perked. All she heard was the rumble of cars on the access road and the occasional roar of a jet lifting off from McCarran Airport, sweeping up like a steel raptor into the starless night sky.

Verna greeted her with a casual nod before turning back to her watch. "You're supposed to be in dreamland, cupcake. What gives?"

Lucy wanted to make small talk. To put off the hard stuff as long as she possibly could. Those words wouldn't come, though. She was angry and she didn't have tools to deal with it, didn't have anywhere for the anger to go, so she just blurted it out: "Why did you try to hypnotize Roy?"

Verna blinked. Her eyelashes fluttered.

"I wrote you," Lucy said, cutting off any chance of a lie before it could reach her lips.

"That answers my question."

"The alliteration is a dead giveaway. At least, for people who know you."

"And you," Verna said, looking her up and down, "know me better than anyone."

Lucy took a deep breath.

"I need you," she said, "to never do that again. Ever."

Verna arched one eyebrow.

"Roy is my friend," Lucy said. "*Our* friend. You don't do that to friends."

"The big guy is useful."

"Useful. You say that like he's some kind of—"

"Important, is that better? Pick a word, babe, pick one you like and stick it right in my mouth, I don't mind. You're the author here. What I mean is, I'm not sure we can pull this off without him. We'd make a good go of it, sure, but there's strength in numbers. So when I thought he might walk, I had to take corrective action."

"He won't leave."

"Why? Because I look like his old flame? I don't know the story there, but a man only looks at a woman like that when he's got one thing on his mind and some experience getting it on the regular."

"For me," Lucy said. "He's staying for me."

"Ohhh," Verna said, drawing out the word with a purr of amusement. "He's got a thing for city mice. Didn't expect that, but you never know taste."

Lucy crossed her arms. "Don't call me that."

"Did he slip into your bed at night, mouse? Sweeping you up in those big mitts, making you feel safe and wanted?"

"Roy isn't like that."

"All men are like that. Only one thing on their minds if they've got room for one thing at all."

Frustration surged up from Lucy's stomach, riding on an upswell of raw disappointment. She tasted bile in the back of her throat. She looked for something to say, flailing and fumbling over ten words at once, battling her fear of a fight and her self-inflicted need to be civil, polite, *nice*. She rammed herself against the wall that normally kept her mouth sealed tight, and broke through all at once.

"I used to think you were cool," she snapped.

Verna froze. She took a step back, then looked Lucy up and down, studying her with new eyes.

"Ouch. I called you a mouse, but kitty's got claws. Tiny, but she does have claws."

Just as soon as she asserted herself, Lucy felt the walls closing in. She wanted to apologize, even though she knew it was ridiculous, even though she was the one being wronged. She still wanted to apologize, smooth things over, make things right. Make things nice.

"But I'll tell you something else," Verna continued. "I think you're just fine living down in mouse-town, eating cheese and cowering whenever anything bigger than a pill bug comes near your hole. And seeing as you've been so kind about sharing your candid thoughts tonight, I'll return the favor and then some."

"You don't need to do that."

"Oh, but I do." Something new glinted in Verna's dark eyes, something wicked. "You need to be shown your proper place. So here's the game. I'm going to hypnotize you. I'll freeze your feet to the parking lot asphalt and hold you here for a few hours. Then I'm going to walk into that room and take Roy for the bedroom ride of his life, whether he wants it or not. Because when I'm done twirling his head around, he'll want it plenty.

Then I'm going to break his heart all over again. A million little pieces all over the shabby carpet, so many you'll never be able to pick them up again."

"Verna—" Lucy said, pleading.

"I'm going to show you, clearly and firmly, who's in charge of this little expedition. Ready? You'd better stop me, Lucy. If you don't, I'll do everything I just promised and then some. Aw, but you can't, can you?"

Lucy's hands twitched helplessly at her sides. She was already rooted, frozen by her own fears. All she could do was beg.

"Please. Don't do this. Roy's a good man, he's trying to *heal*."

"Let him long for it. Listen, Lucy, listen long and loud, listen to lullabies and lies concealed in kinder currents and cunning cat-calls crashing down—"

Lucy's feet were turning to stone. Jagged lines of cold concrete wormed their way through her veins, up from her feet, to her calves, her legs, freezing them solid. Panic rising, she knew she only had a couple of seconds left to do something, anything, to make Verna stop. Pleading wouldn't work, logic wouldn't work. *Nice and polite* wouldn't work. Those were the only tools she had.

"—cross boundary lines, boundaries ne'er broken, fortresses of fear and futile furtive fertile soil—"

Lucy snapped.

It all happened at once. Her fear, her frustration, her anger, welling up from the bottle she kept them sealed inside, surging hard enough to make the cork explode. For the first time in her entire life, her left hand curled into a fist. Then she cocked it back and let it fly.

Her knuckles slammed into Verna's nose. Verna dropped to the asphalt, sputtering, covering her face as droplets of blood squeezed between her fingertips. Lucy stood over her, both hands balled into shaking fists now, her face contorted with fury.

"Don't you ever," Lucy said, "*ever* pull that…that *shit* again, or so help me God you'll get a lot more than a punch in the face. Roy is *my friend*, and *nobody* messes with my friends. Got it? *Got it?*"

Verna had been making a low, keening sound, rocking back and forth, hands cupped over her injured nose and her eyes squeezed tight. Lucy stared down at her as the groans of pain faded to something different. Giggling.

Verna lowered her hands, leaning back on her palms, and let a trickle of blood flow free. It ran along her upper lip, rounding the pert bow of her mouth, dribbling down her chin. Her giggles grew to a hearty, eager laugh as she locked eyes with Lucy.

"There you go," Verna said. "I told you I'd show you who was in charge here."

Lucy stared at her. "What—" she said, lost for words.

"Just like I knew there was a lion lurking behind those mouse eyes and kitten claws. You only needed a little help to bring her out. And now that you know she's in there, ready to stand up and fight, she'll be that much easier to reach the next time you need her. Because you will need her."

Verna held out her hand.

"Help me up?"

Lucy pulled her to her feet. Verna leaned into her. Then her arms encircled her, dragging Lucy into a tight embrace. Their hearts beat against one another, hot and fast. Verna stepped back, still close, still staring into Lucy's eyes. Her fingertip trailed, feather-light, across Lucy's lips.

"Now you're almost ready to face the Duke," she said.

Lucy found a tissue for her. Verna wadded it into a tiny plug, stopping up her bloody nose. They walked together for a while, circling the boundary of the parking lot on a slow patrol.

"I think I finally got you figured out," Verna said. Her tone had changed. It came off like a compliment, not a threat.

"Is that so?"

"I was surprised when we first crossed paths. See, I expected you to be just like the Midnight Jury. Or at least a pale reflection, the flickering shadow of the Jury's bright candle. But that's not you at all, is it?"

"I was afraid a lot, when I was a kid," Lucy said.

That was a half-truth. Her fears had all chased her through the years, and they'd only loomed larger as the demands of adult life, the risks and pitfalls, all joined the chorus of terror. The Jury was never her alter ego. The vigilante was her hero, her protector, the trench-coated knight who would swing in, twin guns blazing, to set the world right when everything felt wrong.

"But then I figured," Verna said, "every writer leaves something of themselves in the mix, don't they? Maybe it's a subconscious thing, but it's there. So I looked at the candidates, weighed the evidence, and came to one conclusion."

She stopped walking. They turned to face one another at the edge of the flickering lamplight.

"I'm you," Verna said. "Your alter ego, your...what do they call it? 'Self-insert character.' I'm the you that you always wanted to be and told yourself you never could be."

"It's more complicated than that," Lucy said.

"Sure, sure. But down at the core of things...I'm right, aren't I?"

They started walking again. Lucy didn't answer, not right away.

"I imagined what I'd be like if I wasn't afraid of my own shadow," Lucy said. "If I could feel...confident, even in a crowd of strangers. If I could talk to people and be charming and witty instead of stumbling over my own tongue."

"And out popped Verna Bell, like Athena from the brow of Zeus."

"I'm not Zeus," Lucy said.

"And I'm not Athena. Believe that. My hands are too dirty for anyone to build a temple in *my* honor. But here's the takeaway: all that strength and courage you dreamed into me? It's inside you too, sister. You couldn't have turned me into a real girl if you didn't have the magic all along. There's a little of all of us inside of you."

Lucy had to smile. "Just not the Roach."

Verna chuckled. Her hand rested easy on Lucy's shoulder. "Maybe not the Roach. Hey. You need to get some sleep. And I'm not saying that because you're some pretty pampered princess who isn't tough enough to hang with me and Roy."

Her hand turned Lucy around, gently.

"I'm saying that," Verna told her, "because when that sun comes up over the mountains, the three of us are going for a little drive. Straight into the maw of a dying world, filled to the brim with walking nightmares and worse. And you, Lucy Langenkamp, lioness-in-training, are the only one who can save us all. So get some rest. Tomorrow's going to be a long day and a much longer night."

Chapter Thirty-one

Roy tried to hold back the dark. He did his best, walking a lonely patrol along the perimeter of the motel parking lot, listening to the crickets and the wind and the rumble of distant engines. Las Vegas was a glowing blob of white light on the horizon, a halo on a dirty angel. Roy measured his watch in footsteps instead of hours, marking away his shift one circuit at a time.

Then he heard the music.

At first he thought it was a flute, soft and lilting and longing, beckoning him toward the access road—sized for delivery trucks and garbage—that ran alongside and behind the motel lot in a sinuous curve. Then he realized it wasn't an instrument at all: it was a woman's voice, perfectly pitched, resonating in his blood. His veins tingled, his bone marrow grew warm, and his feet took him toward the alleyway before his mind could tell them to stop.

One step closer couldn't hurt. He had the single lamp from the parking lot burning behind his back and enough moonlight to see by. Nobody was going to get the jump on him. Two steps closer—three—couldn't hurt. He was awake, alert, beckoned, conjured, it was his choice to take six, seven steps into the mouth of danger—

The voice fell silent.

Just ahead, a shape unfolded from the shadows behind a rusted dumpster. It moved like the petals of a waking flower-blossom, slow and stretching, languid, reaching toward the moon and the distant neon for sustenance. Then the petals became serpents. *No*, he thought, watching purple-black leaves sprout along their uncoiling lengths. *Vines*.

The woman before him was a modern-day Medusa, the curves of her naked body cloaked in darkness and a writhing, undulating nest of vines that sprouted from her living flesh. Her eyelids opened. Her eyes, the color of green glass and segmented like a fly's, glittered in her silhouette.

"Hello, Roy," she said.

She read his mind. Either that, or his next thought was obvious.

"You don't need a weapon, Roy. I'm not here to fight."

Somehow, he found his voice. It came out as a raspy whisper. "How do you freaks keep finding us?"

She chuckled. Then she stretched one arm above her head, tilting her face to the starless sky.

"It's Lucy, don't you see? She's felt like a fish out of water her entire life. Some of that you can chalk up to a lousy childhood, a lack of positive role models, and a bushel of untreated psychological issues. But even if she fixed all of that, she'd still be a woman out of place and time."

She lowered her arm, and locked eyes with Roy.

"She's a dreamer. A big dreamer. The energy that created my world sings out from her soul. She doesn't belong here. She belongs with *us*."

"Agree to disagree," Roy said.

"To draw an...overly simplified metaphor, everything in your world is an apple. Everything in my world is an orange. Lucy is also an orange. The difference is invisible to you, but for the rest of us oranges, she stands out from this place like a spotlight shining in the heavens. There is nowhere she can go, on this side of the doorway, where we cannot find her."

Roy had enough of his wits back to spot the silver lining. *On this side*, he thought. *Once we cross over to the other side, she'll blend in like everybody else. Duke and his goons will be flying blind.*

We just have to live that long.

"So we should expect a visit from the whole clown-car parade tonight," he said.

"Not at all. I'm a bit of a talented mimic, and my perfume...well, you've just had a taste of that. I've seeded several false trails, enough to buy you a few hours. More than enough time to escape this world, if you're smart about it."

His eyes narrowed to a squint. "Why?"

"Because we have some common cause between us. Call me Charikleia, by the way. Some call me the Dryad. Or the 'Dark Dryad,' but—" She let out a tiny sigh. "—I find that a bit too on-the-nose, don't you? Besides, that would imply the existence of a Light Dryad, and I can assure you there's no such being. Can we speak frankly? Under a flag of truce, for the moment?"

"Don't know if we can," Roy said, wary. "I'm pretty sure I didn't walk into this alley under my own steam."

"Like I said, just a taste of my power, to let you know what I'm capable of. Now let me give you a sign of good faith."

Vines rustling, Charikleia emerged from the shadows. She took one slow, doe-like step after another, closing the distance between them on backward-jointed legs. Her jade eyes were fixed on Roy. Her tendrils and blossoms wreathed her, endlessly squirming, a crown of snakes from which her naked body grew.

Her skin was mottled, blue-black, chipped and peeling, like swirls of oil paint slathered onto an antique canvas. Her lips and nails were onyx, her mouth lined with shards of jagged wood for teeth.

"Describe me in a word," she said.

Roy wasn't sure how to answer that. Honesty seemed smart, but at the same time, she was standing close enough to hit him with those whipping vines or her siren voice or any other trick she'd come armed with tonight. Insulting her was a bad idea. He settled on a word, neutral enough, true enough to work.

"Alien," he said.

She smiled.

"If I was using my powers," Charikleia told him, "you would find me unbearably beautiful. You would also be quite incapable of saying 'no' to me, and that wouldn't suit my purposes tonight. I need you to enter this partnership with your eyes—your true eyes—wide open."

"So I just have to take your word for it."

"Of course I could be lying," she said. "Everybody lies."

"I don't think Lucy lies."

"She tells herself that she isn't important. That's the most grievous lie of all. My entire world is going to die without her, Roy. I *like* my world. It's where I keep my things, and my pets, and my pleasures. Over there, I'm the Goddess of the Toxic Green. Over here...well, I don't know what I'd be. This world runs by different rules. Different immutable laws."

"Problem is," Roy said, "your boss wants to bake Lucy into a casserole. I'm not going to let that happen."

The Dryad rolled her eyes. "Let's get one thing clear, yes? Duke Ellery is not my boss or my master. He's a puffed-up peacock of a sorcerer and the only reason I haven't *broken* him is because he has a damnable talent for protecting himself and his throne. I came to your world under the pretense of joining the bounty hunt, but I have no desire to see Lucy land in his claws, any more than you do. The last thing he needs is more power."

"Got an alternative to offer?"

"Me. Duke, as he often does, is going to rash extremes. I believe we can stabilize my world with a bit of strong magic and a little bit of Lucy—with a painless, and decidedly non-lethal, method. There's a book. Beyond rare, one of a kind—"

"The Argisene Grimoire," Roy said. "Sure. Verna Bell's hot to get her hands on that number too."

"Now there's a liar for you."

"All the same, sounds like you two have the same plan. Maybe you should compare notes."

"Roy. Please. If I had any interest in baring my throat to Verna Bell's talons, would I have approached you in private like this?"

"You want me to go behind Verna's back?"

"She's going behind yours," Charikleia said. "I can promise you that much. She's taking advantage of your good nature."

"She already tried taking advantage," Roy said.

"Let me guess, she showed off some of that sideshow carny patter she loves so much." She snorted. "*Hypnosis*. One tiny step up from guessing your weight to win a prize. She was caught, interrupted—and duly chastened, she promised to never ever do it again, cross her heart and pray for hell."

Direct hit, like she'd been riding in the car along with them. Roy still wanted to trust Verna Bell over Charikleia. His gut told him that what he had here, at best, was a choice of vipers.

"It's part of her standard playbook," the Dryad continued. "Show you her blunt knives while she keeps the sharp ones hidden behind her back. Has she seduced you yet?"

"I'm hard to seduce."

"If I enjoyed the company of men, I'd take that as a challenge. But all the same, expect it. She loves to play the wilting, soiled dove, desperate for the protection of a big strong hero." One of the Dryad's tendrils poked at Roy's face, driving home the point. "You're a tool, to her. A tool she can use and then toss away when she's finished."

"Lady," Roy said, "that's what I am to most people. I don't get torn up about it and I don't take it personal."

Charikleia paused. Her insect eyes glittered as she looked Roy up and down for a moment, silent, studying him.

"What if I said you deserved better?"

"I'd say," he replied, "that I know when I'm being buttered up."

"Maybe. But remember this: I came to you unmasked and left you untouched, when it would have been far easier for me to do the opposite. I'm giving you all the honesty I'm capable of. And Verna? She's going to betray you."

"You can read the future, too?"

"I can read *her*," the Dryad said. "And so can you. Watch for the signs, and you'll see the setup in slow-motion."

"What's her real game, if you know so much about her?"

She frowned. Her onyx lips pursed tight.

"All I know for certain is that Verna never backs herself into a corner. She always keeps an escape route open. And after the way she betrayed Duke Ellery, he'll hunt her to the ends of our world. He's not the forgiving type. Unless, of course, she comes up with a suitable apology gift."

Roy didn't need her to fill in the details. He could only think of one gift that might do the trick.

"Like if she handed over Lucy and this magic book everybody wants."

"That's one escape plan. She'll probably have one or two more. And every last one of her schemes ends with you in the morgue and Lucy on somebody's dinner plate. Like I said, don't take my word for it, not when your eyes are sharp enough to see. Watch her. And once you've seen all you need to, why not give me a call?"

"You got phones on the other side?"

"Three-minute calls for a nickel," she told him. "But I've got something more intimate in mind."

Another of her vines unfurled, reaching toward him, swaying like a cobra. The tip was curled around a tiny offering: a knotty twig, stained blueish-black, no more than two inches long.

"Go on," she said.

Roy took the twig. It felt oily to the touch, disturbingly soft and warm.

"Not a gift I give just anyone," she said. "I grew it myself. Of myself."

He almost smiled. After the week he'd endured so far, the idea of a plant-woman giving him a piece of her own body barely even registered on the insanity scale. It was amazing how fast you could get used to chaos when you really had to.

"When you want me, that's how you ring my bell," Charikleia said. "Snap my token in half and carry the broken parts with you. I'll smell the sap inside from just about anywhere."

Roy held up the twig.

"This isn't yes." He slipped it into his pocket. "This is maybe."

"I'll take maybe, tonight."

She glanced to the moon. It shone, reflected, in the alien facets of her eyes.

"Just for tonight," she added.

Chapter Thirty-two

Lucy slept, but she wasn't sure how. She drifted at the edge of consciousness, flat on her back on the cheap motel bed, smelling the musty sheets and the stale air and watching the shadows behind her eyelids. Every night since her life changed forever had been a minefield of danger, and she didn't expect this one to be any different. All she could trust was the promise of the morning to come and the passage to another world.

My world, she thought. Her literal city of dreams in flesh and blood, glass and stone.

She thought she'd be up all night, her restless mind pulled back and forth between excitement and fear, but her body couldn't hold out that long. Out of fuel, aching for rest, she fell asleep like someone had flicked off a switch.

The next thing she knew, the first glow of dawn was pressing against the drapes and a hand was on her shoulder. She jumped, almost launching off the bed, heart-jolt firing an emergency warning that burned through her veins.

"Easy, *easy*," Roy whispered. He squeezed her shoulder. "You're okay."

"We actually—"

"Yeah."

"Made it through the night, without anything weird happening."

Roy glanced away. Just for a second.

"We're good," he said.

"Verna?"

"Bringing the car around."

"Do I have time to take a shower?" she asked, shrugging off the covers.

"Quick one."

Roy gave her a smile, but it didn't quite reach his eyes. They looked tired or troubled, and she wasn't sure which. Maybe both.

"Sure," he said. "Not every day you get to visit another planet. Freshen up."

She slid off the bed, touching down on unsteady feet, cold against the scratchy motel carpet. She turned to the bathroom, then paused.

"Roy—"

"I know."

"This might be a one-way trip."

"I know," he said.

"I mean, it's not going to get any *less* dangerous from here, and there's no telling how this will all end or even what's waiting for us—"

"Hey," he said.

She fell silent, head tilted, her big eyes meeting his.

"This is the part where you tell me I don't have to go with you," he said.

"You don't—"

"And this is the part where I tell you that I'm in this until the end. Bitter, sweet, or otherwise."

"But—"

"And this is the part," he said, "where you make one last half-hearted protest, because you'd feel guilty if I came with you and got my dumb ass killed on your account. Just like I'd feel like the lowest cockroach on the planet if I let you go alone."

She had to smile. "Sounds like you've seen this movie."

"Once or twice, when I was a kid," he said. "Go on. Take a shower. Got a busy day ahead of us."

Verna sat behind the wheel of her alien Ford, fingers restlessly drumming, the engine idling with that broken-glass growl. Roy got in on the other side, checking the side mirror while he settled into the big bucket seat. He reached for the seatbelt out of habit, hand brushing against smooth powder-blue steel.

"I don't suppose this thing has airbags, either."

Verna squinted at him. "What are 'airbags'?"

"Asked and answered," he said. "Does everybody on the other side drive around in deathtraps?"

"Only if you like to move fast. You like to move fast, Roy?"

He looked out over the parking lot, the road beyond, the ribbons of highway winding their way to the distant red-rock mountains. The sun shimmered over the far horizon, turning the dry air amber-gold, bringing the first feather-light brush of warmth to the cold desert dawn.

"Depends," he said.

"On?"

"Who I'm riding with."

"I'm told I'm pretty good behind the wheel." Verna flipped her visor down against the rising sun and glanced over at the motel. "Where's God?"

"Don't call her that."

"If the shoe fits."

"She's already dealing with more stress than any one person should have to. You'll give her a complex."

"You seem cool as a cucumber," she said, looking him up and down.

"I'm a stoic at heart."

"Still," she said, "makes you wonder."

He tilted his head. "About?"

"Well, whatever name you want to give her, Lucy Langenkamp is my creator. She imagined me, she wrote me, she dreamed big...and here I am."

Roy wasn't following. He answered her with a shrug.

"You ever wonder who wrote *you*, Roy?"

Lucy saved him from having to think about it. She emerged from the hotel room, fresh-faced and glowing in the morning sun, and slid into the back seat. Verna swiveled and greeted her with a nod.

"Hey there, cupcake. Ready to go home?"

Roy heard the Dryad's voice in his ears, last night feeling as close as the scent of her flowers. *She doesn't belong here. She belongs with us.*

On a dying planet, Roy thought. *Maybe months from going the way of the dinosaurs. Maybe weeks. Maybe days.*

"We move fast," he said. "We get in, we get the job done, we get out. If it looks like the job isn't doable, we get out. If Duke Ellery latches onto our trail—"

"Relax, big guy. How about you let Lucy answer for herself?" Verna looked back to Lucy. "All set?"

Lucy bit her bottom lip. Then she nodded, resolute, even though her fingers were digging panic-furrows into her knees.

"Ready," she said.

Verna leaned over, reaching across Roy's lap, and flipped open the glove compartment. Amid a clutter of folded maps—roads Roy had ever seen, stretching across territories he'd never heard of—lay a brass charm on a tarnished chain. The amulet looked cheap, dented and flimsy, adorned with a shallow oval of turquoise. It made Roy think of something an "authentic" fortune teller would wear to spice up her act as she waved her hands over a crystal ball.

Verna hooked its chain around the rearview mirror and let it dangle. As it spun and caught the light, Roy noticed an extra detail: a constellation of pinpoint garnets surrounded the turquoise, ringing the outer span of copper. They were cracked, greasy...*dirty*, somehow, several broken and half-missing from their settings. All but the last four, which were neat and pristine and flawlessly cut.

"This little baby is called the Mason's Compass," Verna said. "It was Duke's going-away present to me, not that he knew he was forking it over at the time."

"Skipped the exit interview?" Roy asked.

"I'm not big on long goodbyes. Anyway, the Compass will get us safely across and back again."

Lucy leaned forward in her seat. "Are you sure it'll work?"

"I'm here, aren't I? Even have all my fingers and toes. Believe me, I checked."

Verna backed out of the parking spot and put the car in gear, hooking a hard U-turn that sent Roy and Lucy sliding. Then they were out on the open road, angling for somewhere, picking up speed. They were bound northwest, taking wide highways and tunnels, watching the sleeping resorts of Vegas slide by in the distance. Roy wasn't much of a gambler, but he would have been happy with a quiet hotel bar, someplace to watch the tourists and have a drink or three. Something familiar, cozy, something he could understand.

Instead they ended up on a barely marked off-ramp, then a side road, then hardly any road at all, the Ford growling like a mad dog as its tires chewed up the rough and spat gravel and sand in their wake. It fishtailed on a curve, swinging dangerously out of control, before Verna brought the car to heel with a confident hand.

"Pardon the bumps," she said, as a lurch in the trail made Roy's stomach drop and lifted Lucy off the glossy back seat. "I needed to stash the doorway someplace safe, out of the way. Same time, I knew Duke would send hunters. I was hoping to slow them down."

"How'd that work out?" Roy asked, one hand squeezing the armrest.

"I underestimated the competition. I mean, you've seen Roach's truck. Would you think that piece of crap could go off-road?"

"I'm not sure *this* piece of crap can go off-road," Roy said, gritting his teeth as a front wheel hit a divot with a bone-rattling slam. Verna wrinkled her nose at him.

"It's okay, baby," she said, patting the wheel. "He doesn't mean it. Get ready, folks. We're here."

Roy was about to ask *where*, but then he saw it. Dead ahead, maybe a quarter mile out and coming in hot, stood a perfectly rectangular wall of shimmering air. A heat mirage in the shape of a movie screen.

"Do you smell that?" Lucy said. "Is that...roses?"

"Brace for weirdness. Reality goes a little elastic in range of an interdimensional anomaly. A little *creative*." Verna held up a finger. "Oh. And please: keep your legs and arms inside the ride at all times."

Roy heard sizzling bacon, grease popping in a hot iron skillet, but he smelled roses. The sedan fired toward the rippling movie screen like a bullet and his vision went dark at the corners, blackness closing in, his eyes turning to tunnels. He was in the back seat, next to Lucy. He was in the front seat next to Verna. *Revisions*, a voice that wasn't his explained. *Tiny edits. Have to be consistent, or people start to notice.*

The dangling amulet glowed with more than desert sunlight. The four surviving garnets gathered light from within, shone out, and strobed across Roy's eyes, washing away what remained of the world in a ruby kaleidoscope. He sank back in his seat as the sedan took on a fresh burst of speed, powering across the desert flat, too late to stop now. The screaming engine swallowed everything but the fragmented sound of Verna's voice.

"You may feel—"
and then everything
went
sideways

Chapter Thirty-three

They had arrived.

Roy didn't remember stopping. There was nothing between a hundred miles an hour and a dead stop, nothing but a brutal jolt in the pit of his stomach and a surge of bitter bile in the back of his throat.

"Transitioning can be rough," Verna said. "If you need to—"

The back door yawned open and Lucy fell sideways, head out the door, letting out a string of wet, sputtering coughs.

"—Exactly. *Not* on my upholstery, thank you. Roy? How's your tummy? Made of steel like the rest of you?"

Verna was reaching for the amulet, which dangled from the rearview by its tarnished chain, spinning with some strange momentum all its own. She caught it between thumb and forefinger mid-twirl, stopped it cold, and took it down. Not fast enough to keep Roy from spotting the problem.

On their way across the desert, a miserly circle of garnets had ringed the outer face of the copper disk. They'd been cracked, broken, dull and dark like each one had a blob of oil injected into its heart. All but the last four; those had been shiny and pristine.

Now only one was. The other three stones had shattered down the middle, all of them tainted with that same inky blot of shadow. Roy wasn't a genius, but he could do basic math and he could draw a straight line between two points.

"Help me out," he said.

She answered him with a curious look and a bat of her eyelashes.

"Three people go across." He nodded at the amulet in her hand. "Three stones break."

"I knew you were a sharp one."

"Two people need to go back home once this job is done. One stone left. I'm not here to stay and neither is Lucy, so how are you going to make those numbers add up?"

"Not *that* sharp," she countered, though she smiled when she said it. "I'm not the only world-jumper and this isn't the only Mason's Compass. Duke collects the things. Once he called the hunt down on Lucy's head, he handed them out like candy. All we have to do is get the drop on one of his boys, relieve him of his property, and voila: passage for the both of you."

"That's an extra complication. Did you think about maybe mentioning that earlier?"

"Thought about it, sure." She curled her fingers, reached over and flicked them against his arm. "Come on, big guy. It'll be fine."

Roy thought about the twig in his pocket. And Charikleia's private warning. *I can read her. And so can you. Watch for the signs, and you'll see the setup.* Problem was, he wasn't sure what he was seeing. An innocent oversight, delivered with Verna's usual casual disregard? Or a bigger game in motion? He couldn't find a lie: Verna was right, Duke's hunters had to have their own tokens of passage. *Worst case scenario*, he thought, *I snap the twig and we bargain for the Dryad's. Or take it from her, if we have to. One Compass for Lucy, one for me, and we're homeward bound.*

Roy usually believed in going along to get along. Not much rattled his cage. All the same, he knew there were times when it was good policy to rattle somebody else's. If Verna really was planning something behind his back, it was the best way to force her into a mistake. Before she could tuck the copper medallion away, Roy plucked it from her fingers.

"I'll hang onto this," he said. "For safekeeping."

The woman wearing his dead lover's face tilted her head down and pressed one fluttery hand to her heart.

"Feels like you don't trust me, Roy. That hurts. That hurts a lot."

"You got me all wrong," he said, trying to ignore his still-queasy stomach. "I trusted you enough to come along for the ride, didn't I? But if this little thing is Lucy's ticket home, I'm guarding it the same way I'm guarding her: with everything I've got."

"All right," she said, in a tone that made him half believe her. "Fair enough. Speaking of—"

Lucy had tumbled out of the back seat sometime after her last sputtering cough, and she hadn't come back. Roy shoved his door open, palm flush against the heavy slab of steel, and his shoes touched down on cold, wet grass. He got out, stretched, and took his first breath of alien air.

It was after midnight on the other side of the gateway. He could almost see it: the shimmering movie-screen window about a hundred feet behind the idling sedan, almost invisible save for threads of gold, glimmers that brushed across his eyes before twinkling out of sight. On this side, the only light was electric. The sky was a vast, inky chasm, no stars, no moon, only the vague impressions of oil-paint smears.

He thought they were in the woods at first. Too curated for that, though, the trees too orderly, the lawns shaggy but still far from wild. A park. Gravel-lined paths swirled across the shadowed green, studded with dead lampposts and trashcans caked in scarlet riots of spray paint. And beyond the park, in every direction, filling Roy's vision as he slowly turned in place, was the city.

Skyscrapers that dwarfed the Empire State Building rose all around them, art deco monoliths in marble, granite, and glass. Jammed shoulder to shoulder, they speared up at the void of the sky, topped with chrome spikes and hammered-brass sheeting and, here and there, towering statues like remnants of ancient Greece. The statues kept watch over the endless city sprawl, along with the zeppelins that cruised over the park and drifted, slow and silent, down the wide urban canyons. Spotlights in the zeppelins' bellies carved through the darkness with beams of sizzling white light.

Lucy's voice was a shocked whisper at his back. "Do you see it?"

"Yeah," he breathed. "I see it, all right."

He took another breath. There was a faint, acrid smell on the city wind, a whiff of diesel fuel and musty, rotting trash.

"It looks just like it did when I dreamed it," Lucy said.

Verna stayed in the car. She rolled her window down, shooting a quick glance behind them.

"Switch the cause and effect," she said. "You dreamed it, which is why it looks like that."

Roy couldn't hear what Lucy said, after that. Only the last few words: "...*all of this?*"

"A rare talent," Verna said.

Lucy spun on her heel. The weight of her sudden, excited glee was enough to shatter her fear.

"I want to see it. All of it. The Parthenon, the Serpentine Wall, Golden Acre—"

Verna snickered. "Cool your jets. There'll be time if there's time, but there won't be anything left to see if we don't get moving."

"She's right," Roy said. "And eventually Duke's goon squad is going to figure out they're hunting for you on the wrong world. I don't want to be anywhere near that doorway when they all come back home."

"That's part of the danger," Verna said.

"'Part'?" Roy put one hand on his hip. "More complications you didn't bother mentioning?"

"Just the one you already should have known about if you read Lucy's funny-books. Duke Ellery's a big boss in this town. But he's not the only boss. By now, if the wind's been blowing and mouths have been yapping—like they always do—the competition knows he's making a power move. Which means we need to get out of Eden Park before—"

The ear-shattering roar of afterburners swallowed her voice and sent Roy staggering back, throwing a hand over his eyes to cut the sudden blinding glare and waves of breath-stealing heat. The sound and fury vanished as suddenly as it began, ending with the bone-jarring crash of a ten-foot monolith slamming down to earth. Roy squinted, dazed, trying to make sense of the thing towering over him.

It was a robot, or a person wearing a robot suit, built like a brick and nearly as wide as it was tall. Three blazing red eyes burned from the squat dome of its head, and emerald bulbs traced a jagged lightning-bolt pattern down its chest like stitching on a corpse. Long sinuous strips of supple black leather wrapped the machine's piston-like limbs, crisscrossing over the rusty, pitted metal hull. More leather cord bound the suit in an elaborate harness web, joined by rings of hammered brass.

Pneumatics hissed as the machine twirled an arm that ended in a brutal steel crab claw. It gripped the haft of a sledgehammer too big for any mortal person to lift, let alone swing. It had a long leather-wrapped handle and a massive iron head, flat on one side and honed to a lethal point on the other.

"This guy," Roy said, "was *not* in the comics I read."

Lucy's feet dragged in the grass as she took an uneasy step back.

"My plan for the second major story arc," she whispered. "Duke Ellery's gang goes to war against the East Side Mob. The Midnight Jury had to stop the feud before it consumed the entire city. I never actually got to write it. Just notes."

"And dreams. Big dreams. Right."

A voice boomed from the machine's dome head, the three red eyes strobing in time with the metallic, clicking consonants. "Verna Bell. You are making news tonight. Duke Ellery has put quite the bounty on your head."

Verna leaned out the open window of the sedan, one arm propped on the sill, and looked up at him.

"Don't think you'll be able to collect it, considering he's got one out on you, too. You and the rest of the East Side boys. How about we agree to share a common enemy?"

"Under normal circumstances, perhaps."

The machine swiveled on its rusted torso, ball-jointed like a kid's action figure blown up to nightmare proportions, and focused its glowing eyes on Lucy. Its claw grip spun, twirling the mammoth hammer and bringing the haft to rest against its other hand.

"But these are not normal circumstances. Are they, Lucy Langenkamp?"

"Somebody want to introduce me?" Roy said, getting between them.

"Roy," Verna said, "meet Doktor Impakt. He kills people for money."

"Yeah. That part I could have guessed."

Roy's hand patted his pocket, looking for the comfortable weight of his tactical baton. But it was long gone, abandoned a world away from here, and he didn't have any secret weapons.

"I will take the girl now," the machine announced, as casual as discussing the weather. "You two are of no consequence to me. Stand aside and live. Or obstruct me and die. Your choice is binary."

Maybe Roy did have one little trick. Taking a deep breath, he stood his ground in the towering machine's shadow.

"Don't think so," he said.

Doktor Impakt froze for a moment. Roy still wasn't sure if it was a robot or a suit for a human pilot, but either way, the logic driving the thing wasn't prepared for defiance. He tried not to flinch as the helmet's third eye projected a paper-thin slice of ruby light that sizzled up and down his body, leaving tingling skin in its wake as it studied him from head to toe.

"Weapons scan: negative. Augments scan: negative. Occult-technology scan shows only trace readings of six known energy sources, all acquired through ambient exposure and currently fading."

It lifted one rusty, leather-wrapped leg piston and then brought it slamming down, a piledriver blow that left a crater in the mangled soil.

"You," the machine said, "are defenseless."

"Am I?" he asked. "You sure about that? Because you're a ten-foot-tall Goliath with a sledgehammer, and I've got nothing on me but a dead phone and an empty wallet. Yet here I am. So let me ask you something: am I just crazy, or is there something you missed? Think it over, because you don't want to be wrong."

The last time Roy used this bluff, he was digging for clues in the bowels of an outlaw biker bar. It had worked, too; six guys had him dead to rights with his back against the wall, but none of them wanted to be the first to find out if Roy was some kind of ninja master or if he had a derringer up his sleeve.

Doktor Impakt stood silent for a long three-second count. Then it whirred to life, straightening its back.

"I ran a probability analysis," the machine told him. "Ninety-eight-point-seven percent chance of a bluff. Ninety-three-point-two percent odds that I am effectively immune to small arms fire from your world's weapons, even if you did manage to smuggle something that eludes my sensors. Zero-point-zero-three percent chance of you possessing undetectable occult capabilities."

The machine's crab claws gripped the hammer and raised it high.

"All probabilities are well within risk tolerance settings. Prepare to die."

Chapter Thirty-four

In all the times Roy contemplated his own mortality, all the ways he imagined he might go out in the end, "crushed to death by a sledgehammer-wielding robot" had never come up once. As Doktor Impakt lifted its weapon high above the three-eyed dome of its head, the pointed side of the hammer poised for a killing blow, Verna fired up the sedan's engine.

"Lucy," Roy said, taking a quick step to the side, "get in. Go with Verna."

"I'm not leaving you—"

"I'll lose him in the trees and catch up with you later. *Go.*"

It was a benevolent kind of lie, the kind you tell when you're all out of options. He figured his odds of outrunning this monster were on par with his odds of winning a marathon. He hadn't trained for either race, and the competition was miles out of his league. All he could really do was buy Lucy some time and help her get away. That'd have to be enough.

Lucy was still frozen, torn between Roy and the open back door of Verna's car. Verna shouted for her. Roy needed to keep the machine's attention. He jogged right, sidestepping, keeping the three scarlet eyes fixed on him. He knew he was giving it a perfect angle of attack, that one sweep of that mammoth hammer would leave him crushed, dead or dying. No other choice. He braced himself, bending his legs for one last-ditch leap for survival.

Firecrackers erupted in the dark.

White-hot sparks blossomed along the dome of the machine's head, leaving scorch marks on the pitted, rusty metal. Pneumatics hissed as Doktor Impakt spun, surprised, looking past Roy—and above him. A new arrival stood in the trees, perched like a bird of prey at the end of a long, gnarled limb. For a fleeting second, Roy felt the thrill of hope. In a comic book this would be the moment when the hero returned in long-awaited triumph, there to save the day.

His heart sank. It wasn't the Midnight Jury, and he wasn't here to save them. Roy recognized him from the comics: the ragged ghost-gray overcoat, the leering ivory skull mask, the custom-made rifle cradled in slick black gloves.

"Trigger Mortis," the machine droned. Roy heard clear tones of derision in its modulated voice. "Here to carry out your master's bidding, like an obedient dog?"

Trigger's voice was a ghastly, cold whisper. "Doktor. Still running with East Side trash. Only ones who will have you. *Heh*. Should leave the city, might find gainful employment in a smaller town. Lower standards there."

"Your disdain obscures your logic. I am made of dark alloys, and bulletproof. You are made of meat, and not hammer-proof. I will come out the victor in any projected confrontation between us."

"You mean my opening shots?" Trigger popped the magazine from his rifle, tossing it down to the wet grass far below his perch. He yanked a replacement from his belt and locked it in, slinging the rifle's bolt back. "Heh. Just to get your attention. Now, these...these are *real* bullets. Cooked 'em just for you."

Roy dove, hitting the grass and rolling, as a second salvo ripped through the air. The three-round burst plowed into Doktor Impakt's chest, digging potholes in the rusty metal and chewing up his buckled leather shroud. The shells detonated on impact with ear-clapping eruptions and flares of light that left burning streaks across Roy's vision. He got to his hands and knees and scrambled, crawling fast, another burst whining just over his head and drawing a line of craters up one of the machine's piston-legs. It stumbled back, bleeding oil and spitting sparks.

Doktor Impakt brandished the hammer in one pincer and freed the other, stretching out its gimbaled metal arm. A long, narrow compartment in its right shoulder hissed open.

A buzzsaw blade fired from the slot, screeching as it blazed through the air. The shot went wide, carving into the treetops and spinning wild, trailing fallen leaves and branches in its wake. A second blade, right on its heels, shredded Trigger's perch and turned it into a blizzard of splinters. The assassin leaped farther and faster than any normal human could, firing another burst from his rifle one-handed in midair. His open glove caught another thick branch and he yanked himself upward, landing in a crouch, still high in the twisted boughs.

"I have more bullets than you have blades," he called down.

"More bullets than I have blades: probability ninety-nine percent. More bullets than I have methods of killing you: probability laughable."

Roy didn't care who won this fight as long as he, Lucy, and Verna were long gone by the time the dust settled. Still crawling, he clambered into the front passenger seat of Verna's car, one hand fumbling to yank the door shut behind him. He told her to drive but she was already doing it, stomping on the gas, her showboat sedan fishtailing as it kicked up clods of grass and mud. The tires caught traction and they were off like a rocket, the sudden speed shoving them back against the slick vinyl seats.

A tooth-rattling bass thrum, like a wall of concert speakers all throbbing to life at maximum volume, split the air behind them. Roy squeezed his eyes shut against a lance of burning light, a roiling spotlight inferno like a tube of hot lava. It boiled through the air, crashed into a tree and lit it up like a Roman candle. He barely made out the silhouette of Trigger Mortis, somersaulting in midair, springing for another safe perch with the flames roaring at his back.

"The robot monster has laser cannons," Roy said. He looked back at Lucy. "You gave it *laser cannons*."

"In my defense—" she started to say.

"Save it," Verna said, eyes fixed on the rolling lawns ahead. "The only question is, who does he want more: Trigger, or us?"

The ferocious slam of heavy metal footsteps behind them, like a tank on two legs, answered the question. More buzzsaws screeched after them, guttering into the soil and spinning away as Doktor Impakt aimed for their tires. Trigger, racing along the trees and jumping from branch to branch, offered a counterpoint beat with the pinpoint percussion of his rifle. Sparks erupted from the machine's domed head and one of its three scarlet eyes sputtered out, cold and dead.

"Not even slowing down," Roy said, looking back over his shoulder. He turned to Verna. "Can Trigger stop that thing?"

She thought about it, lips pursed, and gave a tiny shake of her head.

"The problem isn't 'can he stop it.' The problem is that Trigger Mortis is one of Duke's right-hand men."

Lucy sank low in the back seat, keeping her head down and her feet braced. "No matter which one of them catches up to us, we're in big trouble."

"So we don't get caught," Verna said. "Hang on."

She cornered hard and wove between the trees, driving reckless and fast down a tight path built for foot traffic. Cobblestones rattled under the tires, bouncing and jolting them from side to side, the car threatening to spin out of control. Verna handled the beast like a Formula One racer, but she couldn't shake their pursuers. Doktor Impakt and Trigger were close behind them, the machine thundering through the brush while the skull-masked killer flitted, weightless, through the treetops. While they took occasional potshots at one another, now both hunters were more intent on catching up to the fleeing sedan.

Lucy blinked. She leaned forward between the two front seats and craned her neck toward the sloping lawns dead ahead.

"We're heading east," she said.

Verna shot her a sidelong glance. "So?"

"Leave the park by the Thirteenth Avenue exit and take a sharp right."

A buzzsaw chewed into the back bumper, screaming like a dentist's drill. It dug a scar across the thick steel and spun off into the grass. Verna cursed under her breath and yanked the wheel, veering down the hard, steep slope of the lawn. The sedan bottomed out with a stomach-lurching *thump* at the bottom of the slope, driving Roy's heart into his throat.

"How do you know?" he managed to ask Lucy. "Don't tell me you've got this whole city memorized."

"Not a chance, it's way too big. But I know where the landmarks are. Important places. Story places. It's...hard to explain. It's like an instinct. I don't know how I know—"

"But you know," Verna said.

Roy looked back. "So what's the plan?"

"We can't fight," Lucy said. "So we have to lose them, and for that we need a big distraction. I think I might have one."

Chapter Thirty-five

The park's east gate wasn't built for cars.

Two stout pillars dressed in copper sheeting, coated in blue-green patina, rose up to an arch that dripped with weeping-willow vines. Wrought-iron lettering spelled out *Eden Park* in delicate calligraphy, ten feet above a pathway just wide enough for a few pedestrians to pass side by side. Black metal fencing spanned along the park's perimeter in both directions, no way out and no way through.

"We won't make it," Roy said.

Verna's upper lip twitched, curling into a snarl. "I know my car."

"I know *physics*. You're not going to make it."

Thunder echoed at their backs above the roar of the engine as Doktor Impakt stomped in relentless pursuit. Trigger was still weightless, inhumanly light and fast, running along the treetops and firing off three-round bursts that rattled through the dark.

Verna aimed the sedan straight for the narrow opening. Then she stepped on the gas.

The Ford shot through the gate like a bullet, slamming the passengers back in their seats as the side mirrors hit the pillars, shearing off, leaving dangling wires and jagged metal behind. The left pillar scraped the side of the car with a sound like a jackhammer and gutted the powder-blue paint, drawing claw marks along bare steel. Then they were through, and free, and on Thirteenth Avenue. Six lanes of traffic, all one-way and southbound, the rain-slicked streets cast in the shadow of impossibly tall skyscrapers.

Verna lurched the wheel right, leaning into it, throwing Roy and Lucy sideways as the wounded sedan went into a slide. It began to lift, threatening to roll, then slammed back down to earth as Verna veered into the center lane. A truck horn blared behind them and a yellow checkered cab swerved, missing them by inches. She kept driving, darting in and out of her lane, muscling through the sluggish traffic.

Behind them, Doktor Impakt hit the gate shoulder-first and destroyed it in a storm of stone and copper scraps, a shotgun spray of debris that shattered windows and blew out headlights all across the boulevard.

The robot skidded to a stop and turned on its heel, thudding along the sidewalk. Trigger Mortis was right behind it. The skull-masked assassin leaped from the park fence to the roof of a delivery truck, running down the hood and launching himself through the air in a twisting somersault, jumping from car to car with his rifle in hand.

"Left on LeFay Drive," Lucy said.

Verna met Lucy's eyes in the glass of the rearview mirror and answered with a nod. Roy looked back and forth between them.

"What's on LeFay?" he asked.

He got his answer as Verna pulled a fast left turn at the next stoplight, shoving him against the car door. Ahead on the right was a fortress of cold, towering stone, an art deco dream of a medieval tower, bristling with cameras and cast in the roving spotlight of a surveillance blimp. Bulbous black-and-white squad cars with domed rooftop lights, so old they would have been antiques in Roy's world, lined a curving driveway out front.

"Sixty-Eighth Precinct House," Verna said.

Just ahead, one of the cruisers was pulling out. Verna waited until the last second and yanked the wheel, side-swiping the police car with a bone-rattling jolt and the sound of metal being crushed like a soda can. The car's front bumper tore off, rolling along the street. Its dome light flicked on, strobing volcano-red as it spun beneath the tinted glass, and a siren split the air. More cops boiled out of the stationhouse, grabbing their hats and sprinting for their cars.

Doktor Impakt slid sideways at the intersection, one metal piston-foot gouging a broken trench in the pavement. The machine swept its massive sledgehammer back in its lobster-claw grip, raising it high and launching into a charge. Verna swerved and sped up, daring the squad car to chase her—and putting it squarely in the monster's path. The hammer came down on the car's trunk hard enough to lift its front wheels off the ground, crushing the back of the squad car and blowing out its rear window.

Gunfire peppered the machine's hull, throwing off sparks, barely scuffing it. They were answered by big, throaty booms from above. Trigger was perched on the tip of a dead streetlamp, feet tight and knees bent like a bird of prey. He turned his sights on the precinct house, sending cops scattering and diving behind their cars for shelter with a steady stream of bullets.

The stoplight up ahead strobed from green to amber. Verna blew through the intersection, leaving the battle behind. The sounds of gunshots, of screams and tortured metal, chased them through the dark.

"That should keep 'em busy for a while," Verna said.

Roy sank in his seat and let out a gust of breath.

They left the big open boulevards and bright lights behind and drove into the warrens. The streets narrowed, sometimes two uneven lanes divided by spatters of white paint, sometimes a single-car road no bigger than an alley, intersections marked by flashing stoplights and battered aluminum signs coated in graffiti. The concrete canyons still towered around them, but the towers' art deco glory had faded with neglect. These were nothing but hives for human beings, pockmarked with cracked windows and pinned-up sheets.

Down at street level, trashcan fires pushed back the cold. Most of the shops were locked down for the night, armored with steel shutters. Those that remained offered to satisfy a smattering of hungers and sins. Neon signs flashed curvy silhouettes, painting the rainy street in purple and hot pink, promising live sex shows and more. Gin mills and gambling dens jostled for space with peepshows and places whose purpose Roy could only guess at from the arcane symbols and dark bronze letters in ancient Greek nailed over the doors. A video store was open on the corner, electric light flickering behind a wire-covered window. All of the movie posters on display promised violent thrills, power drills and razors and gushing blood, and Roy wasn't entirely sure the blood was fake. An entire city woven from dreams and nightmares.

"Lucy," he said.

Her voice drifted up from the back seat. Hazy, soft, like she was lost in a dream.

"Yeah."

"You were...young, when you made this place," he said. Fumbling around what he wanted to say, the question he wanted to ask.

"I spent a lot of time being scared," she said. "When you're small, the world is so big, filled with wonders and terrors, and nothing makes any sense. Then you get a little older. Old enough that the world notices you. It's different, when you're a girl. The world notices you, and it wants things. It wants things from you before you're old enough to understand and sometimes it just..."

Her voice trailed off. Roy gave her time, held his silence.

"There was supposed to a hero here," she said. "A protector."

Roy spotted tiny bits of hope in the shadows. A soup kitchen, open through the night, serving a line of ragged, hungry wanderers under the light of a purple neon cross. A neighborhood clinic, lights still burning, tending to the sick and injured. A little hope. Just enough to keep going.

"Lucy?" he said.

"Yeah."

"Did somebody hurt you?"

She didn't answer him. She shifted in the back seat, vinyl rustling.

"Verna?" she said.

"Yeah, babe?"

"Tell me the truth. What happened to the Midnight Jury?"

Verna sighed. She drummed her fingers on the steering wheel.

"Best you see for yourself. We're almost there. Oswald Heights is dead ahead. Careful when we get out of the car. That part of town isn't high-scale and classy like this one."

Oswald Heights was a graveyard. A snarl of skyscraper corpses under a muddy sky, where the streetlights were bent and battered along avenues lined with the burned-out husks of old cars. Verna pulled into a vacant lot, tires rumbling over shards of glass, and killed the ignition.

The tower next door had been grand, once. Roy could see hints of past luxury, from the gargoyles guarding the dirty granite outcroppings to the empty sconces flanking the lobby walls. They walked along a grimy black-and-white checkerboard floor to the elevators. Verna tapped a button. It didn't light up, but they heard the reluctant groan of an engine and the rattle of chains.

"Maybe we should take the stairs," Roy said.

Verna gave him the side-eye. "We're headed for the eighty-third floor. You don't want to take the stairs."

She had a point. They waited for the elevator, breathing the musty, dead air, until the door juddered open to reveal a mirror-walled cage. The warped mirrors threw off carnival reflections, the glass slashed and fractured. Roy noticed flecks of dried blood here and there, as if one of the tenants had thrown their bare knuckles at their own distorted face.

The elevator managed to wheeze its way up to eighty-three, doors opening onto a hallway lit by a single bulb in a leaning wall sconce. Dust caked the floor, the old tile scuffed and worn, and a string of pebbled-glass doors with scraped-away lettering told the tale of an office building in sharp decline.

At the far end of the hallway, one tenant remained. Soft light bloomed behind the pebbled glass. Black block letters on the window advertised the current occupant.

Danielle Faust Investigations. Private Inquiries, Occult Consultations, Discretion Assured.

"Well," Verna said. "Here we are."

Chapter Thirty-six

Verna knocked on the pebbled glass. They waited.

Eventually a silhouette, shambling behind the glass, approached. The door swung open.

The woman on the other side was in her late thirties, with curly chestnut hair, messy bangs, and tired eyes. She wore a long black blazer over a corset top, and fishnets traced the distance between the hem of her miniskirt and the rolled cuffs of her leather boots. She held a half-empty bottle by the neck. Some kind of hard liquor, deep brown and dirty, with a label that read *Ole Possum*.

"Hi," Verna said.

The door slammed shut. A lock clicked on the other side. Then a deadbolt slid into place. And another lock.

Verna pounded on the door as the woman, back to a blurry silhouette behind the glass, stalked out of sight.

"Come on, Danielle," she called out. "I wouldn't have come here if it wasn't important."

"Not important to me," said the voice on the other side of the door.

"You don't even know why I'm here."

"I know that I don't care."

"There's somebody you need to meet," Verna said, leaning close to the door.

"Not taking any appointments tonight. See, I'm drunk, and yet not drunk enough. The answer to this paradox may only be found at the bottom of this bottle of hooch, and I'm in hot pursuit of the truth."

"You used to call me when you were on the sauce."

"I call everybody when I'm drunk, mostly ex-boyfriends. It's because I'm desperately trying to get laid and I take great pleasure in making horrible, self-sabotaging life choices that I'll regret in the morning. Now *go away*."

While they argued through the glass, Roy gently tugged at Lucy's sleeve, pulling her back to the opposite wall. He lowered his voice to a near-whisper.

"Are...we in the right place? That can't be—"

"The Jury?" Lucy stared at the door, her gaze distant, thoughtful. "Yes. That's her. I can feel it."

"Hell. Sorry, kid. You know what they say, about never meeting your heroes. Let's get out of here."

Lucy kept staring. Gears moving behind her eyes, putting things together.

"Not yet," she said.

"Pardon me," Verna called out. "I thought you might be interested in saving the world before we all shuffle off for the long nap."

The voice from the other side let out a bitter laugh. "Saving the world? Even at my best I was never that good, and it's been a long, long time since I've been naive enough to think otherwise."

"Like I said, I brought someone you need to meet."

Lucy moved toward the doorway. Slow, ginger steps, her breath shallow, eyes wide.

"Danielle?" she called out. "My name is Lucy."

"Good for you."

"I wrote you."

Dead silence on the other side.

"I wrote...all of this," Lucy said. "And I know it's all falling apart, but I think we can fix it. If we work together."

Verna put her arm around Lucy's shoulder. "You hear that, Dani? I brought God. Never say I'm not helpful."

Locks flipped. The door opened, just a crack.

"You'd better not be fucking with me right now," Danielle said.

Verna shrugged, nonchalant. "So can we come in, or what?"

The office was a shambles, barely holding itself together, a mirror of its owner. Yellowed newspaper clippings drooped from a corkboard over a credenza cluttered with old, dusty books and empty bottles of hard liquor. A few more dead soldiers clustered in one corner of a desk, the bottles catching the amber light from a buzzing, flickering lamp. Danielle had only three mismatched chairs and a fold-out bed. Roy took one look at the rumpled, moth-eaten blankets and decided to stand in the corner instead.

While Danielle fished a bottle of gin from her bottom desk drawer, Verna and Lucy took turns laying down the facts. Roy noticed the way the woman perked up. Once she pushed past her initial reluctance to hear them out—*Suppose I'd feel the same*, he thought, *if someone told me I was a fictional character*—she scooped up a spiral pad and a stub of a pencil and started making notes. She held her silence, listening, then peppered her guests with pointed questions. Roy still didn't buy her as any kind of a heroine, but she had a detective's instincts and an interrogator's sense of timing.

The clippings on the wall confirmed his hunch. Old memories of old glories, with headlines like *Psychic Shocker! Hero Cop Battles Ghosts at Museum of Industry!*

"—so in conclusion," Danielle said, closing her notebook with a flip of the wrist, "we live in a goddamn comic book."

"It wasn't just a comic," Lucy said. "I started dreaming about this place, about you, when I was a little girl. I think the comic just helped it to last longer. Verna says that most—what did you call them? Refractions? Most refractions fall apart right away."

Verna nodded. "Hours, days, weeks at most. We're the rare refraction that actually goes the distance."

"*Went* the distance, in case you haven't been watching the news," Danielle said.

"We can still turn things around," Verna said. "I hired another writer from Lucy's world to try and patch things up. It didn't work, but it held the refraction together long enough for me to find Lucy and bring her across. And it's a damn good thing I did, because Duke wants her like a sailor wants shore leave."

"So she can, what, wave a magic pen around and fill the world with unicorns and rainbows? I don't see what that has to do with me." She fixed Lucy with a hard-eyed stare. "You do realize that every lousy thing that happened in my life is *your fault*, right?"

Lucy slid down in her chair, shrinking, her shoulders tight.

"I didn't— I didn't even know you were real. It was just stories I told myself in the dark, to make myself feel better."

"Every time I got the shit knocked out of me, every time I almost died, every time my reward for saving the day was a kick in the teeth—"

"Hey." Roy stood behind Lucy's chair. He put a hand on her shoulder. "You heard her. She didn't know. Cut the kid some slack."

Danielle sank into a sullen silence, taking a long pull from her bottle of gin.

Roy nodded over at the newspaper clippings. "You were on the job, once?"

"Sure." Danielle held her bottle by the neck, swirling it around. "Was going to help people. Make a difference. Make this city a better place."

"Me, too," he said.

She looked up at him. "How'd that work out for you? Nah. You don't even have to tell me. What do you do now, besides stand around and look ominous?"

"Still trying to help. The badge just weighed me down."

Danielle showed her teeth. "I got disillusioned, fast. Half the cops I knew were on the take, and the other half were too afraid to say jack about it. So I put on the coat and fedora and picked up the guns. I wasn't the first vigilante this burg's ever seen, but I made a hell of a splash."

"But why did you stop?" Lucy asked.

Danielle eyed her like she was sizing her creator for a noose. She started to say something, caught herself, swallowed her own acid and took a deep breath. When she spoke again, her words drifted out on an edge of raw exhaustion.

"Because nothing ever changed."

"But you helped people. You saved lives, you stopped the bad guys—"

"Know what I did? Triage. Triage for a city that was gut-shot and bleeding long before nature decided to turn sideways. I save a store clerk from an armed robbery, another gun goes off a block away. I hand over a crook on a silver platter, and he's out of jail by sunset. And don't get me started on the *real* bad guys. I've lost count how many times I've rounded up every single member of my little rogues' gallery, up to and including Duke Ellery. Either they spring loose on a 'legal technicality'—a technicality that, I swear to you, *did not exist until that moment*—or they break out of Corum Asylum so fast it's like the place has a revolving door out front."

Danielle slumped in her chair. She swiveled to one side, fixing her thousand-yard-stare at the wall over her fold-out bed. Homing in on a memory.

"I stared death in the eye every single night, and the best I could do was break even. Then came one...one particular night. Roach had been hired to take out this poor loser, some parking lot attendant who saw something he shouldn't have. I got there too late. Stopped Roach, but...there wasn't anything left to save, just this smoking ruin that used to be a human being. Roach laughed at me. Said he was ready to go back to the nuthouse, because he got paid in advance."

She cocked her fingers into an imaginary gun.

"I was tired. And I was done. So I shot him. I shot that son of a bitch right between the eyes."

Lucy squinted, not following. "But you couldn't have, he came after us—"

"He came back," Danielle said, suddenly fervent, leaning forward in her chair. "The bastard was dead and buried, and *he came back*. I asked how. He babbled some nonsense about 'ancient mystical secrets' but if you ask me, I don't think he had a goddamn clue."

Danielle slapped her bottle down on the desk.

"That was it. That's when I knew I was in hell. All I could do was tread water, forever. Or get out of the game entirely. Let somebody else save the day for once. I put away the coat, the hat, the scarf and the guns, and hung out my shingle as a civilian. Long as nobody ever connects me to that life, I'm safe. The Midnight Jury is dead. Rest in peace."

"But the dead can come back," Verna said.

"Not this corpse. I'm never putting on that costume again, and the only piece I carry is a very *non*-magical revolver. Legally licensed and everything. Whatever your grand plan for saving the world is, I hope it doesn't involve the Jury. Because if it does, you can hit the bricks right now. I'm not interested."

Chapter Thirty-seven

"Verna's not lying to us," Lucy said.

"You sure about that?"

"She's just...wrong."

She and Roy had stepped outside, out into the hall lined with empty, darkened doorways and scraped-away names, while Verna and Danielle argued it out. Verna wasn't winning, either; the former heroine was digging her heels in, hard enough to gouge trenches in the cheap linoleum.

"I'm inclined to agree." Roy cast a narrow-eyed look at the office door. "This was a waste of time. We should find out if we can scrounge this 'magic book' up on our own, and fast, or we should see about getting another one of those compass gadgets and going back through the gateway before this entire place falls apart."

Lucy shook her head. "That's not what I'm saying."

"What's on your mind?"

"Verna thinks I'm the key, because I—my weird brain, some part of me I don't understand—made this world, right? But the last time I invested any real energy into it was in college, when I was writing the comic books."

"You got discouraged," Roy said. "Understandable, after the way the publisher went belly-up without so much as a wave goodbye."

"But the troubles this world is having..." Lucy's brow furrowed and she looked to one side, thinking. "They're more recent. Look, what does all of the source material—my dreams as a kid, the comics, the book Carolyn Saunders wrote—what does it all have in common?"

Not a hard question. Roy nodded to the pebbled glass window. "Her."

"I'm not the center of this world. *She* is. The Midnight Jury isn't just the city's protector; she's the main character. The star of the show. I never even wrote any background about— Wait a second."

She opened the office door. Verna and Danielle, battling it out across her desk, froze in mid-argument and looked her way.

"Hey," Lucy said, "what's *outside* Noir York?"

Verna looked at her like she didn't quite follow. Her moment of confusion quickly turned to practiced apathy. "Who cares? Everybody who's anybody lives in the city. We've got everything you need right here, and no reason to ever leave."

"I left," Danielle said. "Once. Recently. It was for a job."

"You went to Stettle," Lucy said.

Danielle squinted at her. "How'd you know?"

"Hold that thought."

Lucy shut the door and turned back to Roy.

"I know, because Stettle is the only town outside the city I ever named. I needed it for a side story, just a throwaway reference in a line of dialog. I looked at a map, saw Seattle, and played with the spelling. For all intents and purposes there's nothing outside the city, because there doesn't need to be. The Midnight Jury lives here, and she's the star of the show."

"The Midnight Jury," Roy said, "is a burned-out drunk. And I think she's high on more than cheap booze."

"Why do you think that?"

He pointed to his eyes. "I'm a recovering addict. Functional word is recovering, not recovered. Spend enough time in the gutter and you learn to spot a fellow junkie from a mile away. They can try to bluff, but they've all got tells. Same ones you see whenever you look in the mirror."

"All the same," Lucy said, "I think Verna's wrong. We don't need me. We need *her*. This entire world is a story, and the Midnight Jury is the main character. Without the main character, there's no story. No story..."

She clasped her hands together, then pulled them apart, letting them drift down to her sides.

"...everything falls apart."

"Sounds like she's hell-bent on quitting the job," Roy said.

"The alternative is the end of everything. Literally everything. This world will crumble until there's nothing left."

"I'm not sure that's going to be enough incentive."

"We have to try." Lucy lifted her chin and pushed her shoulders back. "Danielle was right about one thing. This *is* my fault."

"You didn't know. You couldn't have known."

"I'm not saying I was malicious or that I wanted anyone to get hurt. But I created this world, and that makes me responsible for it. I have to find a way to get Danielle cleaned up and back in action. And fast."

Roy gave her a dubious look.

"Back in action? Maybe with a gun to her head," Roy told her. "But she's only going to get clean when she wants to get clean. She'll probably have to hit rock bottom first. God knows I did."

"This looks like rock bottom to me."

"Kid," Roy said, with a faint sad smile in his eyes, "you've never been there."

"All the same. I have to try."

He raised his open palms. "It's your party. I don't like the odds of salvaging a happy ending out of this mess, but that's nothing new."

"You should go," she said. "Take the compass and head back to our world. Verna can help me get another one, and that way...that way, if I stay too long and can't make it back, at least one of us will be safe."

Roy took the amulet from his pocket. His fingertip glided along the ring of burnt-out, cracked garnets, only one pure stone remaining.

"First of all," he said, "this has your name on it, not mine. If we've got to beat down one of Duke's weird-ass gangsters and take their magic doohickey, I think I'm a little more fit for the job than you are, no offense."

"None taken."

"Second of all, just because I don't like our odds doesn't mean I'm not all in. I don't think much of your heroine in there, but I believe in *you*." He slipped the amulet back into his hip pocket. "Besides, now that I've gotten a good look at this place, if I left you alone here I'd never sleep right again."

"You read the comics."

"It's different in the flesh. So. Got a plan?"

"Little bit," Lucy said.

"I'll follow your lead."

"Compromise," Danielle echoed, staring at Lucy like she didn't know the meaning of the word.

"You don't have to put on the coat or pick up the guns—"

"Good. Made my feelings on that pretty clear, I think."

Verna gave Lucy a tiny nod. The look in her eyes was confirmation: she'd tried her best, and at least for now, Danielle wasn't budging.

"—but," Lucy said, "you can still help us, just the way you are. You do detective work now, right?"

"She's a magic detective," Verna said.

"I am not, and don't call me that." Danielle shot her a sidelong glare. "We've discussed this."

"When you do jobs for people, do you do magic?" Verna asked.

"Well, yeah, but—"

"And these jobs. Do they require investigation? Research? Perhaps looking for clues and assembling those clues in the correct order?"

Danielle squirmed in her chair. "Well, yeah, but that's not the—"

Verna dropped an envelope on the desk. It landed with a soft thump, half-covering a ring of dried bourbon.

"You're a magic detective," she said. "Take my money."

Danielle's eyes turned suspicious, hard, looking from Verna to Lucy and back again.

"What's the job?"

"Verna says there's this book, it's called the Argisene Grimoire, and it's connected to other worlds."

Verna nodded. "I think that with the spells in that little powerhouse and Lucy's natural talents, we might be able to strengthen this refraction. Keep our world chugging along and breathing, for a few more years at least. For decades or even longer, if we're really lucky."

Danielle sank into a contemplative silence. She measured out the time with a long, deep pull from her bottle of gin.

"What?" Verna said.

"I don't need detective skills for that. I know exactly where the Argisene is."

She stared at her empty bottle and set it aside.

"I stole it last month."

"You have it here?" Lucy said, eyes wide.

"I said I stole it, not that I have it. It was a commission thing. That trip to Stettle I mentioned. Weird goddamn job, too."

"How so?" Lucy asked.

"For starters, I can't remember who I stole it from. And no, I wasn't on a bender." She paused. "I mean, yes I was, but not the kind where you black out for three days straight. I remember...an office building, and something hunting me down. And when I looked out a window, there was only one moon in the sky."

"Sounds like you were hallucinating," Verna said.

"It's that damn relic. The Argisene isn't your ordinary everyday book of black magic. On the train ride home, it whispered to me. Made everything...hazy, like the world was shifting all around me and I couldn't put my finger on how or why. Dream logic, you know? I kept it locked up tight and made the handoff as fast as I could, just to get rid of the thing."

Verna slid forward, perched at the edge of her seat. "Where is it now?"

Roy couldn't miss the hunger in her voice. *There are three addicts in this room*, he thought. *And whatever's between the covers of that magic book, it's your favorite vice.*

Didn't mean she wasn't on the level. If his own world were falling apart and he'd believed the Argisene Grimoire was the only way to stop the collapse, he'd be motivated too.

Motivated. But he knew from personal experience that *motivated* and *hungry* were two very different things.

"You ever meet Declerc?" Danielle said. "That loremonger who lives out on Crown Point."

Verna tapped her chin, thinking. "Went to a party at his place with Duke once, if I remember right. Gray hair, ponytail, heavyset?"

"That's him. He got a line on the Argisene's location, but he's not much for getting his hands dirty. That was my job. The good news is, Declerc hoards books like a dragon hoards gold. He wouldn't have passed it on to anyone else. The Argisene Grimoire is sitting in his library, right this minute, in a place of pride. All we have to do is roll on over and pick it up."

"What's the bad news?" Lucy asked.

Danielle rose from her chair, remarkably steady considering how much they'd watched her drink over the last half hour or so. She reached for a shoulder holster, the full-grain cowhide dangling from the peg of a coat rack by the office door.

"Bad news is, he won't give it up willingly. And instead of flaming breath, this particular dragon has lots of dirty cash, a very impressive arsenal, and the Crown Point cops in his pocket. Come on. I want to go and get it over with, before I sober up and realize how incredibly dangerous this is. In fact, grab that bottle off my desk for the road. No, the other one. The one with booze in it."

"I'm driving," Verna said.

"Suit yourself."

Chapter Thirty-eight

Danielle cast a gimlet eye at Verna's Ford, with its sheared-off side mirrors and the tiger-claw furrows in the steel, and shot her a look across the hood.

"What'd you do to your ride?"

"Drove it through the Eden Park gate," Verna said.

"That thing's wide enough for three buses side by side."

"Not the car gate. The pedestrian gate."

"I would have used the main road, but you've got a personal sense of style and I respect that."

They rode up front. Roy and Lucy got in back, trying to keep their balance on the slick vinyl seats as Verna pulled back onto the gutted, broken streets of Oswald Heights.

"Take the tunnel," Danielle said. "It's faster this time of night."

Verna shook her head. "The Garza is a shorter trip and the traffic thins out after ten."

"You're nuts. Tunnel's a straight shot to Crown Point."

Lucy leaned forward in her seat, poking her head between them.

"Take the Cornelius Bridge to Fifty-Third Street, then go north on Crown Point Drive," she said. "You save time and you skip the construction in the tunnel."

Danielle looked at Verna. Verna shrugged.

"You," Danielle said into the rearview mirror, "are doing a fantastic job of getting on my nerves. Great work. Keep it up, really."

All the same, Roy noticed, when they rolled up to a bullet-riddled sign pointing east for the bridge, Verna flicked her turn signal on. She had more faith in her creator than Danielle did.

And considering they needed Danielle to hear Lucy out, see things her way, and go back to her old role in the story before this entire planet fell to pieces, that was a problem. Roy thought about the twig Charikleia had given him, plucked from her own body and pregnant with summoning-sap. At some point, and probably sooner than later, they were going to need to consider alternate options.

He would need to, anyway. He had no doubt Lucy would stick it out to the bitter end and go down with the ship she'd built with her dreams. Maybe out of duty, maybe out of guilt, maybe out of some greater nobility that Roy could barely understand. He respected that.

He respected it, but the way he saw things, he had one and only one responsibility here: keeping Lucy alive. And if that meant dragging her out of here while the world collapsed right behind them, so be it. The magic compass in his pocket was only good for one ticket home. He quietly moved "finding a second" to the top of his list of priorities.

Suspension cables, thick as tree trunks, held the gothic span of the Cornelius Bridge aloft over a river of black oil. Boat lights shone in the distance, bobbing, cutting through billowing walls of pea-soup fog. The far shore became a curving beachside drive, granite and glass condos on one side and the hungry wet dark on the other. Every now and then the clouds would part high overhead, baring the curve of a pregnant opal-white moon. And then, to its north, glimpses of a second, smaller moon like a marble of rough blue chalk.

"When we get there," Danielle said, "let me do the talking. You two are tourists from Stettle, first time in the big city, got it?"

"Might help if we told him the truth," Lucy replied. "If he understood how important it is that we get that book—"

"Duke Ellery is the top name in his Rolodex. The only thing Declerc likes hoarding more than scraps of mystic wisdom is cold, hard cash. You've got a bounty on your head, so does Verna, and...well, he doesn't know I used to be the Midnight Jury, I've only ever met him in disguise, but even odds Declerc sells us all out regardless. We'll tell him we've got some hot out-of-town merchandise. He likes to inspect the goods in his library, because it gives him a chance to show off."

"And then?" Roy asked.

She met his gaze in the mirror. The tip of her tongue played across her teeth.

"You mind getting rough, big guy?"

He shook his head.

"Neither do I. We'll have to play this cowboy style. Buffalo him, tie him up and gag him, and make off with the book before his bodyguards figure out what's what. After which the three of you can get out of my life and I can get back to enjoying my well-deserved retirement."

Lucy's eyes widened. Roy knew that bringing her along was part of her plan to get the Midnight Jury back in uniform—hoping, he guessed, that the lure of Danielle's old life would be enough to do the trick—and this wasn't part of the agenda.

"But— We need you for the next bit," Lucy stammered. She looked to Verna. "Isn't that right? For the, uh—"

Verna picked up on her vibe and rolled with it, her lies as smooth as silk.

"The Argisene needs to be deciphered before I can use it. To build a conduit to the spells inside, I need our creator—present—and one of her most important creations, someone with a central tie to our refraction. Now, the way I see it, that's either you or Duke Ellery. And considering Duke wants to devour her soul..."

"Doesn't sound like my problem."

"He thinks he can steal Lucy's powers and become a god," Verna told her. "And I'm not a hundred percent sure he's wrong. Now think about what Duke would do to this world if he had absolute control over it."

Roy chimed in. "More importantly, think about what he'd do to you."

Back in the depths of his worst downward spiral, Roy still had a sense of self-preservation. In the end, it was the only thing that kept him alive and brought him back fighting. Something told him that Danielle was the same way. She stared out at the dark water, thinking, wrestling with herself, then sighed her surrender.

"Fine. Looks like we're pulling an all-nighter at my office, then. Hope you like sleeping on linoleum, because I don't share my bed with anybody."

A white stone wall, mortared in webbed strands of jet black, ringed the outskirts of the loremonger's estate. A brass placard beside a tall wrought-iron gate read *"Declerc House, Est."* And then what might have been a year, the numbers scoured and scratched away, unreadable. Roy realized he hadn't seen a single thing with a date on it since they had arrived in the city. No clocks, either; Verna's dashboard didn't sport one and nobody was wearing a watch. Verna pulled up outside the gate, letting the engine rattle and purr.

"Let me call the man and—" Danielle narrowed her eyes to slits. "Hold up. Something's wrong."

She hopped out of the car and left the passenger door open, approaching the gate alone. The headlights framed her in stark, hard white as she gave the gates a push. They swung wide, silent and oiled, like glass.

Danielle got back in the car. "Drive."

"Supposed to be locked?" Roy asked.

"Always."

The Ford cruised slow up a winding drive, past stone grotesques and mildewed, dry fountains, toward a long white mansion with tall dark windows. Roy noticed that a pair of lampposts, positioned to light up the driveway, were shut off.

"Power outage?" he said.

Danielle answered with his unspoken suspicion: "Or the power's been cut."

"Nobody knows we're coming," Verna said, "so if it's a trap, it's not for us. Dani, is there any chance Declerc tried to arrange a buyer for the grimoire?"

"You kidding me? He practically drooled onto it. No. Declerc sells the cheap relics to keep his operations afloat. The good stuff he keeps for himself. And the Argisene is the definition of good stuff, if you're into that sort of thing."

Verna's eyes twinkled.

"Would he have bragged about it?" Roy asked. He didn't know about magic books, but he knew the perils of loose lips. "Maybe attract the wrong kind of attention, like a rival who wants what he has?"

"Every once in a while, somebody tries to rip Declerc off," Verna said. "They generally don't get far, and if they do, the blowback is...well, if you want to keep what you've got in this town, you have to be willing to make the occasional messy example."

Danielle nodded. "Anyone dumb enough to rob Declerc is also too scared to try."

"You still want to go in like cowboys?" Roy asked.

"Maybe a little quieter."

He looked to Lucy. "Wait in the car. We don't know what's in there."

"Are you kidding me?" She scrunched her nose at him. "We don't know what's out *here*. I'm safer with the three of you than I am by myself."

He couldn't argue with her logic.

Verna killed the headlights before they crested the hill, then pulled up alongside the pillared front porch. They got out, slow and careful, leaving the sedan's doors open to keep anyone inside from hearing them shut. The house's front door was open, too, just a crack. Danielle pushed it with the toe of her leather boot.

It swung wide onto an atrium lit by sporadic flickers of light flashing from emergency beacons. They dazzled Roy's eyes and turned the shadows to mud, playing tricks with his night vision. A leaden hum, like a radio tuned to a dead channel, droned from the shattered console of an alarm system beside the front door. It was nothing but a mangled mess of torn wires and dangling, broken buttons.

They found the first of Declerc's bodyguards down the hall. He sat slumped against the wall, head bowed, with a matted scarf of crimson where his throat had been slashed from ear to ear.

Further along, in a gallery corridor lined with mismatched oil paintings, they found signs of a one-sided fight. Another dead man, and this one had emptied his gun. Judging from the bullets that had pockmarked the alabaster walls and torn through canvas, he hadn't hit a thing. This corpse wore a pair of paper-thin slashes across his face and a second along his jugular vein, turning the carpet beneath him to a sodden, dark puddle.

"We'll cut through the kitchens to the library," Danielle whispered. "We go in, we get the book, and we get out. No detours. Whoever killed these guys is still around and I don't want to meet them."

Roy had no objections. As they crept through the stillness of the house, the air thick with the dank copper stench of freshly spilled blood, his ears perked up. He heard something up ahead, a noise he couldn't quite make sense of. A wet, ragged, squelching sound, interspersed with the crackling of small bones.

Tell me that isn't— he thought, and then rounded the corner.

The emergency strobe flickered across the shadowy cavern of the loremonger's kitchens. Roy caught snatches of Tuscan design, beige and blue tile, commercial appliances and big, brass-detailed ovens. And another body, laid out on the cold, wet floor, with his bathrobe and his skin torn open in ragged folds. His ribcage was splintered, bent back like prison bars to free the tender organs beneath, and the look on the dead man's face said he'd been alive when the ripping began.

The culprit, greedily crouched over him, rose to her full height. Her hands were gloves of scarlet, and her white lab coat wore a riot of red spatters. So did her mouth, her bloody lips curling into an eager smile.

"Mary Contraire," Verna whispered to Roy. "Duke Ellery's right-hand woman."

Roy was normally good at sizing people up, but this world of pulp horror and magic had his calibrations all skewed and he couldn't trust his assumptions anymore. He leaned closer to Verna.

"She more dangerous than the giant killer robot, back in the park?"

"Roy," she replied, "she built the giant killer robot."

Chapter Thirty-nine

Backlit by the slow-flashing emergency light that strobed in a curtain of sapphire blue across the quiet kitchen, Mary surveyed the four people in the doorway. Her twin gloves of blood, coating her in gore from her hands to her elbows, steadily drip-drip-dripped and drizzled upon the tile floor.

She giggled.

"Oops," she said. "Caught me snacking. Hey, Verna. You actually came back. You also just cost me a sawbuck. I had a bet that you'd scamper off to the real world with your tail tucked between your legs and go into hiding."

"The 'real' world?" Roy asked. "This isn't real to you?"

Mary grinned, feral, showing her bloody teeth.

"Are you kidding me? I *love* being a fictional character. I'm rich, I can do anything I want, there are no consequences, and I'm one of the stars of the show. This city is a nihilist's playground. You got a name, handsome?"

"Sure," Roy said. "I have a name."

She snickered. "You, I like. But is that why you came back, Verna? Missed the chaos and the fun? We sure used to have fun together, you and me. No...no, after the way you did my man wrong, you know better than that. You'd only come home if you thought you had some way to squirm out of all the trouble you're in."

"Maybe I'm trying to save the world," Verna said.

"Maybe you're trying to steal Duke's prize out from under him. There are a thousand books in this house, but we both know the one you're here for. Same as me. The Argisene Grimoire." She held up a finger. "But. You'd also need a very special someone. And here's the best part, the one that ties it all together for me: Rumblebones reported in a while ago. Said she almost snatched our girl, only to be thwarted by...how did she put it? A 'heavyweight bruiser.'"

Eyes gleaming, hungry, Mary turned from Roy to the two women at his side.

"So which one of you delicious-looking ladies is Lucy Langenkamp?"

Danielle took a step forward.

"I am," she said. "Let them go, and I'll come with you."

From the look on Lucy's face, she was as confused as Roy was. He thought Danielle had given up the hero thing for good, and self-sacrifice wasn't exactly one of her defining traits. Then it clicked: just like Verna, she wasn't sure about Duke's pretensions to godhood. If he got his hands on Lucy and really did manage to take over this world, there would be nowhere left to hide.

On the other hand, he thought, *by posing as Lucy and giving us a chance to get away—and then to double back and come in for a rescue, since there's no way in hell we're going to leave her in the lion's den...*

Standing one step behind Danielle, he gently touched her shoulder blade. She responded with a small, firm nod. They understood each other perfectly.

Somehow, Mary's manic grin only grew in size, along with the appetite in her eyes. Her response rode on a giddy laugh: "Oh, this is *delightful*. And to think I was supposed to be long gone by now."

She crouched down and casually stuck her hand into the dead man's chest. Lucy let out a nauseated hiss between her teeth as Roy's stomach clenched. Mary twisted her grip, sinew pulling, then snapping, as her victim's heart tore free. She rose up again, contemplating it.

"Imagine being so lucky. I came for the Argisene Grimoire and I'll be going home with the book and my very own author. Two birds with one arrow."

Danielle swallowed, hard. Roy didn't think she was faking the nervous look on her face, either, but she took another step into the darkness and death-stench of the kitchen.

"Fine," she said. "Let's go. But like I said, the others go free."

"I wasn't talking to you, sweetheart." Mary's gaze shifted, locking in on Lucy. "I'm talking to her."

Roy moved to stand in front of Lucy. She shrank behind him, while Verna edged toward the hallway at their backs.

"But I'm Lucy—" Danielle started to say. She was cut off by a short, sharp cackle.

"How many times?" Mary asked

Danielle shook her head, brow furrowed. "Meaning?"

"How many times have we danced, you and I?"

Mary raised the heart to her lips. She bit into it like it was an apple, chewing thoughtfully as corpse-blood guttered down her chin and spattered her white coat.

"Did you think I wouldn't recognize your voice, Jury?"

Danielle didn't answer her. Silent, frozen, locked in a staredown with the cannibal doctor.

"You do have a pretty face. All those times I imagined slicing it off..." Mary paused. "You know, I thought your nose would be bigger. Jury, I *missed* you. Where did you go?"

"I've been making it a rule to stay away from freak shows."

"Cute. That's cute." She wagged the mangled heart at her. "You should run."

Danielle blinked. "Excuse me?"

"Obviously, I'm keeping Lucy. Same with Verna: Duke has plans for her. Nasty plans. When it comes to the big guy, well, Rumblebones has a score to settle, and I owe the little monster a favor. But as for you? I'm not celebrating the grand return of the Midnight Jury with you unarmed and under-dressed. Go. Run. Trust me, I'll come and find you. We all will."

Danielle gritted her teeth. She spread her feet, making her body a psychic wall in front of her three companions.

"That's not who I am anymore. The Midnight Jury is dead."

"Wrong, wrong, wrong. So very wrong. Take it from me: I spent so many years trying to be someone different. So many years fighting my own nature. And I was so very unhappy, until I turned around, faced myself, and embraced who I was always meant to be."

"You're a serial-murdering cannibalistic sociopath," Verna said, her voice flat.

"Psychopath," Mary snapped, glaring at her. "*God*. Does no one in this town understand the distinction? The point is, the Jury isn't a costume you put on. It's you. And no matter how fast you are, how far you go, you can't run from what's inside of you. There's one leading role in this drama and you were born to play it. Isn't that right, Lucy?"

Lucy took a breath. Then she stepped out from Roy's shadow, around him, coming into clear view.

"All I know is, I believe in happy endings," she said. "Which means you can never win. Not in any world of mine."

Mary's smile faded. She rolled her eyes.

"Pfft. Sorry, doll. You've been cut from the show. A replacement writer is waiting in the wings, and he's going to bang out one hell of a finale."

"You talk a good game," Roy said, "but I think you're forgetting some basic math."

"I have a dual PhD in mechanical engineering and medical pathology," Mary fired back. "I can add, subtract, slice, *and* dice."

Roy spread his hands, taking in the room.

"And yet. Four of us. One of you. And I don't see the book, which means it's still somewhere in the house. Now, you might be able to run and grab it. And you might be able to get past everyone standing in your way and get your hands on Lucy. But you can't do both."

"Mm, you're right. Maybe I should bring in a little help, huh?"

The next words from Mary's bloody lips weren't from any language Roy had ever heard before. He wasn't sure they were human. Tangled syllables went to war in his ears, spilling over his brain in a painful static hiss before they faded into echoing silence.

The dead man's eyes snapped open.

He sat up. Ropy intestines spilled from the ruined cavern of his chest, but he didn't seem to notice. He let out a tortured wheeze as he leaned to one side, pushing himself to his feet on the blood-soaked tile.

"When the Nickel Flu hit and people started popping out of their caskets, I knew I needed a sample to study." Mary gave them a little wave. "Hello, official city coroner here. Not just my day job, it's also my passion. Anyway, turns out that wherever the Flu came from, it is *remarkably* easy to weaponize."

She pointed at Lucy and spoke once more. The words, if they were words, washed out Roy's thoughts under a curtain of pinprick electricity. From the way the walking dead man turned, his milky white eyes following the pointed finger, Roy didn't need a translation.

"He won't hurt Lucy too much if she doesn't resist. Maybe some snapped bones, minor spinal damage, but nothing that will keep her from serving her purpose. The rest of you he won't be so gentle with. Meanwhile, I'm going to jaunt over to the library. There's a book on hold, just for me."

She took another bite of the corpse's heart and tossed it over her shoulder. It spattered on the tile at her back. Then she turned, ran...and jumped.

Mary landed halfway up the kitchen wall, her bloody hand clinging effortlessly to the smooth surface. She clambered up like a bug, deceptively fast, the tails of her lab coat dangling as she made her way toward the ceiling. She looked back at Roy with a smile.

"Needless to say, I'll kill anyone who follows me. And if you three split up, that reduces your odds of survival by...oh, let's just say 'a lot.' So there you go, handsome. The question isn't 'which target do I want to go after?' The real question is, 'which one do you want to die trying to save?'"

Chapter Forty

With a sudden lurch Mary loped off into the dark, clinging high to the wall as she skittered through an open archway at the back of the kitchens like a cockroach in human form. She left a string of bloody handprints to mark her passage.

The living dead man let out a wheezing groan, air whistling from his ruptured chest to his tortured throat, and staggered toward Lucy. He moved like a wooden marionette, his legs stiff, arms jutting out toward her with his hands curled into hooks.

"Roy—" Lucy said.

"I know. Get behind me." He looked to Danielle and Verna. "*Go*. Go after her and get the book. I'll protect Lucy."

They didn't stick around to argue. Danielle broke into a run. Verna was right on her heels, pausing just long enough to shout back over her shoulder.

"Meet us outside! We'll rendezvous at the car."

Roy was never much of a horror fan, but he'd seen the same zombie movies as everyone else. He knew the ground rules that all the classics shared: don't get bit, and always shoot them in the head.

Too bad he didn't have a gun.

He had to figure the thing didn't feel pain—after all, it didn't seem to mind that its guts were hanging out, trailing between its legs like wet strings of sausage and stinking like an open sewer main—but Roy still had a size and weight advantage. Careful of the dead man's gaping jaw, he turned one shoulder inward and charged, aiming to hit it high and knock it off his feet.

A stiff, awkward arm swung at him. It almost looked comical, until the impact landed and a starburst of pain exploded in Roy's shoulder. Suddenly he was the one leaving his feet, heel sliding in the puddle of blood and sending him skidding, crashing to the hard tile floor. He twisted his head at the last second, keeping himself from cracking his skull, but his ankle responded with a burning protest when he tried to get up again.

The dead man bent down, reaching for him. He rolled as the hooked fingers groped at his face, slipping aside, his trousers drenched in gore as he slid through the carnage on the kitchen floor. He fought through the pain, forcing himself to scramble back to his feet, buying a little distance.

He didn't need it. The second Roy was out of reach and no longer a threat, the zombie wheeled and fixed its milky-white eyes on Lucy. She backed up, thumping against the marble counter in the far corner of the room, and it stalked toward her on rigor-stiffened legs.

Roy limped to the cabinets and tore them open, rummaging for anything heavier than a saucepan. His hand closed around the handle of a cast iron skillet. He turned, reared his arm back, and let it fly. The skillet hit the corpse in the back of the neck with a jolt that would have stunned any living man, then fell and clattered against the tiles with an ear-piercing ring. It didn't even seem to notice.

Roy needed to use more muscle. And that meant working up close. He ran in, scooped up the fallen skillet, and swung for a home run.

The back of the dead man's skull caved like an eggshell. Sodden, torn skin collapsed over shattered bone. It reeled, wavering on its feet—and kept standing. It turned, spinning around, teeth bared as it lurched at Roy with both hands.

The loremonger's library was exactly that. Before his untimely death and zombification, Declerc had gathered books and folios from around the world—or at least, from traders in the city who *said* they'd been around the world—in stacks that would rival a well-stocked university. The towering shelves ran along both sides of the room, from the floor almost all the way to the sculpted, buttery wood of the arched ceiling, with long and polished study tables running down the center aisle. A pair of crystal chandeliers dangled high above, dead. Only the random flickers of the blue emergency bulbs over the exit doors and the mist-shrouded moons outside the high library windows offered the slightest glimmer of light.

"Magpie magpie *maelzy—*" the rest of Verna's hissed chant became a jarring wash of static and combinations of syllables that shouldn't be spoken by human lips. Danielle, running alongside her, winced and turned her head.

"Don't *do* that when I'm standing this close. You know that makes my teeth ache."

Verna finished the incantation and slapped herself across the eyes. Her vision flared, blossoming and fading, then turned to the sepia of an old photograph. Colors were washed out, details fuzzy, but she could see almost all the way to the far end of the library now.

"Can you see?" she asked Danielle.

"I've got eyedrops."

Verna beamed at her. "The ones I brewed for you? I didn't think you—"

Danielle shoved her, hard. She fell back just in time to see a razor-honed scalpel hiss past her. It punched through the air where she'd just been standing, burying its blade in the library door as she landed hard on the carpet. She scrambled backward on her hands, finding cover behind the closest wall of shelves while Danielle dove in the other direction.

"Come on, Jury," Mary called out. Her voice played off the vaulted ceiling and the rows of shelves, bouncing, sounding like it could be coming from anywhere and everywhere at once. "Do you know how long it's been since I had a genuine challenge? Come on. Play with me. Let's play like we used to."

"How about me?" Verna called back. She grabbed hold of the closest shelf, pulling herself back to her feet.

Mary's response was so vehement it made the windows shake.

"*Nobody invited you, Verna!*" She paused, catching herself. "Ahem. What I mean is, this is a long-awaited reunion and your input is not needed. Or wanted. Or acceptable."

On the opposite side of the middle aisle, hunched behind another wall of shelves, Danielle shot Verna a quick thumbs-up. She mouthed the words, *Keep her talking*. Then she turned and darted off around the corner.

Verna put her back to the shelf. She eased along, sidestepping, eyes left and right as she hunted for any sign of movement in the sepia-tinted gloom. Along the way she grabbed random books and tossed them to the floor, leaving a trail of noise for Mary to follow. Silence answered her. She wasn't taking the bait.

"Mary," Verna called out, inching her way closer to the far end of the stacks. "Mary, tarry twixt these tomes and cherished treasures—"

An arm fired through a gap at her back, hooked around Verna's throat, and yanked hard enough to pin her to the shelf and seal her throat. Spots blossomed in her vision, her half-finished incantation reduced to a squealing wheeze of breath.

"We are all," Mary snarled, "extremely sick of your crap. You should have stayed gone, Verna. If you stayed gone, you might have survived this. That's something you and the Jury have in common."

Danielle plowed into Mary from behind like a bullet in the dark, charging at full speed and hitting hard enough to send her crashing against the shelves. Her arm slipped loose and Verna dropped back to the floor, clutching her throat while she gasped for air.

The impact set the towering bookcase rocking—then tilting, then tipping like a mighty domino. Verna only had a moment to throw her arms over her head, huddling under a hailstorm of falling books, while Danielle and Mary battled on the other side of the mahogany divide.

The dead man set its unblinking, milky eyes on Roy, shambling toward him in a stiff-legged lurch. Roy kept moving, limping on his twisted ankle, barely a step ahead of the creature's hooked claw-fingers. A glancing blow from the zombie had knocked him flat; if it grabbed onto him with both hands, Roy didn't doubt it could rip him to pieces. With his ankle burning, punishing him with a jagged streak of pain every time he put weight on it, he was playing pure defense. No time to do anything but escape the relentless advance, no chance to turn the tables.

"Lucy," he rasped. "Run."

She ran. Not for the exit, but for the long marble counter. As the emergency lights flickered, casting the cavernous kitchens in alternating shades of sapphire blue and ink black, she reached for the tools dangling from a tidy row of hooks and ripped one down.

Lucy spun around with a meat cleaver in her hand. Then she charged in to the rescue.

Roy was about to shout, to warn her to stay back. He had already crushed the back of the zombie's skull along with half of its rotten brain and it didn't even slow the dead man down. So much for movies. As she ran up from behind, though, he saw what she had in mind.

Teeth gritted, her face frozen in determination and fear, Lucy dropped to one knee and swung the cleaver with both hands, putting everything she had into it. The stainless steel blade, polished to a deadly sheen, buried itself halfway into the back of the dead man's leg. She ripped the cleaver free, showering her face and hands in droplets of flying blood.

The zombie teetered on one good leg. It couldn't feel pain, but the doomsday concoction of science and magic that kept it moving couldn't heal a chopped hamstring. Lucy didn't give it a chance to recover, quickly swinging at its other leg. The cleaver sank into the calf, a weaker blow than the first but still enough to tear muscle and chip bone. The zombie turned, grasping at her frantically as it fell, snatching at her hair while she rolled to safety.

It wouldn't stop. Squirming on its belly, the dead man dragged its useless legs and trailing guts across the bloody kitchen tile, pulling itself toward Lucy on its forearms. Roy favored his good ankle. He focused on getting his balance back, working through the pain. He could walk. If he could walk, he could run and he could fight. First things first, though. He held his hand out to Lucy.

"May I?"

With her eyes still wide, lips pursed tight, her face bloodless and pale, she handed him the meat cleaver. He took it from her, gently, and stood over the crawling dead man.

Chapter Forty-one

Verna squirmed out from the narrow gap between the toppled-domino bookshelves. Priceless tomes slid off her back and landed, tattered and splayed, as she pulled herself to freedom on her forearms. Danielle's shoulders hit the bookcase with a floor-rattling slam, driven back by a brutal kick to the gut. She dodged left as Mary lunged in with a bared scalpel, the blade punching through a leather cover and twisting before it ripped free.

The cannibal doctor was a cyclone, all feet and knives, moving faster than the eye could catch. Danielle was out of practice. Slower.

But she hits harder, Verna thought. Mary's head snapped back, a right cross splitting Danielle's knuckles along with Mary's bottom lip, spraying droplets of blood that were black as oil in the pale moonlight. Mary leaped backward, kicking up off her feet and landing on her hands, springing head over heels as she flipped her way down the library aisle. Danielle charged after her, cocking back her bloody fist.

It was a feint. Verna saw it all happening in slow-motion, a train crash she was too late to stop. Mary scampered back, taunting Danielle with her scarlet-toothed smile, stoking the fallen heroine's rage. One of her hands dipped into the folds of her lab coat, showing a tiny flash of steel as she palmed another scalpel. Danielle ran in hard and fast, off-balance, setting herself up for the kill.

Mary wasn't the only one who could feint. Danielle shifted course at the last second. She turned her shoulder, dropping low as the scalpel sliced through the air, the blade close enough to snip a stray curl. She hit Mary like a bull, bowling her over and taking her to the library carpet. They rolled, grappling, Danielle fighting for the scalpel while Mary's teeth snapped at her throat.

Mary broke free, sprang up and leaped a second time, backwards, landing in a birdlike crouch on the edge of a library table. She wiped the back of her hand across her lip, painting a scarlet grin along her gore-spattered cheek, while both women gasped for breath.

"That was fun," Mary said, "but I have to run. My boyfriend's expecting me and I don't want to be late."

Verna watched, staring in silence as Danielle rose to her feet. Danielle's breathing slowed and her eyes narrowed to gunmetal slits. She was ragged but strong. And she didn't have the hat, the coat, the guns, but right now she didn't need them. Maybe it was the heat of battle, maybe it was her repressed hungers opening one sleepy eye, but something had woken up inside of her, even if she wasn't ready to admit it.

The Midnight Jury was back.

"You tell him something for me," Danielle said.

Mary grinned. "I'm all ears."

"You tell him I'm coming."

"We're counting on it. I can't *wait* to have you over for dinner. *Ciao*."

Verna scrambled over to block the library doors. Danielle had the same thought, but as soon as she started to move Mary was spinning on one heel, turning in the opposite direction. She leaped from table to table, streaking toward the far end of the gallery. Verna spotted the prize now: a varnished wood pedestal, a glass case, and a heavy book with yellowed pages resting on a pillow of royal purple velvet.

"Dani," she shouted. "The grimoire! Don't let her—"

The case shattered under Mary's elbow. She scooped up the book, barely losing her stride, and clambered up on top of the nearest bookshelf. Then she jumped from shelf to shelf, twelve feet above the library floor, her final goal in sight.

She took one last leap, spinning in midair. Then she hit the library window like a cannonball. She plowed through the glass, falling free, trailed by a rain of razor shards while she clutched the book to her chest. The darkness swallowed her and a cold night wind washed in through the empty window.

The dead man was still moving, flopping limbless across the kitchen floor, teeth gnashing the air as it struggled to finish its mission. Roy let the meat cleaver fall from his exhausted fingers. The bent, chipped blade clattered on the tile next to his feet. He turned back the way they'd come in. Lucy's hand clamped down on his wrist and she yanked him back, almost hard enough to pull him off-balance.

The move saved his life. Waxy fingers stabbed an inch from his eyes, grasping and hungry. The dead bodyguard from the hallway had gotten up and joined the party. His partner was right behind him, lurching with stiff legs and empty eyes, driven by a hunger for living flesh.

The Nickel Flu was contagious.

Roy and Lucy went the other way. Out the other door, toward the library, following the trail of bloody handprints that Mary had left along the eggshell-white paint. Halfway there, in a gallery where family portraits lined the walls between frosted-glass sconces, they ran into Verna and Danielle coming in the opposite direction.

"More zombies," Lucy said, jerking a thumb over her shoulder. It was all the explanation she needed.

All the explanation she had time for. The air thrummed with the rattle of a rising garage door and the growl of an engine firing to life.

"If she gets away with that book—" Verna gasped, leading the pack as they thundered down the hallway.

"Two outcomes," Danielle said. "Duke gets his hands on Lucy, becomes a god, end of the world. Duke doesn't, end of the world. Pick your poison."

A door opened onto the oil-stained concrete bay of the garage. It was open to the cold night air. They were just in time to see the taillights of Mary's car flash scarlet in the darkness.

They piled into Verna's sedan. This time, Danielle got behind the wheel. Verna tossed her the keys without a word. While she started the ignition, Danielle looked back over her shoulder, locking eyes with Roy.

"Listen to me," she said. "If Mary gets away, you are going to take Lucy and you are going to *leave*, understood? Go back to your own world and never, ever come back here."

Roy caught something in the corner of his eye. Verna's face. She flinched. It was just the tiniest tic, like a poker tell.

"He already sent hunters after us," Lucy pointed out. "He'll send more."

"Then you run and you keep running. This world is falling apart anyway. All you have to do is outrun the apocalypse. This is what we call a self-correcting problem."

She threw the car into gear and stomped the gas hard enough to shove them back against their seats. Then it was a downhill slalom, rounding the twists and turns of the mansion's driveway at lethal speed. Mary was almost to the bottom of the hill, her high-beams flashing toward the open front gate. Her ride was sleek and silver, a vintage roadster with a long narrow nose and a ragtop roof the color of fresh cream.

"If I leave, you'll all die," Lucy said.

"A better death than the one we'll get if Duke Ellery takes over. Sometimes you can't win, okay? Sometimes you just have to pick the least-worst choice. That's life."

Lucy crossed her arms. "The Midnight Jury never gives up."

"I'm *not* the damn—" Danielle started to snap. She caught herself and took a breath. "I didn't say anything about giving up. Only that we have to be realistic about this. Hold on."

The sedan launched through the open gate and veered right, still chasing Mary's tail. The roadster was up ahead, pouring on speed and widening the gap.

"Losing her," Verna said.

Danielle unclenched her gritted teeth. "Not for long. She's headed into Burnside. Tight streets, pothole city. She'll have to slow down."

They slowed down first. As the city closed in, more towering dead tenements like termite hives squeezing tight and blotting out the moons, the streets became a twisted ramble of shredded asphalt and flashing amber lights. The sedan hit a pothole hard enough to make the car bottom out, the transmission slamming pavement. The gunshot-loud impact nearly knocked them out of their seats.

Up ahead, Mary was having the same trouble. The roadster fishtailed, swerving out of control as she blew through a stoplight. From the way the vintage car veered, wild and fast, Roy guessed she was wrestling with the wheel.

At his side, Lucy had her lips pursed. She looked like she was doing a math problem in her head. Before he could ask, she spoke up again.

"Is Duke's hideout still at the old Gran Isle train station?"

"He has a few," Verna replied. "The train station, Apex Chemicals, that tattoo parlor on 28th Avenue. He likes to move around. Why?"

Lucy drew a map in the air with her fingertip.

"Those are...east, south, and west of here." Lucy shook her head. "So why is she driving *north*? There's nothing in Burnside but dead ends and bad news."

"Don't know, but if she doesn't slow the hell down—" Danielle stared dead ahead, eyes in a tight squint, as Mary plowed into the next intersection and spun out. The roadster's tires screamed, drawing long black streaks on the broken road. It shuddered to a stop then suddenly picked up speed, slipping out of sight around the corner.

Two seconds later they heard the hollow *crump* of buckling steel, the blare of a car horn, and the scream of a ruptured engine.

Danielle pulled to a stop just around the corner. Mary's roadster had met a concrete lamppost pedestal head-on, hard enough to rumple the needle-nosed hood and blow out one headlight. The other, still burning white-hot, cast a spotlight on the shabby façade of a dive hotel. The car's driver-side door hung open, nobody behind the wheel.

"She's on foot," Danielle snarled. "We can catch her."

She was feral, a lioness on the hunt as she slapped the gearshift into park and jumped out of the car, leaving the engine running. Verna was right behind her, pointing to faint and fresh scarlet spatters on the pavement. Mary had left a literal trail to follow.

"She's acting more like she used to," Lucy said. "More like herself."

Roy shoved his door open. "I hear a 'but' in your voice. What's wrong?"

Lucy frowned. Following, but her body language was tight as a drum as she got out of the car. Roy paused long enough to shut off the engine and pocket the keys Danielle had left behind.

"Why did she drive *north*?" Lucy murmured.

Roy knew this place. He stared up at the tall cherry-red neon sign clinging to the corner of the hotel, spelling out *Burnside Ritz* in a rococo font. Half the letters were dead, the rest flickering, but he had seen it before. He had seen that sign; it was in the nightmare he had flying from LA to Phoenix, days and an entire world ago. He was on a dying plane, pressing the muzzle of his gun to Perez's forehead, watching the city rise up to swallow them both.

Noir York. Ain't it beautiful? They say this city can make a new man out of you. That you can be anyone you want to be.

Dream-Perez grinned madly at him, gloating, savoring his tiny victory. The woman they both loved was dead, lying on the floor with a bullet in her. Roy's bullet.

But it's no place for you and me, is it, pal? You couldn't change if you wanted to. And me, well, I'm dead.

Verna looked back, wearing his dead lover's face, waving as Danielle darted into the hotel and left the door swinging at her back.

"She's in here," Verna called. "Come on. Let's finish this."

Remember, Roy, said the ghost in his brain. *Dead is forever.*

Chapter Forty-two

The Burnside Ritz wasn't going to win any awards for truth in advertising. Maybe it had, once upon a time, but the jazzy zigzag striped carpet in the lobby was stained with cigarette burns and veins of dark mold ran along paint turned brittle and yellow. A whiskered old man in a battered army surplus jacket snored in a folding chair in front of a boxy television tuned to crackling static snow.

Danielle was already leaning over the check-in desk, as far as she could with the cage of chicken wire that protected the night clerk. He was an emaciated man with greasy, thinning hair and matchstick arms, and he met the new arrivals with sleepy, incurious eyes.

"A woman just came through here," Danielle said. "Lab coat, covered in blood, crazier than a shithouse weasel? Point the way."

"Don't know whatcha mean," he drawled. "Haven't seen anyone all night."

She grabbed hold of the chicken wire and rattled it.

"I will tear this cage down and *beat* you with it."

Now he couldn't meet her gaze. His eyes rolled around the room like they were looking for safe harbor.

"I don't want any trouble, okay?"

Verna stood at Danielle's shoulder. "That woman—that one you claim you didn't see—is a serial killer with a stolen book of black magic, and she doesn't leave witnesses behind. We're here to stop her. Now who do you think is going to cause you more trouble by the end of the night?"

He pointed toward a door marked *Employees Only*.

"She...she wanted to know the fastest way to the back alley. I didn't want to help her, but I mean, she had a knife—"

"Just tell us what you told her," Danielle said.

"Through that door, all the way back through the old kitchens. Restaurant's been closed since before I started working here, but the delivery doors aren't locked. People go out back to smoke sometimes."

Roy had never gone behind the scenes at a hotel, but he was pretty sure it wasn't supposed to look like this. The twisting, winding hallways of unpainted cinder block beyond the door kinked at odd angles and didn't seem to follow any rational floor plan. They ran past chained-shut doors and utility closets, sometimes a string of two or three in a row, under hissing, popping fluorescent bulbs.

Nightmare logic, he thought. *This whole place is built on nightmare logic.*

The blood trail dried up. They had to trust instinct at the occasional intersection, pushing in the direction that felt like it would get them closer to the opposite side of the building. Then they came to a four-way junction with corridors spiraling off at odd angles, the bare floor spotted with stains from leaks in the overhead water pipes.

"This way," Danielle said. Roy kept pace with her, jogging past the intersection.

"No," Verna said, jolting to a stop in the middle of the floor. She pointed. "Other way."

"Everyone—" Lucy said, her halting voice lost in the argument.

"You're nuts," Danielle said. "This is closer. Roy, tell her."

"I'm lost," he said.

"Everyone." Lucy shook her head, all eyes on her now. "We have to go back. Right now. Back the way we came."

Danielle blinked at her. "Why the hell would we do that?"

"Think about it. She had a head start. She blew our doors off at first, but we caught up to her."

"I'm a good driver," Danielle said. "Thanks for noticing."

"She has to take the book to Duke, but she drives north, not toward any of his hideouts. Then she wrecks her car and leaves a convenient trail of blood right to the front door of this place."

"You think she's laying an ambush?" Roy said.

"She *wanted* us to follow her. Remember, the book's only half the puzzle. For Duke to get the power he's after, he thinks he needs one more piece: me."

Verna nodded, thinking it through, moving close to Lucy's side. "She's right. This smells like a trap. Let's get out before she has a chance to spring it."

"And let her keep the book?" Danielle said, exasperated.

"We can steal it back, Dani. But we do it on our terms, not hers. If we lose our author, we lose everything. Let's not be—"

The ceiling rattled.

Roy moved, lunging toward Lucy, not fast enough before a steel grate slammed down in his path. Another rolled down at the far side of the intersection, blocking off the way they came.

"Damn it," Roy grunted, digging his fingers into the metal slats and heaving upward. "Help me with this."

Even with Danielle's help, and Lucy and Verna pulling from the opposite side, the grate wouldn't budge. Danielle took a step back, dusting her hands off.

"Okay. We know Mary's lurking around here somewhere, and we have to assume she's got the rest of Duke's crew on the way. So let's move with purpose. Verna, take Lucy. You two stick together and try to work your way back toward the lobby. If you make it, don't wait around for us: get gone, and we'll meet up back at my office. Roy and I will go this way and see if we can find a path out of this shithole. At least there's some good news."

Roy gave her a sidelong glance. "What's the good news?"

"These grates were supposed to cut us off from retreat. Whatever Mary's planning for an ambush, it'll be right down this hallway ahead of us."

"How's that good news?" Roy asked.

"Well, it's you and me walking into the lion's den, pal. Lucy and Verna are probably going to be just fine. Two out of four ain't bad."

Two bends farther, the corridor weaving like a drunk, the lights went out.

Roy and Danielle stopped at the same time, their last footfalls echoing soft on the concrete floor. Their eyes met in the dark, a mutual understanding.

Roy's hands curled into fists. They started walking again. Slower now, letting their eyes adjust to the gloom, listening to the slow drip of water from the leaky pipes and the occasional distant rattle of plumbing.

Danielle pointed left. There was a door there with a push bar, not chained like the others they'd passed. She gave it a jiggle. Unlocked. *Two choices*, Roy thought. *Is the ambush behind this door, or further up the hall?*

"Can she see in the dark?" Roy whispered.

"Mary? Sure, but so can we. Here. One drop in each eye."

She handed him a tiny plastic bottle. He looked at it, dubious, but he didn't have any reason to doubt. He tilted his head back and gave it a careful squeeze. The drops burned as they hit his open eyes, blotting out his sight in a blurry wet curtain. He blinked, fast—and then stared in surprise as his vision transformed. Colors drained away, grainy hazy light flooded in, and he could see almost as clear as daylight.

The world was a black and white movie. Just like the ones he watched as a kid.

He handed the eyedrops back to Danielle, who treated her own eyes before making the bottle disappear with a twist of her palm.

"Alchemy," she whispered. "Thank Verna if we live long enough to see her again. The girl's got a *few* good uses. The drops last about twenty minutes, give or take."

Roy took point, pushing through the heavy door while Danielle watched their backs. The space beyond was a storage room. Old dusty tarps covered shapeless lumps, too big to be assassins lying in wait. Roy lifted one out of curiosity, finding a stacked pile of hotel room chairs. Another tarp concealed a stack of lumpy mattresses.

"With any luck," Danielle murmured, "this'll connect up to housekeeping or something. If we can make it back into the public part of the hotel, there'll be a hundred ways to get outside. Kick open a door, climb out the window, done. Hold on a second. Check that other door, I need to take care of something."

The knob barely wriggled in Roy's hand. He turned back to tell her it was locked, then froze.

The "something" she needed to take care of came in the form of a fine lime-green powder, poured onto the nearest tarp from a plastic baggie. The color was weird but from the way she was chopping it with a razor blade, forming a pair of neat lines on the canvas, he knew exactly what it was.

The sudden, twisting hunger in his gut was all the confirmation he needed. That old familiar urge on his doorstep.

"The hell are you doing?" he said, crossing the storage room in two quick steps.

"What does it look like? Whatever's waiting for us out there, I'm not facing it without a little marching powder. Besides, I fight better when I'm— *Hey!*"

With a sweep of his arm, Roy blew the orderly lines to a cloud of dust. It billowed through the stale air and scattered across the floor, like radioactive rain.

"*Asshole*," Danielle snapped. "Do you have any idea how much that stuff costs?"

"I lost everything good in my life to that shit, so yeah, believe me: I know how much it costs."

"You want to be sober, good for you, be sober," she said. "I wasn't asking you to snort a line with me. Hell, I wasn't offering."

"You're better than this."

She laughed. "You have no idea how very *not* better than this I am."

"I read your comic books."

Her mocking smile faded. She stared at him like he'd just slapped her across the face.

"Fuck you," she said.

"Are you not the Midnight Jury? Because I'm pretty sure—"

"Blame your pal Lucy for that," she said, sticking a finger in his face. "Do you think I wanted this life? She put her pen to the paper and *made* me this way. I never had a choice."

"We all have choices. Maybe not the ones we want, maybe not enough of them, but we've got choices. If you don't, then tell me one thing: how did you quit?"

She tilted her head. "Meaning?"

"Just what I said. If you were forced to be the Jury, how did you quit? If you don't have any free will of your own, you should still be out there doing the hero thing, right?"

She didn't have an answer for that.

"Lucy set the stage," Roy told her. "Yeah, she wrote you and everybody else in this hellhole city. She didn't know what she was capable of, and if she had, she never would have done it. She was a scared little kid with a power she didn't understand and couldn't control, and she needed a hero. You. You are literally the embodiment of everything she imagined as right and good in the world. The champion who fights the monsters."

Danielle's anger slowly faded, the fire in her eyes dwindling to smoldering cinders.

"Putting a lot on my shoulders there," she said.

"I know," Roy said. "Wasn't fair. Life sucks all over. But that's just where the story began. If you had the power to quit, that means you *always* had the power to quit. You weren't forced to put on the coat and pick up the guns. You did it because, at least until you burned out, you wanted to do it. This is who you are."

She let out a humorless little snort. "Still doesn't give you the right to screw with my coke."

"Call it an intervention." He nodded to the door at his back. "Door's locked, by the way."

"No chain? Fine. I can deal with that. Guard my back while I work."

She knelt in front of the door and fished out a slim green oilcloth case. It opened to bare a row of lockpicks, some in flavors and shapes Roy had never seen before.

"I want to get out of here before Mary's pals show up," Danielle said, sliding a slender tension rake into the lock. "At the very least we know Trigger Mortis is in town, and my old guns are sitting back in my office."

"Could be a good thing. We need to take down one of Duke's people. Preferably somebody who's been on the other side."

She worked a pick into the lock, manipulating it along with the rake, concentrating on the tiny clicks.

"Why?"

"We need their...what did Verna call it? Their Mason's Compass."

She stopped picking the lock. She stood up, crisp black and white in Roy's altered vision, and looked him in the eye.

"Where is *hers*?"

He took it out of his pocket and showed it to her. His finger tapped the one remaining, unblemished garnet on the outer ring.

"Only enough juice for one more ticket back. Verna said we can get one of these gadgets from Duke's hunters and use it the same way."

Danielle's face fell.

"Verna," she murmured under her breath. "You traitorous, evil bitch."

"What? What's wrong?"

Danielle reached out. She put her hand, gentle, over Roy's, holding the amulet with him.

"Roy...Verna lied to you. There is no other Compass. This is it."

"But that means—"

"It means," she said, confirming his worst fear, "that even if we get out of this mess alive, even if we save the day...only one of you is going home again."

Chapter Forty-three

"I don't...I don't get this," Roy said.

That wasn't true. Intellectually, he grasped it just fine. The Compass only had one charge left. One stone equaled one passenger through the gate. He could go home, or Lucy could. Not both. Basic math.

"The Mason's Compass is one of a kind," Danielle explained. "Duke had this thing in his collection for years, studying it, experimenting on it, trying to get the gate to work, before Verna stole it from him. Nobody even knows where it came from or who made it. It can't be fixed."

"This doesn't make sense," he argued, his mind rebelling against the naked facts. "What about his hunters? How did they cross to our world, then? Rumblebones, the Dark Dryad—"

She sighed. "It's a spell. The Navigation Mesh. It's like...I'll try to put this into layman's terms. The Compass opens and powers the passageway. As long as there's at least one stone left intact, the portal stays open. With me so far?"

He nodded.

"Okay. The Mesh piggybacks on the magic that's already there. It lets Duke's crew move across and back again, but only as long as the passage is open. Once it closes, it's closed for good, period. No more travel in either direction. Ever."

"So teach me the spell."

"I don't know it," she said. "And it's not something you can just learn to do, like taking a class. That's why Duke didn't send all his people across and mob you with a small army: he could only teach it to the goons with the most natural aptitude for it. The Dryad and Rumblebones have been doing magic longer than I've been alive and Griffin Malone...well, he's dumb as shit but he's also undead, so magic's literally in his bones. Anyway, I'm no slouch at this stuff but I don't think I could pull it off without getting torn apart by the dimensional flux. You didn't know magic even existed until a few days ago, and Lucy's powers are all in her subconscious mind. I'm sorry. It's just not happening, chief."

"And Verna knew this," he said, his voice flat.

"Sure. Tell me something: why are you carrying the Compass and not her?"

"I noticed she was acting squirrelly about it. Didn't know why, but it felt wrong to me. I decided to hold onto it until I figured out her game." Roy stared into the black and white shadows. "Guess I know now."

"If I had to bet, I'd say you're looking at her last-ditch backup plan."

"This wasn't meant for me *or* Lucy," he said.

"Bingo. If things went from bad to worse, she'd take the Compass and run. With the portal closed, even if we stabilized things on this side, Duke would never be able to hunt her down. Verna Bell, free and clear."

"And now..." He looked at the talisman in his palm. He tucked it away. Too precious to keep in the open air, like the slightest breeze might burst the final stone.

"And now," Danielle said, "we get out of here, we play dumb, and you guard that relic with your life. After that, you've only got one decision left to make. What was it you said to me? Life's not fair, sucks all over...but you do have choices."

Him or Lucy. Two lives, one ticket out of a dying world.

Danielle went back to work on the lock. It didn't take long before the tumblers clicked and rolled. She gave the knob an experimental turn and nodded her approval.

"Do you trust me, Lucy?"

They were lost. Not trapped, but lost. The back hallways of the Burnside Ritz were an impossible maze, without any sense or reason behind the twisting, pointless passages. All they could do was keep moving.

Lucy gave Verna a sidelong glance. "Why do you ask?"

"I was just thinking about when you decked me, back in that motel parking lot."

"You had it coming."

They came to another intersection. Verna held up a hand for Lucy to stop. Then she took a few quick steps ahead, poking her head around the corner, checking each direction for trouble. She waved Lucy up and they kept walking, side by side.

"Sure I did. I just think it's funny."

"How so?"

"You're both changing, my little lioness." Verna flashed a lopsided smile. "You should have seen Dani in the library. She's rusty, a little out of shape, but it was the first time in ages she looked like *herself*."

Lucy perked up. "Do you think she'll go back? To being the Jury?"

Verna waggled her hand from side to side. "Fifty-fifty chance. A few more nights like this might do the trick."

"I don't know if we *have* a few more nights."

"Are you giving up?"

"Never," Lucy said. "I meant what I said: I'm here until the end of the story, one way or another."

"You really are a lot like her, you know."

Lucy had to think about that.

"When I look back..." Her voice trailed off.

Verna arched an eyebrow. "Yeah?"

"Forget it."

"Tell me." Verna took Lucy's hand as they walked. "You know you can tell me anything."

"When I look back..." She paused. "It's just funny. This week I've nearly been killed more times than I can count, I've seen magic, monsters...I've traveled to another world."

Verna squeezed her hand. "Seems like you're holding your own."

"That's the thing. Before this all happened, I was..."

"A city mouse?"

"Afraid," Lucy said. "I was afraid of so much...so much pointless, stupid shit. For no reason."

"You just needed someone to show you what you were capable of."

"I can't go back," Lucy said.

Verna gave her a questioning look.

"To the way I was," she said. "That's not who I am. Not anymore."

"That life wasn't doing you any favors, cupcake."

"You know the first thing I'm going to do when I get back home?"

Verna bit her bottom lip.

"I'm going to march into my boss's office," Lucy said, "and tell him I want a raise, or I walk. No. You know what? I'm just going to quit. Guy's a jerk. I'm *good* at what I do, and I'm going somewhere I'll be appreciated for it. I'm done with apologizing for everything. I'm done with putting myself down, and I'm done with letting anyone treat me like garbage. I'm not perfect, but I'm worth more than that."

The hallway ended in a door. No sign, no markers, no chain on the push bar.

"You sound more like Dani all the time," Verna said. She let go of Lucy's hand and stepped up, gently leaning into the bar. "Or more like me. Hold up, let's see if— *Yes*."

The door opened wide. On the other side, the endless bare cinder block yielded to striped Victorian wallpaper and long rows of brass-numbered doors. The musty air took on the vague smell of potpourri.

"We're out," Verna said. "Just have to make our way back to the lobby, get to the car... Wait. Do you have the keys?"

"I think Roy took them."

Verna shrugged. They picked a direction at random and started walking, letting the utility door swing shut at their backs.

"Should be a train station a couple of blocks from here. We'll hop a ride to Oswald Heights and hole up in Dani's office until the dust settles."

"We should stay," Lucy said. "What if they're in trouble?"

"Sister, trust me: between those two, they can handle it. Now if I haven't totally lost my marbles along with my sense of direction, this should lead us back to—"

A chorus of shrill, panicked squeals from the corridor up ahead cut her off. She staggered to a stop with Lucy at her side.

"What is that?" Lucy's brow furrowed. "That doesn't sound human."

A tidal wave of matted fur and claws came crashing around the bend. Rats. They clambered along the wallpaper and piled over each other on the carpet, a living torrent driven by raw, mad fear. A gout of flame licked the air, filling the hall with the stench of kerosene and smoke.

"Not human," Verna breathed.

Roach lumbered around the corner. His leather-clad bulk filled the hallway, and he cradled his death machine in both hands. Lucy saw herself and Verna reflected in the long onyx ovals of his gas mask eyes.

They ran. Turning, sprinting ahead of the tide of rats and the killer behind them, not caring where they were headed. Roach broke into a lumbering jog, filling the hall with hoarse, wet muffled laughter and short sharp blasts of flame. He turned the swarm into living candles, screeching as their fur ignited, setting the ancient wallpaper on fire and squirming, still burning, under hotel room doors.

The hall ahead ended in a T-junction. They started to break left, but Roach cut them off with another blast of flame, so close Lucy felt like she was standing next to an open furnace. The heat made her eyes water and her nostrils sting. They went right, dodging, desperate to stay ahead of the lethal juggernaut.

He's not trying to kill us, Lucy realized. *He's HERDING us.*

"Over here!" Verna said, pointing to a pair of double doors up ahead. A faded brass sign, marred with tarnish, read *Galaxy Ballroom*.

"No," Lucy said, "that's what he *wants*. We shouldn't—"

Too late. Verna barreled through the ballroom doors, Lucy swept up in her momentum. Then they froze on the gold-and-black zigzag carpet, pinned where they stood at the ballroom's edge.

The cavernous room was empty, angled overhead lights shining down across dusty walls. Chairs were stacked in one far corner next to folded tables, waiting for a party that would never come. They weren't alone. Mary was here, leaning against a wall, lounging in her gore-spattered lab coat and sucking on a lollipop. Trigger Mortis paced, mumbling to himself under his skull-faced mask, chromed revolvers riding on his hips.

And before them, using the overheads like a spotlight, stood Duke Ellery.

"Lucy," he said with a cordial bow, "I have waited so very long, darling. So very long indeed."

Chapter Forty-four

Verna turned to run. She didn't get far. Roach's bulk filled the doorway, driving her and Lucy deeper into the room, closer to the Illustrated Duke.

"Roach," Duke said. "Well done. Did you manage not to set any fires on your way here?"

His gas mask dipped.

"Might be a...small fire," he mumbled.

Duke rolled his eyes. "Well, all right, looks like we'll be leaving shortly. I liked this hotel, Roach."

"Not my fault," he protested. "I got bored."

"Now, as for the two of you..."

Lucy's breath went shallow as Duke approached them, the lean, tattooed man holding one hand behind his tailored white jacket. He locked eyes with her, looming, silent for a moment.

Then he showed his hand, twirling it, and offered her a short-stemmed rose. It was fresh, alive, with petals red as blood.

"A token of respect and gratitude," he said, "from the Duke."

Lucy took the rose, staring at it like it might come to life and bite her.

"We're going to save this world, you and I."

"It won't *work*," Verna protested. "You're insane. You're going to kill us all."

Duke shrugged. "Nah, baby. Just you. I am *absolutely* going to kill you."

"High time somebody did," Mary said. "Let me do her, Duke. I've been wanting her on my table since forever ago."

"First things first, *ma belle dame sans merci*. What's the word on our other guests?"

"Been watching 'em on cam. Should be just about..."

An unmarked door at the back of the ballroom, built for the hotel's custodians, clicked and opened wide. Roy and Danielle emerged, staggering to a sudden stop.

"There we go," Mary said. "Gang's all here."

Duke flashed a toothy smile, fixing his eyes on Danielle.

"Perfect. I smell smoke, so we shouldn't wait too long." He glanced at Roy. "Now, you...you are one unusual cat."

"So I've been told," Roy said.

"You're the only piece of this family reunion that doesn't fit. To tell you the truth, I don't care much if you live or die."

"Except," Mary said.

"Except you had the distinct misfortune of pissing off my girl Rumblebones. She's not the forgiving type. So you'll answer to her."

He trained his sights back on Danielle.

"And you'll answer to me, Jury."

Trigger Mortis was still pacing, skull-mask twitching as he whispered a constant stream of babble, lost in his own world. Then he heard the word *Jury*. He stopped, dead still and frozen.

For a moment, it looked like Danielle might break and run, back the way she came. Her gaze flicked across the room, to each of the gathered villains. Then to Roy. To Lucy. Her eyes stayed with Lucy. The two women, creator and creation, stared at each other across the desolate ballroom. Silence swallowed the world.

She needs something from me, Lucy realized. She tried to decipher the code, to know what to say, what to do. Time was running out. Then it came to her. Four simple words.

"I believe in you," she said.

Danielle nodded, firm, then turned to Duke Ellery.

"You want me, Duke? Well, here I am. You've got me. You sure you're ready?"

Duke snickered. "No magic coat? No magic pistols? Jury, you've got moxie for days but your mouth is writing checks your fists can't cash."

She took a step toward him. Behind her, silent and wary, Roy began inching to one side. Circling the room, making his way closer to Lucy and Verna.

"It's not about the costume," Danielle said. "And it's not about the tools. It's about responsibility. And I've been shirking mine for way too long."

Lucy knew her next words by heart. She had written them herself, years ago, first in a notebook and then in the script for her first comic.

"I am the protector of this city," Danielle said. "I speak for those who have no voices, and I fight for those who can't fight for themselves. I am the Midnight Jury."

She raised her hand, pointing an accusing finger.

"And I find you...guilty."

Duke spread his open hands, taking in the room. Mary was still leaning against the wall, twirling the stem of her lollipop with her tongue, watching Danielle with silent, feral hunger. Roach stroked the barrel of his weapon, raspy breaths drifting from under his mask. Trigger just stood there, statue-still, fingers hovering an inch over the grips of his guns.

"There's no happy ending here," Duke said. "You get that, right?"

Danielle nodded, resigned, ready.

"Then I'll go out doing what I always loved," she said. "Kicking your ass."

Duke grinned and shoved back the sleeves of his tailored jacket. He cracked his knuckles.

"Nobody else touches her," he said. "She's mine."

They both charged at the same time, fists cocked back, meeting with a clash in the heart of the room. No flashy moves, no martial arts: this was bare-knuckle boxing, simple and brutal and stripped to the bone. Duke laid into her with a rib-cracking flurry. She took the pain and sidestepped and drove a hammer-fist into his kidney.

In the corner of her eye, Lucy saw Roy on the move. All eyes were on the fight, and Roach had abandoned his post, shuffling away from the ballroom doors to get a better look. Roy came in from the other direction and hovered right behind her.

"If she loses—" he whispered.

"She won't lose."

Danielle grunted as Duke slammed his forehead down onto her face. Her nose shattered, twisted to one side, spraying blood. Ribbons of wet scarlet ran down Duke's scalp, matting his groomed hair, painting his tattoos. Danielle threw a left, feinted, and her torn knuckles ripped open a gash along his chin.

"Come on, baby," Mary shouted. "Kill her!"

Roach clapped his leather-gloved mitts, grunting his approval. Trigger Mortis was the odd man out. He still stood there, silent, transfixed. His fingers twitched.

Piledriver hits rammed into Duke's gut, dropping him to his knees. Both fighters were drenched in sweat and blood, cut and battered and teetering on the edge of exhaustion. Danielle wavered on her feet, gulping down air, digging for one last burst of strength.

Roy pressed something into Lucy's hand. She ran her thumb over the cold metallic surface. It was the Mason's Compass, with its one last charge, along with the keys to Verna's car.

Duke tried to get up off his knees. He only made it halfway, shoulders slumped, out of gas. Danielle drew back her fist, about to deliver the finishing blow.

Then Trigger Mortis let out a howl of pent-up frustration and raw, seething hate, and stormed across the room. Danielle turned, catching the sudden movement, too exhausted to react in time.

"No," Lucy whispered.

He drew one of his revolvers.

Then he put it against Danielle's head and fired.

She fell in slow-motion, trailed by a spray of red mist. Her body hit the ballroom carpet. Eyes wide open, staring at nothing, with a dark, gaping crater between them. There would be no rescues, no last-second escapes, no happy ending.

The Midnight Jury was dead.

Duke was the first to break the silence, his voice barely louder than a gust of breath.

"Trigger...what did you do?"

"You wanted her gone," he said. "I made her gone."

"Yes, but..." Duke squinted. He reached out and poked Danielle's shoulder. It rocked back and forth against his fingertip. "I'm having trouble with this. Give me a moment."

Mary moved closer. So did Roach. Both of them stared down at the body of their eternal nemesis.

"Damn," Mary said.

"Damn indeed," Duke said.

He rose with a grunt, leaning hard on one leg, and plucked a white silk handkerchief from his breast pocket. He mopped at his face, smearing the blood from his cuts.

"I have to say," he added, "this is a bit anticlimactic."

"Told her she should have stayed gone," Mary said. She looked over at Verna. "She's not the only one."

Duke nodded. "Right. Now for the main event. Lucy, if you would be so kind—"

Roy grabbed her shoulders and spun her around. He stared into her eyes, serious as the grave.

"*Go home*," he said.

Then he shoved her out of the ballroom, into a hallway wreathed with gray, acrid smoke, and slammed the door shut. She heard the lock click and his back thump against it, guarding her retreat with his life.

Roy had one last card up his sleeve. He hoped it was an ace. No telling, with Lucy's nightmare creations all bearing down on him at once, determined to get their author back.

He took Charikleia's twig, the Dark Dryad's peace offering, and snapped it behind his back. Sticky sap smeared his fingers, smelling of fresh pine.

"Heroic, but stupid," Duke snarled. "Roach—"

Roach didn't need to be told. He barreled in, the corroded wand of his weapon raised high in his hands. It swung down and crashed across Roy's skull like a baseball bat. Pain and darkness swallowed him whole before he touched the ballroom floor.

Lucy ran. Through the billowing gray clouds, past flaming corridors, tears stinging her eyes. She couldn't even pretend it was the smoke. Danielle was dead. Roy and Verna were next, if they weren't dead already.

She couldn't believe in happy endings. Not anymore.

She made it to Verna's car, jumped in, and fired up the engine. She pulled away, leaving burning windows and flickering flames in the rearview mirror. And shadows, racing out into the street, making one last effort to chase her down before she left them far behind.

She had the Compass. The last shining garnet on the relic's outer ring was her ticket back. She knew this city, its infinite nightmare sprawl a part of her soul, and she knew she could find her way back to Eden Park. She was as good as home.

Nothing would stop the end from coming now. Once she left, it would only be a matter of days before this entire world—her world of dreams, and nightmares, and heroes and monsters—collapsed entirely. Gone and forgotten. Forgotten by everyone but her.

Lucy realized she was sobbing. Raw grief grabbed her heart like a fist, squeezing the life out of her as she leaned into the steering wheel. She couldn't see through the tears, so she pulled over to the side of the road.

The portal was waiting. All she had to do was drive through it. Her old life was there, just as she had left it.

It was she who would never be the same.

She put her forehead against the steering wheel and took deep, shuddering breaths.

"I believe in happy endings," she whispered. Sending the words up into the night like a prayer as a slow rain began to fall.

I believe in the Midnight Jury.

She wiped away her tears. There was no shame in grieving, but she didn't have time for that now. The spark of an idea ignited inside her. A mad idea, an impossible one.

It felt a little like hope.

Chapter Forty-Five

Roy woke to the sound of a subway train rattling and squealing as it barreled down a tunnel. For a second he thought he was back in Chicago or Detroit or New York, or any of a hundred cities where he'd been a passenger on a hundred trains. It all blended together, just like his work. He didn't know anybody anywhere he went, and nobody knew him. He used to think life was better that way.

As his vision slowly returned, resolving from a blurry mess to floating, nauseating ghosts that swam in and out of sight, he remembered. He wasn't in any town he knew. He wasn't even on his own planet.

But it was a train station, all right. A vintage station with crystal chandeliers and an endless mosaic checkerboard of ivory and amber along the grime-streaked floors. Framed advertisements pitched cigarettes and liquor between polished wall sconces, each one a crowned woman captured in chrome who held out a frosted globe of softly glowing glass. The farthest track, the source of the rumbling sound, was barricaded behind a wall of spray-painted plywood.

A storm had come to the city. It pelted a skylight high overhead, turning the night into a muddy, freezing blur. Roy heard thunder ripple in the distance.

He tried to rub his head, but his wrist jerked short, bound by steel cuffs behind his back. He was sitting in a folding chair near the edge of the track. A familiar voice grabbed his attention.

"Wakey, wakey," said Rumblebones.

Still clutching her teddy bear, the baleful little girl stood watch over him. Him and Verna, cuffed in the chair right next to him. She gave him a helpless shrug. He looked back to Rumblebones.

"Where's your pet snake?" he asked.

Her lips curled in a nasty smile. "Where's your friend Danielle?"

A peal of giddy laughter from the far end of the track turned his head. It looked like the party was just getting started. In front of a wall of mismatched televisions, screens piled upon screens leaning in a dangerously lopsided tilt, Mary—who had changed out her gore-spattered lab coat for a pristine white one—was wheeling out a drink cart. Roach and Trigger Mortis watched, faces unknowable under their masks, while Duke Ellery pointed to the TV in the top right corner.

"Here," he said, fumbling for a remote control and turning up the volume. "Dig it. This should be good."

A reporter's voice rose above the jumbled cacophony of the other screens. "—twelve officers killed in a lethal ambush at the Sixty-Eighth precinct station on LeFay Drive—"

"Fourteen," Trigger hissed. "I counted."

"Maybe you only wounded a couple of them," Roach suggested.

The skull-faced mask snapped in his direction. "I *never* shoot to wound."

"Boys, boys," Duke said, waving his open palm. "You're talking over the show."

"As this plague of violence continues to rise, washing across the city," the earnest-sounding reporter asked the camera, "we ask once again: where is our protector? Where is the Midnight Jury?"

That earned another round of ugly laughter. Roy focused on his breath. In, out. Control. He started working his wrists against the cuffs, hoping to find a little give.

"Knock knock," Mary said.

Duke put a hand to his ear and leaned in. "Who's there?"

"Not the Midnight Jury." She picked up a bottle of champagne from the drink cart.

"Not the Midnight Jury who?"

"Not the Midnight Jury, because she's dead in a ditch with a bullet in her head!"

She cackled and popped the bottle's cork, which flew through the air on a plume of white foam. Roach's wet chortle made Roy's skin crawl. Duke grinned, wild-eyed, and slapped Trigger on the shoulder.

"You hear that, my man? Now who says that women aren't funny?"

"Someone told me I wasn't funny once," Mary said, pouring flutes of golden champagne and handing them out. "So I made his death look like autoerotic asphyxiation."

Trigger lifted the bottom of his mask, just enough to expose sweaty cheek-stubble and chapped lips.

"Heh," he rasped, lifting the flute. "That *is* funny."

"I'm so sorry, Roy," Verna whispered at his side. "I swear, I didn't want any of this to happen."

Rumblebones narrowed her eyes.

"Silence. Both of you. You'll live longer that way." She turned and shouted up the platform. "I could use a drink, myself."

"You're underage," Mary called back.

"I am *literally* over two thousand years old, you impudent—" she finished with a few words that sounded like Arabic, but backwards and put in a blender. Mary feigned shock, putting one hand to her chest.

"Such language from a little girl! I might have to wash your mouth out with soap."

"Must be part of that 'plague of violence' I keep hearing about," Duke said. He turned to Rumblebones and casually sauntered over. "May I remind you, babe, that if you'd done your job and snared our author when you had the chance, we'd all be sitting pretty right now. The end of the Midnight Jury is something to celebrate, not to mention laying hands on the Argisene Grimoire, but we're still riding a dead world on a one-way road to Endsville if I can't patch things up."

"Because of *him*," she snarled, locking eyes with Roy.

Roy met her gaze, unblinking. "Have you been this goddamn whiny for over two thousand years, too?"

She lunged at him. Duke stopped her, fast, barring her with a stiff arm.

"*Down*, girl. Man beats you fair and square, he has the right to needle you a little bit."

"Let me kill him. At least let me kill him—"

"No. Not *yet*."

Duke loomed over Roy. This close, Roy couldn't miss how the tattoos covering every inch of his exposed skin, whirling letters in a dozen dead languages and jagged, disturbing glyphs, rippled like tiny ants. They squirmed across his pale flesh, rearranging themselves on a whim, as if each tattoo had a mind of its own.

"He can be useful to you," Verna said, giving her cuffs a desperate jerk. "We both can. You know how helpful I can be."

He didn't look at her. Instead, he took out a cellophane-wrapped pack of cigarettes and tapped one into his open hand. He offered it to Roy with a question in his eyes. Roy shook his head. Duke shrugged, lit it with a gold-plated lighter, and took a long, slow drag.

"Verna, baby," he said, "trust me when I say that you want me to forget you exist right now. I may seem copacetic, but that's just the afterglow of victory. We still have some debts to settle, you and me. Soon."

Roy felt a tickle along the back of his hand. He almost flinched. Then the feeling of a firm, thorny tendril pressed against his palm. Caressing his skin with a bit of pleasure, a hint of pain, letting him know the score. Charikleia was here. He didn't know where she was hiding, and he didn't dare risk giving her away by turning around, but he felt the cuffs wriggle as a narrow twig slid into the lock.

He needed to keep Duke talking long enough to get loose. He was still surrounded by superhuman killers, lost without a plan or a prayer, but at least he'd die on his feet. These people had Danielle's blood on their hands. Roy silently resolved that no matter what happened, he wouldn't go down without returning the favor. Payback was the only thing he had left.

"You kept us alive for a reason," Roy said.

"The author," Duke said. "What's she to you? You family? Blood? Is she your main squeeze, maybe?"

He shook his head. "Just a friend."

Duke barked out a laugh. "You must be pulling my leg, son. What kind of 'friend' goes on a one-way trip into a dying nightmare without expecting anything in return for it? You could have gotten away back at the Ritz. I saw what you did, passing her the Compass and the keys, guarding that door for as long as you could hold out. There's no way you're getting out of this alive. You traded your life for hers. You know that, right?"

It was a fair question. Roy thought it over, and decided it deserved an honest answer.

"I've been comfortable with the idea of dying for a long time," he said. "More comfortable than any man should be. If you asked me just a week ago what I was living for, I'd have to say I had no idea. It was just *easier* than dying."

"So this is suicide."

"No." Roy shook his head. "The opposite. I finally found a reason to stick around. And when you've got a reason to live, you have to fight for it. Hard as you can. Do you know the Midnight Jury's real power?"

Duke ticked them off on his fingers. "Magic coat, magic guns—"

"Hope," Roy said.

"Well, the Jury's dead. What does that tell you about hope?"

The living twig jostled back and forth in the handcuff lock, quietly shimming it open.

"You don't get it," Roy said.

"Oh?" Duke's eyebrows lifted. "Enlighten me."

"Danielle was right. It's not about the costume. When Lucy imagined her, she gave her those powers to even the odds. To tame her nightmares. But at the end of the day, *anyone* could become the Midnight Jury. All it takes is being willing to stand up to people like you. To fight for the people who can't."

"Oh," Duke said, with the slightest roll of his eyes. "So are you stepping into her shoes, my man? Are you volunteering as her replacement?"

"Right now?"

The handcuffs popped. The steel circlets fell free behind his back. He caught them with one hand.

"You're goddamn right I am," Roy said.

He leaped from his chair and swung the cuffs like a metal whip, aiming for Duke's eyes. At the same time, down the platform, Roach let out a hoarse cry and dropped into the trench of the subway tracks. His flamethrower roared. So did Charikleia, the Dryad bursting from her hiding spot, vines thrashing as they caught fire.

Duke roared with them, half pain and half outrage. The cuffs cut him across one cheek, slicing pale skin and writhing ink. Roy pressed him back, tearing into him with his fists. For one brief, fleeting second, he had the winning edge.

Then Rumblebones kicked the back of his knee, buckling it, throwing him off-balance. Duke did the rest. As Charikleia's howls faded down the subway tunnel, the fires fading, Duke brought his fists together and slammed them down on Roy's shoulder. He dropped, hard, cracking the back of his head against the concrete platform. His vision blurred, body wracked with pain.

Roach came lumbering back up the tunnel and called up to Duke. "She got away."

"We'll settle up with her later."

The sole of Duke's polished leather shoe came down on Roy's throat, pinning him to the floor like a bug. He ground the heel in, cutting off Roy's air, threatening to crush his windpipe.

"You know how lucky I am, my man?"

Roy couldn't even croak a response. He grabbed Duke's shoe with both hands, pushing back, struggling to squirm free. Duke crouched down, leaning in with his full weight.

"I'm so lucky," he said, "I get to kill two Midnight Juries in one night. Careful what you wish for. You might just get it."

Dark splotches erupted in Roy's eyes. His blood was a thundering tempest, rising to block out the world. Duke was still talking, gloating, but he couldn't hear a word. All he could see was the skylight above and the rain coming down, and flashes of lightning in the storm-tossed sky.

It was all right. The last of his strength was giving out and his breath was gone, but it was all right. He'd done his job and he'd done it well. And for the first time in years, the first time in as long as he could remember, he didn't have any regrets.

The skylight exploded.

Mary yowled and dove for cover as spears of glass came crashing down, bursting across the floor of the station like a storm of diamonds. Then came a figure in midnight blue, cloaked in a fluttering, flowing trench coat and fedora, a grappling gun in her hand. The grapple spooled out tactical rope, slowing her descent; she let go and dropped the last ten feet, floating more than falling, a dark angel in slow motion.

She landed in a crouch with the brim of her hat pulled low and her face in shadow.

"No," Duke breathed. He stepped off of Roy's throat and raised a shaking finger. "That's not possible. You're dead. We *killed* you."

She rose to her feet and lifted her head. Roy couldn't breathe so well, but he could muster a smile. Even with a blue silk scarf shrouding the bottom half of her face, there was no mistaking her secret identity.

"You killed Danielle Faust," Lucy said. "I'm the Midnight Jury."

She threw back her coat, baring a pair of .45 automatics nestled in twin holsters.

"And I find you...guilty."

Chapter Forty-six

Trigger Mortis screeched, the assassin's brain filled with hornets and hate. He drew his revolvers. Lucy drew first. Neon runes wreathed her hands, tracing midnight-blue glyphs along the barrels of her automatics. She pulled both triggers and the muzzles erupted with the sound of thunder. One round crashed into Trigger's left revolver, reducing it to a useless lump of twisted metal. The other hit his right hand. He dropped to one knee, howling, clutching his wound as blood guttered between his fingers.

Roy found his second wind. He clambered to his feet and jumped down into the trench, one eye on the rails as he hunted through the trash at the track's edge. A bent metal clip, old and rusted, jutted from the debris. He scooped it up and got behind Verna's chair.

Rumblebones clutched her teddy bear in one arm and raised the other high, chanting in a dead tongue. The curse flowed from her like a heat mirage, a serpent of shimmering air lunging for Lucy's heart. She spun, dropped low and fired a single shot. The toy bear exploded in a flurry of stuffing and pottery, exposing the Egyptian jar—and the ancient, mummified organs, twisted and black, concealed inside. The necromancer's jaw dropped, stretching inhumanly wide, as her little-girl eyes turned to onyx pits. She let out an ear-piercing scream, her curse shattering in the open air.

Cuffs in this world worked the same as back home: cheap and easy to pick. A few quick wriggles of the metal clip and Verna's bracelets popped. She was out of her chair and on the move like a bullet. So was Roy. He had a score to settle. Duke turned just in time to see him charging in with his fist flying. Roy decked him, throwing all his weight behind a single punch, and knocked him flat.

Mary landed on Lucy's back and clung like a monkey, furiously clawing at her eyes. Lucy threw her elbow back into Mary's stomach once, then again, but couldn't shake her loose. Roach lumbered up, flicking a switch to shift his murder machine from napalm to acid.

"*Hold* her," he wheezed, aiming the nozzle. "Hold her or I'll hit both of you."

Verna swooped up behind him. She put one hand on his shoulder and her lips to the black leather shroud of his mask. She whispered to him. Roy couldn't make out the words, but he could hear the sibilant flow, sounds turning to crackles of static that couldn't come from a human throat. The hair on his arms prickled, electricity building in the air. Then Verna punctuated her final word with a light tap on the back of Roach's head.

He howled. He dropped the nozzle, letting it dangle from the hose at his side as his hands batted wildly in front of him, fighting against a nightmare no one else could see. He broke into a panicked, flailing run, vanishing into the mouth of the subway tunnel.

Lucy threw Mary over her shoulder, sending her crashing down onto the platform. Mary rolled fast as Lucy opened fire, a pair of spectral bullets plowing into the tile and erupting in swirls of glowing runes. At Roy's feet, Duke was starting to stir, groaning, pushing himself up with one hand as he clutched his swollen eye.

"If I could offer some friendly advice," Roy told him, "you should stay down."

The corner of Duke's mouth twitched in a grimace.

"Something you'll learn about me: I *never* stay down. Mary!"

The dark lovers moved as one, changing targets while Duke leaped to his feet. Mary spun, a scalpel sprouting between her fingertips, and hurled it at Roy with blinding speed. Roy fell back, the razor-edged scalpel flickering past his eyes, the distraction buying Duke a few precious seconds.

Duke chanted on the run, holding out his open palm toward Lucy. Runes like the ones wreathing her pistols, cast in tones of dark brass and poison green, erupted from his hand and became a rippling shield. Her shots plowed into the shield and burst into a shower of rainbow sparks while Duke scooped his free arm around Mary and yanked her close.

A train was coming. Not from behind the plywood wall this time. Roy heard the horn and the rattling din booming from the tunnel right next to the platform. Sickly light erupted in the dark, bile-green and luminous, the color of deep-ocean algae and the drowned dead.

"My girl and I have a train to catch," Duke shouted over the rising roar of the engine. "But don't worry. We'll be back."

"So will I," Lucy said.

Duke and Mary each took one step backward, gracefully falling onto the subway tracks.

The thing that burst from the tunnel half a second later was no earthly train. It was a glowing, translucent beast, corroded and draped in seaweed, with a whistle that shrieked like a man's dying breath. Roy stood at the edge of the platform, transfixed, catching glimpses of the train's spectral riders. They were eyeless, hollow, motionless as they clung to rotted leather straps.

A moment later, it was gone. Off into the tunnel, taken by the dark, the sound fading into silence.

Roy looked across the platform, over to Lucy and Verna. He pointed to the empty tracks.

"Are they...?"

"Not dead," Lucy said. "That's how they get around the city. The hell-train. I was going to introduce it in issue seven."

"Did I ever tell you," Roy asked, "that you've got a seriously messed up imagination?"

She unwrapped the silk scarf so he could see her smile.

"You might have mentioned that," she said.

Verna walked over to them, nodding back over her shoulder.

"Rumblebones and Trigger got away."

"Usually do," Lucy said.

"So," Roy said.

"So."

He looked her up and down. Then he nodded.

"Coat looks good on you."

Lucy holstered her guns.

"All of Danielle's stuff was back at her office," Lucy said. "I knew where to look."

"I like the hat, too. Very vintage. Good look for you."

"Yeah, I've never had much of a fashion sense, but it fits me."

"Almost like it was made for you," Verna said. "Hey. You feel that?"

Roy glanced at her. "What?"

She held up one open hand. There was no sound, now, nothing but the slowing rain drizzling in from the shattered skylight, droplets dancing on the platform, and the distant rumble of thunder as the storm moved on.

"Nothing," she said.

He understood, though he wasn't sure how. The sense of constant tension he'd felt since crossing the gateway, the reptile-brain fear of some impending catastrophe, was gone. As if this place was finally stable.

Finally whole.

"Got something for you," Lucy said. She held out Verna's car key.

Verna took the key, looking nervous now. "You didn't wreck it, did you?"

"It was already pretty much wrecked."

"True, true."

Lucy turned to Roy. She had something for him, too. She handed him the Mason's Compass. One ticket back to the real world. One ticket home.

"Turns out," she said, "this was for you all along."

"Lucy—"

"I'm staying, Roy. I don't want my old life back. People need me here. Like I told you: I created this place. That means I'm responsible for it."

"So you're going to be a..." he tilted his head. "Two-fisted pulp hero?"

"I mean, I know all the Jury's lines by heart," she said. "After all, I wrote them."

True, Roy thought. *True*.

Chapter Forty-seven

Roy had one night left in Noir York City. A subjective thing, in a town where dawn never seemed to come, but traveling to a parallel, fictional world wasn't something a man did every day. Verna laid on the sugar, talking him into a tiny detour on his way to Eden Park.

"See?" she said. "This burg isn't entirely horrible."

He had to admit she was right. The Skyline Lounge was a slowly rotating disk perched atop the spire of a skyscraper, with a panoramic view of the endless city sprawl. A world of darkness studded with tiny, gleaming lights, like an army of fireflies in the night. He was underdressed for this place; the locals looked like extras from *The Great Gatsby*, and Verna had changed into a scarlet flapper dress lined with wavy fringe. A strand of pearls dangled from her wrist as she lifted her glass in a toast.

He did the same. The local specialty was a frosty concoction, luminous blue and served in a margarita glass, called a Last Waltz. One sip made his head feel like dancing, and he figured his feet wouldn't be too far behind.

"Woof," he said. "What do they put in this stuff?"

"I don't think they have it on your world. See? Plenty of reasons to stick around. You could be happy here."

He chuckled and shook his head. "Nah, not for me."

"Well," she said with a coquettish smile, "I might just have to come and visit you on your world sometime. You can show me the sights."

Except you know damn well you can't, Roy thought, *because the second I take the Compass through the gateway, that's the end of the line. No more gateway. Ever again.*

He pretended not to know that. He had one last night, and he didn't want to sour the mood. Verna was good company. He didn't mind being flirted with, and he didn't mind her taste in booze either.

"I barely knew her, but I'm going to miss her."

"Danielle?"

He nodded.

"Sure you knew her," Verna said. "You read her comic books."

He set his drink on the round table of smoked glass between them. He rapped his fingers on the glass.

"Lucy," he said.

"Had to happen, Roy. You know that. In your heart, even if it hasn't made its way to your head yet."

"I know. But when I'm gone..."

"Mm-hmm?"

"I need you to keep an eye on her. I believe in Lucy. I know she knows what she's doing. But she's also going to have a lot to learn."

"Our paths might cross here and there."

Roy shook his head and smiled. "Cross paths on the right side of the law, okay?"

"Darling," she said, pouting at him. "You make me sound like some kind of...occasional villainess."

"Like you said, I read the comics."

"No promises," she said. Her head turned toward the window at their side, looking out over the canyons of glass and stone. "Ooh. Over there. That's the Falcon Tower."

He gazed out at the distant spire, a needle of neon-lined glass spearing into the overcast sky, painting the streets below in shifting colors of light.

"There's a great casino over there. And a *zoo*. Animals you've never seen before. I'm telling you, Roy, all the action in this town is *way* above street level. You don't know what you're missing."

He picked up his cocktail without looking and drank deep. It hit him with more than a buzz. Something else, something stronger, that made his world start to slide sideways.

Verna reached across the table and took his hand. She rose, slow and elegant.

"Verna—" he tried to say. It came out slurred. His voice sounded wrong. Then it didn't sound like anything at all. She was talking to him, crouching next to his chair, tender and dangerously close, but he couldn't make out the words.

Right before he plunged into darkness, she kissed him on the cheek.

Roy woke up in an alley, slumped against a dank, crumbling brick wall. His head felt like someone had gone to work on him with a jackhammer, and his back was stiff and sore. Wincing, waking up, his first instinct was to check his pockets.

The Mason's Compass was gone.

So was almost everything in his wallet. Verna had taken his cash and credit cards. *Fair enough,* he thought. *Can't use them over here anyway.*

She'd left a note in his pocket, folded primly, sealed with a lipstick kiss. He opened it and began to read.

Roy, she wrote.

I know you won't believe me, but I am sorry about this. After what I did to him, Duke is never, ever going to stop hunting me. The only way I can escape him is to go to a place where he can't follow.

And so, my sweet, I had to take the key and lock the door behind.

I wish things could have been different. I would have liked to have gotten to know you better. I think we could have been good for each other. Or very, very bad. You know I like it either way.

XOXO, Verna Bell

P.S., I meant what I said. You really can be happy here. I always was.

He folded the note, looked up at the churning, dark sky, and smiled.

The Midnight Jury was on duty.

She perched at the lip of a towering rooftop, overlooking the dirty streets and the neon lights far below. The brim of her fedora was pulled down low across her eyes, and the tail of her silk scarf fluttered in a cold night wind.

Behind her, the door to the utility stairwell jolted open. She didn't look back.

"Took you long enough," she said.

Roy held up a brown paper bag, bulging and rolled tight at the top.

"Do you know how hard it is to find good burgers in this neighborhood?"

"Oswald Heights," she sighed, "is not known for its cuisine. Mostly just extortion and manslaughter."

A pair of folding chairs sat side by side. Roy dropped into one, set the sack in his lap, and unrolled it.

"I picked up some soda, too, but...I honestly don't know what kind. One says it's 'violet flavored.' So we're taking some chances tonight. Speaking of, how goes the watch?"

She sat down beside him and passed him a pair of binoculars. He traded her, handing over an aluminum can and a fat cheeseburger wrapped in greasy wax paper.

"The East Side Mob is definitely operating out of that warehouse. Doktor Impakt showed up with a delivery truck about an hour ago. I think they're stashing stolen goods there before divvying them up to their fences across the city."

"What's the plan?" Roy asked.

"Figured I'd go down there and introduce myself." She held up the burger and unfurled her scarf. "After dinner. So. When are you going to tell me why you did it?"

"Did what?" he said.

She gave him a coy little smile.

"Why you let Verna steal the Compass."

He blinked. "What? Now you're a mind reader too? I didn't think that was one of your superpowers."

"No powers needed. I just listened when you told me what happened. Come on, Roy: you mean to tell me that she distracted you and roofied your drink, and you didn't notice a thing?"

"She's very convincing. You wrote her that way."

"And the truth is..." she said, ending with an expectant pause and a steady stare.

"Okay, you got me. I watched her reflection in the window glass. It was obvious she'd put something in my drink. I had a reasonable suspicion."

"But you still drank it."

"Sure did."

She shook her head. "Why?"

Roy leaned back in his folding chair, stretched his arms, and rested his feet on the lip of the rooftop while he stared up at the murky sky.

"She was right. Her note, I mean. Duke would never, ever let her go. And despite all her sins, she didn't deserve that."

"You saved her life," Lucy said.

"The hero business is more your kind of thing. I just did a good deed."

"A regular boy scout."

"That's what they tell me."

"So why the games?" Lucy asked. "If you wanted her to have the Compass, why not just give it to her?"

"Couple of reasons," he said. "You remember when I told you about...my past. About Carmen."

"Your lover. The one who died."

"Who was the spitting image of Verna Bell."

"But they're not the same person," Lucy said.

"Oh, believe me, I know that. But I've carried this picture in my head for the longest time. Not how Carmen was when she was alive, when we were in love, when we were laughing and happy. All I could see was her down on that floor. Dead." Roy tapped the side of his head. "I think...I think I wanted to put a better picture in there. One last look, with her face—even though it wasn't her at all—smiling back at me. So I could finish moving on."

Lucy was quiet for a moment.

"I think I understand," she said. "What's the other reason?"

"Oh, that's easy. You know I watched a lot of vintage TV as a kid."

"Cop shows."

"And film noir," he said.

"Primed you for this place."

He dug into the bag and took out a can of soda. He gave it a dubious look before he popped the tab and it opened with a tiny hiss of air.

"Verna Bell is the *femme fatale* in this story," he said. "And you know what every good *femme fatale* needs?"

"What's that?"

He raised the can in salute.

"To betray the dumb, doomed hero one last time. I played my part and she played hers. In other words, I tossed her a win. Just felt appropriate."

He took a sip of soda and stared at the can.

"It...tastes like the color violet."

"But now you're—" she didn't say *doomed*, but he knew it was on the tip of her tongue. "—you're stuck here. For the rest of your life."

"Not like I ever had a home on the other side, not a real one. Maybe I need a change of pace and a place to put down some roots. This city's good as any other. And a hell of a lot more interesting."

"What will you do?" she asked.

"Well, I know about a vacant detective's office a few blocks away from here where the rent's paid up for another month or two, and Danielle left a spare key under the doormat. I can't say for sure, but I think she would have wanted somebody to have it." He clinked his can against hers. "You're trying to do some good in this town. Maybe I can, too."

"Roy," Lucy said, "I think this is the beginning of—"

"A beautiful friendship?"

She tipped the brim of her hat. "You got me."

"We're already friends," he said. "How about a partnership?"

"You can be my sidekick."

"Nope, equal partners. Fifty-fifty all the way."

"I have magic guns now, Roy. *Magic guns*."

"And I actually know what I'm doing. You never *met* a criminal before last week."

"You never met my old boss."

"I need a cool alias. And a hat. That's the price of my tutorship."

They argued, all smiles, until the last bite was eaten and the soda was gone. And then a little longer, waiting for the right moment to go down to the street and knock on some doors. It felt right, to Roy. *Feels normal,* he wanted to say, though he didn't have a way to measure that word. He'd never felt normal before.

Maybe Verna was right after all. Maybe he—maybe he and Lucy—could be happy here.

He didn't call it a happy ending, because he knew the secret truth. There were no happy endings, because there were no endings at all. Just pauses in the story, from panel to panel, page to page, issue to issue. And maybe they'd still be happy a year from now, or maybe it would all go down in flames tomorrow.

He couldn't wait to find out.

Afterword

It's been nearly a year since my last book hit the shelves, an uncharacteristic gap of time for me; as people who follow my social media know, I had some things going on (I mean, lots of people did, it was that kind of year.) I'm back, healthy, and I have so many stories to share with you. But I hope this one, first and foremost, took you on an adventure. When last year's *The Locust Job* took a one-chapter-long side jaunt to a strange and dark parallel world, I knew right away that I wanted to go back and explore that place; a number of readers told me that they did, too, which meant it was only a matter of time before *Any Minor World* would be born.

(The title, by the way, is a Steely Dan reference. Ask your parents who that is.)

There's power in stories. They can tell us who we are, or who we can be. And it has been my great pleasure to be your storyteller this evening. Of course, I didn't do it alone, not by a long shot: special thanks to Jay Ben Markson for editing this beast into shape, to Susannah Jones for her always-fabulous audio narration, and to Ivan Zann for cover design. And thank you, most of all.

If you'd like to stay in the loop about upcoming releases, you can join my mailing list at https://craigschaeferbooks.com/mailing-list. I can also be found on Twitter at https://twitter.com/craig_schaefer, on Facebook at https://www.facebook.com/CraigSchaeferBooks/, and on Instagram at https://www.instagram.com/craigschaeferbooks/. Be daring, be strong, and I'll see you again soon.

Also by Craig Schaefer

The Daniel Faust Series:

The Long Way Down

The White Gold Score

The Harmony Black Series:

Harmony Black

Red Knight Falling

The Sisterhood of New Amsterdam:

Ghosts of Gotham

A Time for Witches

The Hungry Dreaming

Made in United States
Orlando, FL
28 April 2022